E. Kroll.

# QUEER JUDSON

QUEER TUCSON.

# QUEER JUDSON

## By JOSEPH C. LINCOLN

AUTHOR OF

"Rugged Water," "Doctor Nye," "Fair Harbor,"
"Galusha the Magnificent," "The Portygee,"
"Shavings," "Mary-'Gusta," "The Post-
master," "Extricating Obadiah,"
"Thankful's Inheritance," etc.

A. L. BURT COMPANY

Publishers       New York

Published by arrangement with D. Appleton & Company
Printed in U. S. A.

# QUEER JUDSON

# QUEER JUDSON

## CHAPTER I

CAREY JUDSON swung about on the high stool behind the tall, ink-spattered cherry desk and hitched up one long leg until the heel of the shoe upon the foot attached to the leg was hooked over the upper round of the stool. Then, resting the elbow of a long right arm upon the upraised knee, he lifted a hand—long and thin like the rest of him—drew down a lock of hair until it reached the bridge of his nose, twisted the end of the lock between his thumb and finger, and gazed drearily out of the office window.

A snapshot of him taken in that attitude would have been a far more characteristic likeness than any posed photograph could possibly have been. It would have emphasized the angularity of his figure, the every-which-wayness of his thick light brown hair, the odd manner in which his clothes managed not to fit him, although they had been made by a fashionable city tailor. It might have caught the lines between his brows and at the corners of his wide, pleasantly attractive mouth, perhaps a ghost of the expression in his eyes, eyes which, in their dreamy wistfulness, were curiously reminiscent of those of Abraham Lincoln. In fact, such a snapshot, taken at this time, would, omitting such details as beard and coloring, have been rather like a picture of the great President. Not, however, as to age, for Carey Judson was only thirty-four.

His full name was James Carey Judson, as had been his father's before him, which was, of course, the reason why he, the son, had always been called Carey. Captain James

Carey Judson—*he* had always been called, locally, "Cap'n
Jim-Carey"—was dead, had been dead seven years. Carey
had been very fond of his father, but now he was thankful
that the old gentleman was no longer living. And, on the
whole, he envied him. To be comfortably dead must be infinitely preferable to being uncomfortably alive. Captain
Jim-Carey had not wanted to die. He enjoyed every minute
of the life allowed him, and was accustomed to speak en-
viously of another mariner, Noah, who, he said, "was spry
enough to put to sea in command of the Ark when he was
six hundred and odd. A man," affirmed the captain, "was
given time enough to learn how to navigate in those days.
Now, just as a fellow is beginning to catch on to the ropes,
he is called aloft." Captain Jim-Carey had no wish to be
called aloft; he would have much preferred staying aboard
this world. His oldest son, on the contrary, would not have
minded dying, but considered himself obliged to live. An
odd fact, as the son thought of it, but very typical of the
kind of world it was.

The room in which he sat, sprawled upon the high stool
behind the tall desk, was the office of J. C. Judson & Co.
The desk and the stool and the old eight-sided clock on
the wall were part of the office equipment purchased by
Captain Jim-Carey when he gave up going to the Banks,
in 1851, and set up business there in Wellmouth, his native
town. J. C. Judson & Co. was the name on the weather-
beaten sign over the door of the good-sized building at the
foot of Wharf Lane. The printed letter and bill heads in
the desk drawer announced that J. C. Judson & Co. were
"Wholesale Dealers in Fresh and Salt Fish. Terms Thirty
Days Net." When Carey was a little boy he used vaguely
to suppose that the "Net" referred to the method by which
the fish were caught. The "Co." upon the letterhead and
upon the sign had puzzled him then. He used to wonder
if Mr. Ben Early, the manager, was the "Co." or was it
Jabez Drew, the wharf boss? When he asked his father,
the latter only laughed. When he asked Jabez, Jabez

solemnly admitted that he was not only the "Co.," but the entire establishment. "I'm the Company and the fish, too," vowed Mr. Drew. "Don't you believe it? Why—why! I'm surprised! Don't I smell as if I was wholesale fish?"

He certainly did. For the matter of that, the whole building, and the wharf, and the neighborhood in which it stood reeked of fish. And at the end of the wharf lay always one, and sometimes two or three, schooners from which fish were being unloaded, or which were just starting after more fish. The skippers and crews of those schooners smelled fishy, so did Mr. Early's office coat; even Cap'n Jim-Carey, when he came home to eat supper with his two sons and Mrs. Hepsibah Ellis, the housekeeper, brought the odor with him. Carey had smelled fish ever since he could remember smelling anything. And he loathed the smell. He was loathing it now, as he sat upon the stool, looking out of the window.

The outlook had changed little. It was very like what he remembered seeing through that window twenty-five years earlier. The wharf, the piles of barrels, the inevitable schooner at the end of the wharf, the coating of fish scales over everything—they looked about the same. Jabez Drew was out there, chatting with the mate of the schooner. Jabez had changed, of course, since the days when his employer's little son suspected him of being the "Co." on the sign. As a matter of fact, the "Co." was, and always had been, a fiction. Cap'n Jim-Carey, sole owner of the buildings and the wharf and fleet, had added the "& Co." to his name merely because he liked the looks of it. Since his death, George Judson—Carey's brother, two years younger than he—who fell heir to the business, had left the lettering of the sign and the firm's stationery as it was. "Father liked it that way," he said, "and it is a name that stands for something, so why change it?" Even his wife's repeated declarations that it was ridiculous not to put his own name there where it belonged had, so far, been without effect.

Which was unusual, for, as all Wellmouth knew and repeatedly said, Mrs. George Judson was "boss" in that family, even though her husband was boss of so many things outside it.

The ancient, but reliable, eight-sided clock marked the time as half-past five. The calendar hanging beside the clock was torn off to a Saturday in July of a year early in the eighteen eighties. And Carey Judson, bachelor, thirty-four years old, college graduate—a far greater distinction in those days than now—so recently junior partner of Osborne and Judson, bankers and brokers, with offices in State Street in Boston—Carey Judson, now a bookkeeper in the employ of his younger brother, and occupying that by no means exalted position merely because of the relationship, twisted the lock of hair between his finger and thumb, and, as he gazed pessimistically out of the window, reflected that his first week's labors in that employ were at an end.

Benjamin Early, store manager, and George Judson's trusted right-hand man, came briskly through the rear door leading from the warehouse and shipping rooms into the outer office. Carey remembered him as, in the old days, a little, straight up and down, precise young man, able, efficient, and recognizing a joke only when he saw it labeled as such. In those days his dearest dissipation was the annual picnic of the Methodist Sunday School, in which school he taught a class. He was no longer young, of course, and his once shiny black hair, the little left of it, was iron gray. He was just as careful of it as ever, and the few remaining locks sprouting at the sides of his narrow head were encouraged to grow long and were plastered across the shiny desert between. He had been superintendent of his loved Sunday School for eight years, was a director in the Wellmouth National Bank, and his character, both as a Christian brother and a business man, was above reproach. He was careful of his conduct, careful of his dress, and very careful of the stray pennies. In every respect a sharp contrast to the new bookkeeper.

He walked smartly and precisely over to the closet in which the office employees of J. C. Judson & Co. were, under orders, accustomed to hang their street apparel. He removed his seersucker shop jacket, washed his hands at the sink beside the closet, and tenderly relaid and replastered, with the brush suspended by a chain from the hook by the mirror, the strands of hair bridging the waste places above his forehead. A careful inspection of the reflection in that mirror seemed to convince him that the engineering feat was a success, for he turned again to the closet, took from the shelf a pair of celluloid cuffs, secured these to his wristbands with nickel "cuff holders," donned a respectable—almost pious—black coat and lifted from the same shelf an equally impeccable straw hat.

Then, turning toward the occupant of the desk stool, he smiled between two sets of absolutely regular and orthodox false teeth, and observed:

"Well, Carey, I think we can go home now."

Only two years before, when the junior partner of Osborne and Judson last visited, in that capacity, his native town, Early invariably addressed him as "Mr. Judson." And there was no condescension in the tone of the address then, quite the contrary. Carey, of course, had noticed the change, but he did not resent it. It was a part, a to-be-expected part, of the general change in the world's attitude toward him, and the very least of his troubles. He paused in the twisting of his forelock, tossed the latter away from his eyes with a jerk of the head, and replied to Mr. Early's observations with philosophic calm.

"Yes, so it is," he agreed. "Good night, Ben."

Early took a step toward the outer door. Then he hesitated and turned back.

"Got along all right to-day, have you, Carey?" he inquired.

"What? Oh, yes! Yes. I have got along."

"No trouble with the books? Nothing has come up to—er—fuss you? Nothing you didn't understand?"

Judson shook his head. "Well, Ben," he said, "I wouldn't

want to say that, quite. There has been nothing that I haven't *thought* I understood. That is the most I can swear to to-night."

The manager did not understand exactly, but he never admitted non-understanding of anything.

"That's good—that's very good," he declared.

"I don't know whether it is or not. Wait till next week. My thoughts haven't had time to get to the bank. They haven't been certified yet."

More non-comprehension on Early's part. He coughed and tried again.

"Don't forget what I've told you before, Carey," he said, graciously. "At any time when anything happens—any little matter comes up that you ain't—aren't sure of, just come to me about it. Never mind whether I'm busy or not. Don't let that keep you from speaking to me. I'll be glad to help you at any time."

"Much obliged, Ben. I'll try not to come too often."

"Any time, any time. No trouble at all. How did you get along with the pay roll?"

"Well, I paid everybody that asked for their wages. And I don't remember any one who was too shy to ask."

"Eh? . . . Oh! Oh, yes, I see! Ha, ha! No, I don't imagine they would be. Well—er—how do you like the work here, so far as you've gone?"

For the first time Carey Judson smiled, and the smile lighted up his thin face in a surprisingly agreeable way. Members of the opposite sex had, in the old days, been known to observe that when he smiled he was really quite good looking.

"Ben," he observed, "that isn't exactly the question. It doesn't make much difference how I like it. The real conundrum is 'Can I do it?' I guess that is the question in your mind, isn't it?"

Early, in spite of his self-importance, was a little taken aback and showed that he was.

"Why—no, no!" he protested; "there isn't any doubt

you can do it. No, no! I—we haven't any doubt of that at all."

"Haven't you? I shall be glad to lend you a little. *I* have a surplus of doubts."

"Oh, no, no! You mustn't talk that way. Of course, it's natural that you find it hard—a little mite hard at first. The wholesale fish business is different from the stockbroking business. Yes, it is different."

He delivered this nugget of wisdom with intense solemnity. For an instant the bookkeeper regarded him with a look of suspicion, as if, in spite of long acquaintance, he was uncertain whether or not a sarcasm was intended. The unworthy suspicion must have been dismissed, however, for his reply was given with a gravity approaching reverence.

"You're right, Ben," he vowed. "Yes, you're right. I have noticed the difference myself."

Mr. Early coughed again. He was about to make a little speech and when he made little speeches to his Sunday School he always prefaced them with coughs.

"Yes," he went on, "it's different. And the bookkeeping in a wholesale fish business like ours is what you might call considerable—er—complicated. What makes it more mixed up and troublesome is the retailing we have to do. If it was left to me altogether—" he spoke as if at least seven-eighths of it *was* left to him—"I think I should do away with retailing. Yes, I think I should. But Mr. Judson—George, I mean—doesn't hardly like to give it up on account of the cap'n—your father—being so set on it, as you might say. Cap'n Jim-Carey always said that so long as his neighbors in Wellmouth wanted to buy fish for them and their families to eat, they should have the privilege of buying it here. George and I have talked matters over a good many times since the old man—since the cap'n passed on, and, although we realize the bother of keeping two sets of accounts, George feels—we feel that we ought to go on doing it because it would please him. Now there ain't a mite of use," he added, growing a little more heated and consequently losing a trifle of his platform manner and language, "in a firm like ours here peddling out codfish to every Tom, Dick and Harry that wants to lug one home for dinner. And no profit that amounts to anything, either. It's a pesky nuisance, and—"

His feelings were running away with him and he pulled them up with a jerk, settling back upon the platform again with another little cough and a smile of resignation.

"But there, there!" he said. "We hadn't ought to complain, I suppose. And we don't. Your brother George says oblige the neighbors for the cap'n's sake, so we keep on obliging 'em. He's a very fine man, Mr. George Judson is. Wellmouth is proud of him."

It may have been an over-tender conscience working upon a sensitive imagination, but to Carey Judson it seemed as if the emphasis in Ben Early's concluding sentence was upon the last word in that sentence. He suspected that it might be intended as a dig in the ribs of a member of the Judson family of whom Wellmouth was anything but proud. He winced a little inwardly, but he showed no outward sign of the hurt.

"George is the best there is," he declared. "You ought to be proud of him."

"Yes—yes, indeed, we are. Oh, by the way, where is he? Has he gone home?"

"George? No, he is in there—in the private office. Cap'n Higgins is with him."

"Which Higgins?"

"Tobias."

"Cap'n Tobe? Sho! What does he want, I wonder? . . . Oh! I see. Probably come to talk a little more about that seven hundred dollars of his. Humph! I wonder that George bothers with him. It isn't any worse for him than it is for the rest. . . . Oh, by the way, things are pretty well settled up for you by now, Carey, I presume likely. Eh?"

Carey did not answer. He was looking out of the window once more. Mr. Early tried again.

"I say, George has got your affairs pretty well fixed up by this time, hasn't he?" he repeated.

Judson's long body shifted uneasily on the stool.

"I guess so," he answered, curtly. "Good night, Ben."

The manager did not take the hint. He looked as if he were about to make another little speech. Just then, however, the knob of the outer door was jerked from his fingers and the door pushed violently open. A plump, red-faced little woman, her outward apparel seemingly all at loose ends and fluttering, bounced into the office, panting in her haste.

"There!" she exclaimed, triumphantly, "you *ain't* all gone home, be you? I was afraid you would be. I was up to Sophy Cahoon's and we got to talkin' about this, that and t'other thing until I declare if I didn't forget all about the time! And I don't know's I'd wouldn't be forgettin' it yet if her settin'-room clock hadn't banged out six right 'longside of my head. I jumped much as a foot right clear out of the chair I was settin' in. 'My soul and body!' says I. 'Don't tell me that's six o'clock already! I was on my way down to George Judson's store to pay my fish bill, got the money right in my hand to pay it with,' I says, 'and here I've set and set and now 'twill be too late to catch 'em 'fore they close up. And I don't know *when* I'll get down to the village again. It's too bad!' 'No, 'tain't too bad, neither,' Sophy says; 'it's all right. That clock's all of fifteen minutes fast and you can fetch there yet, if you hurry.' And if I *ain't* hurried! Don't say a word! Whew!"

She paused to dab at her forehead with a crumpled handkerchief. Her hat was askew already and the dabs pushed it still farther toward her left ear. Carey remembered and recognized her now. She was "one of those Blounts," from the settlement in the woods beyond Wellmouth Neck and was married to Uriel Hope, a member of "that Hope tribe," long resident in the same locality. She and her husband were town "characters"—weak ones.

Judson regarded her with mild interest and she regarded him with what appeared to be apprehension.

"Well, Mrs. Hope," he asked, "what can we do for you?"

She was still breathing shortly and her little eyes were opening and shutting like those of a nodding automaton in a Christmas window. She must have heard Judson's question, but she did not answer. Early spoke.

"Come, Melie," he snapped, impatiently, "what is it? Want to pay your bill, you say? All right, pay it at the desk. Mr. Judson'll take care of you."

Mrs. Hope moved toward the desk, but she moved slowly and with evident reluctance. She paused and opened a reticule which looked as if it were made of oilcloth, extracting therefrom a dirty piece of paper—evidently the bill—and a very small packet of equally dirty bank notes, folded and refolded. She moved forward again until she stood before the opening in the grill. Carey Judson extended a hand toward that opening.

"All right, Mrs. Hope," he said. "Give it to me. I'll take it."

But the lady did not give it to him. Instead, clutching the notes and the bill in her hand, she turned her troubled countenance toward the manager.

"Is—is it all right to pay it to—to *him*, Mr. Early?" she asked, anxiously.

"Why, of course it is. Come on, Amelia, come on! You're in a hurry and so are we."

She did not "come on." She glanced fearfully toward the man behind the grill and then at Early.

"I—I'm payin' it in money," she said. " 'Tain't no check, it's money."

Early laughed, impatiently. "We'd just as soon have your money as your check any day, Melie," he declared. "Maybe a little sooner. It's all right, give it to Mr. Judson. He'll receipt your bill for you."

Carey Judson smiled. "You don't quite understand, Ben," he said. "Pay Mr. Early if you had rather, Mrs. Hope. You *had* rather, hadn't you?"

Melie hesitated. "I—I'd just as soon," she faltered.

Early looked puzzled. "What in the world—?" he demanded.

Judson was still smiling. "Just sound business caution on her part," he observed. "If you don't mind, Ben. . . . Thanks."

He slid from the stool and started over to the window. Early impatiently jerked the bank notes from the caller's clutching fingers, made change from the cash drawer, and hastily receipted the bill. Melie talked all the way from the desk to the door and, still talking, was pushed through that door by the manager. The latter turned and looked at the bookkeeper, who was gazing out of the window.

"Pesky fool!" snorted Early.

Judson turned. "Yes?" he queried. "What is it, Ben?"

Early stared. "What's what?" he demanded. . . . "Eh? Why, good Lord! You didn't think I was talking to you, did you, Carey?"

"Weren't you?"

"No. Well, yes, I was. But I wasn't calling you a fool, 'tain't likely. I was talking about that Melie Hope and her husband. There ought to be a law against half-wits like those two running loose and getting married. One ninny is bad enough, but when that one marries another as bad as she is, what have you got then?"

"More, in the natural course of events, I should say."

"Eh? What? . . . Oh, I see! Yes, yes. Well, *that* hasn't happened yet, thank goodness."

He regarded his companion for a moment and then added:

"Say, Carey, you aren't letting things like that bother you, are you? That woman is just a fool-head, and everybody knows it. Don't pay any attention to her actions. She don't count."

"All right, Ben."

"But I mean it. And don't you let what folks say trouble you, either. They'll talk some for a while, but they'll forget it. You've done all you could. You're going to pay as much on the dollar as any sensible person could expect you to do—

yes, and more than the law would have made you. George has handled things mighty well for you, and don't you forget it."

"Thanks. I'll try and remember, Ben."

"That's right. Let 'em talk. You stick to your new job here and forget what's past and gone. They'll forget, too, by and by. You aren't the only man that's failed in business, not by a good deal."

"All right, Ben."

"Yes. You just go right along, just as if nothing had happened. Don't hide yourself nights and evenings and Sundays. Go out and meet folks and hold your head up. After all, you're George Judson's brother, you know, and that covers up a lot here in Wellmouth. Oh! and speaking of Sunday—that reminds me. Why don't you go to church to-morrow? Our minister, Mr. Bagness, is the smartest preacher in Ostable County. You drop in to-morrow forenoon. 'Twill do you good to hear him. And it won't do you any harm to be seen in church, either."

Judson's hand moved toward his forelock.

"He's going to preach about the prodigal son, I believe," he said. "I noticed the title of his sermon on the church notice board."

"Is that so? I hadn't heard. Well, that always makes a good sermon."

"Yes. And my attendance would be *apropos,* I admit."

"What?"

"Nothing. Thanks for the invitation, Ben. I'll think it over. Good night."

"Better come, Carey. Well, good night."

The door closed. Carey Judson, left alone once more in the outer office, stood gazing from the window, his hands in his pockets. One of the hands encountered a service-worn briar pipe. Absently he drew it forth and lifted it to his lips. Then, remembering the sign above the desk, "Positively No Smoking," he sighed and returned the pipe to the pocket again.

Seen through the not overclean windowpanes was the wharf end, with the little fore and aft schooner made fast to the rings in the stringpiece. Beyond was the harbor, shining, a golden blue, in the sunshine of the late afternoon. Scores of sea birds, gulls and terns and sandpipers, sailed and swooped, or fluttered and dipped, in their everlasting hunt for food. He regarded them with a sympathetic, understanding interest. They, or their relatives and ancestors, were old friends of his. He alone, of the two thousand and odd citizens of Wellmouth township—a township including Wellmouth Center, East, South and West Wellmouth and Wellmouth Neck—could have tagged each species of sea fowl with its ornithological name, could have told where it nested in the nesting season, how many and what sort of eggs were likely to be found in the hit-or-miss nests in the sand, how the fledglings were fed by the parents, everything concerning the birds, big or little. He envied them out there in the sunshine. He would have changed places with any one of them. As a man he was a complete failure, but as a gull—well, he believed he might have been a pretty decent, perhaps even a successful, gull.

He was brought back from the air to the hard pine floor of the office by a voice behind him. It was a hoarse, masculine voice, and there was a distinct note of sarcasm in it.

"Well," it drawled, "hard at work, I see!"

Judson turned. The man who had spoken was a thickset individual, with a long but rotund body, supported by a pair of short and substantial legs. The legs had a decided outward bow. The face above the body was broad and smooth-shaven and sunburned to a clear, fiery red. The nose was red and large and bulbous, and the eyes, small, blue and twinkling, were set under heavy reddish gray brows. The figure was dressed in a suit of blue cloth, the trousers and coat faded and wrinkled, but the waistcoat bright as new. Mr. Sherlock Holmes, noting the condition of the garments, would have drawn the inference that, whereas the coat and trousers were worn almost every day, the vest was donned only on important, dress-up occasions. Above the red face was a forehead, the full extent of which was not visible, as it was covered by a broad-brimmed, high-crowned, brown derby hat, canted well to port. In the starboard corner of the mouth was the stump of an extinguished cigar.

Judson knew the man, of course. He was Captain Tobias Higgins, retired skipper and part owner of the whaling ship *Ambergris*. He had been in conference with George Judson in the latter's private office, a conference dealing, so Carey guessed, with the affairs of the late firm of Osborne and Judson. He stood there, his big feet well apart, chewing the stump of the cigar and eying the new bookkeeper with a look of ironic solemnity. Carey met the look with one of bland interrogation.

"I beg your pardon?" he said.

Higgins grunted. "You needn't," he observed. "I forgive ye."

"Much obliged. But you said something, didn't you?"

"Now you mention it, seems to me I did. I said you 'peared to be hard at work."

"Did I? I'm sorry to disappoint you."

"Humph! I can stand up under the disappointment. You was pitching in about as hard as I expected."

"Good! You give me courage to keep on."

Captain Tobias pushed the brown derby backward until it hung at the last possible angle of safety. He rubbed his left eyebrow.

"Humph!" he grunted again. "Well, Carey, I don't know as I ought to mention it, but after all this good sensible talk of ours so fur, do you cal'late you could come down to somethin' light and frivolous like business? I had a notion of payin' my bill. Phœbe, my wife, seems to think I owe this consarn of your brother's a little somethin'. It can wait a spell longer, though, if it's necessary. I hate to take you away from what you was doin'. I spoke twice afore you heard me, so I judge 'twas interestin'."

"It was. I was looking at the gulls. Did you ever think you would like to be a gull, Cap'n?"

Captain Higgins stared. "A gull?" he repeated. "What in thunder would I want to be a gull for?"

"I don't know. So far as that goes, why should any one want to be anything? And what difference would it make if he did? However . . . now about that bill of yours?"

He walked behind the tall desk and opened one of the books upon it. "According to the records," he said, "you owe this corporation seven dollars and eighteen cents. As they aren't my figures, but those of the fellow who had this job before me, I shouldn't wonder if they were correct. What do you say, Cap'n Higgins?"

Apparently the captain did not think it worth while to say anything at the moment. Puffing a little with the exertion, he pulled a fat black wallet from the inside pocket of the blue coat, loosed the strap which bound it together, and from the midst of a mass of papers selected one. Then, from another compartment he took a small roll of bills secured by a rubber band. He glanced at the paper in his hand.

"Seven eighteen is the figger," he announced. "And seven eighteen she is."

He rolled to the desk beside Judson and, thrusting a bulky thumb into his mouth for moistening purposes, counted off one five-dollar bill and three ones.

"There you be," he said, pushing them across the desk.

Judson took the money and, unlocking the cash drawer, counted out a sum in silver and copper.

"And there you are," he added. "Count it, please."

Higgins grunted again. "I was cal'latin' to count it," he retorted. "I most generally do count what's comin' to me. It pays to be careful in this world."

"So they say. You aren't as careful as some people, though. Amelia Hope was in here just now to pay her bill and she is more careful than you are."

"Eh? Who? 'Melia Hope? Melie G., you mean? There

ain't enough in her head to make a meal's vittles for a hen. What do you mean by her bein' careful?"

"She wouldn't pay her money to me. She insisted on paying it to Ben. She doesn't take any chances, you see. Don't you think you are rather reckless?"

Captain Tobias glanced quickly at the speaker. "That depends on how you look at it," he announced, with a grimly appreciative grin. "I'll chance seven dollars' worth. Anyhow, you hadn't ought to expect me to be as smart as Melie G."

He paused again, glanced shrewdly at the face of his companion, and added, in a tone a little less gruff: "How are you gettin' on in your new berth, Carey? Kind of a rough passage 'long at first, is it?"

Carey smiled. "I suppose I am doing as well as might be expected," he announced. "That depends—"

"Depends on who is doin' the expectin', eh?"

"That's it exactly."

"Um-hum. Well, stick to the wheel. George seems to cal'late you'll make your ratin' all right."

"George is optimistic."

"He's what? . . . Well, never mind, never mind. I might not know any better when you got through tellin' me, *I* ain't ever been to college. But let me give you this one p'int. It ain't my business to set your course for you, boy, but if I was you I'd quit lettin' the Melie G.'s and the rest of 'em make me sore. Forget 'em. See? . . . Well, why don't you answer me? What are you starin' at? Nothin' the matter with my face, is there?"

Judson shook his head.

"No," he answered. "No, your face is perfect."

"Humph! It is, eh? I want to know! Then what are you owlin' at it that way for? You make me nervous."

"I was looking at your cigar."

"My cigar!" The captain took the cigar stump from between his lips. "What ails that cigar?" he demanded. "It's a good one. I paid ten cents for it."

"I know. But it makes me envious, that's all. They won't let me smoke in here."

He pointed to the "No Smoking" placard. Higgins looked at the sign and snorted disgustedly.

"That's Ben Early's doin's," he sneered. "He's too good to live, that feller. Don't you pay too much attention to him, neither. *I* don't. . . . And *now* what are you laughin' at?"

"I wasn't laughing. I was just thinking."

"Thinkin'! You've always been thinkin' ever since I knew you. If you'd done less thinkin' and more doin' you'd have been better off. What are you thinkin' about this time?"

"I was thinking that you and Ben seem to agree."

"We do, eh? Then it is the first time. What are him and I agreed about?"

"Why, his advice seems to be the same as yours. He says not to trouble myself about what people say—or think. He tells me to forget, just as you do."

Captain Tobias' red face grew redder. The statement seemed to irritate him.

"Is that so!" he sputtered. "Well, it's easy enough for him to forget. What's *he* got to remember? Nothin'. He ain't seen the money that he'd saved up and cal'lated to put by safe for a rainy day go plumb to blazes. He ain't seen it stole and carted off by a damned swab that— Humph! Well, I'm talkin' too much, I guess. Good night."

He turned to go, but paused at the threshold.

"I'm sorry I let off steam like that, Carey," he grumbled. "What I meant to do was just give you a little mite of a straight tip, that's all. This ain't liable to be a real happy v'yage you've got ahead of you for the next six months. No, and accordin' to my notion it hadn't ought to be. When a feller ships as mate it's his job to see that the skipper don't run the ship on the rocks. It ain't enough to just stand by and—and look at the—at the—"

"At the gulls?"

"Why, yes," his indignation rising again. "That's just it, if you want to put it so. My tip to you, now that you've come back to Wellmouth here, is to forget what's gone and past and do your level best to make good. George has done all he can to help you. He's stood by you better than a whole lot of brothers would do, I can tell you that. Seems to me it's up to you to buckle right down to hard work. I don't suppose you like keepin' books in a fish store. Seems like consider'ble of a comedown, I don't doubt, but—"

Judson stirred uneasily and lifted his hand.

"Never mind that, Cap'n," he interrupted.

"Eh? Well, it's so, ain't it? I was a good friend of your father's; and I'm one of the ones that lost money by that thievin' partner of yours. Yes," in a still louder tone, "and by your carelessness in lettin' him steal it. So I've got the right to talk, ain't I?"

"No doubt of it. Every right."

"Seems so to me. Well, then! Your job is to work hard, whether you like it or not. Keep your mind on the books and not out of the window and don't make any more mistakes or let anybody else make 'em. . . . There! I've got that off my chest. Good night."

"Just a minute, Cap'n Higgins. Speaking of mistakes. Did you count that change I just gave you?"

"Course I did. I make it a p'int to count money—yes, and look after it, too. Always did—whether 'twas mine or my owner's," significantly. "Why?"

"Ninety-two cents, wasn't there?"

"That's it. Ninety-two is right."

"No, ninety-two is wrong. Eighty-two is right. You owe Judson and Company a dime."

Tobias Higgins hastily did a sum in mental arithmetic. The result seemed to embarrass him. He muttered something and reached into his trousers pocket for the superfluous ten-cent piece.

"There!" he exclaimed, returning to slap the coin upon the desk. "Now we're square, ain't we?"

"Now we're square."

"Humph!" suspiciously. "That was a fool trick, I must

say. How did you come to find out you'd given me ten cents too much?"

"Oh, I knew it when I gave it to you."

"You did! Then what did you give it to me for?"

"Well, to tell you the truth, I expected you to find out the mistake yourself. I judged you would expect me to make mistakes and I hated to disappoint you. I aim to please, you know."

Captain Tobias was, for the moment, speechless, an unusual condition for him. He choked, scowled and then shook his head.

"By the everlastin'!" he growled. "I don't believe you've changed a mite, in spite of everything. You're just as big a—a crazy-head as you ever was. . . . Well, I'll be darned!"

He departed, slamming the door behind him. Carey Judson smiled, then sighed, swung off the stool and, walking over to the window, relapsed into dreamy contemplation of his friends, the gulls.

A few minutes later George Judson came out of the private office. He was, in every respect, a marked contrast to his older brother. The latter was tall and thin. George was of middle height and thickset. Carey was light-haired, George was dark. George was careful and neat as to dress, Carey was indifferent to what he wore or how he wore it. George was, and looked like, a successful, practical man of business. Only about the eyes and when they smiled could one notice a resemblance. But between them was a deep and sincere affection.

When George spoke, his tone was brisk and authoritative, another point in which he differed from his brother.

"All right, Carey," he said, cheerfully. "We can call it a day, I guess. Lock up."

Carey turned from the window, took the books from the desk, placed them in the safe, swung the heavy door shut and whirled the dial of the combination lock.

"Come on," urged the head of the firm of J. C. Judson & Co. "We'll be late for supper, I'm afraid, and Cora won't like that a bit, especially as Aunt Susan is there, you know."

Carey looked at him.

"Oh, she came, did she?" he said.

"Yes. Came on the afternoon train. The train was late, nearly half an hour, and she sputtered about that, just as she did when she was here last. That was years ago and she hasn't changed a bit. She asked about you, of course. She'll be glad to see you."

Carey Judson did not answer. He did not deny his brother's assertion, but he doubted it, at least in the meaning in which it was uttered. If Aunt Susan Dain would really be glad to see him it would be only because she could then have the opportunity of letting him know what she thought of him.

He took his smart straw hat—relic of last year's fancied prosperity—from the hook in the closet and, in company with his brother, went out to face again the ordeal which he dreaded, that of walking through Wellmouth streets under the eyes of the Wellmouth citizens whom his incompetency and criminal carelessness had defrauded.

## CHAPTER II

IT was an evening in early June, that on which George and Carey Judson left the office of J. C. Judson & Co. and started on the walk to the home of the former. Wellmouth was quiet and peaceful, its serenity undisturbed, its Saturday night suppers of baked beans and brown bread already on the tables of its householders or awaiting the arrival of fathers or sons on their way home from stores and shops—or, in rarer instances, of belated summer boarders or city relatives "down on vacation," who, out "codding" or "mackereling," had allowed sport to render them forgetful of time. The Boston morning newspapers, brought down by the noon train, had been distributed and read long before and nothing in their contents was of particular, intimate interest to Wellmouthians. A sensation—even a sensation such as the Osborne and Judson failure—becomes an old story in six months and, although Wellmouth had not forgotten it, and, because of its disastrous consequences to so many citizens, was not likely to forget it for many a year, it had ceased to regard it as the only worthwhile subject of conversation. Even Carey Judson's progress, in his brother's company, from Wharf Lane to the Main Road and along the Main Road to the remodeled towered and dormered residence on Lookout Hill was no longer of such interest as to distract the attention of an impatient housewife from the consequences attendant upon an indefinite delay of supper.

Such a housewife, peering from the dining-room window, may have sniffed disdainfully at the sight of the brothers as they walked home together. She may have declared, as some of them did, that she should think Carey Judson would be ashamed to have the face to be seen among the folks he had swindled; but it was merely a casual remark expressive

21

of a settled conviction. Carey Judson was a disgrace, and every one admitted it, but the reasons why he was a disgrace had been discussed and dissected and vivisected at homes and at sewing circles and after and before church on Sunday until even those who had suffered most were tired of the subject. When the disgrace himself first returned to the village his shame and its course were subjected to a second picking to pieces, but he had been in Wellmouth for a fortnight now, and even his brazen effrontery in coming back and his brother's soft-heartedness in allowing him to do so were getting to be old stories.

The mine had exploded late on an evening in the previous December. A telegram to George Judson first brought the news. George had said nothing concerning it, and the station agent—who was also the telegraph operator—could not have disclosed its contents, for he was supposed to keep all telegrams a secret. But some one told, and that some one told others. Before Wellmouth went to bed that night rumor of the disaster which might mean not only the shattering of an idol, but financial loss to so many, was buzzing in every dwelling from Wellmouth Neck to South Wellmouth.

The next morning the buzz had become a roar. Those who hastened to see George Judson at his office found that he had taken the early morning train for Boston. Then to Captain Benijah Griffin came a reply to his telegram of inquiry, the latter sent to a nephew, a Boston business man. The message was brief, but as sharply pointed as a lancet. "Osborne and Judson failure announced four o'clock yesterday. Looks bad. Morning papers give all known about it so far."

That was all, but, like the announcement of a fatal accident, it was a sufficiently definite declaration that the worst had happened. Osborne and Judson—the firm to which at least fifty men and women of Wellmouth had intrusted their surplus or their savings for investment—Osborne and Judson had failed and the failure "looked bad." "For further particulars see morning papers."

That noon Griggs' Store, at the junction of the Main Road

and Wharf Lane, was crowded with what the *Item* later described as a "seething mob." There were at least thirty-five people in Griggs' store when the depot wagon drew up at its platform, and all of the thirty-five were eagerly and, in so many instances, anxiously excited. Outside, by the platform and moored to the hitching posts near it, were horses attached to buggies and surreys and carryalls and blue "truck wagons." The horses gnawed at the already well-gnawed tops of the posts and pawed at the clam-shells of the frozen road. Inside, at the counter near the rack of letter boxes— Isaiah Griggs was postmaster as well as storekeeper—their owners fought for copies of the Boston dailies.

The depot wagon had brought the bundles containing the latter and, behind the counter, Sam Griggs, the postmaster's son, was opening and assorting the contents. Distribution of the morning papers was always a lively session, particularly during a political campaign or on the day following elections, but then there was loud laughter, joking, and boisterous confusion. Now, as the men pushed and crowded about the counter, no one joked and no one laughed.

Young Griggs, his sorting finished and the papers arranged in piles, found it difficult to keep them out of reach of clutching hands.

"Hold on, there!" he ordered, indignantly. "Let alone of those *Journals*, can't you? You'll get yours, Eben, in a minute. Give me time! Take your turn! . . . Now then: Sam Davis, one *Globe* . . . James Snow, one *Advertiser* . . . Eben Bailey, one *Journal*. There! you've got it; I hope you're satisfied . . . Tobias Higgins, one *Globe*. Eh? What do you want two for? I don't know as I can spare you an extra *Globe* to-day, Cap'n Higgins. . . . Well, well! take it then, take it! Can't stop to argue with you now. Take it and clear out. Only, if somebody else has to go without, you and him'll have to settle it between you. . . . Moses Gould, one *Journal*. . . . Stop your shovin'! Take your *turns!*"

Captain Tobias, his two copies of the Boston *Daily Globe*

tightly clutched in a sunburned fist, elbowed and pushed his
way through the struggling crowd. Having fought his way
clear he folded one of the papers and jammed it into his hip
pocket and, crossing the shop to a comparatively secluded
spot by the side window, he spread open the other, adjusted
his spectacles, and gazed fearfully at the front page. Almost
instantly he found what he was looking for. The headlines
jumped at him.

"Disastrous Failure of a State Street Banking House.
Firm of Osborne and Judson Bankrupt. Senior Partner
Missing. Rumors of Crookedness and Embezzlement.
Sensation in Financial Circles."

This was the scarehead. Beneath it were two columns of
fine print, the second column ending with "Continued on
page 2." Tobias Higgins began to read.

The Boston business and financial world received a shock
late yesterday afternoon when announcement was made of the
failure of Osborne and Judson, bankers and brokers, whose
offices were located at No. — State Street. The firm, although
not an old one—the partnership having existed less than eight
years—was considered one of the soundest in the city, and its
collapse, under circumstances which are reported to be most
suspicious, was a complete surprise to the public. Particulars
are as yet unobtainable, no authoritative statement having been
given out, but the senior partner, Graham G. Osborne, is neither
at the office nor at his Marlboro Street residence and it is said
that he cannot be located. A rumor, as yet unconfirmed, declares that a warrant for his arrest has been issued and that
the police are in search of him. Other rumors are to the effect
that practically all the securities intrusted to the firm by investors have disappeared and it is feared that they have been
sold and the proceeds dissipated in speculation by Osborne. The
junior—and only other—partner, J. Carey Judson, is said to be
in a state of collapse and, at his bachelor apartments at No. —
Mount Vernon Street, it was declared that his physician permitted him to see no one. Those in charge at the State Street
office decline to give any information, but will, so it is said, issue
a statement to-morrow.

The firm of Osborne and Judson was founded in 1876. Graham Osborne, the senior partner, now missing, is forty-two years of age. He was for twelve years in the employ of Jacoby, Coningsby and Cole, the well-known banking house on Congress Street, where he was highly esteemed and, during the later years of his employment there, occupied positions of trust and responsibility. He—

Captain Tobias, having read thus far, skipped the two paragraphs following and began again at the third.

James Carey Judson, the junior partner (he read) is thirty-three years old. He is the son of the late James Carey Judson, of Wellmouth, Cape Cod, where his younger brother, George Judson, carries on the wholesale fish business founded by the father. The Judson firm is one of the best known in its line on the Cape and the family is one of the oldest and most prominent in that section. James Carey Judson, the elder brother, graduated from Amherst in—

Higgins read no further at the time. A cursory glance at the remainder of the article showed him that, so far as news was concerned, it was entirely lacking. There were more historical details concerning the late Captain Jim-Carey Judson and the Judson family generally, but Tobias, like every Wellmouth citizen, was acquainted with those. He folded the paper he had been reading and jammed it into the hip pocket containing the other and unopened copy. Then, without waiting for the distribution of the mail—a most unusual omission on his part—he moved between the groups of townsfolk crowding the store and headed for the door.

These groups made way for him only under physical compulsion. Each member of each group was clutching an open newspaper in his hand and tongues were busy. The general hum of excited conversation was punctuated by exclamations and outbreaks either of wrathful indignation or sorrowful surprise. Of these emotions the former were by far the

more prevalent. Tobias caught snatches of the talk as he
pushed by.

"In a state of collapse, eh? He ought to be. If he showed
his head down here 'twould be collapsed for him. . . . Not
a cent! No, sir-ee, I never let 'em have a cent of *my* money!
I know better. . . . This will be some knock in the eye for
Cora T., won't it? She'll have to come down off her high
horse. Brother-in-law a thief and bound for jail, she won't
be puttin' on so many airs, maybe. . . . Well, his *partner's*
a thief, anyhow; it says so in the paper."

The group next near the door were discussing the sensation
from another angle. The remarks caught by the captain, as
he passed, were in a lower key.

"Cap'n Bill Doane will be hit hard. He put about all he
made when he sold his half of the *Flora* in Carey's hands to
invest for him. Told me only last week he was getting five
and a half per cent on the average. . . . Old Mrs. Bangs—
Erastus' widow—will lose about all her insurance money if
this turns out to be so. She swore by the Judsons. Erastus
worked for the Judsons till he died. . . . How about the
Sayleses? Lawyer Simeon Sayles and Cap'n Jim-Carey were
chums all their lives. I *know* a lot of their money was bein'
taken care of by Osborne and Judson, because Desire Sayles
told my wife so, herself, last time Desire and Emily were
down here—last summer 'twas. . . . Enough to make Cap'n
Jim-Carey turn over in his grave. Young Carey was his
pet. . . . Mighty tough on George Judson, too. George
swore by Carey, he did."

At the door Captain Tobias encountered the Reverend
Ezekiel Thomas. Mr. Thomas was—and had been for
thirty years—pastor of the old First Church, the aristocratic
"meeting-house" of Wellmouth. The minister's white hair
was little whiter than his face as he acknowledged Higgins'
good morning. He paused to ask a question.

"Is it true, Tobias?" he inquired, anxiously.

Tobias nodded.

"It's true," he replied. "The papers have got a lot about

it. They've failed—busted to smash. Don't seem to be any doubt of that."

Mr. Thomas caught his breath.

"Oh, dear!" he gasped. "Oh, dear me! And—and is the rest of it true? Is it as bad as—as they say it is?"

"Bad enough, I cal'late. Looks as if Osborne was a thief and had run away—cleared out. The police are after him."

"And—and Mr. Judson? Carey, I mean?"

"I don't know. All it says here is that Carey is sick abed and the doctors won't let anybody run afoul of him. Don't know whether he helped with the stealin' or not."

"Oh, I hope not! I hope not! I have known him since he was a boy. He was one of my boys in Sunday School. I can't think *he* is dishonest."

"Humph! Well, it's kind of hard for me to think so. I never cal'lated he had—"

"Yes? Had what?"

The captain grunted. "Had ambition enough to take to stealin'," he answered. "He's always seemed to me *too* darned lazy for that."

The minister shook his head.

"I know what you mean, of course," he admitted. "But I— Oh, dear! He is unlike his brother, that is true. Mr. George Judson is—"

"He's a worker, that's what he is. And always was. He was a smart boy and now he's a smart man. Look what he's doin' with his father's business. *He* never had everything he asked for and a whole lot he didn't. If Cap'n Jim-Carey had treated his oldest boy the way he done George, Carey might have amounted to somethin', too. But he didn't —he sp'iled him. And I never see a sp'iled young-un come to anything yet."

"But Carey was always such a *good* boy."

"Good! He was always too lazy to be anything *but* good. When George was pluggin' away in the old man's office and Carey come down here on his vacations—what was he doin' then? Nothin'—nothin' at all! A dozen times when I've been over on the beach, gunnin' or hand-linin' or somethin', I've run afoul of Carey Judson and every time he was just settin' sprawled out in the sand with a pair of spyglasses, lookin' at all creation in general and nothin' in particular, so far as I could find out. Watchin' the gulls and coots and shelldrakes and critters like that, that's what he said he was doin' when I asked him. Healthy job for a grown-up young feller, that is—spyin' at a passel of birds! If he'd had a gun or a line with him I'd have understood. I like to shoot and fish as well as anybody. But he—why, my godfreys; he had the face to tell me once that he didn't like to kill things unless 'twas needful. Said he always felt as if 'twas only good luck —or bad, he said he wasn't sure which—that they picked him out to be man instead of one of them ducks off yonder. I flared up; a feller's patience will stand about so much and no more. Says I, 'Well, Carey, I don't know about a duck, but I cal'late you'd make a pretty fair *loon*. And you wouldn't have had to change much neither.' That's what I said, and I walked off and left him. . . . Good! Bah! He was *good* enough, fur's that goes. But it ain't much of a trick to be good when there's nothin' worth while bein' bad for."

Mr. Thomas sighed. "He was always so kind and—and generous," he observed.

The statement seemed to ruffle the captain more than ever.

"Generous!" he snorted. "Anybody can be generous with money that comes as easy as his did. And good natured! Say, if he hadn't been so everlastin' good natured I'd have had more patience with him. I like to see a feller get mad once in a while; shows there's something *to* him. Take it that time when I called him a loon—did he get mad then? Not much he never! *I'd* have knocked the man that called me that halfway acrost the beach. But all he done was grin, in that lazy way of his, and says he, 'Well, Cap'n,' he says, 'I don't know but bein' a loon has some advantages. A loon generally gets the fish he goes after.' And he knew darned well I'd been heavin' and haulin' that line of mine the whole forenoon and hadn't had a strike. Bah!"

"But every one liked him."

"Well, what of it? You don't call that anything to brag of, do you? When you find a man that all hands like it's my experience you want to keep your weather eye on him. You never heard that everybody liked me, did you? You bet you never! . . . Well, there!" he broke off, disgustedly. "What's the use of all this kind of talk? They won't many of 'em say they like him now, I cal'late. There's too many hard earned dollars been—" . . . He paused and then added, with some hesitation, "Say, Mr. Thomas, it ain't any of my business, but I do hope *you* wasn't soft-headed enough to trust any of your money with that Osborne and Judson gang. *You* don't stand to lose anything by 'em, do you?"

The minister tried to smile, but the attempt was not a success.

"Oh, a little," he confessed. "A little, that's all."

Higgins looked troubled. "I see," he said. "A little, eh? But a little too much, I presume likely. Well, accordin' to what I hear, some people in this town are liable to lose a lot. It's too bad! It's a shame! Why don't they stick to savin's banks and solid places like that? . . . Well, maybe 'tain't so bad as it looks to be now. You can't always tell by the newspapers. I've seen 'em have a Republican all sot and elected one day and the next have to crawl and come out with the truth about the decent candidate winnin'. Maybe it's all a mistake, the worst of it. I hope so."

"So do I. Indeed I do! And not entirely on my own account, I assure you. Poor Carey! At all events, I am very glad you didn't have any money invested with them, Tobias."

Captain Higgins had turned to go, but now he turned back.

"Don't be too glad," he said, dryly. "I've got seven hundred dollars planted there, waitin' for the tombstone."

"You have? You! Why, I thought you said—"

"I say a lot, but I don't always do what I say. I'm as big a jackass as anybody, when the average is struck. Yes, I handed over seven hundred when I sold my cranberry swamp last April. . . . Well, to-morrow we'll know more and feel better, maybe. The 'statement' will be out by then."

The statement issued by the insolvent firm was printed in the papers the next morning, but it was anything but reassuring to the anxious creditors of Osborne and Judson. And the developments which followed confirmed their worst surmises and forebodings. These developments came thick and fast for weeks. Graham Osborne, traced by the police to a hotel in a southern city, shot himself when the officers came to his room to arrest him. He had less than a thousand dollars with him and the problem of what had become of the firm's capital and that placed in its care by trustful investors was solved only too quickly and completely for the peace of mind of the trustful ones. Osborne's life was not a long one, but the last five years of it must have been merry, if indulgence in every sort of expensive luxury, legitimate or otherwise, furnishes merriment. The list of his race horses and card clubs and establishments of various kinds was lengthy and there were items in it which supplied Wellmouth circles—particularly its sewing circles—with scandalous material sufficient to keep them busy all winter. The horses were supposed to be fast, but they had failed to prove that supposition on the tracks. The bets at the card clubs were said to have been high, but they merely lowered the resources of the bettor. As for the establishments—well, their fastness was sufficiently proven, goodness knows, but they merely put their maintainer further behind.

The rest of it, so far as Osborne was concerned, was the ancient story of attempted recuperation by way of the stock market with the inevitable result. Such personal means as he possessed were exhausted early in the game; those of the firm and its customers were sent in vain pursuit. There remained of the wreck little more than a heap of worthless notes and some equally worthless securities. The banking and broking house of Osborne and Judson was as dead as the senior partner who had killed it and himself.

But the junior partner still lived and upon his head fell

the wrath of every sufferer. The creditors wanted to know—
the newspapers wanted to know—the great crowd of casually
interested readers of those papers wanted to know what on
earth he had been doing while the pilfering was going on.
If he, himself, was not a thief—and it looked as if he was
not—then where had he been all the time? What sort of a
partner was he to neglect the business, to let his associate
walk off with everything portable and, when the crash came,
be, apparently, as dumbfounded and overwhelmed as, for
example, Uncle Gaius Beebe, who declared himself so took
aback he just lay to with his canvas slattin', knowin' that he
ought to pray for strength, but too weak even to cuss. More
so, for Uncle Gaius said a great deal, whereas Carey Judson
said absolutely nothing.

The papers said it for him, however. It being evident that
the surviving partner of Osborne and Judson was a promising
subject for interesting development, the editors set about de-
veloping him and his history. Reporters came to Wellmouth
and obtained the stories they were in search of. Readers of
the Boston dailies learned of Captain Jim-Carey's rise from
skipper of a Banks schooner to one of Cape Cod's
wealthiest and most influential merchants. They learned and
wrote and printed the life story of J. Carey Judson, Junior:
how he had been his father's pride and pet; how he had
attended the local school until, quoting from Uncle Gaius
and others, "that wan't high-toned enough for him" and he
had been sent to an expensive private school and then to
college. And how, when his college years were ended, Captain Jim-Carey had set him up in business with Osborne at
considerable expense.

In order [wrote one capable reporter] to understand why so
many of Judson's fellow townsfolk were led to invest their savings with him and his associate, the correspondent interviewed
a number of Wellmouth citizens. It seems that Captain Judson, Senior, had, for years before his death, been accustomed
to help his friends and neighbors with their investments. In
every case, apparently, his judgment was good and the invest-

ment profitable. He was a director in the local bank, prominent in town and county affairs, and respected and trusted by every one, not only in his own community, but in much wider circles. When he provided the capital to start his older son in business it was taken for granted that he knew what he was doing, as he usually did. He carried on his own somewhat extensive buying of securities through Osborne and Judson and he encouraged his friends to do the same. After his death the custom continued on their part. Carey Judson was a Cape man, and the son of one of the most honored and honorable men on the Cape. It was, therefore, natural that when Wellmouth citizens had money to invest they should continue to ask the son of their friend and mentor in money matters to take care of it for them. Mr. George Judson, now head of J. C. Judson & Co., is as respected and trusted locally as was his father. It is reported that he and his firm have lost much by the Osborne and Judson failure but he, George Judson, refuses to believe a word concerning his brother's possible knowledge of Osborne's crookedness or implication in it. He declares—and a considerable portion of Wellmouth, including some who have suffered heavy losses, seems to agree with him—that Carey Judson was entirely innocent of any actual wrongdoing. He—George Judson —stated in a short interview, the only one he has given the press, that his brother was never a business man, that he never cared for or seemed to understand money matters and that, in his opinion, at the time and since, Judson Senior made a great mistake in insisting upon making a banker out of his elder son.

"He seemed to be doing well," Mr. Judson went on to say. "When I asked him about the business he always appeared satisfied, and he always had plenty of money when he came down here on his vacations or to spend a holiday. But he never talked about financial matters of his own accord and his interest was, I believe, as it had always been, elsewhere. He was very fond of nature and natural history and I have heard father tell him, more than once during his college years, that he knew a lot more about the birds and animals up around Amherst than he seemed to know about his studies. He graduated with fair marks, however, and I think he worked hard there, but principally to please father. The old gentleman was proud of him and doted on him, and Carey returned the feeling. That was why he consented to be a banker, to please father. I know that, because he told me so. But it was a mistake, a bad mistake. A slick scamp such as Osborne seems to have been could wind Carey around his finger—and that is just what he did, of course. Carey is as transparent and honest as the daylight. Every one trusted him and he trusted every one. There isn't a crooked bone in his body; I say so and I know. He is taking all this terribly hard, but his friends are going to stand back of him, don't forget it."

This from George Judson; but from others, less charitable, came stories of Carey's eccentricities, his "queerness" and his impracticability. They were interesting tales, funny, some of them, and they made good reading. Thousands of people chuckled over them during that December and January. Carey, himself, slowly recovering in the hospital, from the collapse and nervous breakdown which followed the shock of the failure, read some of the stories, in spite of the care of the nurses to keep the papers out of his hands. He did not chuckle. Every sneer, every jibe at his carelessness and the ridiculously incompetent manner in which he had neglected to keep the slightest watch upon the actions of his partner or the money intrusted to him by people whom he had known all his life, seared his sensitive conscience like the touch of a red hot iron. He did not resent the sneering criticism; he felt that he deserved it all and more.

George had promised to stand by him through his trouble and he kept that promise. It was George who undertook the Herculean task of helping the receivers straighten out the tangled affairs of the bankrupt house. Carey's first thought, when he grew strong enough to think clearly of anything, was concerning the friends and neighbors who had lost their money through him. He had a few personal possessions and these, he made his brother promise, must be disposed of and the proceeds used to help pay the little which could be paid. His father had left him some real estate on the Cape and that was sold. He owned half of the house and land, the former residence of Captain Jim-Carey on Lookout Hill, and George, who owned the other half, bought Carey's share and moved into the old home himself, something his wife had been urging him to do for years. Carey's carefully collected library, including the rare volumes on the birds and animals of New England, went to the auction rooms. Even the furniture of his apartment in Mount Vernon Street went with the rest. Everything, even the few bits of jewelry, family heirlooms, were sold, everything but Captain Jim-Carey's gold "repeater," presented to him by the people of Wellmouth as a thank offering for his labors in bringing the railroad to the town a full year ahead of the scheduled time. That watch George flatly refused to sell. He kept it himself, but only in trust for his older brother.

During the months while the Osborne and Judson snarl was in process of straightening, Wellmouth's resentful animosity toward the betrayer of its trust had slackened just a little. George's attitude and his unswerving confidence in his brother's innocence of intentional wrongdoing helped to soften the feeling. Then, too, there was the hope that some of the invested money might be returned to the investors. But when preliminary announcements were made and the hopeful ones realized how little of each dollar was to come back to their pockets, much of the resentment came back also. Again Carey Judson's name was spoken at every breakfast, dinner and supper table, and, although pity was expressed, very little of it was wasted on him.

Then came the news that the black sheep was to be led back to the home fold. He was to return to Wellmouth, to live with his brother in the big house on the hill, and to keep books in the office of J. C. Judson & Co. Ed Nye, the former bookkeeper, had accepted the offer of a job in Boston, and Carey was to have his place.

Then the tongues wagged. The cheek of the fellow! The bare-faced effrontery of him—his "everlastin' gall," Captain Tobias Higgins called it. To come back to his native town, to live and work among the neighbors he had cheated—it was unbelievable, it could not be true. Or, if it was, he would find Wellmouth the chilliest spot this side of

the North Pole. They would let him see what they thought
of him. Even if he was George's brother—and George was
a smart man and an honest man and a good fellow—even
so, George was carrying things a little mite too far, and they
would make that fact plain to him. They would do almost
anything for George, but they would not take that thieving
brother of his to their bosoms, not by a considerable sight
they wouldn't.

The Reverend Mr. Bagness preached a sermon dealing
with the wages of sin and during his discourse he raised the
sinner's salary.

"And he's going to live in his own father's house," cried
Mrs. Captain Horatio Loveland, one of the local aristocrats,
whose own jig-sawed and cupolaed residence was also on
Lookout Hill and fronted a spacious yard with two green
iron deer and a black iron fountain in it, not to mention an
iron hitching post at the gate, the post representing a negro
boy holding aloft a ring. The paint on the negro boy's
face was scaling off in spots, giving him a leprous appearance, but his attitude was indicative of pride and prosperity.

"He is going to live *there*," repeated Mrs. Loveland. "In
the very house that belonged to the father he disgraced. I
never heard of such brazen—er—brassiness in my life. I
must say I should think George Judson would know better.
But he is like Cap'n Jim-Carey, when it comes to being silly
about that brother of his. Well, I wonder what Cora T.
thinks of it. I rather guess *she* doesn't like the idea—much."

Mrs. Loveland's guess was correct. "Cora T."—her
maiden name had been Cora Tryphosa Peters—was George
Judson's wife. She had lived in South Harniss before her
marriage and her family were everyday people, her masculine parent getting his living by providing the community
with clams and lobsters in the season. But when this fact
is called to mind it should also be mentioned that Mrs. Judson had carefully forgotten it. What she took pains to
remember, and have others remember, was that she was now
the wife of the head of J. C. Judson & Co. She was a

good-looking, dark-haired woman of ample proportions, and her chin, beneath its fleshy upholstery, was squarely framed.

When her husband announced his intention of not only bringing Carey back to Wellmouth, but to a room and meals in their home, that chin became squarer than ever. Also it moved rapidly. She declared she had never heard of such a crazy idea in her life. And she did not intend to hear any more of it.

She did, however, hear a good deal more. George went on to explain. He was worried about Carey. The latter was in miserable physical condition, and his mental state was worse.

"He is half sick," he continued, "and almost crazy with the dreadful experience he has been through."

"Well, he ought to be," snapped the lady. "And as for his coming back to Wellmouth, to say nothing of your bringing him here to live with us—well, I should say you were as crazy as he is. He can't come here. He shan't. I won't have him. What do you think the folks he's cheated will say? What do you think the Lovelands will say? And the Halls? And Emily Sayles and her mother? What do you think everybody will say? Living here, with us, in comfort and luxury, just as if nothing had happened, as if he was as honest as—as you are."

Her husband interrupted. "He is honest," he declared. "There never was a straighter fellow than Carey."

"Rubbish! You can't make me believe any such nonsense as that, George Judson. And you don't really believe it yourself. You only pretend you do because he is your brother and you have always let him make a perfect fool of you. Don't I know? Haven't I seen it ever since I knew both of you? He was always your father's pet and could have every blessed thing he wanted by just asking for it, while you had to work and work like—like a man digging sand in the road—to get the little you have got. While your father lived, and before we were married it used to make me *so* mad to see how that Carey always had his own way, did just what he wanted to, and you—"

George broke in again. "You're wrong there, Cora," he said. "If Carey had had everything he wanted he never would have gone into business. He hated business. He wanted to be a naturalist, or a scientist, one of those fellows that work for the museums and such places. He would have done well at that, I'm sure."

"Then why didn't he do it? Don't talk so silly! If he had told your father he wanted to do that, he would have been let do it. Of course he would, no matter how ridiculous it was."

"No, he wouldn't. Father was set in his mind about that. The only times I ever saw him lose his temper with Carey were when they got on that subject. Carey told father he would never be any good in the banking business. Yes, and I said so, too. The only real row we three ever had was when I took Carey's part and said it was a mistake to try and make a stockbroker out of a man that didn't know a dividend from an assessment. But, you see, father was awfully stubborn in some things. He always planned exactly what we boys were going to do. And—"

"Oh, don't tell me any more about it! I tell you I won't hear it."

She turned angrily to the door, but her husband was standing on the threshold and he made no move to let her pass.

"I want you to hear it, Cora," he persisted, mildly. "You ought to hear it, you know. You don't understand Carey as I do."

"I understand him well enough and I understand what he is, too; just the way all the folks in town understand. And *you* might as well understand, once and for all, that he shan't come to work in your office, to say nothing of living here with us. That's final."

George shook his head. "I wish you wouldn't feel so, Cora," he urged. "It is all planned for Carey to start in on the books a week from Monday after next, and I am going

up to Boston to get him and bring him down to the house
the first of next week. He can have the room over the back
parlor. He will be by himself there, and he won't be in the
way or the least trouble to anybody."

Then the storm broke. The weather had been increasingly
threatening ever since the beginning of the interview, but
now there was what the weather bureau would have called
"high winds, increasing to gale force, accompanied by heavy
rain squalls." Cora T. was accustomed to rule her husband
and, usually, he accepted the rule with meekness and docility.
But on rare occasions he stood his ground. It was so now.
Mrs. Judson stormed and threatened and pleaded and, at
last, wept. But George remained firm and, like the house
founded upon a rock, refused to be blown—or washed—
from his foundations.

"Carey is the only brother I've got, Cora," he told her.
"He is in trouble, awful trouble, and, if he was left alone, as
helpless as he is and feeling as he does, I don't know what
he might do. I want him here where I can keep an eye
on him. He needs me and I am going to stand by him. He
has stood by me—yes, and taken more than one licking for
me, when we were kids."

His wife, seated in the rocking chair, a picture of despairing abandonment, raised her head and fixed a pair of stream-
ing eyes upon the Rogers group on its stand by the window.

"And—and I'm the—the only wife you've got," she
wailed.

"Now, Cora, dear—"

"Don't you 'dear' me. . . . Well, I suppose I've got to
have him here. When you get this way you're as pig-headed
as your father ever thought of being—and worse. But I
tell you this, George Judson, if you expect me to be palaver-
ing and soft-soaping to that scamp of a brother of yours
you'll find yourself mistaken. I'll treat him just barely
decent—you'll make me do that, I suppose—but I *won't* have
him associating with my friends, and when I have parties,
and—and—"

"There! there! You needn't worry. He'll be the last to want to come to parties. I am awfully sorry you feel this way, Cora, but I've got to do it. It's—well, it's my duty, as I see it, and it is going to be done. Forgive me, Cora, dear, and—"

"I won't forgive you. And as for forgiving *him*—o-oh! . . . Well, I tell you this much more: you've got to hire another girl for me and get her right away. The Lovelands keep two now, and Emeline Hall told me she expected she'd have to keep two pretty soon. And you've got as much money as her husband has, I *hope*. If another great hulking man is going to be here to cook for and wait on I'm going to keep extra help, that's all."

"Why—why, of course, Cora. Get another girl, if you can find one. I told you that before. Now kiss me, and—"

"I shan't kiss you. You can kiss that Carey, if you want to. I wonder you don't. You think a lot more of him than you do of me. When I ask you anything—when I beg you on my bended knees—do you pay any attention to me? Indeed you don't! I've been telling you all winter that I need a new sealskin coat."

"Get your coat, get your coat. I said I wanted you to have one."

"Yes, you did!" sarcastically. "But you didn't tell me where I could find one at the price you said you could afford to pay. Sarah Loveland has got one—oh, yes! she has got one! *Her* husband can afford *anything*. If that precious Carey of yours wanted sealskins or diamonds or anything else all he would have to do is hint, just as he hinted that he wanted to come down here and have us take care of him—"

This was too much. George Judson's eyes and mouth opened. "Here! Hold on!" he ordered. "What is that you say? That Carey *asked* to come down here to Wellmouth to work—and live! My heavens and earth! I've been trying for over a month to make him see that he ought to come—that he must come. And for the first three weeks of that month all he would say was no; and even yet he hasn't really promised. And if he ever does agree to do it, it will be only to please me. I want him here because I'm scared to let him go anywhere by himself. Being in this town, as sensitive as he is and feeling as he does, is going to be hell for him—just plain hell."

Mrs. Judson bounced from the rocker.

"There!" she cried, wildly. "That's enough. That's the last straw. Swearing at your wife is something new for you to do, but I might have expected it. It goes along with the rest. I suppose you'll be striking me next. Go away from me. Go down to your old fish store. There is plenty of swearing down there, from what I hear, and you'll be right at home. . . . Go, this minute!"

George went. And, as he walked briskly down to what his wife contemptuously called his "old fish store," his sense of amazed resentment at her idea that it could be Carey who had asked to return to that store and the town in which it was situated—to say nothing of occupying a room in the house which had been his boyhood home—grew and grew. If Cora only knew! If she might have been present at some of the interviews between the brothers.

When the subject was first broached by George, Carey had flatly refused to listen. So, at the second broaching and the third. Carey did not know what he should do and, apparently, did not care. If he were unfortunate enough to recover from his present illness he supposed he should have to go somewhere and do something, but they would be a somewhere and something which would take him as far as possible from all who had ever known him.

"Why, good God, George!" he said, raising himself on his elbow in the hospital cot. "What are you talking about? Do you suppose I shall let myself be a burden on you for the rest of my life? Haven't I made trouble enough for you already and for everybody else who was unlucky enough to have anything to do with me? I can't get away from you now. You and the doctors and nurses have got me down and you're about five to one, so I can't fight my way up—yet. But when I do—well, I'm going somewhere, and it won't be Wellmouth."

George gently forced him back to the pillow.

"There, there, Carey!" he said. "Don't be foolish. There is only one place for you to go, only one I'll let you go—for a while anyhow. And that is where I can watch you. And, as for being a burden, that's nonsense. I need you. Yes, I do. I need a new bookkeeper. I've got to find one right away. You needn't laugh; I mean it."

Carey was not laughing. He was smiling, and was almost too weak to do that. The perspiration stood out on his forehead.

"George," he observed, feebly, "if I were you I wouldn't waste as good a joke as that in a hospital. I'd send it to one of the comic papers. Me—a bookkeeper! I would be a wonderful bookkeeper, wouldn't I? Just about as good as I was a broker. And your customers would enjoy having me handle their accounts. . . . There, there, old man, don't say it again, I know what you're doing for me, and what you have done, and—and the Lord knows I appreciate it. I—oh, here comes that confounded nurse! Keep her away, will you? She's as good a woman as ever lived, and she's been mighty nice to me, so I don't want to kill her. I haven't got the strength to make a clean job of it, anyway. Tell her to clear out and let us alone. Tell her!"

George did not tell the nurse to clear out, of course. Instead he went away himself. But he came back often and each time he came he renewed his persuasions and arguments. He—Carey—was not fit to go away among strangers, and, even if he went, wherever he went, he would have to earn a living. "And what could you do?" he asked.

Carey shook his head. "I don't know," he admitted. "But I know what I can't do, and that is keep books."

"Yes, you can. You can keep my books. It isn't much of a job for a fellow with your education, but—"

His brother waved a thin hand in protest.

"Suppose we forget my education, George," he said. "I have forgotten most of it, myself, and I would sell the rest cheap. I only wish I could pay my debts with it."

"But, hang it, Carey! Talk sense. You've got to do something the rest of your life, haven't you? What do you want to do?"

Another faint smile. "Give it up," was the dubious reply. "If you hear of any one who raises chickens I might be of some use to him. I could understand anything that wore feathers, perhaps. And the hens might like me; my brain and theirs ought to be about on a level. . . . No, George; stop talking about it. It isn't any use. And tell me now about the other thing. Have you sold everything of mine I told you to? How much are the poor devils that trusted me likely to get out of the wreck?"

It was that of which he wanted to talk always and insisted upon hearing. And it was along that line that his brother finally made the approach which led to his consenting to return to Wellmouth.

One day, during the latter part of his stay in the hospital, he first spoke of the idea as a possibility.

"George," he said, "I've been thinking this whole miserable business over since you were here last."

The younger brother nodded. "I know you have," he agreed. "That is the trouble. You don't think of anything else. It is that kind of thinking that has kept you from getting on your feet before now."

Carey's mild eyes showed an unwonted flash.

"Well?" he demanded. "Are you surprised at that? I don't believe you are. I know you pretty well. Suppose you had muddled things as I have. Suppose your bungling and incompetence and general damn-foolishness had lost your father's money, and your brother's and your friends' and the Lord knows how much more. Suppose you had seen yourself held up as a nincompoop in the papers and made a standing joke for everybody to laugh at—those who weren't too sore to laugh. And realizing all the time that you deserved a lot more than you were getting. You would think of it—say, once in a while, wouldn't you?"

George had no honest answer to make. "I wish I might have been there when that partner of yours shot himself," he growled, vindictively. "I think I would have been willing to pay high for a front seat at the show."

"No, you wouldn't. Neither would I. Osborne was made the way he was and he paid high for his own show, such as it was. I am a whole lot more disgusted with myself than I am with him. But say, George; I want you to tell me this: How much money do I owe—oh, well, never mind, then! How much money does that precious firm of mine owe the folks in Wellmouth? Never mind the other creditors for the minute. A good many of them were trying to get rich in a hurry and they gambled. It was a crooked deal they were up against, but never mind them. How much do I owe in Wellmouth?"

George lied a little; that is, he stretched the truth backwards as far as he dared.

"Oh, not very much," he said. "I guess thirty or forty thousand would cover the whole of it down there."

"You're sure? All that I owe the widows and orphans and crippled sea captains and the rest?"

"Yes, I should say so."

"Humph! And if I were to try and keep books for you— Lord! what a crazy idea it is!—I shall be earning something, I suppose? At least you will be paying me something?"

"Of course. I shall pay you what I paid Ed Nye. Perhaps I might pay you a little more."

"No, you won't. And if it wasn't for my debts I should never let you pay me that. But—well, I've got to do something about those debts, those Wellmouth debts. See here, old man, if I did come down there and worked and paid just a little to those—those poor people I've swindled, do you think they might come to see I was sorry and meant to be as honest as—as I could be, with my limited intellect?"

George Judson leaned forward. "Carey," he said, earnestly, "don't let us have any mistake about this. If you come back to Wellmouth it is going to be hard—darned hard, for you at first. You'll have to expect to be slighted and—well, snubbed."

"Of course. Why not? I ought to be. Go on."

"That at first. But I honestly do believe if you come there and work hard and—if you feel you want to, though there is no earthly, legal reason why you should, for your firm's settlement will be as straight and a lot more liberal than other bankrupt concerns I've known of—if you want to try and pay a few dollars now and then on your own hook, I honestly believe you will do more to square yourself with Wellmouth and the Cape than you could ever do any other way. That's the truth; I mean it."

Carey Judson twisted the lock of hair above his nose; he was sufficiently himself by this time to resume old habits. Then he sighed. "Yes, I guess you do, George," he said. "And I know you want me to do it, heaven knows why. And I know, too, that it is going to be mighty hard for you. . . . Well, I—I can't say anything about how I feel towards you. It's no use."

"You needn't. You would do as much and more for me."

"Maybe. Just now I haven't enough confidence in myself to believe it. But, as for your plan, George, I—well, maybe I'll say yes. Maybe I'll come with you and see how it works."

"Good! Good enough!"

"Bad enough, it is more likely to be. But I guess I'll try it."

So, in the end, he came. And now, his first week's labor ended, he was walking, with his brother, to the latter's house —the house in which he had spent his childhood and boyhood and the happy vacations of his youth—to face again the frigid and contemptuous countenances of his sister-in-law and the servants, and to meet his aunt, Mrs. Susan Dain, from Cleveland, Ohio, who had not seen him for at least four long years.

# CHAPTER III

THERE were no cast-iron animals in the yard of the "Cap'n Jim-Carey place," although the path from the front gate was flanked by a pair of iron benches, of the scrolled and curlicued cemetery variety. The path led straight to the front steps, the top step having a scraper at either end. Above that step was the formal front door, its upper panels of ground glass ornamented with designs of fruit and flowers. These, however—and the door itself—were hidden by closed green blinds, for the Judson front door, like all front doors in Wellmouth at that period, was strictly for ornament and almost never for use. As a matter of fact, that particular door had not been opened since the day of Captain Jim-Carey's funeral.

George and Carey Judson did not attempt entering the house by way of the front door. They would as soon have thought of entering by the chimney. Midway of the yard, the walk forked and they took the branch to the left, that leading to the side door and side entry. In this entry, on a walnut rack, they hung their straw hats and, George leading the way, they went on into the sitting room. The sitting room was bright and cheery and livable and in it, in rocking chairs each with a crocheted "tidy" on the back, sat Mrs. Judson and Aunt Susan Dain, sewing. No, Mrs. Dain was sewing; Cora T. was making a splintwork photograph frame. The ladies put down their work and rose. The brothers came forward to meet them. Mrs. Judson spoke first.

"Well," she observed, tartly, "you're here, aren't you. I began to think you wasn't coming at all. What sort of state supper's in, the land only knows. It's been waiting for you half an hour."

Her husband hastened to apologize.

45

"I'm sorry, Cora," he said. "I was all ready to shut up and come home when Cap'n Higgins came in to see me, and you know how hard it is to get rid of *him*. Well, Aunt Susie, here's Carey. You and he haven't seen each other for a long time. Looks about the same, doesn't he?"

Aunt Susan Dain—she was a younger sister of Captain Jim-Carey—did not answer for the moment. She was a brisk little woman, with sharp blue eyes and a snappy manner of moving and speaking. She looked her older nephew over from head to foot.

"No," she said, "he doesn't. He's a lot thinner than he used to be and he's as white as a Sunday handkerchief. He always did look like a picked Shanghai chicken, but now he looks as if he didn't get enough to eat—or didn't want to eat it, one or the other. . . . Well, Carey, why don't you say something? Aren't you going to kiss me? Or have you forgotten how? For the matter of that, you never did know how very well. George was different. I guess likely he had had more lessons."

George laughed. Carey smiled and bent to peck at his relative's cheek. Cora T. watched the performance with impatient disapproval.

"Humph!" she sniffed. "Lessons aren't necessary for some things, with some people. I guess likely that precious partner of his could have given 'em to him, if what the papers have been printing is true. And you needn't worry about his not getting enough to eat. George looks out for that. My soul, George Judson," she added, turning to the latter, "what in the world did you send home all that halibut for? There's enough for a regiment. What did you think I was ever going to do with it?"

Her husband's brow puckered. "Why, Cora," he protested, "you told me you wanted a good piece of halibut for to-morrow's dinner. That was as fine a piece as we've had come in at the wharf this year. And 'twas caught only yesterday."

"What of it? If you'd caught a whale yesterday, I sup-

pose you'd have sent half of that home, wouldn't you? . . .
Oh, never mind, never mind! I suppose the hens will have
what the rest of us leave, as usual. Well, if you're ready
I am sure supper is—too ready, and spoiled, probably."

At the supper table Aunt Susan was placed at George's
right hand, opposite and as far away from Carey as possible.
Mrs. Judson was affectionately gracious to the old lady. The
latter was, in spite of her loss of several thousand by the
Osborne and Judson failure, still in possession of a good
deal of money and her two nephews were her only relatives.
The covered dish of baked beans and the heaped plate of
brown bread were deposited in front of George by the new
servant. The latter was an importation from Boston, and
about her, and everything she did, was a haughty air of
conscious superiority. She bore the dishes in from the
kitchen with uptilted nose, as if the odor of such plebeian
rations disgusted her, and her attitude, as she stood behind
her master's chair, awaiting their apportionment, was that
of self-contempt at finding herself in such a humiliating
position. Mrs. Judson had secured her through the influence of the Loveland cook, also a Bostonian of Hibernian
extraction, and Cora T. proudly told her husband that she
had worked for some awfully rich families. Why she no
longer worked for those families, but consented to take a
situation in the country, was something of a mystery. Mrs.
Judson's own cook—her name was Hepsibah Ellis; she had
been Cap'n Jim-Carey's housekeeper and there was nothing
of the Bostonian about *her*—confided to personal friends
that the newcomer thought herself "some punkins" and was
always talking about the big bugs she had been used to waiting on, but she—Hepsibah—had already found out it was a
good plan to keep the cooking sherry locked up. The new
servant's name was Maggie.

George Judson bent his head and pattered through a hasty
blessing. Then he proceeded to his business of serving the
baked beans. Maggie slid each plate before its recipient with
a contemptuous flourish, thrust the platter of brown bread

under each nose, and then distributed the teacups as Mrs. Judson filled them.

"That will do, Maggie," said Cora T., grandly. "You can go now."

Maggie departed, her skirts swishing disdain as they brushed the doorway. There was a general relaxing of tension following her exit, particularly noticeable on George's part. He began to talk to Mrs. Dain, as did his wife. Aunt Susan talked to both of them and, occasionally, to Carey, who said very little. George asked questions concerning matters in Cleveland; Mr. Dain had been an Ohio man, and his widow's home was in that city. Cora T. talked of society happenings in Wellmouth, dwelling largely upon the new piazza which the Halls were adding to their home.

"Piazzas are getting to be quite the thing," she observed. "People sit outdoors in the summer time so much more than they used to. I think it is real nice in warm weather. I have ordered a hammock myself. Tobias Higgins is going to make it for me. He makes lovely hammocks out of cod line. The Lovelands have got one. It is made just like a fish net. They have it hung out in the front yard between the syringa bush and the lilacs."

Her husband laughed. "That was Nellie's idea, I shouldn't wonder," he observed. "Nellie is the Loveland daughter, Aunt Susie; maybe you remember her. She's been trying to land a fish for the last three or four years, but up to now they have managed to get away. The other evening, when I was going down to lodge meeting, I noticed she had young Bennie Hall hung up in that hammock. Maybe *he* won't be able to wiggle out, you can't tell."

Mrs. Judson regarded him with disapproval.

"Don't talk nonsense, George," she ordered. "Bennie Hall is only a boy. He isn't through Tech yet. And Nellie is— well, she is older than he is."

George chuckled. "That statement isn't what you'd call an exaggeration," he declared. "But maybe she's old enough not to be too particular. The younger you catch 'em the tenderer they are, you know. Ho, ho! That's so, isn't it. Carey?"

Carey looked up from his plate. "What, George?" he asked. "I didn't hear you. I was thinking of something else, I guess."

"As usual," commented Mrs. Judson. "George—"

But her husband was still chuckling.

"There was a time here, half a dozen years ago, Aunt Susan," he explained, "when we didn't know but Nellie would have Carey hooked. He is older than she is, of course, but he was pretty tender in those days. He—"

"George!" snapped Cora T. "Be still and pay attention to your business. Pass Aunt Susan the brown bread, why don't you?"

Mrs. Dain accepted a second slice of the bread. She regarded her older nephew through her spectacles.

"Humph!" she sniffed. "I didn't know that Carey was ever interested in any girl—except one, perhaps. What has become of that Emily Sayles? I always liked her."

"Who? Emily? Oh, she and her mother are in Hartford, I guess. They live there winters. Lawyer Simeon Sayles— Emily's father; of course you knew him, Aunt Susan— owned that old white house on the Trumet road. Desire and Emily used to come there summers, but for three years they've been away, down in Maine, I believe, and this sum- mer—well, I don't know what they'll do this summer. There is some talk of the Sayles place being put up and sold. . . . Probably that is just talk, though," he added, hastily.

His wife looked wise. "I shouldn't wonder if it was a lot more than talk," she announced. "Sarah Loveland told me that she had had a letter from a cousin of hers—a very nice person who visits her once in a while, *so* pleasant and refined, and worth a *great* deal of money. I know her *very* well. . . . This person said in the letter that she met Emily in New York and that Emily told her she and her mother were considering selling the old place. Emily said they hated to think of doing it, but they might have to."

Aunt Susan seemed surprised. "Have to?" she repeated. "Why should they have to if they don't want to, for mercy sakes?"

Cora T.'s air of wisdom became more profound.

"I don't know," she said. "Of course I don't *know*—but I might guess. Maybe it's because they need the money."

"Need money! Why should they need money? They've got money, haven't they? In my day here Simeon Sayles used to be called rich."

George put in a word. He appeared uneasy.

"Oh, I guess he never was anything like as well-off as people thought he was," he explained.

"Well, he had considerable, I know. And there was nobody to leave it to but his wife and daughter. They have always lived pretty well since his death, too. When I saw them the last time I was East here they certainly didn't look poverty stricken. What have they done with their money?"

George fingered the handle of the serving spoon. He tried to change the subject.

"I—I don't know, I'm sure," he stammered. "Er—can't I help you to a few more beans, Aunt Susan?"

"No, of course you can't. You gave me enough for a day laborer in the beginning. And I have eaten them, too. I ought to have more sense, at my age. But what makes you act so queer? What have the Sayleses done with their money? I believe you do know. At any rate, Cora does. What is all this mysterious stuff, George Judson?"

George did not answer, nor did his wife, although she seemed about to do so. It was Carey who spoke.

"Everybody knows, Aunt Susie," he said, quietly. "They invested a good deal of it through me and my late partner. It isn't much of a mystery."

Aunt Susan said "Oh," and that was all. George said nothing, but he frowned. Cora T. smiled slightly and begged her visitor to have another cup of tea.

There was a good deal of talk during the rest of the meal.

but it was very general and a trifle forced. Aunt Susan chatted of this and that, but she carefully refrained from addressing her older nephew, although she glanced at him shrewdly from time to time. After supper was over they went back to the sitting room. A few minutes later Carey announced that, if they did not mind, he would excuse himself and go to his own room.

"I am going to bed early," he explained. "I am rather tired, for some reason."

Mrs. Dain's bright little eyes looked him straight in the face.

"Working pretty hard, are you, Carey?" she asked.

"Oh, not too hard."

"A little harder than you've been used to, maybe."

"Perhaps. . . . But—"

"But what? You mean you wouldn't have to kill yourself to do that?"

Carey smiled. "You're a pretty good mind reader, Aunt Susie," he said.

"Humph! It never was much of a trick to read *your* mind, young man. It always was pretty large print. Well, I shall see you in the morning, I suppose."

"Eh? Oh, surely! Yes, indeed."

"All right, I want to. Good night."

After he had gone upstairs she turned to George.

"Takes it pretty hard, doesn't he, George?" she inquired.

George nodded, gloomily. "Mighty hard," he said.

"Humph! Yes, he would. Well, that won't hurt him any. May do him good. And he deserves it."

Cora T. dropped the splintwork frame in her lap. "There!" she exclaimed, with great satisfaction. "If it isn't a comfort to hear you say that, Aunt Susan! It is exactly what *I* say, and what I tell George. He does deserve it. When I think of all the poor people in this town, and so many other places, who have lost their money through him, I —oh, I lose all patience!"

Aunt Susan threaded her needle. "Then I wouldn't think

of them," she said. "It doesn't do them any good, and most
of us need what spare patience we've got."

"But *some*body ought to think of them."

"Well, somebody does," with a jerk of her head toward
the stairs. "I imagine *he* does, for one. . . . George, read
me some of the town news in the *Item*. It has been a long
time since I was here and I want to know who is having his
barn shingled. You can skip the death notices; I have reached
the age where they are altogether too much like a time-table."

Upstairs, in the bedroom over the sitting room, Carey
Judson, too, was reading, or trying to do so. He was
sprawled in the Salem rocker, by the table with the lamp upon
it, and the book in his hand was one he had taken from the
shelf on the wall at the head of the bed. It was one of his
own books, one he had bought with money which Aunt
Susan had sent him on his fifteenth birthday, a juvenile
yarn of hunting and adventure. All the books on that shelf
were similar—boy's stories which he had owned and loved
when a boy. For that room had been his ever since he was
old enough to have a room of his own and, for a wonder, it
had been allowed to remain pretty much as it was, untouched
by his sister-in-law's improving and modernizing hand. Cora
T. had not yet, as she said, got around to "doing over"
that room, although some of these days, she prophesied, she
was going in there to "pitch out" most of the dreadful rubbish
it contained. The wall paper was the same which Captain
Jim-Carey and his wife had selected when the house was
built. The furniture was old-fashioned painted pine and
maple, not new black walnut. The "rubbish" was Carey's
own accumulating, a moth-eaten stuffed squirrel on a stick;
a moulting stuffed gull hung from the ceiling by a wire; a
pair of stuffed quail in a homemade and lopsided glass case;
the cabinet—also homemade—containing his collection of
birds' eggs; the long muzzle-loading shotgun Judson, Senior,
had once owned and later presented to his oldest son in
defiance of family and neighborly protest. To Carey that
room was home and it was the one spot connected with home

for which he felt the old affection. In that room, at times
since his return, he could still experience a sense of "belong-
ing" and a measure of forgetfulness.

Not this evening, however. The story he tried to read
was too youthful and impossible to hold his attention, and
he laid it down. He walked to the window and stood, looking
out over the town, its lighted windows agleam. Every house,
every back yard in sight, was familiar to him. He had been
in each house, had played in each yard. At the beginning
of how many happy vacations had he eagerly hurried from
school or college to the train which would bring him back
to Wellmouth! Acquaintances and friends had often urged
him to spend a part of those vacations with them elsewhere,
but he only infrequently accepted the invitations. But once—
when he went on the three months' trip to Labrador with
Professor Knight, the head of the Ornithological Department of the Museum of Natural History in a middle-western
city—had he missed spending at least a part of a summer
in Wellmouth. The Professor used to visit a sister in the
town—she was dead now—and he had taken a fancy to the
young fellow who knew and loved and understood birds so
well. Carey had had a glorious time on that excursion. He
had not seen the Professor since, although for a time they
corresponded. As he stood there at the window he found
himself wondering what the old chap was doing. Still put-
tering with his specimens and chasing here, there and everywhere after others, probably. It must be a glorious life and
fortunate the man who could live it, whose parents—even
if they believed him to be an idiot—had permitted him to go
his own idiotic way, be the consequences what they might.
At least they could never be as disastrous as those which had
followed upon Captain Jim-Carey's stubbornness in driving
him into business and his own careless, weak-spirited yielding. He might have—probably would have—failed at anything he tried, but at least those people down there behind
those lighted window shades would then have been able to
speak of him only as an honest and foolish failure, not as

a crook. Why—oh, why—had Aunt Susan Dain dragged Emily Sayles' name into the supper table conversation!

He swung away from the window, picked up the book once more, and read a few lines, then gave it up and did what he had told his aunt he intended doing—went to bed.

He rose early the next morning and came down to the sitting room. The George Judson family followed the ancient New England custom of lying late on Sunday morning and the Sabbath breakfast was usually served about nine-thirty. Carey had arranged with Hepsibah to eat alone in the kitchen and go out for a walk before his brother and Aunt Susan and Cora T. made their appearance. Hepsibah had been "hired help" in that house ever since he could remember and he and she had been co-conspirators on many Sunday mornings in the past. Since the failure and his return in disgrace her attitude toward him had been a peculiar combination of impatience and indulgence. On the evening of his arrival she had greeted him with a sniff and a perfunctory handshake; but later on, when, following a boyhood custom, he went out to the kitchen for a drink from the pump, she had appeared at his elbow with a handful of molasses cookies and the announcement that there was a piece of apple pie in the pantry if he felt like eating it.

"I saved it for you," she said. "It's awful stuff to eat just afore you go to bed, pie is, but you've ate enough of it in your time and it ain't killed you yet, so maybe you'll take the risk. Only don't blame me if you suffer afterwards."

He accepted the pie, not because he wanted it but because he knew his doing so would please her, and while he was eating it she sat in the kitchen rocker knitting and regarding him steadily. Maggie, the new maid, was out and they were alone.

"Well," she observed, after an interval of silence, "you've come back to Wellmouth to stay put this time, eh?"

He nodded. "It looks so," he said.

"Um-hum. Well, you might come to a worse place. I

'don't cal'late you feel that way just now, though. Goin' to keep George's books for him, so I hear."

"I'm going to try."

"Huh? I guess likely 'twill *be* a trial—for you, I mean. What do you know about keepin' books?"

"Nothing."

"Well, that's some satisfaction, maybe. When a body knows they don't know anything they're generally in better shape to learn. You're goin' to work for a good man. Did you know that?"

The nod this time was emphatic. "No one knows it better," he said.

"Yes, George Judson's a good man. He's got a lot of your father's generousness and common sense and there's enough of your mother in him to keep the sense from runnin' to pig-headedness. You don't remember your mother very well, of course. She was a fine woman. I thought a sight of her."

Carey was busy with the pie and made no comment. Mrs. Ellis went on.

"Maybe if she had lived," she said, "she might have made Cap'n Jim see that settin' you up in that bankin' business was a fool notion. Might as well turn a canary bird loose in a room full of cats. Anybody that knew you would know that Boston gang would have you clawed to pieces and swallowed in less 'n no time. *I* wasn't surprised when it happened. Only surprisin' thing was that it took so long. . . . Well? Have you had enough to satisfy you till mornin'? There's plenty more cookies. I wouldn't let you eat any more pie if I had it to give you."

Carey rose. "I have had quite enough, thanks, Hepsy," he said. "It was as good as it always used to be."

"Huh! Why shouldn't it be? I guess I know how to cook well enough to satisfy the average man, even if I never hired out to Boston big bugs. You always had a sweet tooth. Well, come out here any time when you get the cravin'. What you get in there," with a movement of her thumb in the direction of the dining room, "may have consider'ble pepper along with the sugar. . . . My soul!" with apparent irrelevance, "it is astonishin' how sensible a man can be in most things and what a dummy he's liable to be when it comes to pickin' a woman to live with all his life. . . . Well, good night."

"Good night, Hepsy. Thanks again for the cookies."

"That's all right. They'll always be here when you want 'em. Don't pay any attention to that Maggie one; you come right to me."

She was awaiting him in the kitchen when he entered it this Sunday morning, and his breakfast was ready. He sat down at the table there and she stood by and watched him.

"Goin' off by yourself, same as you used to, I suppose probable?" she asked.

"Yes. I thought I might take a walk along the beach."

"Um-hum. I'd have guessed that if you hadn't told me. Comin' back in time to go to meetin' with the rest of 'em?"

"I doubt it."

"So do I. Well, I suppose you know what she'll say. She's a great go-to-meetin' hand."

"She," of course, meant Mrs. George Judson. Hepsibah usually referred to her as "she." Carey smiled dubiously.

"I know," he admitted. "But—well, honestly, Hepsy, I haven't got the—call it courage, if you want to—to go to church here yet. Everybody knows me and—and—"

"And you cal'late they'll be payin' more attention to you than to Mr. Thomas' sermon. I shouldn't wonder if you was right. But you'll have to go sometime, won't you?"

"I suppose so. But I can't make up my mind to do it to-day."

"Well, then, don't. Go when you get good and ready and not before. Only *when* you get ready—go, even if you have to go alone. Say, Carey, I don't know as my advice amounts to much, but, such as it is, I'll hand it you free gratis for nothin'. You do what you feel is right to do and don't let anybody else talk you into doin' the other thing. You've done that other thing too often; that's part of what's the matter with you. . . . Eh? Good land, who's this comin'! I didn't suppose there was anybody up but you in that end of the house yet awhile. Who's sick, I wonder?"

No one was sick, but Aunt Susan Dain was up and dressed, and apparently very wide awake. She opened the door from the dining room and looked in.

"Good morning," she said, briskly. "Carey, when you've finished breakfast I wish you would come into the sitting room a minute. I want to see you before the others come down."

The door closed again. Carey twisted his forelock.

"How on earth did she know I was out here?" he asked.

Hepsibah sniffed. "She's known you and your tricks about as long as I have," she declared. "She's a smart woman, always was, way back afore she was married. And she comes of smart able people. *Her* father never peddled clams for a livin'—or, if he did, his customers never found 'twas safer to smell of 'em afore they paid the bill."

When Carey entered the sitting room Mrs. Dain, who was sitting by the window, looked up from the *Item* she was reading and motioned to him to take the chair next hers.

"Sit down, Carey," she ordered. "I've been wanting to talk with you alone and I guess this is as good a chance as any we're likely to have."

Carey obediently took the chair. It was Cora T.'s pet rocker and his occupying it was close to sacrilege.

"All right, Aunt Susan," he said. "Here I am. Talk."

"I'm going to. I'm going to talk about you. That's what I got up so early for. It probably won't be much of a novelty for you—being talked about. I should imagine you must be used to it by this time."

Her nephew nodded gravely. "I am," he admitted; and then added, "measurably."

"Humph! Well, you didn't expect not to be talked about, it isn't likely?"

"No."

"And you deserve to be. You know that, too, don't you?"

"Yes."

"Um-hum. Perhaps it's been mentioned to you before. And will be again. Well, that is what you must expect. People who dance have to pay the fiddler. . . . Now what are you twisting your front hair for? What were you going to say?"

Carey's slim fingers paused in the twisting. He smiled.

"I wasn't going to say anything," he answered.

"Probably not. But you were thinking."

"Why, yes, I was. I was thinking that some people don't seem to be able to do either."

"Humph! And what does that mean? Either what?"

"Either dance or pay."

"I see. You never did dance much, that's a fact. It might have been better for you if you had. Then you would have been where you could watch the others. That partner of yours danced considerable, didn't he?"

There was no answer. Carey's hand moved upward again toward his forehead. Mrs. Dain's sharp command halted its progress.

"Let your hair alone," she snapped. "It will go fast enough without your pulling it out by the roots. Carey, I am all out of patience with you. What in the world did you ever get into this mess for?"

He shook his head. "Why does a hen cross the road?" he asked.

"Oh, my soul and body! *Can't* you talk like a sensible person? No, I suppose you can't; anyway you never have since you were old enough to talk. Well, I always heard a hen crossed the road because she couldn't go around it. But she looks where she's going, at least. Why didn't you look and see where that business of yours was going? It must have been plain enough."

He stirred and started to rise from the chair. She caught his arm.

"You sit right down," she ordered. "I haven't said a

word of what I wanted to say yet. We'll leave what has happened to take care of itself. Talking won't help it, now that it is done, and it was your father's fault more than yours. I *should* like to talk to *him;* but he has gone where I can't get at him. . . . Carey, what did you ever let George tease you into coming back here for? To keep books, of all things! You—keep books! You couldn't keep a—a fish line and keep it straight. . . . *Now* what were you going to say?"

"I was going to agree with you, that is all."

"Oh, dear me! If you would only stop agreeing with folks and say no once in a while, for a change! If you had said no to your father— But there! we were going to forget that. You came here because George wanted you to, of course. That is part of what I wanted to talk to you about. You've picked out about the hardest thing you could possibly do. You're going to have a dreadful hard time of it. Working in that office, walking the streets of this town where everybody knows you, facing the very folks whose money has gone to pot on your account, living in this house with—well, with those you've got to live with. It is too much. Whether you deserve it or not it is altogether too much. See here, Carey, suppose I could find something for you to do out in Cleveland, some sort of work—the land knows what it would be—anything you could do, I mean—would you do it? Would you give up this foolishness—and come out and try it?"

He shook his head. "No, Aunt Susan," he said.

"Humph! . . . Well, you said no prompt enough that time, I'll have to admit. Why won't you, for mercy's sake? Do you *like* to be here?"

"No."

"Of course you don't. That was a silly question, and I shouldn't have asked it. Then why not come?"

"Because—well, because I have made up my mind to stay here. Thank you just as much, though."

"Never mind the thanks. And don't make the mistake of thinking that I have forgiven you for making such a spectacle of yourself, because I haven't. You deserve to be punished and you're bound to be—only—well, I believe there is a law against cruel and unusual punishments and I suppose I've got some of the family soft-heartedness—or soft-headedness, whichever you want to call it. If you've made up your mind to be a martyr—and you say you have—I can't stop you. But I want to tell you this, young man: martyrdom is a beautiful thing for other folks to read about, but I sometimes doubt if the martyr himself appreciated the beauty of it while it was going on. And it generally takes the rest of the world at least a hundred years to realize it was a martyrdom and not just burning rubbish. If you act as brave and long-suffering as—as any Saint What's-his-name that ever was boiled in oil, you won't be praised for it down here in Wellmouth. I hope you realize that."

"I do."

"But you're going to stay just the same?"

"I am going to try to stay."

"All right. I guess there's some of your father's stubbornness in you, after all. And, it is like his, too—showing up in the wrong place. I shall be interested to see how it works out. You're going to hoe your row, and you'll have to hoe it alone. I've offered you a chance—mercy knows why, for you don't deserve one, that's sure—and you won't take it. But that's all I can do for you. You mustn't expect any help from me—money help, or any other kind. You have had money of mine—you and your partner—and it has gone where the woodbine twineth."

Carey's hand, which had again strayed toward his forehead, moved impulsively in her direction.

"I'm awfully sorry, Aunt Susan," he said, sadly. "That is one of the things I am most sorry about."

"You needn't be. I can afford to see it go better than a whole lot of others can. Only," with a sarcastic reference to some of the newspaper stories concerning the late Osborne's extravagance, "if I'd known it was buying orchids for other women I *should* have liked the privilege of picking the women. What I want to say, Carey, is just this. You mustn't expect any more money from me—while I'm alive or after I'm dead. That is plain enough, isn't it?"

Carey untangled his long legs and stood up.

"Perfectly plain, Aunt Susan," he said, quietly; "and common sense besides. If I had any fault to find with it, it would be that it was a little superfluous. I haven't expected any money from you. I have never thought of such a thing."

She regarded him shrewdly. "Haven't you?" she observed. "Well, perhaps, being you, you haven't. But I shouldn't be paralyzed with surprise if there were some folks who had— and do. However, I guess probably you haven't. You never were enough interested in money to think about it much. *And*—which does make a difference—you've always had all of it you wanted. Well, you won't have it from now on, which may be a good thing for you. . . . What? Don't mutter; say it out loud."

He was looking at her with a peculiar expression. Now he smiled.

"I am thinking about it," he said. "In fact, I expect to think about it for—well, for the rest of my life, perhaps."

She straightened in her chair. "Now what do you mean by that, I wonder?" she demanded. "You mean something. When you get that queer look in your eye it means there is something up your sleeve. I've seen you look that way too many times not to know. Humph! And you won't tell me what it is, of course? No, you never would. Oh, Carey Judson, you *are* a provoking good for nothing! Did you know it?"

His smile broadened. "It seems to me I have heard something of the sort," he said. Then the smile faded, and he added seriously and more briskly than was his usual habit of speech, "But I don't mean to provoke you, Aunt Susan. You have always been mighty good to me."

"Stuff and nonsense! And never mind whether I have or not. I'm not going to be good to you any more. I'm through with you and you must understand it. . . . Now where are you going? Down to the shore to moon up and down the sandhills, I'll bet! Why don't you stay at home and go to church like a respectable person?"

"Now, Aunt Susan!"

"*Stop* looking at me that way! I suppose you mean you aren't a respectable person. Well, you aren't. Clear out! Go away! You'll spoil my appetite for breakfast. But don't you forget what I've said. You mustn't expect me to help you any more, alive or dead. I've taken you out of my will, Carey. I'm sorry, but my conscience wouldn't let me do anything else. If I left money to you I should crawl out of my grave every night and sit on the tombstone wondering who had got it away from you. You're better off poor, and that's what you will always be, as far as I am concerned. Poor folks have to work, and hard work is a change that may do you good. I did think that I might take you somewhere where the hardness wouldn't be quite as hard in one way, but if you had rather stay here—why, that is your own lookout. . . . There! I've said my say. Now you can go beachcombing, if you want to."

# CHAPTER IV

THE day was clear and sunshiny. There was a light breeze blowing from the southwest, a breeze which, although bringing with it more than a hint of the coming summer, had still in it a tang of coolness invigorating and salty. Carey's thin nose sniffed it with zest and his stride quickened as he moved down the road leading from Lookout Hill toward the shore. The road was deserted. Smoke arose from kitchen chimneys of the houses he passed, indicating that breakfasts were in process of preparation, but the shades in the front portions of those houses were still drawn tightly to the sills. Over the dozing village hung the stillness of Sunday morning, a stillness which belonged to it and was a part of every Sunday he could remember.

He walked along the main road for a short distance, then, turning to the right, swung over the cedar rail fence bordering the field beyond the Methodist church and took the path "across lots" which led directly to the beach. The path climbed a little hill and, winding through a thicket of cedar and white birch, continued along the top of the dyke separating Eben Crosby's cranberry swamp from Cahoon's pond, the little sheet of water where, as a boy, he had navigated the first rowboat he ever owned. The water of the pond was blue and upon its slightly rumpled surface floated a party of his friends, the gulls, enjoying the luxury of a fresh water bath. Beyond the dyke the path entered a grove of pines and, emerging from these, came out at the top of the first of the row of sand dunes bordering the bay.

From this dune the view was, except for its foreground, exclusively wet. Right and left the beach stretched in low white lines, backed by yellow sand hills. To the right it ended at West End, with its lighthouse: to the left at East

End, marked by a barrel on a pole. Within those arms was Wellmouth Bay, and, beyond and between, a glimpse of open sea. The bay, ruffled by the wind, was an expanse of blue, or light and dark green, broken only by the fish weirs, their spidery poles and nets rising here and there as if traced with a pen dipped in brown ink. The air came cool and fresh from the water, the light surf creamed and frothed along the strand, and above its tumbled lines more gulls, large and small, swooped and soared and dived. Flocks of sandpipers scurried along the beach, just above the ripples' edge.

At Carey's left, a half mile away, the village began abruptly with a row of fish and clam shanties and, beyond these, the wharf of J. C. Judson & Co., the schooner moored at its outer end, and other bay craft anchored here and there. There were, at this period, but few dwellings in sight. Most Wellmouth householders either were spending or had spent the larger part of their lives upon salt water and, when at home, preferred to look out upon the roads and streets of their native town rather than upon the element which was, or had been, their workshop. There was one notable exception. Halfway between the wharf and the spot where the path followed by Carey Judson emerged from the pines stood a square house of medium size, with the railed platform called a "whale walk" in the center of its roof. Before it, at the water's edge, was a long boathouse and behind it a barn and cluster of sheds and outbuildings. House and boathouse and sheds were painted a gleaming, spotless white. The window blinds were a vivid green. The little front yard was surrounded by a picket fence, whitewashed until it glistened, and in the yard was a flagpole flying the stars and stripes and, below the latter, a banner exhibiting a spouting whale in red and the letter "H" in bright blue.

Every one in Wellmouth—yes, and practically every adult citizen of Trumet and Bayport—knew that house and that banner. They knew the story connected with them and enjoyed telling it to casual strangers or summer visitors.

Captain Tobias Higgins had been a Wellmouth boy. Like many Wellmouth lads of his generation he left school and went to sea as cabin boy when just entering his 'teens, but, unlike the majority, his first voyage was made aboard a New Bedford whaler. And, from that time until his late forties Tobias spent the greater part of his life in the Arctic or Antarctic oceans hunting the sperm whale or the right whale or the finback. He had risen to command of a whale ship by the time he was twenty-one and when thirty owned a share in that vessel. He married Phœbe Baker—she was a Wellmouth girl—and she accompanied him on the long voyages of two, and sometimes three years. His ship, the *Ambergris,* soon acquired the reputation of being a "lucky" craft and he of being a lucky skipper. People said he was making money and saving money, but, in spite of this, they were greatly surprised when, at the age of forty-seven, he and his wife returned to their native town to announce that they were through with seafaring forever.

"Yes, sir-ee!" declared Captain Tobias, "we're through, me and Phœbe are. We've spent years enough keepin' company with polar bears and walruses and Huskies and critters like that. We're goin' to drop anchor and lay up amongst Christians for the rest of our days. . . . Eh? What's that? No, I won't say I've made all the money I want. I don't believe anybody ever did that, John Jacob Astor nor anybody else, but I've made enough to pay for my three meals and lodgin' ashore and ashore's where I'm goin' to stay from now on. I've harpooned whales and cut up whales and tried out blubber, till, by thunder, now that I've got to where they have hot weather once in a while, I don't expect to sweat nothin' but pure ile. Where *I've* been there wan't no chance to sweat. Cold! Why, the only baby we ever had come to port was born one winter when the old *Ambergris* was froze in up in Hudson's Bay, and when the child died all hands had to turn to and chisel a hole in an iceberg so's it could be buried decent. Yes, sir, my wife and I have had enough of that. We're through. You can rate me from

now on as A. B. L. L.—able-bodied land lubber. I never
cal'late to be where I can see salt water again—no, nor even
smell it."

By way of proving the truth of this declaration, he bought
land, not on the main road, but on the hill fronting the bay
and erected thereon the square white house with the whale
walk on the roof. Within a year he had built the boathouse
at the shore, and now, moored in front of it, was his catboat,
the *Ambergris Junior*. In that boat, or gunning or fishing
up and down the beach, he spent most of his spare time in
the summer months. During the winter—when "iced up,"
as he called it—he puttered about the house, driving his wife
nearly frantic, or loafed about the store and post office,
squabbling over local, state, and national politics and invariably espousing the unpopular cause because it happened
to be unpopular. Town meetings had livened up tremendously since Captain Tobias Higgins "retired." Every morning, stormy weather excepted, he hoisted the flag of his
country to the top of the pole in his yard and, beneath it,
the banner with the red whale and the blue "H." This
banner had been his private signal in his years of active
service. "I run her up now to show that the old man's
aboard and able to stand watch," he explained to those who
questioned.

Carey Judson, from the top of the dune at the edge of
the pines, noticed the flags flapping lazily in the breeze and
inferred that Captain Higgins, like himself, was an early
riser that Sunday morning. The thought of Tobias called
to mind their interview in the office the previous evening
and he smiled as he recalled it. It had amused him to catch
as positive a person as the captain in a mistake. He wondered if Higgins had told his wife the experience. Probably not, for Mrs. Higgins—in spite of her husband's out-
of-door boasting—was distinctly in command of the domestic ship and Tobias, so the stories affirmed, played a minor
fiddle in his home orchestra.

Carey stood but a moment on the dune. Then, his long

legs moving in their characteristic swinging stride, he walked to the beach, and, turning to the right, followed the shore for a mile or so. Then another dune pushed itself out from the main, forming a miniature cape, the further side of which was out of sight from the village, even from the Higgins' whale walk. He turned at this point and there seated himself, his back against the bank and his feet half buried in the loose sand. This was his destination and, having reached it, his first act was to search one pocket after the other until he located his ancient briar pipe and a stained and worn tobacco pouch and matches. When the tobacco in the pipe was alight he again dove into the numerous and capacious pockets of the old canvas shooting coat he was wearing and from them extricated, one after the other, a series of articles which, if they could have seen them, would have puzzled the Wellmouthians. They had never seen them; as a matter of fact, no one save himself knew of their existence.

The first of those articles was a shore bird of the variety known locally as a "beetle-head." It was not a living bird, of course, but, except for the absence of legs—a foot long iron spike occupying the place where legs should have been —it looked astonishingly like one. It was the exact size and shape of a living "beetle-head," its body poised exactly as in life, its wings loosely closed as if the creature had just alighted. The coloring, to the smallest feather, was natural, neither under nor overemphasized. Yet it was merely a painted wooden effigy and Carey himself had carved and painted it. He turned it over in his hands, his eyes regarding it dreamily, and then, leaning forward, drove the spike into the sand. So placed it became, from a short distance away, a genuine shore bird, resting, after flight, upon the beach.

Then, from a second pocket, he tugged forth another block of wood, roughly shaped and partially carved to resemble the finished product before him. Next he spread his handkerchief upon the sand and took from a third pocket various little tools and knives. These he arranged upon the handkerchief. By that time he remembered to pull at his pipe, but found the result unprofitable because, having received no encouragement for some few minutes, the pipe had gone out. He was not surprised, but calmly relighted it and, picking up the wooden block and selecting one of the little tools, he set to work. Before long the pipe had again gone out but he did not seem to mind and sucked serenely at the stem, unconscious of everything except his carving.

For a long time he sat there, his feet settling deeper and deeper in the sand, the smokeless pipe clenched tightly between his teeth, his long fingers busy with one tool or another as he cut or grooved or gouged, leaning forward occasionally to gaze at his model. He worked swiftly and deftly and if his brother or Cora T. or Mr. Ben Early could have seen him just then they would have been surprised. Since his return to Wellmouth he had labored hard at the books of J. C. Judson & Co., but it was always apparent that he did so because of a fixed resolution, not because the task itself interested him. Mr. Ben Early, a shrewd observer within limits, summed it up when he told his wife: "Yes, he's doing well enough. Hasn't made as many mistakes as I thought he would. But he'll never amount to anything at the job. He's doing it because he knows he's got to, not because he wants to. No, there's nothing about him that'll ever set me to worrying so far as my getting that partnership by and by is concerned. He'll peter out, you see, and get as careless and slack and don't care about the bookkeeping as he always has about everything else he's ever tackled. I kept those books myself once, but I was crazy about keeping 'em just so. That's why I'm where I am now in the business. If there was any kind of work that Carey Judson *liked* there might be a chance for him, but there ain't. . . . Just name it 'Work' and that settles it, so far as he is concerned."

And yet, even to Mr. Early, the careful, engrossing industry with which that same Carey Judson carved and shaped that wooden block might have seemed like work. The practical Benjamin, however, would not have called it that. "Tomfoolery" would have been his name for it.

Carey whittled and dug at his tomfoolery for more than an hour without shifting from the position he had taken when he sat down. Then, attempting to shift, he awoke to the realization that there was something the matter with his right foot. Awaking still more, he became aware that that foot was not keeping the rest of his body company in the awakening but remained fast asleep. Dragging it from its grave in the sand it came slowly to life, but a life which was full of prickles. He muttered impatiently, turned over and rose clumsily, stamping as he did so to restore circulation. Then he saw a man walking along the beach about a hundred yards away coming from the direction of the village. The man he recognized as Tobias Higgins, and Tobias, at the same time, caught sight of him.

Carey's muttered exclamation was profane this time. He did not wish to meet any one, had journeyed to that secluded spot on purpose to avoid such meetings. However, he had been seen and he could not run away or hide. Hastily he picked up his tools, the handkerchief and the block of wood and jammed them into the pockets of his shooting coat. Then he strolled slowly forth from behind the dune. Captain Higgins advanced toward him. On the Captain's part there had been no recognition as yet.

It came a moment later. Tobias, pulling his cap brim further forward to shade his eyes, squinted uncertainly— he scorned spectacles—and then hailed.

"Eh?" he called. "Who—? Oh, yes, yes! I see! It's you, ain't it? Humph!"

He turned from the hard wet sand of the beach and rolled and plowed up the slope. Carey advanced to meet him.

"Good morning, Cap'n," he said. Tobias growled acknowledgment of the greeting.

"Humph!" he grunted, puffing with the exertion of the

climb and pausing to mop his forehead with a blue and white bandana handkerchief. "So it's you, eh?"

Carey nodded. "Exactly, Cap'n," he said. "As the story books say, 'The solitary horseman was none other than our hero.'"

Higgins stared. "What kind of talk's that?" he demanded. "You ain't on horseback, fur's I can see."

"No, and I'm not solitary, now that you ve come. It's a fine morning, isn't it?"

Captain Higgins ignored the weather.

"I might have known who 'twas," he declared. "Nobody else would be stuck away out here in a sandheap at the fag end of nowhere at the time when respectable folks were gettin' rigged up for meetin'. "

"True enough. You are already rigged, I suppose?"

"Eh? Rigged? What— Oh! Well, I wasn't cal'latin' to go to meetin' this mornin'. Phœbe wanted me to, but I told her I figgered a tramp alongshore would do me about as much good. A man can't be expected to turn out *every* time the bos'n pipes for prayers. I didn't sleep's well's I might last night. on't know what 'twas ailed me, but 'twas somethin'."

"You weren't worried over that ten cents, were you, Cap'n?"

"Hey? . . . See here, young feller, don't you get sassy. I presume likely you think I wouldn't have found out you'd given me the wrong change. Well, I would. How do you know I didn't find it out then and kept quiet just to try you out? Eh? How do you know I wasn't doin' just that?"

"I don't, of course. But, if that was it, I'm surprised at your taking such a chance."

"'Twould have been pretty reckless, wouldn't it?"

"Very, everything considered."

"Yes. Well, as a matter of fact, Carey, I didn't know anything about it. You had one on me that time, I'll have to own up. What are you doin' out here all alone by yourself? Makin' believe you're a gull or somethin' like that?"

"Not exactly. Making believe isn't much satisfaction."

"Sometimes 'tis. Ben Early now—he seems to get a lot of satisfaction makin' believe he's the Lord A'mighty. I'm surprised he didn't ask you to go to church along with him."

"He did say it wouldn't do me any harm to be seen there."

"I bet you! . . . Well, I must be gettin' under way again. I thought I'd cruise out as fur as West End maybe, and have a smoke along with Ezra Pollock at the lighthouse. Keepin' light ain't a job I'd hanker for, but there's one good thing about it—you ain't expected to tag your wife to church every time the bell rings. Won't keep me company, will you, Carey?"

"No, thanks, Cap'n, not this trip."

"Humph! Ezra 'd be glad to see you. A feller that keeps light is always glad to see *any*body."

Carey nodded gravely. "That's another advantage, isn't it," he said. "He doesn't have to be particular."

"Eh? Particular? Oh, good Lord! don't take it that way. . . . Say, look here; if I had a—a conscience like yours I'd bile it so's to see if I couldn't toughen it up. I asked you to go along with me, didn't I? Don't you suppose I'm as particular as a lighthouse keeper? Now you haul those big feet of yours out of that sand and walk out to West End with me."

"Not this time, Cap'n Higgins."

"Huh! Not this time nor any other time, you mean. You'd rather roost here listenin' to the gulls squawk. Well, there! I can't waste any more breath on you. So long."

"Pleasant walk, Cap'n."

"Ugh!"

With this farewell grunt the irritated ex-whaler turned on his heel and headed for the hard sand of the beach. He headed diagonally this time and his third stride—or wallow—took him to the end of the projecting dune. There he stopped short and stood still, staring intently at some object on the other side. An instant later he came tiptoeing back again, his red face blazing with excitement.

"What is it, Cap'n?" queried Carey, lowering his voice involuntarily.

Tobias flapped a cautioning hand. "Sshh! Sshh!" he whispered. "Give me a rock! Give me a *rock!* Thunder mighty! Ain't there a rock 'round here nowheres?"

Rocks are scarce on the south side of Cape Cod. On the north side, from Ostable to Bayport, water-worn boulders, relics of the glacial drift of the ice age, are plentiful as raisins in an old-fashioned mince pie, but about Orham or Trumet or Wellmouth a rock bigger than an egg is a rarity. And, even if they were plentiful, why on earth Tobias Higgins should be so frantically demanding one Carey could not imagine.

"A rock?" he repeated. "A rock, did you say?"

The captain flapped both hands this time.

"Sshh! Sshh, can't ye?" he whispered. "He'll hear you and fly away. He's settin' there not twenty foot off and I can nail him easy as not. Give me a rock! . . . A-ah!"

The exclamation was one of triumph. He stopped and picked up a pebble half the size of his fist and, clutching this in his right hand, crept cautiously around the point of the dune. Carey followed. Tobias peered over the bank. A sigh, apparently of relief, came from his lips, and he took another forward step and drew back the hand containing the stone. His companion, who had noticed the direction in which he was looking, and had also looked, seized that hand just as it swung forward to throw. The stone flew straight up in the air and descended not a dozen feet from where they were standing.

Captain Higgins gasped. Then he turned.

"What in the blue blazes did you do that for?" he demanded.

Carey grinned. "What were *you* doing?" he asked, on his own account.

"Doin'? *Doin'!* I was cal'latin' to kill that beetle-head yonder. Didn't you see him? Settin' right in plain sight he was, not twenty foot off. I could have knocked him— Oh, you *divilish* fool! What did you grab me like that for? I've a good mind to—"

Carey laughed aloud. "There, there, Cap'n," he put in. "Keep your hair on. He's there yet, isn't he?"

"There yet! Yet! What do you think he is; as big a numbskull as you be, yourself? Course he ain't there. You've scared him to Jericho by now. Oh, good Lord, I—"

"Sshh! He *is* there. See."

Captain Tobias looked. "Well, I swan to man!" he gurgled. "He is, ain't he. Don't that beat all! Got a broken wing, or somethin', I bet you! Or maybe he didn't hear us after all. Give me another rock. Let go of my arm! Let *go!*"

But Carey would not let go. He clung the tighter. Higgins struggled violently and then, noticing the expression on the younger man's face, stopped his struggles.

"Eh?" he demanded. "What— Say, what is this, anyhow?"

Carey, still laughing, released his hold.

"You leave that beetle-head to me, Cap'n," he said. "I'll get him."

"You'll get him! *You* will! Why. . . . Well, I'll . . . be . . . darned!"

For his companion had calmly walked over to where the bird was resting, had pulled the iron spike from the sand, and was returning with the beetle-head in his hands.

"There you are, Cap'n," he said. "It is easy enough to catch 'em when you know how."

Tobias snatched at the wooden bird. He turned it over and over, his eyes and open mouth expressing much emotion.

"Whew!" he whistled, slowly. "Well, if that ain't. . . . Humph! got another one on me, ain't you. Well, I swan! Where did the thing come from, anyhow?"

"It came from me. I put it there."

"You did? When?"

"An hour or so ago, when I first came."

"Sho! What did you put it there for; so's to have another chance to make a fool out of me?"

"No, indeed. I didn't know you were coming. I didn't think any one but me would come along here on a Sunday morning. When I caught sight of you I—well, you surprised me and I forgot it altogether."

"Pshaw! Sho! I want to know! Well, you did make a fool out of me, whether you meant to or not. Gettin' to be what you might call a habit of yours, seems so. . . . You'll have to give in that I wasn't much to blame. A—a thing like that would make a fool out of anybody. That's the best decoy I ever see in my life. 'Tain't a decoy—it's a beetle-head, that's what 'tis. Just a beetle-head, settin' there waitin' for some jackass to come and heave rocks at him. Where did you buy a thing like that, Carey Judson?"

Carey hesitated. Then he said:

"I didn't buy it; I made it."

"Eh? Made it? *You* did! . . . Say, now, lay to; come up into the wind, Carey. You've had your fun, now tell me the truth. Where did this thing come from?"

"I made it. That is the truth. I made it last winter. Birds are a—well, a hobby of mine."

"Humph! Yes, I know you can stuff birds. I've seen them you've got up in your room; George showed 'em to me one time. But this one ain't stuffed, it's—it's wood, ain't it? And it—it—why, no stuffed bird ever looked like this, never looked half so natural. No, nor no live one neither. I've shot a couple of thousand beetle-heads in my time and they wasn't nary one of 'em as natural as this. . . . Where did you get it, Carey?"

"I made it. It isn't such a job. I was making another one when you came along."

"Go on! . . . Where's the one you was makin'?"

"Here." Carey took the partially carved wooden block from his pocket. "It is only about half done, of course, but you can see what I'm after."

Captain Higgins examined the work, examined it at length and with care. Then he drew a long breath.

"Was you cal'latin' to go on makin' it if I hadn't come?" he asked.

"Why—er—yes."

"All right. *Go* on. I want to watch you. That is, if I won't make you nervous."

Carey twisted his forelock.

"You won't make me nervous," he said; "but I don't see why you want to. It can't be very interesting—to watch. Besides, you were going down to smoke with Ezra Pollock."

Tobias consigned Mr. Pollock to a place where smoke is supposed to be thick.

"I can see Ezra any time," he declared, "but I don't often get a chance to set around and see somebody do miracles. Turnin' water into wine ain't so much—I've drunk plenty of wine that had had that done to it—but when it comes to turnin' wood into beetle-heads I want a seat up front. Set down and turn to, Carey. Don't mind me. I'll try to keep quiet. If I swear once in a while 'twill only be my way of sayin' 'Hooray.' "

So, although he was not very keen at the prospect of pursuing his hobby before a witness, Carey did return to his former seat in the lee of the sand bank and resumed his carving and shaping. Tobias Higgins curled his bowed legs under his round body and, to the accompaniment of grunts and short-breathed exclamations, sank down beside him. In a few minutes the carver had forgotten all except his beloved task. Another hour passed and, after that, still another. Then the captain ventured to speak.

"Say, Carey," he observed, breathing heavily, "I hate to nose in on you, and I wouldn't if 'twasn't kind of serious, but if I squat here much longer my legs'll grow crookeder than they are now—and that would be gildin' refined lilies, as it tells about in Scriptur'. Besides, it's edgin' up to twelve o'clock, did you know it?"

Carey came out of his trance. "What?" he asked. "Did you speak, Cap'n Higgins?"

"Yes," gravely, "I did. Now I'm gettin' ready to speak again, so, if it ain't too much trouble, I'll ask you to pay attention. It's most noon, and my legs have commenced to grow backwards. Otherwise than them everything seems to be shipshape. When was you cal'latin' to head for home?"

"Why—why, I don't know. I guess I hadn't calculated much about it."

"No, I don't suppose you would. Well, don't you think it might be a good idea to get out a pencil and piece of paper and commence figurin' along that direction? What time do they expect you up to your house?"

"Oh, around dinner time, perhaps."

"Humph! What would happen if you didn't report for dinner? Would they ring the meetin'-house bell and send up rockets, or anything like that?"

"I doubt it."

"Just go ahead and have dinner without you, wouldn't they?"

"Probably."

"Um-hum. I guess likely they wouldn't be worried to death. They must know you pretty well. Your brother and Hepsy Ellis do, anyhow. All right, you come right along and have dinner with Phœbe and me. . . . Now we won't argue about it. That's what you're goin' to do. Heave ahead and get under way."

"But, Cap'n Higgins—"

"Didn't I say we wouldn't have any arguin'? Who's cap'n of this ship? Say, Carey, what are you cal'latin' to do with those beetle-heads when you get 'em done? Wouldn't sell 'em, would you?"

"Why—"

"Because if you would I'd like to put in a bid. I'll give you—I don't know's I wouldn't give five dollars for the pair of 'em."

Carey, who had risen and was storing his tools and the

wooden birds in the pockets of his canvas jacket, smiled, but did not answer. Tobias repeated his offer.

"Why don't you say somethin'?" he asked. "That's a fair offer, ain't it?"

"Fair enough."

They were under way by this time. Judson moving in his long-legged stride and his companion taking two steps to his one.

"If it's fair why don't you take it up?" demanded the captain. "Are wages so high up there at the fish house that money ain't any object to you?"

Carey shook his head. "Not exactly," he replied. "What do you want of the things, Cap'n Tobias?"

"I don't know. What did the whale want Jonah for? Probably because he'd never run afoul of anything like him afore and thought he'd like to have him for a curiosity. I never saw anything like those beetle-heads afore. I want 'em. Sell 'em to me; will you, Carey?"

"I can't, Cap'n. They aren't mine."

"Aren't yours? What kind of talk's that? Course they're yours. You made 'em, didn't you? I've seen you makin' one."

"Yes, I made them. But I'm making them for some one else. I've—well, I suppose you might say I have an order for a dozen of them."

"Sho! You have? I don't wonder, but—who ordered 'em?"

The reply was given after some hesitancy.

"I don't know that I ought to tell you—or any one else," Carey said. "There isn't any secret about it, but I had just as soon not have it talked about down here. You see—well, no one knows I do this sort of thing, and if they did—"

"If they did, bein' none of their business, they wouldn't talk about anything else for a spell. That's true enough. All right, you needn't tell me, if you don't want to. If you do want to you can rest easy that I shan't let it go any further."

"I'm sure of that. And there isn't any real reason why— Well, you see, for a year or two I have amused myself with this sort of foolishness in my spare time. I did it for fun, of course. I like birds and—and I think I can say I know birds pretty well—our birds around here."

Tobias nodded. "Know 'em!" he repeated. "If you had feathers you'd *be* a bird. You've got the build of—of one of those long-shanked squawks that's always flappin' 'round over the cedar swamp at East End. Well, never mind my compliments. Heave ahead with your yarn."

"So," Carey went on, "as stuffing and mounting birds— real birds—was almost impossible up there at my rooms in Boston, I thought I would try my hand at making them out of wood. I had a sort of idea that I would make a specimen of each kind—not life-size, all of them, you know—but the bigger ones in miniature. I tried two or three and they came out pretty well, so I went on. Then—then came the smash and—and I stopped—everything stopped."

His story stopped also. After a moment Higgins ventured an encouraging "Um-hum. Sartin; 'twould naturally."

"Yes. Well, I had some friends up there, some of them with a good deal of money. Most of them dropped me, as they should have, but one or two hung on, came to see me at the hospital and were a lot more decent than I deserved. One was a chap named—but you don't know him, so his name doesn't matter. He was a wealthy fellow, fond of shooting and fishing, and gave a lot of time to that sort of thing. Just before I came back here he asked me what I was intending to do with my collection. I said I hadn't thought about it, except to, perhaps, sell as much of it as I could. He bought the whole affair."

"Sho! Did, eh?"

"Yes. Then he asked me if I had ever thought of making any more of the wooden birds, like these I have here. He said they were so much better than any decoys he ever saw that he would like immensely to have a set of—well, the different kinds of shore birds and the ducks, and so on, to use on his own shooting trips. Probably he didn't mean that, really."

Tobias interrupted. "No, course he didn't," he put in, sarcastically. "Probably he'd seen so many beetle-heads like that one I tried to heave a rock at that he'd ruther spend his money on the average decoy, them that look as if they'd been hacked out with a broad-ax. He was crazy in the head and just ravin'. Let it go at that. What next?"

"Well, of course I had never thought of making the things for money. I never thought any one would wish to buy them, or cared for them the way I did. And, really, even he didn't care for them that way. He wanted them for—"

"There, there! You've told me what he wanted them for. Did he get 'em? that's what I want to know?"

"He hasn't yet. I didn't believe I could make them well enough to be paid for doing it. I would—I might have tried making him a few for nothing, just as a present, you know—he'd been awfully kind—but he wouldn't let me."

"Wouldn't, eh? He *was* crazy, wasn't he? Go on."

"So, at last, I agreed to try making a dozen of these beetle-heads at his price. It was a ridiculous price, but—"

"How much was it?"

"Well," Carey hesitated again. "Well," he said, "I am almost ashamed to tell you. It was such a ridiculous price that—"

"Go on! Go on! Tell me all the ridiculousness, so I can laugh, too."

"You will laugh. He insists on paying me ten dollars apiece for them. That is ridiculous enough, isn't it?"

If it was, the announcement did not have the effect of making the captain laugh. Instead of laughing he stopped short, gazed earnestly up into his companion's face and whistled slowly.

"Ten dollars apiece!" he repeated. "You ain't foolin', Carey?"

"No. That is the price he insists on paying. He would have paid more if I had let him. Why—you'll hardly believe it, but he actually offered to pay twice as much. He did, for a fact. Of course he was a good friend of mine and he has all the money he wants, so—"

Tobias broke in. They were walking on again and he seized the tail of Judson's shooting jacket.

"Here, here, here!" he panted. "Lay to! What do you think this is, a race? Let me get it straight. He's goin' to pay you a hundred and twenty—a hundred and twenty *dollars* for a dozen of those beetle-head images?"

"Yes."

"And he would have paid two hundred and forty if you had let him?"

"Yes. I know it sounds foolish. Of course he was doing it just to help me out, that's all."

"Um," thoughtfully. "I wonder. And he wanted more than the beetle-heads, didn't he?"

"Yes. Oh, he would have ordered a dozen of everything— brant and plover and shelldrakes and black duck, and—all sorts. And he pretended to believe he could get me lots of orders just like his. He couldn't, of course, but he said he could. He is a wonderfully fine chap. . . . So, in the little spare time I have had down here, some evenings, and last Sunday and to-day, I have been working as I was when you caught me at it. It is slow work but it takes up my mind and I like to do it. And I need all the money I can earn because—well, that doesn't matter."

His lips closed and he strode on in silence, his brow puckered and the loose lock of hair blowing, beneath the floppy brim of his canvas hat, across his eyes. Captain Tobias, rolling and puffing beside him, was silent also. It was he who spoke first.

"You say you do some of this evenin's, Carey," he observed, after the interval. "Kind of hard work to do it up there to the Jim-Carey place, ain't it?"

Judson blinked and came to life. "Eh?" he queried. "Oh! Yes, it is. In fact I've given it up—doing it there, I mean. It is a messy job, shavings and chips all over the floor, you know; and I can do it only in my bedroom. I'm not alone anywhere else and—and I don't care—well, you see, I had rather the folks—George and—and—"

"And Cora T. Um-hum. You'd rather they didn't know what you was up to, I expect."

"Yes. Ye-es. They are awfully kind to me, but—but perhaps they wouldn't understand. It does look like child's play, I admit."

"Oh, it does, eh? I wouldn't go so fur as to say that. However, I know Cora T. and that's education enough of its kind. So you've given up the evenin' work, and just work out here on the beach Sundays. Humph! How long do you cal'late it's goin' to take to finish up that feller's order for the first dozen beetle-heads at that rate of sailin'?"

Carey's smile showed that he appreciated the sarcasm.

"Oh, possibly fifty years," he replied.

"Humph! Yes, yes. We-ll, it looks as if I might have to put on those specs Phœbe's always at me to wear if I cal'late to see the last one done. My timbers are average sound, but they may be creakin' a little by the end of another fifty year. . . . Humph! Say, Carey, suppose you had a place all to yourself, a place where you could work nights when you wanted to, and Sundays and holidays—any time when you felt like it—"

It was Carey who interrupted now. "Oh, I feel like it all the time," he observed. "But it wouldn't be work. Work, for me, means doing something worth while, something profitable and practical."

"Yes. Sartin. But there's a sort of floatin' smell of practicalness hangin' around a hundred and twenty dollars, ain't there? Seems to me there is, but I ain't never been in the bankin' business. . . . Sshh! Never mind, never mind. I'll forgive myself for sayin' that if you will. . . . A hundred and twenty dollars a dozen. . . . Humph! Sho!"

His muttering faded away and he said no more just then. Carey was not anxious to talk so he, too, said nothing. It was not until they came opposite the Higgins' front gate that the captain came out of his reverie. Then he again clutched the rear of the canvas jacket and stopped its owner in his stride.

"Here we are in port," he declared, "and Phœbe's been waitin' dinner. I know she has because I can see her keepin' lookout through the kitchen deadlight. . . . Now *don't* talk any more. Of course you're comin' in. I'll need you, man, to keep her from bendin' the best sasspan all out of shape on my head. . . . Phœbe! Oh, Phœbe! Here's Carey Judson, he's goin' to have dinner with us. I know I'm late, but don't blame me. I'd been here an hour ago if it hadn't been for him. He didn't want to come. Seemed to be kind of shy of tacklin' your cookin'. . . . You go in first, Carey. She's swingin' that sasspan now."

# CHAPTER V

IF there was one thing certain it was that Carey had not intended to accept the Higgins' invitation to dinner. When Tobias first tendered it, up there behind the sand dune, he had not flatly refused because the refusal would mean a long argument and he always avoided argument if he could. So he neither accepted nor refused, postponing the decision until he and the captain should have reached the latter's home. And now that they had reached it he found that refusal next door to an impossibility. When he announced that he could not accept but felt that he must go on to the Cap'n Jim-Carey place, Tobias, still clinging to his coat tail, vowed that if he went he would have to "take a tow," because he did not intend to let go his hold until he was dragged across George Judson's threshold.

"And it's liable to be hard haulin' for you up that hill," he prophesied. "You'll have wind and tide against you, Carey, and my keel will be scrapin' sand all the way. You may fetch me in in time for to-morrow mornin's breakfast, but nothin' sooner. And we're likely to attract consider'ble attention, besides."

When Mrs. Higgins came out and added her protestations to her husband's Carey's resolution broke. Phœbe Higgins was a little woman, but, as her husband phrased it, she had "the power of an ocean liner, even if she did look like a tug boat."

"Of course you'll stay," she announced, "I shan't let you do anything else. Come right straight in. Don't stop to talk about it. Heavens to Betsy! you don't want my dinner sp'iled any more than 'tis, already, do you?"

The Higgins' dining room was as nautical an apartment as a room on shore could be. The clock over the mantel was a ship's clock. The barometer hanging by the door was a ship's barometer. On the west wall, between the windows, was a glaring oil painting of the *Lucy Winslow*, the whaler aboard which Captain Tobias had made his first voyage as mate. A pair of whale's teeth, polished, and ornamented with fanciful feminine portraits, stood at either end of the mantel and above them and the clock was suspended a cane made from a shark's backbone. The sole ornament lacking the salt sea smack was an engraving of the Honorable Franklin Pierce, the candidate for whom Tobias had cast his first vote in a presidential election. The painted floor—a gray, thickly spattered with white dots—the white woodwork, the ceiling, the windowpanes, the window shades, the table cloth, were spotless. Through the doorway leading to the kitchen Judson could see the cookstove, its nickel work glittering.

He and the captain "washed up" at the kitchen sink and then joined Mrs. Higgins at the table. Tobias said grace, a nautical grace beseeching the Almighty not to forget those "afloat on the wide waste of Thy waters," and then proceeded to carve the chicken. His wife served the vegetables and issued orders concerning the carving. He bore the criticisms for a minute or two and then ventured a protest.

"All right, all right," he said. "I wasn't cal'latin' to give him the neck, nor the piece that went over the fence last. Who's gettin' this critter to pieces, you or me?"

"You are," was the prompt reply. "And it looks as if you was doin' it with a hammer. He's been so used to cuttin' up whales," she added, addressing the guest, "that anything smaller bothers him."

During dinner they talked of many things, but the subject of the wooden "beetle-heads" in which Tobias had seemed so interested, was not mentioned. Nor, to Carey's relief, did Mrs. Higgins refer to his return to Wellmouth or his bookkeeping for J. C. Judson & Co. They discussed local news items, such as the prospect of the Reverend Bagness having had a "call" from a parish in a New Hampshire town and whether or not he might be likely to accept. Only once was mention made of a member of the Judson household.

"Your Aunt Susie's here visitin' up to your house, they tell me," said Phœbe. "I ain't seen her since before she was married. The cap'n and I—" she invariably spoke of her husband as "the cap'n"—"were at sea the other times she's been here. A real smart woman, your Aunt Susie is. You like her, don't you?"

Carey nodded. "Very much," he said.

"Yes, well, you'd ought to. I wonder how she and Cora T. cruise in company. Get along all right, do they?"

"Why—why, yes; I suppose they do."

"Um-hum. I was just wonderin', that's all. Two skippers aboard the same vessel—even if one of 'em is a passenger— ought to make things lively for the crew. How's George?"

"Well, thank you."

"Is, eh? I—Mercy on us, Tobias, why don't you look out for folks? Can't you see his plate hasn't got anything on it but bones?"

Captain Higgins hastened to replace the bones with something more edible. He winked at his guest as he did so.

"Only one skipper aboard *here,*" he muttered, under his breath.

After dinner the captain suggested that he and Carey go outdoors for a smoke.

"Unless you need me to help with the dishes, old lady," he added.

"I don't. I've got too much respect for the dishes."

"Just as you say, Chippy. I took to callin' her 'Chippy,' Carey," he explained, gravely, "'way back afore we was married. She was always hoppin' around so pert and lively, you know, like one of them little two-for-a-cent chippy sparrows that build nests out of horsehair in the hedge bushes. Pretty good name for her, don't you think so?"

Carey, repressing a smile, agreed that it was. He had heard of the Higgins' "pet name" before; it was one of Well-mouth's standing jokes

"And what does she call you?" he asked.

Tobias opened the outer door before he replied.

"We-ll," he drawled, "there was a spell when she used to call me 'Tootsy.' That was a long time ago, though. Now she calls me most anything she happens to lay her tongue to."

Mrs. Higgins made an ominous motion with the gravy ladle just then and he dodged into the yard.

The back yard was as neat and trim as the inside of the house. The captain produced a pair of mammoth cigars and Judson accepted one with outward gratitude and an internal shudder.

"You ain't ever been out aft here afore, have you, Carey," observed Tobias. "Got quite a nice little layout, I have. Nothin' fancy—no Cunard trimmin's, of course—but good enough for an old hulk alongshore. Here's the barn."

They inspected the barn, with the fat, middle-aged horse placidly chewing or dozing in the stall and the Higgins' buggy and carryall—the latter draped with a white cotton cover—in the carriage room. They went out and on to the henhouse and the pigpen. Beside the henhouse was a long low building with a broad double door and windows in each side.

"Come in here, Carey," invited the captain. "Here's my white elephant. You ought to see him."

There was nothing to see. The building was empty, save for workbenches along each side, equipped with vises and spread with carpenter's tools, and an ancient stove and stovepipe at the farther end.

"How do you like the elephant?" inquired Tobias. "Nice bulky critter, ain't he?"

Carey twisted his forelock. "Wonderful," he said.

His host had evidently not expected this sort of reply. He stared. "Wonderful?" he repeated. "What's wonderful?"

"The elephant."

"What in time—? Say, what are you talkin' about?"

"Why—the same thing you are talking about, I suppose."

"Same—! What am *I* talkin' about; do you know?"

"No. . . . Do you?"

Captain Higgins took three long, odorous pulls at the big cigar. Judson, whose own cigar had been considerate enough to go out, laughed.

"Sa-a-y," drawled Tobias, after a moment, and speaking through the haze, "I . . . well—but there! you ain't account- able, I suppose. Do you mind tellin' me if you rave like this part of every day?"

"No. Only when I'm out seeing the elephant."

"Humph! . . . I see. Well, *this* is the elephant, this buildin' here. I built the darn thing to make boats in. Cal'lated I'd been in and around boats long enough so's I ought to know how to make 'em. I tried makin' one. When I got part of it done I asked Phœbe out to give me her opinion of it."

He paused. "Did she give it?" asked Carey.

"Um-hum, she did. The hog is havin' his dinner out of it now. So I quit, and this place has been standin' empty ever since. That's why I call it my white elephant. . . . But 'twould make a pretty able-bodied workshop for a feller that could work, wouldn't it?"

"I should say it would."

"Um-hum. Well . . . that's all of that. Finished your cigar, have you?"

Judson, carefully concealing the unconsumed cigar by thrusting the hand holding it into his trousers' pocket, said that he had. Also he firmly declined the offer of another. They strolled back to the house, where the visitor, after a short chat with his host and hostess, announced that he must go. Mrs. Higgins urged him to stay longer but, somewhat to his surprise, the captain's insistence was rather perfunc- tory.

"It's all right, Chip," he said. "We mustn't keep him if he feels he hadn't ought to stay. Probably he's afraid Cora T. or his Aunt Susie or somebody will think he's got one

of his absent-minded streaks and forgot the way home. He
doesn't want the constable to be out with a bell and a lantern
huntin' for him. We'll let you go this time, Carey, but you
must come again. Come often. We'll probably have dinner
'most every Sunday—'long as the butcher cart'll trust us.'"

At the gate, whither he walked with his departing guest,
he seemed more reluctant to say good-by. There appeared to
be something on his mind.

"Carey," he said, hesitatingly, "I cal'late you wonder
what—I presume likely you don't see why I. . . . Humph!
. . . Well, maybe I'll drop in at the office to-morrow."

Judson and he shook hands and the former strode away
in the direction of the village. Only in its direction, however.
As soon as he was out of sight from the Higgins' house he
turned back across the fields and between the dunes to his
seat in the lee of the sand bank at the point. There he carved
blissfully at the wooden "beetle-head" until it was time to
return to the Jim-Carey place and a supper for which he felt
neither appetite nor inclination.

He was questioned, of course. George wanted to know
where he had been, so did Mrs. Dain and Hepsibah. Cora T.
evinced no interest whatever, treating him with lofty disdain,
until he mentioned dining with the Higginses. Then her sniff
expressed much.

"Oh!" she observed. "So they took you in, did they!
Well, I'm a little bit surprised, I must say, considering the
kind of remarks Tobias Higgins has been making around
town for the last six months. I hope they made it pleasant
for you."

"They did, thank you."

"Umph!"

After Carey had gone to his room Aunt Susan asked a
question of her niece.

"What did you mean by Cap'n Higgins making remarks?"
she inquired. "What kind of remarks?"

Mrs. Judson's answer was tart enough.

"The same kind that the whole town has been making,"

she snapped. "Why don't you ask George? He has heard as many of them as I have. He can tell you—if he will."

George stirred uneasily in his chair.

"Oh, just the usual thing," he said. "Cap'n Tobe had seven or eight hundred dollars with Carey's firm and—well, he was as sore as the rest, naturally. He talked about it considerably. He always says a lot more than he really means. He is a mighty good fellow, underneath."

His wife sniffed again. "Oh, how can you!" she exclaimed. "I tell you this, Aunt Susan, if I had said half the things Tobias Higgins has said about a person I wouldn't ask that person to my house to dinner. I wouldn't be so two-faced."

Mrs. Dain looked up from the *Item*.

"I remember the Higginses real well, of course," she said. "Tobias was a great friend of Jim's. They always seemed to me very good people."

Cora T.'s eyes flashed. "They're good enough, I suppose," she admitted. "Although that depends on whether a man who swears the way Cap'n Tobias does is what you call good. *Good* enough, maybe—but common—oh, my soul!"

Carey Judson had paid little attention to the captain's intimation that he might drop in at the office the next day, in fact had forgotten it altogether. Therefore he was a trifle surprised when, just before closing time that Monday afternoon, the door opened and Tobias rolled forward to the desk.

"Carey," he said, hastily, "got anything 'special to do tonight, have you?"

Carey, whose attention had been centered on a knotty problem in bookkeeping, unwound his legs from the rounds of the stool and tugged thoughtfully at his hair.

"We-ll," he mused, dreamily. "I didn't know but I might go to the opera this evening. Either that or call on Mr. Bagness. He missed me at church yesterday, I understand. A prodigal son sermon without any prodigal is—"

"Oh, shut up! I'm talkin' sense. *You* better try it, for a change. Can you run down to my house after supper?

I've got somethin' to say to you, somethin' that—well, that may come to somethin', if you think as well of it as I do. . . . Hurry up, hurry up! Let your crimps alone. Say yes or no. Will you come?"

"Yes."

"All right. I'll be expectin' you. . . . Say, don't tell anybody you're comin'."

Even then Carey's curiosity was only mildly excited. What it was that Higgins wished to see him about he could not imagine, nor did he speculate greatly. After supper, however, he walked down to the captain's house. It was a lonely place after nightfall; even the gulls had gone to bed.

Tobias was wide awake, however, and awaiting him in the dining room.

"Set down, Carey, set down," he ordered. "Phœbe's gone to some kind of a hen party—church committee meetin' or somethin'—up to Elkanah Saunders', so we've got the ship to ourselves. Now listen; this is what I wanted to talk to you about."

He went on to make a proposal. Briefly put—which was by no means the way in which he put it—it amounted to this: The building—his "white elephant"—in the yard by the henhouse was not used by him or any one else. He had built it for a workshop and some one ought to be at work in it. He and his wife—for he never did anything without calling her into consultation—had decided that Carey Judson was that some one. They offered it to Carey, free of charge, as a place in which he might, evenings, holidays, and Sundays, whenever he had spare time on his hands, make his decoys unmolested.

"There 'tis," declared the captain. "Lots of room, two big kerosene lamps and a ship's lantern, carpenter bench, couple of vises—everything except your own special kind of tools, and them, of course, you'd want to fetch, yourself. 'Tain't any use to me, and I should think it might be consider'ble use to you. What do you say?"

Judson said a good deal. The proposition did appeal to

him greatly. Seclusion, light, warmth in winter, conveniences —they were alluring indeed.

"But I don't think—it doesn't seem to me that I ought to use your premises for nothing, Cap'n," he protested. "It is awfully kind of you, but it is too much. You might have a chance to rent the building to some one else and then—"

"Sshh! I could have rented it two or three times over if I'd wanted to. But I didn't want to. Phœbe and I don't want tenants; they're a pesky nuisance, always findin' fault and wantin' this and that done. I've been a tenant myself and the names I called my landlord was the only satisfaction I ever got out of it, except havin' him call 'em back and give me a chance to call more. No, sir-ee! I wouldn't rent that boathouse to nobody—Saint Peter or Ben Early or nobody. And don't make a mistake and think I'm doin' this because I am generous. I ain't generous. I'm selfish as the Old Harry himself. I want you in there so's I can have a place to set in a comfortable chair and watch you whittle out those beetle-heads and the ducks and coots you'll make by and by. I'd ruther do that than go to a show. Now you be decent enough to give me the chance, will you? You owe me that much. You and your darned partner owed me seven hundred dollars, fur's as that goes."

"Well, if you put it that way, Cap'n—"

"I'll put it a thunderin' sight worse if you don't say yes and head me off."

Carey twisted and untwisted his legs, pulled at his forelock, and went through the various gymnastics which indicated that he was considering deeply.

"Well, I tell you, Cap'n Tobias," he said, after a little. "I don't think I shall say yes unreservedly."

"Unre—which? What does that mean? You can say it with finger-signs so long's you say it."

"I mean that I don't want to use your building without paying you for it in some way. How would this do? Suppose I gave you a commission—a sort of percentage on what

I get for making those things—provided I ever really get anything."

Tobias grunted. "I cal'lated you might be heavin' overboard some such offer as that," he admitted. "Anybody but you—anybody that was any kind of a business man—would see that here was a chance to get a good thing for nothin' and take it; but you're no business man, and never was. Suppose we settle it this way: You work along in there for a spell for nothin'. Then, by and by, unless I miss my reckonin', you'll want more contraptions to work with—a foot lathe, maybe, or a jig saw or somethin'. *When* you want 'em I'll buy 'em and we'll say I'm so much of a partner in the shop. Then we can arrange about that percentage; but you try it as you are fust and see how you make out."

"But, Cap'n—"

"Be still. You're a fool banker, Carey, but you can whittle out beetle-heads to beat the cars. Besides, after all, you're Cap'n Jim-Carey's son and it would take a lot more than seven hundred dollars to square my debt with *him*. . . . And there's one more reason."

"Yes? What is it?"

"This town is loaded to the guards with pig-headed Republicans. Every last one of 'em think because I'm a Democrat I ain't got any sense. They all swear you're no good. I tell 'em that I give in you're no good in a bank, and maybe won't be much more good at bookkeepin', but at the right *kind* of job you'd be A No. 1. If that ain't so, I say to 'em, then you're the fust Judson that ever turned out that way."

"But, see here, Cap'n Tobe, they mustn't know I'm doing this. I may fail at it as I have at everything else. And it never will amount to a great deal, anyway. You mustn't tell them a word."

Tobias laughed scornfully. "*I'll* never tell 'em," he declared. "I'll know it myself. I'll see you makin' good and showin' them up for idiots and that'll be enough for me. They're Republicans, I tell you. They wouldn't know anything if they did know it. They ain't capable of knowin' anything, or they'd be Democrats."

In the end it was settled that way. Carey accepted the offer and the boathouse on probation and the very next evening he brought his models, his skins and stuffed birds, and his tools, down there and set to work, with Mr. and Mrs. Higgins as interested spectators. At first he found their presence a little embarrassing, but, as they asked few questions and were careful neither to suggest nor interfere, he soon forgot them altogether. And, by the end of the first week the novelty had worn off and Phœbe visited the boathouse only occasionally. Tobias was more regular in attendance, but his chatter and comments on village happenings were amusing and Carey began to miss them when he was absent.

There was some curiosity at the Cap'n Jim-Carey place, of course. Cora T. asked questions concerning his repeated evenings out and made caustic comments when those questions were not answered satisfactorily. Mrs. Dain's remarks were characteristically blunt and to the point.

"You don't intend to tell, that's plain enough," she observed; "and, so far as I know, there isn't any law to make you. But, whatever you are up to, I do hope it is something that won't get you into more trouble. Look here, you haven't got a girl, have you?"

Her nephew shook his head.

"No," he replied, gravely.

"You are sure?"

"Why, moderately so. Do I look as if I had?"

"You look the way you always look and that's like nobody else on earth. You're sure some woman hasn't got you in tow? You're just the kind of a moon-struck innocent that a woman could tie to her apron strings if she set out to."

"Much obliged. But you are a little rough on the sex, aren't you?"

"The what? Women, you mean? Not a bit. There are plenty of women that can't get along without a man hanging around 'em and they aren't too particular what kind of a man it is. Whatever else you do, Carey Judson, don't you get in the habit of having some woman tell you she's the only one that understands you. That sort of game is more risky than banking, even with a partner like the one you had."

Carey told his brother about the Higgins' boathouse and the work he was doing there, but he told no one else. There was a distinct let-up in the family questioning thereafter and so he judged that, either from George or another source, they, too, had the answer to the riddle. And, from certain remarks dropped by Mr. Early and others he soon came to realize that his "secret" was not much of a secret, after all. To keep a secret in Wellmouth was much harder than making wooden "beetle-heads," marvelous as Captain Higgins still seemed to consider that accomplishment. The captain kept guard over the boathouse and permitted no trespassers on his property, so Judson did not mind. So long as he was left alone and his hobby not interfered with he was happy, as happy, that is, as a community disgrace might ever expect to be.

His aunt Susan's visit was to terminate on July first. She was going back to Cleveland then. Mrs. George Judson was sweetness itself to her husband's relative and did everything she could think of to show her affection for the latter. As Hepsibah Ellis told Carey, when he was eating an early Sunday morning breakfast in the kitchen: "The way she pours butter and sweet ile over that old woman is enough to make an eel too slippery to swim straight."

"I should think your Aunt Susie would see through it," she went on to declare. "I used to think she was sharp-sighted enough to see the whys and wherefores of anything, but she don't act as if she suspicioned a mite now. She just takes all the 'You're *sure* there isn't anything you'd 'specially like for dinner, Aunt Susie' and the 'Oh, Aunt Susan, *can't* you plan to stay a little longer? We *shall* miss you so after you're gone!'—she takes all that the way our cat takes the fishheads, as if 'twas what was comin' to her and no more. I'm surprised at her, I snum I am!"

Carey sipped his coffee. "Well, it *is* coming to her, isn't it?" he inquired, placidly. "She is George's aunt and she is very fond of him. And he is fond of her. So am I. So is everybody who knows her."

Hepsibah looked steadily at him for a moment. Then she breathed heavily. "Sometimes I wonder," she observed, irrelevantly, "how much of some folks' dumbness is real dumb and how much is make-believe. If you can't see. . . . Well, maybe you can't." Changing the subject, she added, "She's plannin' to have a big time here at the house one night just before your aunt goes away. A reception is what she calls it, though I told her, says I, 'I always cal'lated a reception was to say "Howdy do" to folks, not "Good-by."' But she's plannin' to have everybody come to the thing from Dan to Beersheby—all the big bugs, that is—and so she's been waitin' for Desire Sayles and Emily. George has heard that they're goin' to open their house first of next week. You'll be glad to see Emily, won't you? It's been a long spell since you two run afoul of each other, I guess."

Carey did not answer, nor did he finish his coffee. His forenoon at the Higgins' workshop was pretty well spoiled. He was not anxious to meet any one, least of all the girl whom he had known so well in the days when he was a care-free young fellow home from college on vacations.

He and Mrs. Dain had had few confidential talks since that in which she told him his name had been erased from her will and that he must hoe his own row. The disinheriting had not troubled him in the least. He had expected it, and felt that he deserved it. He was particularly glad that the old lady had been considerate enough not to mention it again. For her part, having freed her mind on that subject, she treated him just as she always had, and was as crisply cordial with him as with the other members of the family.

The Cap'n Jim-Carey house possessed an heirloom. It possessed many antiques, but antiques in the eighties were regarded as incumbrances, not as valuable assets, and many an Adam or Sheraton highboy or dresser was by Wellmouth householders relegated to the woodshed for use as a repository for seed potatoes, its place being taken by a marble-topped black walnut atrocity. The Judsons' woodshed and garret had its share of these castaways, but they were not spoken of as heirlooms. There was only one "heirloom" and that was a crude, and huge, painting in water color of the brig, *Glory of the Wave,* the vessel in which Ebenezer Judson, Jim-Carey's grandfather, had made his first voyage to the East Indies as captain. This masterpiece had been executed—and executed is the word—by a native artist who concealed his talent by a residence on the island of Mauritius. Captain Ebenezer had superintended the execution there and had brought the remains proudly back to Boston with him, where he preserved them in a dreadful gilt frame. When he died the heirloom was inherited by Captain Sylvanus Judson, Jim-Carey's father, who, when his time came, handed it on to Captain Jim. Each succeeding heir had inherited with it the pride of ownership. When, after the Osborne-Judson failure Carey had sold the old house to his brother, the heirloom went with the rest, but Cora T., breaking the family tradition, did not welcome it with pride. She promptly pronounced it a "horror" and sentenced it to the attic.

One evening, during the latter part of her visit, Mrs. Dain referred to it. Carey was out, as usual, but George was there and his wife also.

"There!" exclaimed Aunt Susan, suddenly, and dropping her knitting in her lap. "I knew I'd missed something since I've been here and it has only just this minute come over me what it was. Where's that picture of Grandfather Ebenezer's ship; the 'Hosanna of the Wave,' or whatever it is? Father used always to have it hung over the sofa there. What has become of it?"

George Judson looked at his wife and she returned the look. It was Cora T. who answered.

"Oh, that old thing," she said, lightly. "It's around the

house somewhere, I guess. It was *such* a sight, Aunt Susan; so dingy and dirty and the frame all chipping off and showing the white plaster under the gilt, that I couldn't bear to look at it. I put it up in the attic, I believe."

Her husband seemed surprised at the statement. He opened his mouth to speak, but Cora T.'s look became very expressive indeed, and he closed it again. Mrs. Dain may or may not have noticed the look and its effect. At any rate she seemed to have no idea of dropping the subject.

"You put it up in the attic!" she repeated. "Why, what on earth did you do that for? Father thought more of that picture than he did of about anything in the house—and so did Jim."

George would have spoken had his wife given him the opportunity, but again she cut in ahead of him.

"I know he did," she admitted, with a laugh. "He did, and goodness knows why. I'm sure you must have forgotten what that picture looked like, Auntie. You haven't seen it for years and it had gotten to be a terrible thing. All wrinkles and fly-specks—and oh, my goodness! When we first took the house I had left it hanging where it always did—over that sofa, as you say—and Nellie Loveland and her mother came here to call. I don't know as you know it, Aunt Susan—perhaps I didn't tell you—but Nellie paints, herself, awfully well—"

Aunt Susan interrupted. "Paints herself!" she repeated. "What does that mean, pray?"

George broke out in a vigorous "Ha, ha," but Cora T. squelched the merriment.

"George!" she exclaimed, indignantly. "George, don't act so foolish. I mean Nellie paints pictures. She's got an awful lot of talent, everybody says so, and she's been taking lessons of a *very* well-known man up in Boston. She came here that time with her mother and when she saw that picture of great-grandfather Ebenezer's old ship I thought she would *die*, she laughed so at it."

Mrs. Dain made another comment.

"I don't know why she should," she observed, rather sharply. "It couldn't have been the first time she had seen it. She used to come here when she was a little girl. I've seen her here, myself."

"Yes. Oh, yes, I know. But a child—well, you know a child doesn't notice things. And Nellie's—er—genius hadn't begun to come out, as you might say, in those days. But now—now, you see, she knows about art and—and all like that. She was right fresh from studying real pictures and that old ship one almost killed her. She made *such* fun of it, and had so many real bright, cute things to say about it, that her mother and I almost died, too. But, in spite of my laughing so, it did make me kind of ashamed, and after they had gone I took it right down and marched it straight up attic. 'There!' says I. 'That's where you belong and that's where you'll stay.' When I told George about it he agreed that I'd done just right. Didn't you, George?"

George did not answer as promptly as he, perhaps, should.

"Didn't you?" insisted his wife.

"Oh—oh yes—yes! Seems to me I did. It *was* pretty funny, that old picture—when you come to think of it."

Aunt Susan picked up her knitting.

"Things—and humans—are apt to be funny when they get old," she remarked. "I'm getting funny, myself. . . . Well," after a moment, "is it up attic now?"

Again her niece and nephew exchanged looks. And again it was the former who answered.

"Why—why, yes. I—I shouldn't wonder if it was," she said. "Why, Aunt Susie?"

"Oh, nothing much. Only, if you and George don't care about it and have thrown it away I thought perhaps you wouldn't mind my having it. Would you?"

Another moment of hesitation, particularly noticeable on George's part. His wife, too, seemed a little disturbed.

"Aunt Susan!" she cried. "You're making fun. You

don't really want that old picture? You wouldn't carry that away out to Cleveland with you. You wouldn't want it in your great lovely home out there."

"I don't know as my home is so lovely. And it certainly isn't great. And, as for the old ship, I rather think I might want it. It would remind me of the folks who used to own it and take pride in it and anything that reminds me of them is worth while."

"But how could you get it there? It is so big and clumsy."

Mrs. Dain held her knitting closer to the lamp and carefully picked up a dropped stitch.

"Don't talk any more about it," she said, calmly. "If you don't want me to have it—if you don't want to part with it, I mean—that is quite satisfactory and I don't blame you. I shouldn't have asked for it if you hadn't told me you had thrown it away—or put it in the attic, which is the same thing. That's enough about it, anyway. Read me the *Item*, George. The new one has just come."

Later on that evening there was a heart to heart conversation in the big bedroom, that occupied by Mr. and Mrs. George Judson.

"*Don't* say you can't get it," snapped the latter, irritably. "Of course you can get it. It's hanging there in Carey's room and all you've got to do is take it down and give it to her. What on earth she wants it for, I don't see, but she does and so, I suppose, she'll have to have it. What makes old people get such cranky notions I don't see. She's had one after the other ever since she came here and there are times when I'd like to shake her. If she was my relation instead of yours I guess I should have done it. She's going pretty soon, which is a mercy. Well, now you get that picture and give it to her."

George was troubled. "How can I get it, Cora?" he pleaded. "It isn't mine, it's Carey's. The very day after you took it up attic he asked what had become of it and when I told him you had thrown it away he asked if we would mind giving it to him. Said he was rather fond of it—said it in that queer, bashful kind of way he has, you know, and—"

"Know! Who should know it better than I do? Don't I have to put up with it and with him every day? Well, you did give it to him, like a ninny—as if you hadn't given him enough already—and now he's got it, worse luck."

"But, Cora, I asked you before I gave it to him and you said—"

"Never mind what I said. Tell him you've changed your mind. Ask him to give it back to you. He'd give you his head if you asked; you know it."

"Now, Cora, I don't like to ask him for it. He'll wonder why, and— See here, why not tell the old lady the truth? You can say you forgot that you had given it to him, and it will be all right. . . . Eh? Great Scott! you don't suppose she has seen it hanging up in his room?"

"Indeed she hasn't! I've taken good care that she hasn't been in his room since she came. There are too many things there that it wouldn't do us any good to have her see. She pretends to be dreadfully down on your precious Carey, but he always was her pet baby, and I'm not sure that she hasn't got a soft feeling for him in spite of his being a—all but a jailbird."

"Come, come, Cora! That's enough of that."

"Oh, don't get mad. I didn't mean it exactly. I lose my patience sometimes, and I wouldn't be human if I didn't. But I don't mean for your aunt to see all those story books and boy things that Carey keeps up there and that he has hung on to all these years. She gave some of them to him herself and she's got a sentimental streak in her just as he has—yes, and you have, too. No; unless she has sneaked up to that room all alone by herself—which isn't likely—she hasn't been in it. Now what are you going to do about that ship picture?"

George seemed to feel that he had a bright idea. "Why, do what I said," he urged. "Tell her we gave it to Carey, and then she can ask him for it. He'll give it to her, I'm sure."

Cora T.'s face was a picture. "You're sure, are you?" she mocked. "Is that so! Yes, well, I'm sure too. That *is* a wonderful notion, now isn't it? He'll give it to her and she will know that he loved the thing so much that he saved it after we threw it away. And that *will* make us solid with her, for certain! Oh, have some sense, George Judson! I tell you we can't take chances like that. She's down on Carey now—and she's got to stay down. She likes you—oh yes! You're one of her own. But whether she likes me or not is—well, sometimes I wonder. But, anyhow, we can't afford to risk the least little thing that may make us stand higher with her. George, you ask your brother for that picture to-morrow morning. And when he gives it to you— which he will—then you give it to her. And don't you tell her where it came from, either."

George walked up and down the room. Then he turned. He was resolute enough with all except his wife, and on some occasions with her. This was one of the occasions.

"No, Cora," he said, firmly. "I can't ask Carey for that picture. It's all he has now of father's and mother's things and I gave it to him because I could see he really wanted it. I won't ask him to give it back again and then give it to somebody else."

She glared at him.

"You won't?" she repeated.

"No, I won't."

"Then do you know what I shall do? I'll go straight into his room, after he has gone to the office to-morrow morning, take that picture from the wall and carry it downstairs and give it to her, myself. And I shan't let her know that he ever had it."

"Cora!" sharply. "You won't do anything of the kind."

"Won't I? You'll see! Oh, if some of the people around here who think you are so wonderful—always telling me what a lovely husband I've got—if some of them only knew!

If they could see and hear you now! Oh, I should think you would be ashamed! I—"

And so on, long after the lamp was extinguished and they were in bed. But Mrs. Judson did not take the picture of the *Glory of the Wave* from the wall of her brother-in-law's room the following morning. It still hung there when the owner of that room came home at noon for dinner. And that evening when he was alone in the Higgins' boathouse and hard at work on the fourth "beetle-head" the shop door opened, and Mrs. Dain walked in.

He gazed at her in a sort of paralysis. She greeted him as if her visit was as casual a happening as finding a patch of Mayflowers in the April woods.

"Hello, Carey," she observed. And then added: "Got anything here that a person with a moderately clean dress can sit down on? I'm tired. This is a longer walk than I generally take at this time of night."

"Why, Aunt Susan!" he gasped. "Is—is—"

"Don't say, 'Is it you?'" she broke in, tartly. "It sounds like somebody in a play, and it is silly besides. It *is* me and, as far as I know, there is nobody around here that looks like me. Is that chair sound and whole? It appears to be."

He was sufficiently awake by this time to seize the chair to which she was pointing, give it a brush with his handkerchief and place it before her.

"I think it is moderately strong," he said. "Cap'n Tobias uses it a good deal."

"Who? Tobe Higgins? Humph! Well, then I'll guess it'll hold *me* up. . . . So, young man, this is the place where you make your playthings, or whatever they are, is it?"

She gave the boathouse a thorough looking over. "It is kept clean, anyhow," she observed. "Who keeps it that way—Cap'n Higgins or his wife? It looks like a woman's job to me."

He was twisting his forelock and wondering many things. So, instead of answering her question, he asked another.

"How in the world did you know I was here, Aunt Susan?"

he asked. "I thought—I haven't told any one, except George."

"And so you supposed, on that account, it was a dead secret. That's just like you, Carey. Well, it isn't a secret and hasn't been for ten days or more. Cora knows it and Hepsibah knows it. So does the whole town, I imagine. Did you think you could go wandering off practically every night in the week, not to mention Sundays, and have nobody interested enough to find out where you went—yes, and why you went? Well, you couldn't—not in this town, or any other of its size. And if you thought you could tell George anything that his wife wouldn't find out it shows that—well, it shows you have never been married, for one thing. I have been intending for more than a week to come down here and see what you were up to. George and Cora have gone out to call on her wonderful Lovelands, and I stayed at home with a headache. That's why I am here now."

Carey was disturbed. "A headache!" he repeated. "And you walked away down here with a headache. And alone— and at night. You shouldn't have done it, Aunt Susan."

She sighed. "Mercy me!" she exclaimed, resignedly. "It's no wonder that Osborne thief could pull the wool over your eyes. There was wool enough there to make a blanket out of before he started. Don't worry about my headache. There was only enough of it in the beginning to make an excuse, and now there isn't any. As for walking—well, if I can't walk a mile on a fine night like this then I wish you'd tell me why."

"But all alone—"

"Well, why not alone? Do I look as if I needed somebody to lead me by the hand? . . . There, there! That's enough silliness. Show me that bird thing you are making."

He handed her the partially finished "beetle-head" and she examined it carefully. Then she asked to see a completed specimen. Over the latter she shook an admiring head.

"Well, I declare!" she said. "I do declare! And you made that creature all yourself, Carey Judson?"

"Yes. It was easy to make. It isn't work, really. I have always liked birds, you know, and I suppose that is why I enjoy making these wooden ones."

"Humph! So you don't call making a thing like that work? What do you call it—play?"

"Yes. It is play for me. . . . And it keeps me busy, so—"

"So you don't think too much about other things. I see." She turned the decoy over and said again, "Well, I declare!" Then she added:

"George said something about your having an order for a dozen like this. Some friend of yours wanted to buy them. Is that so?"

He said it was and told her the same story he had told Captain Higgins that Sunday morning on the beach. She listened until he finished. Then she asked more questions.

"So you will get a hundred and twenty dollars for the dozen," she said. "What do you want of the money down here in Wellmouth? George pays you wages enough to live on, doesn't he?"

"Oh, yes! He is very generous. He pays me more than I am worth there in the office. I have told him so more than once."

"Have you? I shouldn't wonder. Then what do you want to make more money for?"

He hesitated. "I want it—" he began. "You see—well, I have had a sort of idea—a hope— Oh, it is crazy, I know—but. . . . Do you mind if I don't answer your question, Aunt Susan? I haven't told any one and I'd rather not tell even you—just yet. It will probably end as most of my hopes do—in nothing."

To his surprise his refusal appeared to please her.

"Of course I don't mind," she declared. "Don't tell me or anybody if you don't want to. I'm glad you've got back-bone enough not to tell. It is a good sign. Now go on and work. I want to watch you and probably I shall do talking enough for both of us."

She did not talk much. Later on, however, she spoke of a matter having nothing to do with his occupation.

"I see you've got that picture of your great-grandfather's ship, the *Glory of the Wave,* hanging up in your bedroom," she said. "I went up there by myself, day before yesterday, when Cora was downtown shopping, and I saw it. By the way, you needn't tell her I was up there. She has never offered to take me there, so perhaps she wouldn't like it if she knew. How did you happen to get that picture, Carey? I supposed, of course, that went with the rest of the things when you sold out to George."

Carey squinted along the back of his beetle-head and then removed a minute shaving from that back.

"Yes—yes, it did," he replied. "But after I came back here to live I missed it—it wasn't hanging where it used to, over the sofa in the sitting room, and when I asked George he said his wife thought it was too disreputable for public exhibition and had thrown it away, put it with the rest of the rubbish in the garret. So I asked him if I might have it and he gave it to me."

Mrs. Dain nodded. "I see," she murmured. "Yes, yes. Well, I guessed that was about it. What did you want of it, Carey?"

Her nephew was hard at work and his answer was absently given.

"I don't know," he said. "I—I fancied it, for some reason or other. It had always been a part of the old place as I remembered it and—and I knew father was tremendously fond of it, so—well, as George and Cora didn't seem to want it, I did. That's all. Why?"

"Nothing in particular." She was regarding him intently. "Carey," she said, quietly, "it was a good deal of a wrench for you, selling the place and everything in it, wasn't it? Your share, I mean?"

He bowed assent. "Yes," he said, shortly. Then he added, "But George was mighty fair about it. He paid me all and more than my half was worth."

There were a few moments of silence. Then said Mrs. Dain, with a half smile:

"It's a troublesome thing, this having sentiment in your make-up. You've got it, Carey, and so have I."

He turned. "You!" he said. Then, with a short laugh, he added, "You're joking, of course. I should scarcely call you sentimental, Aunt Susan."

"No, with your wonderful judgment of human nature I guess you wouldn't. But I am—in spots. For instance, I like that old ship picture and I'd like to own it and take it back to Cleveland with me to hang up where I can see it every day. It makes me think of Jim and your mother and the old house more than anything I know. You wouldn't want to give me that picture, would you, Carey?"

He was surprised, but his answer was prompt and hearty. "Why, certainly I would," he said. "You may have it and welcome, Aunt Susan. I shall be glad to give it to you."

"Thank you. . . . And you won't feel that I am taking away the one thing you care most for?"

He smiled now. "If I did it wouldn't make any difference," he declared. "But I don't, of course. The *Glory of the Wave* is yours, Aunt Susan."

Her eyes brightened and she leaned forward as if about to speak impulsively. But, if this was her intention, she changed her mind. What she did say was commonplace enough.

"All right, and thank you again," she said. "You bring it down from your room and give it to me to-morrow at breakfast time. You needn't say anything about our talk to-night. Perhaps you might just as well not tell any one I came down here by myself to see you. George and Cora will only think I am a stark lunatic to do such a thing— which is what you are thinking this minute—and I shall have to do a lot of explaining about that 'headache' besides. Just give me the picture as if it was your own idea. You thought perhaps I might like it. Do you see?"

He did not see at all, but he did not feel like further questioning, so he said he understood. He carved and whittled and measured for another half hour and then his visitor announced that she must go.

"And you haven't got to go with me," she asserted. "I can get along by myself perfectly well. Stay and make your playthings just as if I hadn't come at all."

He would not stay, of course, so when the lamps were extinguished and the boathouse door locked they walked home together. The Higginses were out that evening, having driven over to Trumet to what Tobias called a "Free Mason time" at the town hall there, so their exit from the yard, like Mrs. Dain's entrance to it, was unobserved.

It was a beautiful clear summer night and Aunt Susan, although she said little, appeared to enjoy the walk, trotting briskly on beside her tall, loose-jointed nephew. In the middle part of the ascent of Lookout Hill, however, she suddenly stopped and Carey thought he heard her utter a gasping exclamation.

"What is it, auntie?" he asked, bending over. "Anything the matter?"

She was panting, but her reply was serene and business-like.

"Nothing unusual," she said, breathing quickly. "When a body gets to be as old as I am they must expect to have pains, I suppose."

"Pains? What sort of a pain? Do you want to rest—to sit down?"

"Of course I don't. Would I sit down in the middle of the road, is it likely? But when that doctor tells me that I can't have a pain because he can't find anything wrong where I say the pain is—well, then I say he'd better look where it isn't. Because smoke comes out of a chimney that doesn't signify that the fire's on the roof. . . . There! I'm all right again. Go ahead."

Just as they entered the yard of the Cap'n Jim-Carey place she spoke again.

"Carey," she said, still panting, "I am ever so much

obliged for that picture and when I die you shall have it back again. I'll see to that. But you mustn't expect anything else. I have told you about my will and I meant what I said."

He pressed her arm a little impatiently—for him. "Please don't tell me that again, Aunt Susan," he begged. "I don't expect anything. I don't want anything. I don't deserve it and you don't need to remind me of that because no one knows it better than I do. You've done exactly right and so we won't talk about it any more. . . . That is, if you don't mind."

"All right, we won't. As I see it now, money would only mean more trouble for you, Carey, and you've got enough of that. You go on and make your wooden birds. Anybody that can make such things the way you do ought not to be plagued with money for other folks to get away from him."

# CHAPTER VI

THE presentation of the heirloom took place the next morning. Carey, following his aunt's instructions, brought the picture downstairs at breakfast time and gave it to her. His explanations of the reason prompting the gift were brief and, although he tried to make them plausible, his manner was not as convincing as his words. There was an element of deception about the affair which he did not like. So far as he knew, there had never been any secrets between George and himself—certainly none on his part. But Mrs. Dain had insisted that her request to him for the ship painting be not mentioned, and he had promised her that it should not be.

"I just—er—thought you might like to have it, Aunt Susan," he faltered. "You—er—I remember you always liked it and—and—er—"

Mrs. Dain hastened to help him out.

"Indeed I did," she agreed. "And I am awfully glad to have it, of course. Thank you very much, Carey."

"Yes. That's all right; you are welcome. I knew George and Cora wouldn't mind your having it. They had decided not to keep it in the sitting room and gave it to me. But I have so many other things of the kind that when you said —I mean when you spoke of it—er—"

Cora T. broke in.

"Oh!" she exclaimed. "Then you had spoken to Carey about it, had you, Aunt Susan? I didn't know that.'

Aunt Susan was not in the least perturbed. Unlike her older nephew she seemed to be enjoying the situation, and was entirely equal to it.

"Yes, I believe I did say something to him about missing it from the wall there," she said. "But that wasn't until after you and George and I had had our talk. And what a coincidence it is, isn't it—his giving it to me now? Enough to make a person believe in this mind reading the papers tell so much about. Just think, Cora! Only night before last we were talking about this very picture—you and I and George here—and I said I'd missed it from the place where it always hung, and when you said you didn't care about it, I asked you to give it to me. And now Carey, who wasn't there at all, comes trotting downstairs with it as big as life. Isn't it astonishing?"

Mrs. Judson admitted that it was. In fact her astonishment appeared to be quite as great as Mrs. Dain's. The looks which she gave her husband expressed that astonishment, and suspicion as well.

"I should think it was astonishing," she observed, with emphasis. "Very astonishing indeed—to me. Perhaps it isn't quite so miraculous to George and Carey, though. I shouldn't wonder if they knew more than they have told. . . . Humph! Yes, considerable more."

George, however, expressed absolute innocence and looked it. "If you mean that I told Carey to give it to her," he protested, "you're dead wrong, Cora. I didn't know he had such an idea in his head."

Before Cora T. could speak again, Aunt Susan put in a word.

"But I understood you to say it was up attic where you had stowed it, Cora," she said. "You never said a word about Carey's having anything to do with it. Not a single word."

This was something of a poser and to answer satisfactorily and promptly strained even Mrs. Judson's capabilities. But she did answer and as convincingly as she could.

"Why—well there, Aunt Susan!" she exclaimed, contritely. "I don't wonder you ask that. And I guess George doesn't wonder, either. It is his fault. You see, he—he had given that picture to Carey—after I put it in the garret, you know—and—and when you spoke of it he forgot all about Carey's having it. It wasn't until—it wasn't— Oh, you tell her, George!"

George looked at her, then at his aunt, and then at Carey. His expression was that of one who, having been unexpectedly thrown into deep water, was undecided which way to swim.

"Why—why, I guess there isn't anything more to tell," he stammered. "I—I forgot—that's all there was to it. I'm sorry, Aunt Susie."

"You needn't be. There's nothing to be sorry about. Anybody's apt to forget things. I know I am. And I've got the picture, which ought to satisfy me, I should say. Thank you very much for it, Carey. And for being so thoughtful. I shall take it to Cleveland with me, of course, and every time I look at it I shall think of this old house and you people in it. All of you."

That night there was another animated dialogue in the George Judson bedroom. Mrs. Judson was, as usual, the prosecutor and her husband the defendant

"I didn't, I tell you," he vowed. "I give you my word of honor that I never mentioned that ship picture to a soul but you—Carey or anybody else. That's the truth, whether you believe it or not. I don't know why he took it into his head to give it to her. All I know is that I didn't put him up to it."

"Humph! Then perhaps you'll tell me who did?"

"I don't know who did. Maybe nobody did. Probably he just happened to think she might like it, that is what he said."

"Oh, *do* try to have *some* sense! Somehow or other she found out it was in his room and *some*body—she or you or somebody—got him to give it to her. That is sure."

"Well, what of it? You don't want the thing. I would have kept it where it always was, in the sitting room, but you declared you wouldn't have it in the house."

"Yes. And then you gave it to Carey. *You* did."

"You said it was all right for me to. What harm is there in it? You don't want it, and apparently Carey doesn't want it. She does want it and she's got it. So it is all right, I should say."

"All right! All *right*, is it? *He* gave it to her and we—you and I—were made to look not only as if we didn't have any family sentiment at all, but like a pair of liars. . . . What's that you say?"

George had muttered something. Now, driven to desperation, he repeated it aloud.

"Well, so far as that goes," he said, "we did lie. And we got what liars usually get. . . . Now go to bed and forget it."

Cora T. did not forget it, of course, nor did she permit him to do so, but she was so very busy during the days and evenings immediately following that she did not dwell upon her humiliation or the mystery accompanying Carey's presentation of the heirloom to his aunt. The reception to that lady was to be given at the Cap'n Jim-Carey place on Thursday evening of the next week and the household was busy with preparations. The date had been fixed, after much discussion and at least a half dozen changes, and the invitations, printed at the *Item* office in Trumet, mailed. The list of guests was a long one and, when completed, contained the names of almost every adult in Wellmouth and vicinity. There were many names on that list which Mrs. Judson did not wish there, but which, after much consideration and heated argument with her husband, she was forced, for diplomatic or business reasons, to add.

"The idea of asking those Baileys," she sneered, during one of those differences. "They wouldn't know a reception from a strawberry festival. But they'll come. Oh, heavens, yes—they'll come! You couldn't keep them out with a barbed wire fence. And what do you suppose the Halls, or Nellie Loveland and her mother—ves, or the Sayleses—will say when they see them here?"

George did not know what might be said, but he was certain that the objectionable ones must be invited.

"Joshua Bailey has sold our firm his fish ever since he was

old enough to command a schooner," he declared. "Father dealt with him long before I had anything to do with the business. And he and his wife knew Aunt Susie before she was married. Talk about saying things! What do you suppose they would say if they weren't asked to her party?"

"It isn't her party, it is my party, in my house. Just because you and Father Judson have bought their old fish is no reason why they should come and smell of it in my parlor."

"But Aunt Susan would wonder—"

"Oh, be still! She is worse than you are. If she has her way she'll invite every quahaug raker in town."

Considering the occupation of her own masculine progenitor this remark was risky, for it opened the way for a pointed rejoinder by her husband. But whatever the latter thought he said nothing, being, apparently, content with seeing the names of Captain and Mrs. Joshua Bailey added to the list of guests.

Cora T. was right when she intimated that Mrs. Dain was far from backward in supervising and extending the said list. Captain and Mrs. Tobias Higgins might not have been invited except for her insistence, and there were many others. Her niece-in-law declared she did not know where she was going to put such an army, to say nothing of feeding them.

The weather, on the fateful Thursday evening, was fine, in spite of morning clouds and a doubtful noon. The Cap'n Jim-Carey place was brilliantly illuminated. Not only the sitting room and dining room, but the huge front parlor and the little front hall were thrown open and shared the glitter. Even the front door was unlocked, its green blinds hooked back, and its ground glass panels, with their cut designs of grapes and flowers, dusted and washed. In the parlor, in the corner where the whatnot usually stood, were chairs upon which were to be installed the performers in "Beebe's Four-Piece Orchestra," a costly importation from Bayport.

The whatnot, with its collection of shells and ivory carvings, the alabaster image of the Leaning Tower of Pisa, and the card receiver made by gluing more shells to a pasteboard box, had been moved to the other corner by the square piano which no one had played since Mrs. Cap'n Jim-Carey's girlhood. There were many other curios on the shelves of that whatnot, including an "alum basket" and an apple tightly stuck full of cloves. The huge "base burner" stove, thanks to Hepsibah's strong arm, had been polished to ebony glitter, and at one side of it, beneath the mantel, hung a design made by crossing a whiskbroom and a poker, gilding their handles and tying them together with bows of yellow and black ribbon. This work of art was balanced on the other side by a gilt-handled dustpan and shovel, also becomingly ribboned. The mantel displayed more curios and photographs in splint-work or worsted and cardboard frames, while upon the walls were oil portraits of Captain Philander and Mrs. Sophronia Judson—George and Carey's grandfather and grandmother—painted about 1840 by an artist who was making a pedestrian tour of the Cape and was willing to "work for his board." There was another oil painting on the parlor wall—"Highlands of the Hudson," it was called—and when Carey and George were little shavers their admiration of it centered upon the fact that the sail in the foreground did look something like a sail from a point near the sitting-room door, but like just a daub of white paint when one drew nearer to examine. And its reflection in the light blue water was but another daub of the same paint. It must be great to be able to fool people like that.

There were many things in that parlor—the portraits and the clove apple, for example—of which Mrs. George Judson disapproved. But, just as in the case of the "rubbish" in Carey's bedroom, she had not yet found time to pitch them out. There was another reason for her delayed action in this respect. Her husband professed to like that parlor just as it was. It was as he had always remembered it and he wished it kept that way.

Supper that evening was a hurried and perfunctory meal, served hit or miss in the kitchen, in order that Hepsibah and Maggie, like the other members of the household, might have time to dress and prepare for the grandeur to follow. There had been some discussion as to whether or not George and Carey should don evening clothes. Carey had owned such an outfit since his college days, but George's was a more recent acquisition. And now, to his wife's disgust, he flatly refused to wear it.

"Of course I won't, Cora," he declared. "Nobody wears a dress suit down here and do you suppose I'm going to strut around to-night in the only swallowtail in the crowd? My Sunday suit is almost new and it is good enough. When I show off it won't be in the town where everybody has known me since I was a kid. And I guess Carey feels the same way. Don't you, Carey?"

Carey certainly did. The thought of the reception and the ordeal of meeting all those people, some of them creditors of his own bankrupt firm, was a horror which kept him awake at night. His first idea had been not to attend the affair, but to spend the evening in the Higgins' workshop. Aunt Susan's insistence, however, had forced him to change his mind.

"Of course you'll stay right here, Carey," she announced. "It is my party and I want all the family to enjoy it with me."

Carey, writhing, and tugging at his forelock, uttered one more protest.

"Enjoy!" he repeated. "Well, Aunt Susan, I must say I don't like your choice of words. I might endure the confounded thing—I suppose I shall have to, if you insist—but nobody on earth could make me *enjoy* it."

"How do you know? I shouldn't wonder if you had a pretty good time. You'll know every one."

He groaned. "Yes, and they know me," he muttered.

"Certainly. I see your point; but let me tell you this, young man: if you think they'll talk about you any the less if you stay away you're making a big mistake. They'll notice you're not here and every living soul will say you were ashamed to meet them."

A savage jerk at the lock of hair. "If they say that they will be speaking the truth," he vowed. "I am ashamed."

"All right, be ashamed then. But don't run off and hide, like a coward, because then you'll have that to be ashamed of, as well as the rest of it. Face the music, even if it's the kind of music that What's-his-name's orchestra is likely to play. . . . Come, come, Carey! When I saw you the other night making those wooden bird things I was—well, I must say I was pleasantly surprised. I decided that you must have—well, never mind. Only don't spoil everything by not coming to my party. I want you there."

So he promised to be on hand and donned his own "Sunday suit" with the feelings of a victim dressing for the scaffold. When he came downstairs the others were ready, Mrs. Dain serenely majestic in black silk, with Cora T. resplendent in the new gown the Wellmouth dressmaker had made for the occasion. The receiving line formed in the parlor, and Maggie, nose in air as usual, was stationed at the front door to admit the guests. In spite of her disdain she wore a triumphant expression, having that very afternoon forced her mistress to raise her wages under threat of immediate resignation if the demand was refused.

The hour set for the reception was eight, but a number of the townsfolk arrived before that. The Baileys—Mrs. Judson's detestations—made their appearance at seven forty-five. Captain Josh explained their forehandedness.

"Fust ones to report on deck, ain't we, George," he observed. "Well, that's my wife's doin's. She's so used to goin' early to Uncle Tom shows and such like at the town hall so's to get a front seat—her bein' kind of hard of hearin', you know—that she can't seem to get out of the habit. Hello, Susie!" shaking Mrs. Dain's hand with enthusiasm. "Ain't seen you since you made port this time. Look about the same as you always done, 'bout as big as a pint of cider. Why don't you fat up? Ask my wife—she'll tell you how. She weighs over two hundred nowadays."

Carey, whose place in the receiving line was at Cora T.'s left—so fixed by his aunt's orders—remained there no longer than was absolutely necessary. When the throng began to fill the parlor he slid unobtrusively away and retreated to the sitting room. Beebe's Four-Piece Orchestra was in full career by this time, rendering "After the Ball," a then popular ditty which its leader seemed to consider fitting. Even in the sitting room Carey was by no means alone, but he felt himself less conspicuous.

The Lovelands, in all their glory, made their entrance at the aristocratic hour of eight-thirty, almost immediately followed by the Halls, who may or may not have been watching them. The parlor overflow trickled into the sitting room. Carey, in his corner, was noticed and greeted by many. Most of the greetings were cordial enough, but some were frosty and distant. Captain Horatio Loveland, retired and wealthy, shook hands with him, asked bluffly how he was getting on and walked off, attended by admiring satellites. Mrs. Loveland's nod was short and her "Oh, how d'ye do?" decidedly snippy. Miss Nellie Loveland seemed inclined to be more companionable. She was a vivacious young woman, with flashing teeth and a flow of conversation which at any time was likely to become a freshet. She informed Carey that she had been just dying to meet him again; he was the most talked about man in Wellmouth; did he realize that?

"I think we all owe you a vote of thanks, Mr. Judson," she declared. "Some of us would have died of the blues if you hadn't given us something new to talk about. I was *so* sorry when I heard about your business trouble. Of course it was all that awful Mr. Osborne's fault. He must have been a dreadful man, but I don't wonder he fooled you. He fooled everybody else. I met him once—at the Seaburys' in Boston. Do you know them? They are the loveliest people. But of course you know them. They said they knew you."

Carey admitted that he knew the Seaburys.

"Yes. Well, Mr. Osborne came there to call, the very day—I mean at the time when I was visiting there—and everybody was fascinated by him. I know *I* was absolutely fascinated. He was so good looking and charming and such a wonderful talker. When I told him—just happened to mention it, you know—that I was studying art, he was *so* interested and asked such understanding questions. I declare I think I must have fallen in love with him—mother always scolds me for being so impressionable, you know. Yes, I think I did fall in love with him. Ha, ha! Isn't that a dreadful thing for me to say?"

She appeared to expect Carey to make some sort of comment, so he said, "Yes," explaining a moment later that he meant "No, not at all."

"Well, I couldn't help it, anyway," went on the impressionable one; "and you can imagine my feelings when I read what the newspapers said about him. But everybody was awfully sorry for you, Mr. Judson—for you and your brother and dear Mrs. Judson and all. And I think it is awfully brave of you to come back to Wellmouth to live and work in that old fish place, after what you have been used to, you know. Father says Mr. Early told him you were doing surprisingly well with the books, too. That is exactly what he said—surprisingly well. But don't you just *hate* it, bookkeeping, I mean?"

He murmured something to the effect that he liked it well enough. The remark was inane, but it answered the purpose. In a chat with Miss Loveland, the remarks of other people served merely as punctuation to her monologue.

"I do hope we shall see something of you now that you are here," she went on. "Do come and call. I am dying for some one—some cultivated person—to talk to. Bennie Hall —he is a nice boy, but only a boy—will be home from college on his summer vacation pretty soon and he calls a good deal, but—oh, well! *You* know, don't you? Do come and see me—us, I mean." . . . She paused and then, bending forward to whisper confidentially, added, with a giggle, "Isn't this just the weirdest crowd you ever *saw?*"

Members of the weird crowd came over to speak and the Loveland confidences were broken off, a fact for which Carey Judson was profoundly grateful. But those who succeeded her had altogether too much to say concerning their sympathy for him when they heard of his disaster in business, their surprise at learning of his accepting the bookkeeper's position with J. C. Judson & Co., and their hope—always, it seemed to him, with an unexpressed doubt attached—that he might "get along first rate" with his new duties. And invariably coupled with the surprise and hope were words of praise for his brother's action in providing him with that employment. If there had been any question in his mind concerning Wellmouth's conviction that that action was purely a deed of charity this evening's experience would have answered it.

Mr. Benjamin Early espied him as he stood there in the corner and approached, his wife in tow. Mr. Early's attire was faultlessly respectable; the most casual onlooker would have recognized him at once as a person of worldly importance and orthodox piety. Mrs. Early—her Christian name was Patience—was a moon-faced, hesitating woman who always looked at her husband before making an observation or venturing a reply.

Mr. Early said, "Good evening, Carey." His wife, after looking at him, said "Good evening" also. Benjamin observed that it was fine weather for the reception. "Pashy," after the look, affirmed that the weather was as nice as if it were made on purpose. Early, his shirt bosom creaking, declared the assemblage "about as representative a crowd of the right kind of people as you were likely to find anywhere." Before his wife had time to concur he leaned forward and whispered.

"Good chance for you to make yourself solid, this is, Carey. Stir around and shake hands with Cap'n Loveland and Squire Hall and folks like that. The more you're seen talking with their kind the better it will be for you. I'll send a few of the right ones over your way when I get the chance. . . . Ah, good evening, Cap'n Snow. Good evening, sir. You're looking well to-night. Fine gathering, isn't it?"

The sitting room was, by this time, almost as crowded as the parlor and Carey, fearful that the diplomatic Early might be sending some of the "right ones" in his direction was seriously thinking of leaving his corner, when Captain Tobias Higgins came plowing alongside. Tobias was, as usual, red-faced and short of breath, but his handshake was hearty and his greeting free from condescension. He and Carey were exchanging small talk when Mrs. Dain appeared.

"Oh, there you are!" she exclaimed. "I couldn't imagine what had become of you. My soul and body! Were you ever in such a jam in your born days! Come right into the parlor with me. There is some one there you ought to meet and who wants to meet you. Come right along. You'll excuse him, won't you, Cap'n Tobias?"

Captain Higgins grinned. "Sartin sure," he declared. "Glad to get rid of him. I can see him any time and there's folks here I ain't seen for so long I begun to think they was dead."

Carey did not want to return to the parlor and he was quite sure that he did not wish to meet any one who might want to meet him, but he obediently followed his aunt. The parlor was packed from wall to wall and above the clamor of tongues Beebe's Four-Piece Orchestra could be heard playing—for no discernible reason—Mendelssohn's Wedding March.

Aunt Susan, who had never let go of his arm, dragged him—not to the receiving line—but to a comparatively sheltered nook in the lee of the square piano. An elderly woman with a pleasant face and white hair was seated there and, although she did not rise, she leaned forward to extend a welcoming hand.

"Why—is it possible!" she cried. "Yes, of course it is. I can see that it is now. Carey, how do you do?"

Carey, accepting the hand, colored and was embarrassed. She had aged much during the five years since they last met.

"Good evening, Mrs. Sayles," he said.

He was glad to see her in one way—very. In another not so glad. She was one of the unfortunates a portion of whose money had been "taken care of" by Osborne and Judson. Her husband, Simeon Sayles, and Cap'n Jim-Carey had been great friends, and it was the former who suggested his son's firm handling the "investments." In his boyhood days the Sayles' house on the Trumet road had been a place where he had had many good times. Now, according to town gossip, there was possibility of that house being sold and the reasons prompting the sale had been repeated in his presence more than once. If, as his aunt had declared, Mrs. Desire Sayles wished to meet him, he could think of no agreeable reason why she should so wish.

She was cordial, however, surprisingly so.

"Let me look at you," she said. "Sit down beside me where I can see and talk to you. Your Aunt Susan and I have been saving this chair until she could find you. You are even thinner than you used to be, I do believe, and you never were what I should call plump. And you look older, a great deal older. Well, we all grow old, and I suppose young people show the change more than we who haven't been young for a long time. Emily hasn't changed a great deal. She looks much as she used to. She will want to meet you. She was here a moment ago, but I don't see her now, do you?"

He did not see her and was glad that he did not. Ever since he had learned that Desire Sayles and her daughter were to visit Wellmouth he had looked forward with dread to the time when he should meet them. He knew, of course, that they had been invited to the reception, and it was his principal reason for hoping he might be permitted to be elsewhere.

"She has gone into the other room, I guess," went on Mrs. Sayles, "but she will be back soon. Susan—"

But Mrs. Dain had wandered off and was chatting with

another group by the door. Mrs. Sayles turned again to look at him.

"Yes, you look much older," she repeated. "I suppose you feel even older than you look, don't you?"

He tried to smile. "Perhaps I shouldn't answer that," he said. "I may not be a competent witness—as to my looks."

She did not seem to understand, for the moment. Then she, too, smiled.

"Meaning that you haven't paid much attention to them, I suppose," she said. "Well, as I remember you, you never did do that. You have been through a great deal since I saw you. I am awfully sorry, Carey."

Here it was—the loathed subject again.

"You can't be as sorry as I am," he vowed, bitterly.

"No, I suppose not. But I am sorry. Emily and I have thought and spoken of you very often since it happened."

"I can imagine that. Mrs. Sayles, I—well, there is no use trying to ask you to forgive me. And I shouldn't ask it if there were. But—I wish you would tell me this—is it true that you are thinking of selling your property here in Wellmouth?"

Her answer surprised him.

"No," she said. "We have decided not to sell. We did think of it at first. You see, we were afraid we might have to. But we couldn't make up our minds to let any one else have the old place. So we sold our Maine cottage instead and gave up the little apartment we had in New York and we are coming to Wellmouth to live."

He turned to face her.

"To live!" he exclaimed. "To live the year around?"

"Yes. Why not? I lived here when I was a girl. I lived in that very house until my husband died. I always loved it more than any other I ever lived in. I am sure we shall be very comfortable in it now."

He did not comment on this statement; he could not. He

knew, of course, that they had lost heavily, but he had not understood what sacrifice that loss might mean.

She must have read his thought, or a little of it, for she put her hand on his.

"Now don't worry about that," she said, cheerfully. "Nor about Emily and me. We are going to be very happy there, I tell you. Emily is delighted with the idea. She always loved the place and she likes Wellmouth. . . . Tell me about yourself. How do you like your work at the office?"

He tried to answer, but he was not certain of what he said. She made the stereotyped remark that George Judson was a very good man indeed.

"I am glad you are going to be with him," she declared. "He always was your very best friend, Carey, and you will be safe with him."

He twisted the lock of hair between his thumb and finger.

"What did you say?" she asked.

He looked up. "Did I say anything?" he queried. "I did not mean to. I was thinking, that was all."

"What were you thinking?"

"I was thinking that you must wonder at his risking his own safety by having me about."

"Nonsense! Carey, will you take an old woman's advice? If you will, it is just this: Don't fret about what has happened. That you can't help. . . . I judge by your expression that some one has told you that before."

"At least some one. Yes."

"Well, it is good advice. . . . Now you haven't asked me a word about myself or about Emily. Aren't you interested in the doings of old friends?"

She did not wait to hear whether he was or not, but went on to tell of her trip to Europe with her daughter four years before, of their little summer home in Maine—that which had been sold—and of Emily's studies in music, which, it appeared, was a hobby.

"She is planning to give piano lessons here in Wellmouth," she said, and added hastily: "Oh, just for fun, of course.

She will want to do something and that will be fun for her—
that and the housekeeping. I shan't be as much help as I
should like to be. Since I had that wretched 'shock,' or whatever it was—"

He interrupted. "Shock!" he repeated, aghast. "What do
you mean, Mrs. Sayles?"

She shook her head. "There!" she exclaimed. "I didn't
intend to mention that word. No one in this town knows
about it yet—which is remarkable, considering the town—and
I didn't mean for them to. Perhaps it wasn't a shock—a
paralytic shock. The doctors gave it some Latin name or
other, but, to be honest, it seemed to me to be at least first
cousin to what old Doctor Doane who practiced here when
I was a girl would have pronounced a 'slight shock.' The
New York doctors said it was due to my nerves, or something. . . . Whatever it was it was a nuisance, for it has
left me good for not much, so far as stirring about is concerned."

He was regarding her intently. "When did you have it?"
he asked.

"Oh, last fall or in the early winter. Just before Christmas,
as a matter of fact. A delightful Christmas present, wasn't
it? It came, as such things usually do, without any warning.
I was—"

He did not hear the rest of the particulars. Just before
Christmas was the time when the news of the failure of
Osborne and Judson was spread abroad. It did not need
extraordinary imagination on his part to connect cause and
effect. He rose from the chair.

"Why, you are not going to leave me, are you, Carey?"
asked Mrs. Sayles. "I was relying on you to keep all those
other people away. I don't feel a bit like shaking hands with
the whole village. Do stay. Emily will be here in a minute,
I am sure."

But he would not stay. He muttered some transparent
excuse about "seeing George" and elbowed his way to the
sitting room. His own pet corner was occupied, but he did

not mind that. He hurried on to the little entry leading to the side door and from that door stepped out into the yard. The night was starlit and balmy, but had it been black and stormy it would not have made any difference to him just then. The thoughts in his brain were black enough and, his hands thrust deep in his trousers pockets, he paced up and down, through the alternate patches of shadow and light from the windows, thinking those thoughts.

He strode to the door, then turned and walked back toward the corner of the house. There was an iron seat there, one of the pair which had stood by the front walk. Cora T. had had it moved to that spot after a call from Nellie Loveland, who had remarked upon the lovely view from the corner. As he approached this seat he was startled from his unpleasant reverie by a movement in the shadow and a feminine voice which spoke his name.

"Why, Carey!" said the voice. "Carey Judson, is that you?"

He stopped in his stride. The figure in the shadow rose from the seat and came forward into a beam of light from a window.

"It is you, Carey, isn't it?" said Emily Sayles. "Why, how do you do?"

She extended a hand and he took it. He even smiled. The humor of the situation was tinged with irony. His reason for leaving the house had been largely the fear of meeting her and, had he remained inside, the meeting might have been avoided.

His greeting was not enthusiastic, but she did not seem to notice.

"Why, how odd that I should find you here—or we should find each other—in this place," she exclaimed. "Once before I caught a glimpse of you, in the sitting room it was, but before I could get away from Cap'n Loveland, who had me penned in a corner, you had disappeared. I do believe, though, that I have met every one else I ever knew in Wellmouth. *What* a crowd! Where do they all come from?"

He shook his head. "I don't know," he replied, "but they have all come, there is no doubt of that."

"Yes. This must be one of the parties with hundreds of invitations and no regrets. I feel as if I had been fighting my way through a parade. I was so tired of saying 'How do you do?' that I came out for a minute's rest. I suppose you were trying to escape, too, weren't you?"

He nodded. "Yes," he said.

"Mother was very anxious to have me find you. Have you seen her yet?"

"Yes. I have just been talking with her."

"I'm glad. You—and old Cap'n Tobias Higgins were the two people she especially wanted to meet to-night. And Mrs. Dain, of course. She is just as dear as she ever was, isn't she—your aunt, I mean. She says she is going back to Cleveland soon."

He told her what he knew of his aunt's plans for departure, and she referred again to the size of the crowd and the people—old acquaintances most of them—whom she had met. Then she asked:

"Did mother tell you that she and I were going to live here in Wellmouth now—permanently, I mean?"

"Yes, she told me."

"Isn't it a wonderful idea? It was my own, and I am very proud of it. And you hadn't heard?"

"No. I did hear that you and she thought of selling your property in Wellmouth, but I think it isn't generally known that you mean to live here. Do you really?"

"Of course we do. Why do you ask it in that tone? It isn't a calamity."

It seemed one to him and he could not believe it to be anything else to her. He did not answer her question. She went on to tell of how the decision had been reached.

"It came to me like a flash," she said. "I think it must have been in mother's mind for some time, but she did not mention it because, I suppose, she was fearful that I might not like it. But I do. I love the old home, and I like the town and I have—oh, so many plans about fixing up the rooms and changing things about. And the housekeeping, for just two of us, will be fun. And there is my music. Did she tell you I was planning to give piano lessons?"

"Yes."

"You must have felt like laughing. I do myself when I think of my daring to attempt such a thing. Perhaps you remember my playing. I don't see how any one could ever forget it. But I have studied a good deal, and I *think* I have improved. And the pupils I am likely to get—if I get any—will be only beginners. And it will be a—a plaything for me—something to keep me interested. They say every one should have a hobby of some sort. . . . Oh, and that reminds me, one of the first things I heard after our arrival yesterday was that you were playing at that old hobby of yours, bird making. I supposed, of course, that you were stuffing and mounting specimens, as you used to do, but Cap'n Higgins—he and I had a long talk this evening—tells me that it isn't that at all. According to him you make birds out of wood, and he says they are—well, he says that when you finish one of those—what is it? beetle-heads—it lacks absolutely nothing but the chirrup."

She laughed gayly as she said it. They were still standing by the end of the seat and she had been chatting rapidly and, it seemed to him, a little nervously. He understood the reason for her nervousness. He turned toward her impulsively.

"Emily," he said, "I—I tried to tell your mother a little of how I feel about your being forced to come here to live. She didn't say you were forced to do it, of course, but I know you were—and what forced you. I—well, what is there for me to say? You must have been amazed when you heard I was brazen enough to come back here—to live—and try to work, after—after—"

She interrupted. "Oh, of course I wasn't amazed," she declared. "We knew—mother and I—why you came back. You did it to please your brother. He wrote us all about it—

we have been in touch with him ever since—he has been
advising us, in business matters, you know, and—— But there.
I don't want to talk about that. I want to tell you more about
my plans about the house and about my precious music teaching scheme. And I *very* much want to hear more about your
wooden birds. . . . Are you so very anxious to get back into
that crowd?"

"No. I am glad to be away from it. But—"

"So am I, and thankful. And it is such a glorious night.
Sit down here on this bench. It does remind one of a grave-
yard, but even that has a welcome hint of rest after those
packed rooms. Do sit down and talk to me, or let me talk
to you. I must talk to some one and you always were a good
listener, even if you didn't always pay attention. Come."

So, because he could not think of a good excuse for refus-
ing, he did sit beside her on the iron seat while she went on to
speak of the new wall paper which she had purchased for
their parlor, which was, she said, to be no longer a "parlor"
in the Wellmouth sense, but a room to be lived in daily and
used. She asked his advice about the paper and begged him
to suggest a carpenter for the repair work. At first his suggestions were few and his replies to her questions absently
given, for heavy upon his conscience was the weight of
responsibility for the downfall of the Sayles family fortunes
and its accompanying sense of shame and guilt. Again and
again he attempted to return to that subject, but each time
she refused to listen and went on with her rambling chatter
concerning her own plans and intentions. Little by little,
she broke down his reserve and reluctance to talk about
himself and her evident real interest in his bird making led
him to talk about that, about the Higgins' workshop, the con-
templated purchase of a foot power lathe and saw, about the
probability of more orders in the future—about the one actual
interest left to him in life. And not once—this did not occur
to him until afterward—did she mention the drudgery in his
brother's office, ask him how he liked bookkeeping, or any
of the questions which every one else asked and which he

hated. In fact, from being particularly miserable, he began actually to enjoy this conversation with the girl whom he had so dreaded to meet.

"I am crazy to see those birds of yours," she declared. "I like birds too. Do you remember I helped you prepare some of those you had in your room upstairs? I did, whether you remember it or not."

"Of course I remember. By George, you did, didn't you! Why you stuffed one yourself and it was a tip-top piece of work. It was a robin and it is up in the room yet. I'll show it to you some time."

"Will you? I should like to see the poor thing. I can't imagine how it could have looked much like a robin after I finished with it. I should have supposed it would be more like the dog the boy started to draw and, as he said, it 'came out a lamb.' But I do want to see those wooden birds of yours and, some day, after the 'pupils' have gone—or while I am waiting for some to come—I am going to walk down to the Higgins' establishment and sit and watch you work. May I?"

"Certainly, if you want to. Although I can't see why you should."

"I can. And I shall come. Probably on a Sunday. You are always there Sundays, so Cap'n Higgins says."

"Almost always. I suppose I am regarded as more than ever wicked for doing such things on Sunday. Even George doesn't like it, and Cora, of course, is scandalized. But— well, so far as going to church here in Wellmouth is concerned, that is an ordeal that I haven't had the courage to face."

"I know. Of course I know. . . . Well, I shall come, probably some Sunday afternoon. . . . What is all the excitement inside there? Something unusual must be going on."

The click of plates and the odor of hot coffee supplied the answer to the query. Miss Sayles rose.

"Refreshments are being served, of course," she said.

"And I mustn't leave mother any longer. You may bring us our share there by the piano, if you care to, Carey."

They fought their way back through the crowd, against the tide which was setting toward the dining room, and leaving her in her mother's company, he joined the masculine whirlpool about the end of the table where Mrs. Loveland, assisted by Mrs. Hall, was "pouring."

After midnight that evening, when Desire Sayles and her daughter were again in their own home, the former said:

"So you had a long talk with him, did you, Emily? How did he seem to you?"

Emily shook her head. "He is dreadfully despondent, mother," she said. "Any one could see that, especially any one who has known him as you and I used to."

"He has grown ever so much older, hasn't he?"

"Yes. And he is so—well, sad and—oh, hopeless. I pitied him as much as I ever pitied any one in my life. Poor helpless, innocent thing! Trying to find comfort and forgetfulness with those wooden birds of his. I suppose every single person who spoke of him to you was condescending— if nothing worse."

"Most of them would have been worse if I would have let them. He *is* innocent—and was innocent all through, daughter, I know that. But his kind of innocence is so near to wicked carelessness that it probably deserves punishment—and always gets it. I hope you didn't let him know how pinched we really are."

"Of course I didn't," indignantly. "He tried to talk about it and would have cross-questioned me, if I had given him the chance. Which I didn't."

"Well," with a sigh, "I wish I could believe that he would ever get anywhere in this world. I'm afraid he won't. So long as George Judson lives he will, I suppose, be tolerated as bookkeeper in that office. But if anything should happen to George—I don't know what he would do. He is, I think, the most impractical person I ever met—and one of the most likable. You can't help liking him."

No, you can't. I liked him when he was a boy and I like him now. And even if his 'carelessness,' as you call it, has forced me into giving music lessons, I am just as sorry for him as I can be. Almost as sorry as I shall be for the unfortunates who pay for the lessons. Mother, you must go to bed this minute. This has been a frightfully dissipated evening for you."

Carey had not yet gone to bed, but having helped the Judson family, its Cleveland relative, and the servants with the cleaning up, he was at that moment on his way to the stairs. Aunt Susan came out of the dining room and beckoned to him.

"Well, Carey," she said, "you managed to come through it alive, didn't you?"

Carey smiled. "Yes," he said. Then, as if the fact surprised him as much as it could any one else, he added, slowly, "I—why, to be honest, Aunt Susan, I feel as if I had had a pretty good time."

Mrs. Dain's lip twitched. "I thought perhaps you might," she said. "Well, if you are invited to any more receptions or parties I should advise you to go. They are pretty good prescriptions for some kinds of people."

# CHAPTER VII

MRS. DAIN'S visit came to an end the Tuesday of the week following the reception. George and Cora begged her to stay longer, but she refused. She was a person of determination, who did her own thinking and settled her own problems. And, having decided that she should go, she went.

"I have played long enough," she said. "I left my house in Cleveland in the care of the cook and housemaid. They are good servants and they have been with me a good many years, but they are jealous of each other and quarrel like cats and dogs. They both promised me to keep the house and the peace while I was away, and I think they both meant it. But I have had letters from each of them and I can see it is high time I went home. I don't mind seeing my name in the society notes of the newspapers, but I *am* fussy when it comes to its getting into the police items. . . . And I planned to go back about this time, anyway."

Carey was sorry to have her go. Her manner toward him was uncompromisingly blunt and her criticisms of his character and habits outspoken. They were honest criticisms, however, and shrewdly wise. He found no fault with them. Since her unexpected call at the Higgins' workshop it seemed to him that she had been more tolerant of his failings. She had not called there again, but she occasionally asked him how his "bird dolls" were getting on and he learned from Captain Tobias that she and the captain had had at least one long conversation concerning him and his "hobby."

Higgins chuckled as he told of it.

"She's a smart woman, that aunt of yours," he said. "I'll bet there don't anybody fool her much. She got me in a corner that night of the sociable—or reception, or whatever you call it—and by the time she was ready to cut cable and let me cruise by myself she had me pumped dry. I wasn't cal'latin' to say much about you, Carey. I knew you didn't want your work here talked about and did my best to keep my main hatch closed; but sho! she cross-questioned me the way my mother used to when I'd hooked jack from school to go swimmin'. And she done it so clever, too. While I was talkin' with her I felt pretty satisfied with myself; figgered I hadn't told a thing that I didn't mean to tell. 'Twan't until I got home that night that I realized she'd found out all I know about you and a lot more that I only guessed. I'm sorry; but that's how 'twas."

Carey was indifferent. "I don't mind," he said. "You couldn't tell her more than she knew already. The whole town knows what I do down here in this shop. The people who come into the office ask me about my 'decoys' continually. I judge they think you and I are running a sort of toy factory."

Tobias grinned. "Let 'em think so," he grunted. "They ain't many of 'em drifted in here to bother you while you are workin', have they?"

"No. No, they haven't. I guess they aren't interested enough for that."

"Ho, ho! Don't you believe it, son. The very reason that you don't want 'em here would be enough to get 'em interested—some of 'em. If half of the gang here in Well-mouth was as interested in gettin' a livin' as they are in interferin' with other folks's doin' it taxes would be a consider'ble sight lower than they are. They'd come if they was let come, but Phœbe and I see that they don't. The minute you go into this shop, that minute our dinin'-room window shade goes up and we commence to stand watch. Between us I presume likely Chip and me have headed off about fifty loafers that was on their way to help you whittle by settin' around borrowin' your tobacco and matches and doin' the heavy lookin' on."

Carey pulled at his forelock. This was news to him.

"I'm very much obliged to you, I'm sure," he said.

"You needn't be. After all, these are my premises and I'm particular whose boots wear off my grass."

He shook his head reflectively and then added: "There was one thing Susie Dain didn't get out of me. She didn't find out what you was cal'latin' to do with the money you earned beetle-head makin'. I couldn't tell her that because I didn't know."

If the captain was doing a little fishing on his own account the result must have been disappointing. Judson made no comment. Tobias threw over a fresh bait.

"When I came to think over what she said," he observed, "it seemed to me that was one of the things she 'specially wanted to learn. I judged 'twas her notion you had some sort of plan of your own about what to do with that money."

Another pause. Carey was busy with his paint brush.

"The funniest of all was what she said at the end," went on Higgins. " 'I don't know much about his private plans,' I told her. 'If he's got any he don't tell 'em to me.' And all she said to that was, 'Good! A person's bein' able to keep things to himself is a proof that he's got some character of his own, after all. Isn't that so, Tobias?' 'Course I said it was; but it was funny all the same her talking that way, wasn't it, Carey? Eh?"

Carey, reflecting upon his talk with the captain did think it a little odd that his aunt should be so interested in what he intended doing with the money he might earn from bird-making. He remembered she had asked him why he wanted that money and he had hinted at a secret plan—or hope—concerning the use of it. But when he had asked her to excuse him for not revealing that plan, even to her, she had applauded his silence. Then why had she cross-questioned Higgins? He could think of but one possible reason, which was that she wished to make sure he was speaking the truth when he said he had told no one.

The thought was distinctly unpleasant. He knew Mrs. Dain's opinion of him. She had declared him to be a careless incompetent, helplessly impractical in a practical world, and therefore unfit to be entrusted with money. He quite agreed with her and did not resent the estimate. But he did not wish her to think that his reason for wishing to earn more than his salary as bookkeeper had in it anything selfish or dishonorable. He did not care to have that reason known in Wellmouth, but she was leaving Wellmouth. He determined to tell it to her before she went.

The opportunity came on Monday afternoon, the day before her departure. Dinner was over. Cora T. was in the kitchen, playing a poor second in a peppery dialogue with Maggie, whose high mightiness was becoming unendurable and who was threatening to sever connections with her employers. The reception was the final straw for Maggie. She told Hepsibah—and did not lower her voice because of Mrs. Judson's proximity—that "such a boonch of hayseeds *I* never seen and I'll break me back cleanin' up afther no more of thim."

George, having an appointment at the bank, had hurried away, leaving Carey to finish his meal at leisure. He had finished it and, as he came into the sitting room, could hear Aunt Susan moving about in her room overhead, whither she had gone to finish packing. It occurred to him that here was his chance for a talk with her. He went up the stairs, knocked at her bedroom door, and found her on her knees beside the trunk and surrounded by intimately personal items of apparel. She looked up at him over her spectacles.

"Carey Judson," she snapped, "what is it? If Cora sent you you can tell her I'll come down as soon as I can. I've got troubles enough without settling any fights between her and that Maggie. If the saucy thing worked for me she would have been settled before this. . . . Oh, dear me! *Where* shall I put this dress? It came in this very trunk, so I suppose it's got to go back in it, but *how* the Lord knows! Go and tell Cora what I said and don't bother me."

Her nephew did not obey orders. Instead he seated himself upon the edge of the bed and crossed his long legs.

"Aunt Susan," he began, slowly. "I want to tell you something."

She barked at him like an excited puppy. *"Get* up this instant, you great lumbering thing!" she commanded. "How many times a day do you think I want to make that bed? Get *up!"*

He did not appear to hear her. As a matter of fact he did not hear. What he had come to tell was tremendously serious to him, but he realized it was likely to sound silly to others.

"Aunt Susie," he began again. "I hate to bother you, but—"

"But you are going to; I can see that. Well, go ahead and bother and get it over with. I shall keep on packing. I don't believe anything you are likely to tell me is important enough to interfere with that. What is it? You haven't changed your mind and decided to go to Cleveland, after all? That isn't it, is it? I hope not, for I've changed mine and now I think you had better stay where you are."

He looked at her in surprise.

"No," he announced. "Why, no. I guess—I guess I had forgotten that you suggested my going to Cleveland. No, that isn't it."

"Well, then, what is it? Come, come! Hurry! Let your hair alone, if you can—and *talk."*

He pulled harder than ever at the forelock.

"It's just this," he said. "You remember asking me what I wanted to make the money for—the money for my birds, you know? And I said—well, I told you I had rather not tell?"

She was refolding the dress. Now she stopped and looked keenly at him.

"Cerainly, I remember," she declared. "And I remember telling you not to tell anybody, unless—or until—you wanted to."

"Yes. Well, I want to tell you now."

"O-oh! You do. Why?"

"Because there isn't any good reason for not telling you. I want that money to—to pay my debts with."

She let the partially folded gown slip from her hands to the floor.

"Your debts!" she repeated. "What debts? My soul and body! You don't mean you owe debts that I don't know anything about. *More* debts?"

"What? More? No, indeed! They are those you and every one else know about. But—"

"Wait! You can't mean the debts of that banking firm of yours. Those are being taken care of. Your creditors know how many cents they are to get on a dollar. They should be thankful to get that much, I suppose, and some of us are. Those debts are settled—or as much settled as they ever will be."

"Yes. . . . Yes, most of them are, I suppose. But there are some that—that—"

"Carey Judson, I declare you frighten me! You look as guilty as a henhouse thief. What are you trying to tell me?"

He did look guilty. Now that the point had been reached when he must put into words his cherished dream, he found it very hard to do so. It seemed so picayune and childish, after all. He was afraid of being laughed at.

"Well, Aunt Susan," he stammered, "you see—I feel as if—as if I must pay some of those debts myself. Dollar for dollar, I mean. There are people here in Wellmouth, people I have *got* to pay. I must pay them. . . . Good Lord, I *must!*"

Packing and all connected with it was apparently forgotten. Mrs. Dain rose to her feet. She came over and sat beside him on the bed.

"Carey," she said, gently, "don't look like that. Or talk like it. Stop it this minute! You have been worrying over this miserable business until you are half sick again. You mustn't do so. What's done is done, and to fret yourself into another nervous breakdown only makes everything worse. . . . Perhaps, after all, you had better come to Cleveland with me."

He smiled, crookedly. "My nerves are all right," he observed. "So is my mind, as right as it ever was. At any rate it hasn't cracked sufficiently to make me believe I can pay all my debts, even all here in Wellmouth."

"I should say not! George says the folks in town here lost over forty thousand dollars. Some could afford to lose and some couldn't; but what *is* the use—"

He interrupted. "I think there may be some little use," he said. "I'm hoping there is. If I could I would square up with every old friend of father's and George's and mine to the last nickel, but that I can't do. I can pay a little, here and there—or I think I can—and if I can I shall. It is those people who can't afford to lose I am talking about. People who lost a few thousand dollars, about all they had put by. I can pay some of them, a little at a time, and the others needn't know anything about it. For instance, I shall get a check for a hundred and twenty dollars any day now. And I have orders for more birds. I imagine I can get orders enough to keep me busy a long time. I don't want the money for myself. George pays me more than I'm worth, and it is more than I need. But, don't you see—"

She laid a hand on his knee. "Wait a minute, Carey," she said, quietly. "I guess I'm beginning to understand. This was the idea you have had all along? The plan you wouldn't tell me about when I asked you down at your workshop?"

"Yes. I said it was, didn't I? There was no real reason for my not telling you then, but—"

"Never mind that. Tell me now. Tell me everything about it."

He went on to tell, mentioning names of those whom he hoped to pay first. She learned that he had kept a list of the Wellmouth creditors and had checked those to whom Osborne and Judson owed little and who could least afford to part with that little.

"It wasn't my own idea, exactly," he told her. "Something George said there at the hospital when he was coaxing me to come back here—that set me to thinking. He said if I cared to, and could, pay a few dollars here and there in Wellmouth, on my own hook, it would do more to square me with the people I know there than anything in the world. Really that was the deciding factor. I am sure I shouldn't have come if it hadn't been for that. His idea, I suppose, was that I might save a little from my salary. I am doing that, too. But afterwards the bird-making plan occurred to me and it looked pretty good."

He paused. His aunt made no comment. After a moment he went on.

"I don't know how this sounds to you, Aunt Susan," he said, with a twisted smile. "It sounds idiotic and silly enough to me as I say it. I realize I am talking like the poor, but honest hero of a Sunday School book, but I'll be damned if I feel like one. . . . Excuse the emphasis, please. I forget my manners sometimes."

Mrs. Dain sniffed. "I'll excuse it," she declared. "Go on."

"I have gone about as far as I can. There is nothing heroic about it, and precious little common sense, I guess. And, to be honest, I am doing it more for my own sake than any one else's. It— Humph! well, I suppose the idea fools me into thinking I have some self-respect to keep up. . . . That's it."

He twisted a corner of his coat into a ball and squeezed it tight. She saw his knuckles whiten with the force of the grip. He drew a long breath and rose from the bed.

"I am telling you this," he said, more briskly, "because I didn't see any reason for hiding it from you. Don't tell any one else, that's all. Cora would think me a jackass— which I am—and why should George be worried? Now I must go. I shall be late at the office."

She did not detain him. "Thank you for telling me, Carey," was all she said.

"That's all right. I didn't want you to think I was going

to follow Osborne's example and buy orchids with my surplus, that's all."

He hurried out, leaving her still seated on the hopelessly rumpled bedspread. It was some time before she resumed her packing.

Next morning Carey, because his aunt insisted upon his doing so, went in company with his brother and Mrs. Judson, to the railway station, to bid their visitor good-by. He and she had no opportunity for another lengthy talk, but just before she boarded the train she led him to one side and begged him to write regularly.

"I shall expect a letter from you once a week," she whispered. "You won't disappoint me, will you?"

"No, Aunt Susan. I'll write, if you care to have me."

"I do. And I want to hear all about your paying those town debts of yours; who you pay and all about it."

"All right, I'll report progress—if there is any."

"Good! Take care of yourself and don't worry any more than you can help. I was going to say don't worry at all, but, knowing you, that would be foolish. And I shall write you all the Cleveland news, including how I get along with the servants and my pains, and all my troubles."

There was a note in her voice as she uttered the last sentence which caused him to glance at her quickly.

"Your pains?" he repeated. "You haven't had any more of those pains such as you had the other night, have you?"

She smiled, grimly. "I have them, more or less, a good deal of the time," she declared, "and probably shall have them till the final one comes. But I don't want you to tell any one that. Pains are some of the things that aren't helped by advertising. . . . There! Kiss me, and run along. Cora is beginning to glare at us, which means she suspects we have a secret. . . . Well, perhaps we have, but, so far as I am concerned, it shall be one. Good-by, Carey."

Mrs. Judson's farewells were much more effusive. Her handkerchief was in use when the train pulled out. As they drove back to the Cáp'n Jim-Carey place she asked a question.

"Well, Carey," she inquired, with elaborate carelessness, "what were you and Aunt Susan whispering so earnestly about? Was she afraid George and I might neglect you after she had gone, or something like that?"

Carey shook his head. "I guess she wasn't greatly afraid of that," he said.

"Humph! She looked as if she was afraid we might hear what she was saying, I noticed that much. What did she say?"

George, to his brother's relief, put in a word.

"Probably she was telling him what she told me, to be a good boy and behave myself," he said. "She is a lively soul, Aunt Susan is. The house will be lonesome for a while now that she has gone."

Cora T. sniffed. "It will be quieter, at least," she declared. "If she had stayed much longer I should have had to lose Maggie, that's sure. She and Aunt Susie hated each other. I do not see why some people feel it necessary to boss everything, no matter where they are."

The Cap'n Jim-Carey place was particularly lonely for Carey after Mrs. Dain's departure. The old lady was sharp-tongued and outspoken, but he was fond of her. And she was the one person to whom he had confided his dream of paying a few of the Osborne and Judson debts. He had not told her until the last moment, but, having broken the ice and finding the water by no means as chilly as he expected, he would have enjoyed asking her advice and discussing names and means. Between George and himself there had always been the most complete confidence, but to tell George was equivalent to telling George's wife, and that he could not do. At the end of the first week he wrote his aunt a long letter, announcing shipment of the dozen "beetle-heads" and promising to report receipt of the check when it arrived.

Time at the office dragged heavily for him. The novelty attached to learning the routine of the bookkeeping was over; he was as good a bookkeeper now as he was ever likely to be and the fact was forced upon him that he would never be a shining success in the position. He could add and subtract and multiply and divide, when he had to, and post and credit with fair accuracy, but doing none of these things interested him. His interest was elsewhere, out along the beach with the gulls and sandpipers, or in the Higgins' shop where, on the chance of disposing of them to some one, he had begun work upon the first of a dozen black duck. Occasionally he took a Sunday dinner with Captain Tobias and Phœbe Higgins, and twice he had accompanied the former on sailing trips in the *Ambergris, Junior*. At home with his wife, the captain's authority was pretty much pretense, but aboard his catboat and on salt water he was a martinet. He treated his passengers as he had treated his foremast hands aboard the whaler.

"Slack up that peak halliard," he would bellow, from his seat by the wheel. Most catboats were steered with a tiller, but the *Ambergris, Junior* was not of these. A tiller was a "no-account fresh water contraption" and Tobias Higgins would not tolerate it. His boat had a wheel and as near a "man's size" wheel as her build permitted.

"Slack up that peak halliard," roared the captain. "Do you want her on her beam ends? What are you sittin' there for? Think you've growed fast. What the blank crash bang ails you? Lively!"

When the crisis was over he would apologize.

"Wonder you don't haul off and lam me with the boat hook, Carey," he was likely to observe. "I know I hadn't ought to go for you that way, and I don't mean to. You see I've been used to speakin' out what's on my mind when I'm aboard a vessel—when I'm on deck anyhow—and since I've been hauled up on dry land I've kind of had to muffle down. Out here, away from women folks, the old habit sort of comes back. Godfreys! It seems good to be able to let go once in a while, but I don't mean nothin' by it. You won't hold a grudge against me, will you, Carey?"

Carey rather enjoyed being ordered about by Tobias. The

latter's outspoken roars of fault-finding were a pleasant contrast to the condescendingly suave nagging of Mr. Ben Early
in the office of J. C. Judson & Co. The manager was always
outwardly friendly, almost effusively so, but his was the
ostentatious kind of friendship which made Carey long to
slip from the high stool and kick him. His encouraging comments, his solicitous offer of aid "whenever anything comes
up that bothers you, Carey," and his very obvious conviction
that things of that sort were continually "coming up," were
hard to bear. And harder still because there was a measure
of truth in that conviction. The problems connected with
the bookkeeping were bothersome.

Carey's second trial balance was a trial indeed. Early
had helped him with the first one, but the second he attempted drawing unaided and the confounded thing would
not come right. He labored over it long into the night, laid
it aside until the next night and then tackled it again. The
amount needed to make it square was small but the error
remained unlocated. George and Cora supposed him to be
at the Higgins' shop busy with what the latter contemptuously
called his "playthings," and he did not undeceive them. He
stubbornly set his teeth and resolved to win the battle himself, without any one's aid, least of all Early's. The
ubiquitous Benjamin had that very afternoon casually inquired concerning the balance and Carey had lightly answered
that it was all coming along right. There was—or it seemed
to him there was—a hint of ironic suspicion behind the
inquiry and the bland smile accompanying it. He was almost
certain that the manager suspected that it was not all right,
and was rather pleased than otherwise. Well, it should be
right; he would make it so.

So, at eight-thirty the third evening, he again entered the
office, pulled the window shades down as near the sills as
he could get them—one of them was out of order and refused
to come all the way—lighted the hanging lamp above the
desk, took the books from the safe and began poring over
them once more. It was a warm evening and he had left a

window open to relieve the stuffiness and moderate the ever present scent of fish.  The partially drawn shade flapped occasionally in the summer breeze.

He labored with the figures, and labor it was.  He hated it—oh, how he hated it!  To save his life he could not concentrate his thoughts upon the drudgery; they would stray to the black duck which he had left lying, partially complete, upon the bench in his shop.  He was not quite certain whether or not the pose of the neck was exactly what it should be. He must carefully examine his photographs and the stuffed model before he went any farther with it. . . . Then, with a guilty twinge of conscience, he shut the duck from his mind and resumed his bookkeeping.

Some one knocked at the door.  He looked up from the ledger page with a start and a feeling of intense annoyance. Some one—Early or George probably, or perhaps old Jabez Drew, the wharf boss—had seen the light in the office, or had been told of it by some one else, and had come to investigate.  He slid off the stool and walked to the door.  He did hope it might not be Early.  Anybody but that fellow, until that balance was struck.

But when he opened the door he found Emily Sayles standing on the platform.

"Good evening, Carey," she said.  And then: "Why, don't look so thunderstruck!  Nothing has happened.  I haven't any bad news.  I was passing and your window shade was up and I saw you sitting at the desk.  There was a question in my mind that I wanted answered and when I saw you it occurred to me that you would be just the one to answer it. That isn't such a miracle, is it?"

It was not, of course.  Only a few people used the Wharf Road after nightfall, although some did, and any passerby would have noticed the light.  But why she should be walking along that road at nine o'clock in the evening he could not imagine.  He had not seen her since the night of the reception, although he had heard much.  All Wellmouth was talking of her and her mother and their decision to make the old Sayles house their permanent abiding place; also, of course, the piano lessons.

"Won't you come in?" he asked.

She hesitated. "No," she said, "I won't come in. . . . I guess. . . . Well then, I will, for just a minute. But you are busy, I know, and I promise you not to stay."

He made no comment upon her change of mind. She entered and he closed the door. Then he walked to the window and tugged impatiently at the refractory shade.

"Never mind that," she said, laughing. "We are not likely to be seen, and if we are I am sure I don't mind."

No doubt she expected him to laugh also, or at least smile, but he did neither. Nor did he voice the thought, whatever it might be, which was obviously in his mind. Possibly she guessed it, for she colored slightly, and spoke again.

"Of course you wonder," she said, quickly, "how I happen to be here. I have been up to Cap'n Obed Cahoon's, to see Mrs. Cahoon about Elsie—their little girl, you know. They want her to come to me on Tuesdays and Fridays for music lessons. I talked with her mother and Cap'n Obed—he doesn't know a thing about music, says the only scales he is acquainted with are those on a fish—and I talked with Elsie herself. And she is my question. She came to the house last Tuesday and I spent two miserable hours with the child. *She* doesn't want to play the piano, says she *hates* it. And, truly, Carey, I think she is determined not to learn. She is spoiled utterly and she has a will like iron, whether inherited or not I don't know."

Carey twisted his hair.

"I do," he observed. "I know her father."

"I see. Now the question is what ought I to do? I am tempted to tell the Cahoons exactly how I feel and that, in my opinion, sending Elsie to me as a pupil will be a waste of their money and my time. She told me that she would not practice and, judging by what I have seen of their control—or lack of it—over her, they won't force her to do so. I wanted to say no to them just now—to-night, but I did not because—well, because I feared it might not be a diplomatic thing to do. I have a bad habit of telling people exactly what I think and mother says only very rich people can afford to do that. I was turning the matter over in my mind and wishing there was some one—somebody who knew the Wellmouth people better than I did—who could advise me. Then I saw you—and here I am. Now tell me what to do."

The lock of hair in the center of Carey's forehead was by this time twisted into a sharply pointed wedge extending downward to the bridge of his nose. He left it hanging there and dropped his hand to his chin, which he rubbed thoughtfully.

"How did you happen to be down here on the Wharf Road?" he asked.

"Oh, I didn't tell you that, did I? It just happened, that is all. It is a gorgeous night and the water looked so lovely in the moonlight that I walked around this way instead of going directly home. Besides, I wanted to think and I didn't want my thinking interrupted by meeting people. Now tell me what to do with Elsie Cahoon."

He shook his head. "You say you are not a diplomat,"
he observed. "Did you ever hear any one call me anything of the sort?"

He asked the question solemnly enough, but the look accompanying it caused her to smile.

"No," she confessed, "I can't remember that I ever did. But, perhaps, after all, it isn't diplomacy that I want to hear. Tell me just how you feel about it. The problem must be settled and the sooner the better."

Carey stopped rubbing his chin and his slim fingers strayed to the "scratcher"—the ink eraser—upon the desk, and began playing with that. That "scratcher" was Early's particular horror. Its use upon the books of J. C. Judson & Co. he considered almost as great a sacrilege as making wooden birds on the Sabbath. Because the sacrilege in both cases was committed by the brother of his employer his objections were not made openly, but were confined to hints. Carey, if he recognized them as such, did not heed them. He continued his Sunday bird-making and he continued to correct mistakes with the scratcher. To his particular kind of bookkeeping that scratcher was as necessary a tool as a pen and was always kept within easy grasp.

Now, while considering his visitor's problem, he stood the scratcher on end, reversed it, and then dug absently at an ink smear on the desk. Miss Sayles began to lose patience.

"Do tell me," she urged. "I stopped here especially to have you tell me and I *mustn't* stay any longer. If you were in my place, what would you do?"

Carey, having removed the ink smear and a little varnish with it, looked up.

"If I were in your place," he said, "I suppose I should tell the Cahoons that I couldn't give lessons to their daughter."

She nodded. "I see," she said. "Well, that is what I wanted to do, of course . . . but—"

"Wait. That is what *I* should do and so it makes me feel pretty certain that you mustn't do it."

"Now, what in the world, Carey Judson—?"

"I think you had better give her the lessons. If you don't some one else will and you will have the Cahoons down on you, besides. Cap'n Obed has a good deal of influence in town and his wife—well, she is blessed with what the papers call an easy flow of language."

"I see what you mean. She and he will say all sorts of horrid things about me. Well, so far as that goes, I shouldn't care if they did. I would have done nothing to be ashamed of."

He dropped the scratcher and his tone changed.

"You should care," he said, earnestly. "In a town of this size it is not pleasant to be—talked about in that way. I know it."

She moved nearer the desk.

"Carey," she said, impulsively, "I am sorry. I wish I had not stopped here to worry you with my little troubles. Oh, why *do* I always act on the spur of the moment?"

"That is all right. As I see it, you may as well give the Cahoon girl her music lessons. If you succeed in teaching her anything why, well and good. If you fail, why—"

"Why, then her father and mother will say it is all my fault."

"That is probably true; but in the meantime you will have made progress with your other pupils and will be in a better position to answer criticisms. . . . There, that is my advice. I think you had better not take it."

"Not take it? . . . Oh, I see. Because it *is* yours, you mean."

"That's it."

He picked up the scratcher again. She turned to go.

"I shall take it, I think," she said. "And thank you very much for giving it." Then she added, smiling: "You have surprised me a little bit. You said you were not a diplomat and I have heard people call you impractical; but I should say you had answered this question of mine about as practically, and certainly as honestly, as any one could. I am sure mother will say exactly the same thing when I tell her. Oh, by the way, when are you coming to call on us at the house? Mother says you promised her you would come."

He had no recollection of making any such promise. Nor, when he spoke, did he refer to the invitation.

"I hate to let you walk home alone," he said, "but I am afraid I can't leave here yet. If I were a diplomat I might have concluded a treaty of peace with this confounded trial balance. As it is the war is still on. Excuse me, won't you?"

"Of course. What is the trouble with the balance? Won't it come right?"

"I suppose it might if I gave it the chance. The trouble is with me. As a bookkeeper I am a first-class bird stuffer."

"Wouldn't Mr. Early help you if you asked him?"

"Yes."

The monosyllable was sufficiently expressive. She laughed. Then, after another instant of hesitancy, she walked again to the desk.

"I wonder if I might not help?" she said. "I like figures and—I never told any one in Wellmouth this and perhaps there is no need of their knowing—I did some bookkeeping over in New York. I was a bookkeeper in an office there for three months, and they *said* I was a pretty good one."

He looked at her.

"When?" he asked.

"Oh, this past winter. You see—well, it was before we sold the Maine cottage and decided to come here. It was more for fun than anything else," she added, hastily. "The firm who employed me was—the head of it was a friend of ours—and I wanted something to keep me busy, so—I did that."

She finished the sentence in some confusion. He understood her reason for embarrassment. And he realized only too well why she had taken employment in that New York office. It was necessity—not fun—which had been the compelling force. The Osborne and Judson failure again. He pulled the ledger toward him and took up his pen.

"Good night," he said, and bent over the book.

But she did not go. Instead she came around behind the desk and stood at his side.

"I am going to try and help," she declared.

He shook his head.

"No," he said.

"But I think perhaps I can; and I want to. Why not?"

"Because you—well, to be perfectly honest, you shouldn't stay here any longer. If any one should see you—"

"Nonsense!"

"I want you to go."

"I know, but I am not going—yet. And if you don't want me to be very angry indeed you won't say another word about people seeing me. Do you suppose I should be here if I were ashamed to be seen?"

Her tone was crisp and there was heightened color in her cheeks. He sighed, wearily.

"Emily," he persisted, "if you really want to help me you

won't give the people of this town any new opportunity to talk about me. You *must* understand what I mean."

"I understand exactly what you mean. And I should stay here now if I hadn't intended to before. You and I have known each other ever since we were children, and if we can't be seen together without— Oh! if Wellmouth is *that* kind of a place I am sorry I am going to live in it. . . . Now tell me about your trial balance. How much is it out of the way?"

Even then he tried to insist upon her going, but she ignored his insistence entirely, so he reluctantly informed her concerning the difference in the balance. It was a small amount.

"That sounds like an error in posting," she said. "Of course you have checked your ledger."

He shook his head. "I have checked the ledger and the cash book and the petty cash," he declared. "Also the bills and the bank account. I haven't counted the postage stamps yet, nor the fish in the barrels, but I'm not sure I shouldn't."

She laughed. "Before you do that," she said, "I would suggest checking again. I will call the items from the journal to begin with. No, you call them, and I will check them in the ledger."

So the—to him—wearisome process began once more. He read the items and she proved their transfer to the ledger. Fifteen minutes passed. Then she interrupted his reading.

"Wait a minute," she said. "What was that last amount? Four dollars and thirty cents, was it?"

"Yes."

"And it is bill payable, not receivable?"

"Yes."

"Then here is your mistake. You have posted it on the wrong side. Put it over here, where it belongs, and you make a difference of eight dollars and sixty cents, which is just the amount you are out of the way. And now you are all right. . . . Why, that was easy, Carey."

He tossed the journal upon the floor and, rising, looked

over her shoulder. He frowned, pulled at his forelock, sighed and then smiled.

"You'll notice, perhaps," he observed, "two pencil marks beside that four-thirty? Yes. Well, that is where I checked it twice before and made it right both times. By George, I *am* a good bookkeeper!"

"Oh, that is nothing. Every bookkeeper makes mistakes."

"Don't say that. You hurt my pride. I like to think I am unique. . . . Well, I am ever so much obliged."

"Don't mention it. Now I must go. Mother will think I have been kidnaped."

He was strongly tempted to ask her to wait until he put the books in the safe and then escort her home. But he remembered that there was a sociable that evening at the church presided over by the Reverend Bagness and that, at about this time, people would be leaving. For her to be seen walking along the Main Road with him would be putting a strain upon certain imaginations which, so far as anything connected with him was concerned, were already cracked in a good many places. For himself he did not greatly mind— he was past that—but she must not enter upon her Wellmouth residence and those music lessons under any unnecessary handicap. So he did not yield to his temptation, but merely accompanied her as far as the office door.

"Good night, Emily," he said. "And, of course, all the thanks in the world for saving the day—or the night—with that balance. I shall stay here and make a brand-new clean copy now. One that will shake Brother Early's trust in righteousness to the foundation."

"He expects you to have to call on him for help, I suppose."

"If he doesn't, then his looks the past day or two belie him."

"I am glad he is going to be disappointed. Now, Carey, when are you going to call upon mother and me?"

"Oh—oh, pretty soon. Yes, pretty soon."

"I don't believe you mean to come at all, really. Very

well, then I know how to make you. Mother has been saying she intends asking you to take supper with us. I shall tell her to do it at once. And I am going to come down to Cap'n Higgins' some Sunday and see your birds. Good night."

## CHAPTER VIII

CAREY'S premonition that Mr. Early cherished suspicions concerning the trial balance was confirmed next morning. The manager made it a point to enter the office precisely on the stroke of eight and, therefore, it not infrequently happened that the Judson brothers found him there on their arrival. This particular morning George was a little later than usual and, as they always walked down together, Carey was late also. When they came into the office the latter found the safe already open and the books spread upon the desk. Early was the only one, other than George and the bookkeeper, acquainted with the combination, so, although he was not in sight, it was evident that he had been there. He came in from the back room a moment later.

"Good morning, good morning, Mr. Judson," he said, with deferential cordiality. Then, still cordial, but without the deference, he added, "Morning, Carey. . . . A fine day, Mr. Judson. Very fine indeed. Yes."

George was not in a talkative mood that morning. In fact, or so it had seemed to his brother, he had not been in his usual spirits for several days. The change had followed a short business trip to Boston which he had made at the end of the previous week and from which he had returned—or so Carey imagined—rather downcast and taciturn. He had offered no explanation and when Carey asked if anything had gone wrong said, "No, indeed. Of course it hasn't. What do you ask that for?" It seemed almost as if he resented the question and his brother did not press it. As a matter of fact it was only in business hours—and then but occasionally—that the latter believed he noticed the depression and low spirits. At home George was even more cheerful than usual.

153

He replied to Early's greeting with a gruff "Good morning," and then, as though realizing the acknowledgment had been somewhat ungracious, paused on his way to the private office to observe: "Well, Ben, you beat Carey and me out this morning, didn't you? I see you've opened the safe. Some one been in to pay a bill? Or in a great hurry to collect one?"

Early smiled, as he always did when he suspected facetiousness on the part of his employer. "Oh, no—no," he replied. "No one has been in. I just opened the safe—to—er—to save Carey the trouble, that's all."

Carey, however, was already behind the desk and had noticed things.

"You found the balance all right, didn't you, Ben?" he inquired, casually. "I see you have been looking at it."

Mr. Early did his best to smile. He displayed a liberal expanse of teeth, but his attempt at ease was not a complete success.

"Eh?" he queried. "Oh, yes! Yes, Carey, I—er—saw the balance there and I—I—er—glanced it over—glanced it over. A very neat job, I call it. Carey's doing pretty well with his bookkeeping, Mr. Judson. He'll be up to our standard if he keeps on. Yes, indeed."

"What *is* your standard, Ben?" asked Carey, politely. The manager opened his mouth, closed it, and then decided not to hear the question. Instead of answering it he began to speak with George concerning a recent shipment of fish.

The following Sunday afternoon, as Carey was in the Higgins' shop, alone and hard at work on the second black duck, some one knocked at the shop door. He went to open it with a strong feeling of impatience. He was busy—happily busy—and he had no wish to be interrupted, even by Tobias Higgins or Phœbe.

The person who had knocked was neither of the Higginses, however, but a huge man with shaggy eyebrows and a thick gray beard. This man looked at him keenly, as if to make certain of his identity, then smiled and extended a hand.

"How do you do, Judson?" he said.

Carey recognized him. His own face lighted eagerly and he seized the hand and shook it.

"Why, Professor Knight!" he exclaimed. "Is it possible!"

His caller smiled. "Quite," he said, dryly. "Well? May I come in?"

Carey, who was still clasping his hand, almost dragged him across the threshold.

"I should say you could!" he declared. "You are about the last person I expected to see, but I am tremendously glad of the chance. Where on earth did you drop from?"

The professor was almost as tall as Judson himself, and infinitely broader. His face, under a broad-brimmed Panama hat, was sunburned and he stepped with the vigor and snap of a football player. He took off the hat, exposing a thatch of curly gray hair, and looked about the shop with interest.

"So this is where you hide yourself," he observed. "You are guarded well, did you know it?"

"Why? What do you mean? Sit down."

"I will in a minute. I want to look around first. What do I mean by guarded? I mean just that. Who is the peppery lady in the house in front here? She hadn't the slightest idea of letting me get at you. Who is she?"

Carey smiled. "That was Chippy," he said.

"Chippy?"

"That is her husband's pet name for her. She is Mrs. Higgins, wife of the old chap who lets me use this place. Did she hold you up?"

"She did. I was marching out here as bold as brass when she appeared at the door and wanted to know where I was going, who I was, why, and what excuse I had for interrupting you. She cross-questioned me like a lawyer and I had to explain that I was an old friend, that you had been to Labrador with me, and that I was responsible for your interest in birds and such things, before she would consent to my knocking at your door. Even then I think she wanted to come with me to make sure I wasn't lying."

He laughed heartily, the thick beard shaking like a bush in a wind. Carey laughed, too.

"I think," went on the professor, "that it was my reference to the Labrador cruise which finally turned the trick. She seemed to have heard of that."

"Yes, I told her and the captain about it. They are good friends of mine, the Higginses, and they know I don't, as a usual rule, like to have people running in here to bother me when I am at work—or play—whichever you care to call it. This is a small town, but there are an amazing number of people in it who love work—when it is done by some one else. . . . I am sorry she troubled you, though."

"Not a bit. She has the right idea. I'd like to hire her to sit outside my door at the museum. Well, let me look at you. You were a youngster when I saw you last. . . . Humph! You've grown older, my son."

"Yes, I have. But you haven't."

Nor had he, to any appreciable extent, so far as outward appearance went. The hair and beard, which Carey remembered as black, were gray, and he wore spectacles, but the eyes behind those spectacles were just as keen as ever and the motions of the broad shoulders and big hands were just as quick and purposeful as they had been during that memorable expedition in the Labrador wilds, the happiest summer in Carey Judson's life.

"You aren't a day older," declared Carey, and meant it.

Knight laughed. "Don't you believe it," he scoffed. "I ought to know a fossil when I see one and I am moving up into that class. But I mean to have a little more fun before I petrify. . . . Well, now tell me about yourself. I only arrived last night, but I have heard you spoken of."

"I am sure of it. Tell me first why you came, what you are doing here—yes, and what you have been doing since I heard from you. Your last letter was—oh, years ago."

"And it wasn't answered, as I remember. . . . Oh, well, never mind, probably it was and I was in Kamchatka or Timbuctoo, or somewhere. I plug away in civilization till I can't stand it any longer and then I trek. I'll tell you why I am here now. . . . By the way, you said something about sitting down, didn't you? What would you suggest my sitting on? Not that chair, I hope."

It was the only chair in the shop. Carey usually sat on an upturned packing case when at work. He twisted his forelock.

"That chair I keep for any visitors who get past the guard," he confessed. "It occasionally breaks down and sometimes they go home then. If you don't mind a box?"

"Not a bit, if it's a solid one. And if you have a spare pipe—?"

Carey produced the pipe, a charred corncob which his visitor regarded with approval, also tobacco and matches. Professor Knight seated himself on the box, blew a succession of smoke rings and then observed:

"I came here—well, I don't exactly know why I did come. I always liked this place and while—my sister—was living I have had some good times here. It wasn't spoiled then by a lot of city visitors. Hope it isn't yet."

"Not altogether."

"Humph! It will be some day. Judson, it is a good thing for fellows like you and me that we are living just at this period. There are still plenty of decent cannibal islands to run away to when civilization gets wearisome. A hundred years from now they'll be going through Patagonia in Pullmans. Well, I was in Boston, seeing some of the Harvard men about an expedition I am hoping to finance and go out at the head of—I'll tell you more about that by and by, probably—and I saw an idle Sunday ahead of me. It occurred to me that Wellmouth was only a little way off, so why not spend that Sunday looking the old place over? I came down on the afternoon train, put up at the Travelers' Hotel—God help me!—spent the morning loafing up and

down over the dunes and am figuring to spend a good deal
of the afternoon with you. That is my story—part of it."

The final sentence was divided in what seemed to Carey
a peculiar way.

"Part of it?"

"Why, yes; I was wondering whether I had better tell you
the other part. I think I will. I had another reason for
coming to Wellmouth. I came—not entirely, but partially—
to see you again."

Carey picked up a shaving from the floor and began tearing it into strips.

"I see," he said, slowly. "They—some one told you that
I had come back here."

"Yes. A fellow named Moore told me."

"Oh! Ed Moore? Yes, he knew, of course. How did
you happen to see him?"

"In regard to this proposed expedition of mine. He is
with a firm of financiers in Boston and expeditions cost
money, more's the pity. This young Moore's father used to
be interested in natural history—birds particularly—and he
helped me finance a previous trip. He is dead, but his son
seems to have inherited a little of the old man's taste, as well
as his millions. In the course of our conversation your name
was mentioned. Moore said he knew you. Then he told
me a lot about you and ended by speaking of some decoys
you had made for him. He has been away on a fishing trip
and has just returned to find the decoys waiting for him."

"I see. That explains why he hasn't written me about
them. I was beginning to be afraid they weren't satisfactory."

"You needn't be. He did not want to talk about anything
else. He insisted on my coming home with him that evening.
He pretended he wanted to give me a dinner, but the real
reason was that he wanted to show me those birds."

"He liked them, then? I am glad of that."

"Liked them! He bowed down and worshiped them.
According to him, Judson, you would have been an invalu-

able help to Noah aboard the Ark. If the old fellow had happened to omit a sample pair of any bird species from his assorted cargo you could have made a couple of wooden ones and no one would ever have known the difference. He served those decoys of yours with the soup and talked of nothing else all through the meal. He says that if you care to undertake the work he can keep you supplied with orders to the end of time."

Carey made no comment. The news that his friend had found the "beetle-heads" satisfactory was gratifying, but the realization that Moore must have told his guest many other items of his own recent history was not as pleasant.

The professor refilled the corncob from the tobacco tin on the bench and then went on.

"Of course I had to see the things," he continued, "and— well, son, I don't wish to swell your head unduly, but I was almost as enthusiastic as he was. The only fault I have to find is that a fellow who knows birds like that should be wasting a part of his time trying to keep books in an office. I understand that is what you are trying to do."

Carey stroked his nose. "I notice you say 'trying,'" he observed. "Every one who mentions those books to me never goes farther than to say I am trying to keep them."

"Hum! How on earth can a sane man think anything else? No one in the least acquainted with you could imagine your keeping them well. And that isn't all. I hear you tried to be a banker."

"No. . . . No, I didn't."

"What? You were a banker, weren't you?"

"No. I pretended to be one, because my people seemed to think I ought to be. But I didn't try. If I had I might have saved my friends a little of the trouble, perhaps."

"Nonsense! If you had tried night and day you couldn't have been a banker any more than I could. And who wants to be one, anyway?"

A slow shake of the head. "I don't, certainly," said Carey, gloomily.

"Of course you don't. What use are bankers, except to supply money occasionally to people who are doing something worth while? . . . Now show me some more of those birds of yours. You are making more. You couldn't stop if you tried."

Carey, with some diffidence, handed his friend the finished black duck. Knight examined it with care. His inspection was thorough and took some time. Then he nodded his big head.

"Good," he declared.

"You think it is all right, then? I wasn't quite sure about the neck. The one I am at work on now will be a little different. I don't intend to make them alike, you know—their positions, I mean. No bird is exactly like another. . . . But it isn't necessary to tell you that."

"No, it isn't. But why not make them alike? It would be easier, I should say. And as decoys they would be almost as satisfactory."

"Why, yes, perhaps they would. But I shouldn't get as much fun out of making them."

"I see. What does Moore pay you for them? If you don't mind telling me."

"Not in the least. He offered me ten dollars a piece for the other lot, the shore birds. I don't know what he will pay for the ducks, but I guess he will pay that."

"Hum! Yes, I should imagine he might, if you pressed him. How long will it take you to make the dozen?"

"Oh, I don't know. That one—the first one—took nearly two weeks of my spare time. The next won't take quite as long, I hope."

"Hum! And you get ten dollars for each one! Judson, it is easy to see why you didn't make good as a banker. What *are* you wasting your time down here for?"

Carey did not quite catch his meaning.

"Why, I thought you understood," he said. "I came here because George—my brother—was anxious to have me.

And, after all, I had to go somewhere and do something. You see—"

He went on to explain how George had urged him to take the bookkeeper's position in the office, his own reluctance and final yielding.

"George—you used to know him, Professor," he said, in conclusion, "has been tremendously kind to me. He has stood by me as no one else ever could—or would. Besides, he is a first-class business man; that isn't my judgment, of course, for I haven't any business judgment, but those who know about such things say so. I took it for granted he knew best what I ought to do. He said come, so I came. He was willing to hire me, and I can't think of any one else who would do as much."

His visitor nodded again. "Yes," he said. "Well, I had heard practically all that before. This bird making, however, was your own idea, not his. What does he think of it?"

"Oh, he likes to have me do it. It keeps me amused, he says. And it does. Honestly, I don't know how I could have stood the—well, the living here and meeting all the people I know and—and so on, if I hadn't had my playthings to turn to. That is what they call them," he added, with an apologetic smile, "my playthings."

Knight rose to his feet and looked at his watch.

"I must be going," he said.

Carey was greatly disappointed. "I thought you were going to spend the afternoon with me," he declared. "I hoped you would tell me about this new expedition of yours."

"I want to tell you about it. That's why I am leaving now. If I go now I can make the call or two I want to make and have my evening free. I must take the early train for Boston to-morrow. Can you come to my rooms at the hotel after supper to-night, for another talk?"

There was no hesitancy in the reply.

"I'll come," said Carey, emphatically.

"Good! I'll be waiting for you about eight o'clock."

He tossed the corncob pipe on the bench, scattering ashes in a way that would have shocked Phœbe Higgins' orderly soul, and strode out of the shop without even a good-by. Carey, peering after him through the window, heaved a sigh. With him went romance and adventure, the atmosphere of out of doors and the great, free joy of life and labor at their completest. More than once, in the old days, Carey had heard Wellmouth people characterize John Knight as a "crank," and, since knowledge of his own bird making became widespread, he knew the same name was often applied to him. It appeared that there were lucky and unlucky cranks. And the former variety deserved their good fortune, of course. Only a short time before, his sister-in-law had observed, in a supper table conversation, that people usually got about what they deserved in this world.

He turned back to his workbench and the black duck. It was harder to concentrate upon the poise of the wing than it had been. Memories of that glorious summer in Labrador kept occurring to him. They were useless, even tormenting memories, but in a way they were pleasant. At last he laid the duck down and, his knees crossed and his empty pipe between his teeth, sprawled upon his packing case seat, his back against the bench, and allowed his mind to drift unhampered toward the Arctic Circle.

There came another knock at the door, but he did not hear it. Then, after a moment, that door opened a little way, and some one said:

"Carey, are you there? May I come in?"

He sprang up and the packing case fell backward to the floor with a clatter.

"Eh?" he cried. "Why—oh, yes! Yes, of course. Come in."

Emily Sayles accepted the invitation.

"Good afternoon," she said.

He was regarding her oddly. They had not met since the evening of her visit to the office and, having been favored with no sly hints or sarcasms concerning that evening's hap-

penings he was convinced—and thankfully so—that no one
had seen her there. Now, however, his expression as he
stood before her was not so much astonishment at her presence as of concern. And his first remark was, to her, in-
explicable.

"I was expecting you," he said.

If he were not surprised to see her she certainly was by
his statement.

"You were expecting *me?*" she repeated. "Why?"

"Eh? Oh, I don't know. I was, that's all."

"I don't know why you should have been. I didn't tell
any one I was coming here. I wasn't quite sure I should
come, myself."

"No? . . . Well, it doesn't make any difference."

"But it does. I don't understand why you should have
expected me. Do you have what people call premonitions?"

"No-o. Not as a usual thing. But I must have had one
now. Perhaps it was because I was thinking of you and—"

He paused and might have changed the subject, but her
curiosity was aroused.

"Why in the world should you be thinking of me?" she
asked. "Wasn't that trial balance right, after all?"

"Yes. Yes, that was right. And why I should have been
thinking of you I—I don't know, exactly. . . . But I was—
yes, I was thinking of you just at the moment when you
came. I don't wonder you were surprised at that. I am
myself."

The confession was so frankly ingenuous that she could
not help smiling. It was true, however. He had been thinking of her. For a half hour his thoughts had been busy with
the Labrador trip, and Knight, and then, somehow or other,
they had returned to Wellmouth and to her. And, with this
realization, came the discovery that he had thought a great
deal about her of late. It was, as he had said, odd—very
odd. Of course she had helped him with the trial balance
and his interview with her at Aunt Susan's reception had
made that evening bearable, but—yes, he had thought of her

a *great* deal. . . . Humph! He groped for a reasonable explanation.

"I think it must have been that I was afraid you would come," he said, gravely.

She looked at him in amazement and then burst into a laugh.

"Well, I must say I like that!" she exclaimed. "Carey Judson, you are the most— But there, you can't make me angry. I know you too well. Of course I came. I told you I was coming here soon to see your birds and the place where you make them. I meant to come before."

He shook his head. "You know you shouldn't," he said. "I told you not to. Mrs. Higgins saw you. She is a good woman, but—she belongs to the sewing circle."

She interrupted. "Carey," she said, quickly, "are you going to say the same silly things you said the other evening at the office? Unless you promise me not to speak another word of that kind I shall go this minute and never come back. If you really want to get rid of me you understand now how to do it."

His fingers, as always when he was perplexed or troubled, strayed to his hair.

"I—I didn't mean to offend you, Emily," he protested.

"Well, you have. Shall I go?"

He twisted the lock of hair into a tight knot. There was a momentary pause. Then he said, "No."

"And it is thoroughly understood that what people may say is not to be mentioned by you to me again?"

"Yes."

"Very well. . . . What? Did you speak?"

"Eh? No. At least I didn't mean to. I was thinking about my aunt—Mrs. Dain. She must be a remarkable judge of character. . . . Sit down. . . . No, not in that chair. That is for company."

"Well, I am 'company.' "

"Not that kind of company. . . . Please don't sit in the

chair; it has acquired a habit of breaking down. May I offer you a—er—box seat?"

She did not understand about the chair, but she accepted the seat on the packing box, just as Professor Knight had done. He turned toward the bench.

"Now I suppose you want to see some of my playthings," he observed.

"Playthings! Oh, the birds? Yes, of course I do. I am crazy to see them. But wait a minute. What did you mean by saying Mrs. Dain was such a wonderful judge of character? Were you and she discussing my character?"

"Eh? Oh, no! No, indeed! She was discussing mine. She said I hadn't any strength of mind."

"Why, the idea!" indignantly. "I thought she was fond of you."

"She is. . . . That is, I hope she is. But she was quite right. She meant I was like the young fellow·in *Simon Martin, or His First Glass,* that old-fashioned total abstinence book we used to have on the shelf at home. It isn't there now; Cora has pitched it out long ago. Simon, as I remember, died eventually in the gutter, or a canal—or a ditch—somewhere where there was water. Lord knows why, for nobody hated water worse than he did. But his principal trouble seemed to be that he couldn't say no. I can't say it either—except in places where I should say yes."

She reflected. "I see," she said, after an instant. "You mean you should have said no when I insisted upon staying here. Well, it isn't too late yet for you to say it—if you wish to."

He smiled. "I never did wish to," he answered. "And I have already said yes. So that is settled. . . . Here is the sort of creature I am turning out in this factory. It is meant to look like a duck. Sometimes I think it does."

Her exclamations at the sight of the black duck were so sincere in their wonder and admiration that contrition at his weak-mindedness was, for the moment at least, forced from his thoughts. And for a long time it did not return. Urged by her eager questions and evident real interest he exhibited his finished duck, the one he was at work upon, the model from which he had made his beetle-heads, the stuffed birds from which that model was made, his paints, his carving tools, and, at last, the new foot power lathe which had just arrived from the manufacturers and had the previous evening been taken from the crate.

"I shouldn't have bought that," he confessed, guiltily. "I haven't the money to pay for it and shan't have, until I get the check from Ed Moore, the fellow who ordered the beetle-heads. Cap'n Tobias urged me to get it—and goodness knows it will be a help and a time-saver—but I didn't mean to buy anything yet awhile. Tobias kept after me and insisted that, if there was any long delay, he would be responsible for the money and so—well, it was another case of 'Simon Martin'—I yielded. . . . But I shouldn't—I shouldn't. I had another use for that money."

It was on the tip of her tongue to ask to what use he referred, but the expression upon his face caused her to refrain. Instead she began to speak of the Higginses, what dear, kind, whole-souled people they were. It was the right note, for, in praise of his friends, he forgot himself. He quoted Tobias' jokes, told of the latter's pet name for his wife—Emily had not heard it and it amused her immensely—and of the "cruises" he and the captain had taken in the *Ambergris, Junior*.

"He is a remarkably well-informed man," he declared enthusiastically, referring to Higgins. "He is, really. And he—he understands, too. Now when he saw me at work on that shore bird, that very first Sunday, he was as interested as if he cared for birds as—as I do. Of course he doesn't," relapsing into his customary tone of apology when speaking of his own hobby. "Nobody else cares for them like that, no practical, businesslike person; but he seems to care a good deal and—and, honestly, he, as I say, seems to understand. I suppose you don't just get what I mean by that. There is no reason why you should."

She nodded, her eyes shining.

"I think I do," she said. "Because—well, because I am sure that I understand—a little."

"Eh? Do you? Yes, I guess you do. If you didn't you wouldn't let me bore you like this."

"But you haven't bored me. I am more interested than I have been for—well, certainly since I came back to Wellmouth."

"Truly? . . . That's odd. Most people who come here think I am a little crazy. No wonder they do. If I were like them I should think so, too."

"Be thankful you are not like them—most of them. What do they or their opinions amount to?"

"Oh, a good deal. You mustn't get the idea that I have a poor opinion of the people here in this town. They are my people; they were father's people. They are all right and—well, I am the one who is wrong. But I can't help it. . . . And," with another deprecating lift of the lip, "it is pleasant to find some one like you and Professor Knight who are—who must be—a little wrong, too."

"Professor Knight? Who is he?"

He had been sitting on the bench, swinging his long legs and bending forward to speak. Now he straightened in surprise.

"What!" he exclaimed. "Why, by George, that's queer! Is it possible I haven't said a word to you about Knight? Not a word since you have been here?"

"Not one word."

"Well. . . . Well, by George! . . . Why, he was here just before you came. Walked in at that very door and I never was more surprised to see any one—or more glad. And I haven't mentioned his name! I was thinking of him when you came."

"Were you? I thought you said you were thinking of me."

"Why, yes. Why, yes, I was. I was thinking of him and about that gorgeous summer he and I and those other chaps had in Labrador, and—and then, somehow or other, I drifted from that to you. I was thinking of you when I heard you call me. . . . Hum! . . . I don't see why. There is no reasonable connection between that Labrador expedition and you; now is there?"

His question was so seriously asked that she laughed.

"I can't see any," she replied; "but perhaps I may when you tell me more about this Mr. Knight."

"Not Mister—Professor. He is—oh, he is a wonderful fellow. Why, he—"

He began to sound the praises of the great man, of his discoveries in ornithology, of the honors paid him in this country and abroad, of the expedition to Labrador and his own part in it; then, at last, of the professor's call upon him that afternoon and of the hint of the new expedition.

"Where is it to be this time?" she asked, breaking in on his flow of excited enthusiasm.

"I don't know. He hasn't told me yet. He will to-night, though. I am sure. I am going to see him again to-night, at his room up at the hotel. I am sure he will tell me all about it then."

She leaned forward. "Carey," she said, eagerly, "you don't suppose—you don't suppose it is possible he is going to ask you to go with him on that expedition?"

He stared at her. "Ask me?" he repeated. *"Me?* Why —why no, why should he?"

"Why shouldn't he? You went with him before. And he likes you, or he wouldn't have come here to see you. He might be going to ask that very thing. I am almost sure he is. . . . Oh, wouldn't that be wonderful for you!"

She was quite as excited now as he was. More so, for, after the first flush of the amazing and rapturous idea, the myriad objections to it were forming in his mind. Slowly he shook his head.

"He wouldn't ask me," he said. "There are hundreds of better men than I am who would be crazy to go. And they could go. . . . I couldn't, even if I had the chance."

"Why not? Of course you could. You would. You wouldn't *think* of doing anything else."

"I couldn't think anything *but* something else. How could I go? Expeditions like those he goes on are expensive. Very often the chaps who go out furnish a part of the money. Where would I come in there?"

"But I thought the museums and—and societies, whatever they are, furnished the money."

"Sometimes they do. Sometimes the trip is financed by private individuals, persons interested in science, you know. And I judge from the little Big Jack said—that's what we used to call him, 'Big Jack'—that this particular trip he is planning will have to be financed that way. And, in that case, it is almost sure that every one going on it will have to pay his own way. No, I guess—but we needn't worry. Of course he has no idea of asking me."

"I am almost sure that is just what he means to do. Oh, Carey, don't you *see?* He came to Wellmouth on purpose to meet you again. He was so interested in the birds you were making. He— And you are going to see him this evening. I shall be dying to learn what he does say to you. Will you promise to tell me all about it?"

"Why, yes, certainly; if you really care to know."

"I do. Good! . . . Carey, were you planning to work here to-morrow evening?"

"Yes. . . . But," anxiously, "you mustn't come down here, Emily. I—I know I promised not to say any more about your being seen with me, but—well, it just won't do, that's all. I like to have you—you must know that—but—"

"Hush! hush! I have no idea of coming here to-morrow evening."

"Haven't you? . . . Oh! . . . Well, that's right."

"If I wanted to come I should, of course, but I don't—to-morrow evening. You are coming to take supper with mother and me to-morrow evening, Carey."

"What? . . . Oh, no, I can't."

"Why not? Mother has been charging me for more than a week to see you and fix a time for your having supper with us. Now that time is fixed. You are to come tomorrow at six o'clock."

"But I can't, Emily. Don't you see?"

"No. I don't see. You can spare an evening from your ducks as well as not."

"It isn't that."

"It mustn't be anything else. Carey, you deserve a good talking to and I am going to give you one. You are behaving ridiculously. You are going about town here, hiding from every one, those who would like to be your friends as well as those who aren't. If you had committed some mean crime you couldn't act more guilty or shamefaced."

He shrugged his shoulders.

"I have done just that," he said.

"You have done nothing of the sort. You were unfortunate in business. Lots of others have had that happen to them, even here in Wellmouth. You think every one is whispering about you and saying how wicked you are. They aren't. The worst they have ever said is that you were careless and let your partner deceive you. And they are not saying even that now; you are an old story and they have other things to talk about. They have practically forgotten you and, if they hadn't, the surest way to convince them that you are wicked is to slink and hide and run away. I said there were people here who would like to be your friends, and would be if you gave them the chance. Why not give it to them? . . . Oh, do say something! Don't sit there as if you were deaf and dumb. And don't smile, either. What satisfaction do you suppose I get out of lecturing a person who just sits still and smiles that irritating smile?"

The smile broadened a little. "You are preaching the same gospel they all do," he observed.

"All? Who are 'all'?"

"Oh, Aunt Susan and George—and Cap'n Tobias. Yes, even Ben Early, although he doesn't say it as bluntly.

Benjamin usually sends his advice by the around the corner route."

"You notice I am not sending mine that way. And, no matter how or from whom it comes, it is good advice. Carey, *won't* you take it?"

He clasped his knee in his hands and rocked back and forth on the bench. She waited, fighting her impatience, until he spoke. And when, at last, he did, his reply was, to her surprise, merely a monosyllable.

"Yes," he said.

She gasped.

"You *will* take it?" she cried. "You mean—"

"I mean that hereafter I shall slink and hide no more."

"Oh, please don't be offended. I shouldn't have used those words."

"They were the right words. Slinking and hiding were pretty nearly what I have been doing. Now I am through. I have been paying attention to my own counsels. I don't know why; I never counseled myself well, as I remember. My only excuse might be that, pretty often, when I have followed the advice of other people the results have been as bad—or worse. Never mind; I am willing to try once more. From now on I shall slap Cap'n Elkanah Snow on the back and call Mrs. Loveland by her Christian name. I forget what that name is, for the moment, but no doubt she will tell me, if I ask."

This was not altogether satisfactory. Miss Sayles shook her head.

"Oh, dear!" she sighed. "I am afraid you are impossible."

"I am. And now I am going to be impossible in another way. What time shall you expect me to-morrow evening; six, was it?"

"Yes; but, Carey, I don't want you to come if you come unwillingly."

He ceased to smile. Leaning forward on the bench he spoke slowly and with earnestness.

"I shall come willingly enough," he told her. "I have

wanted to come very much. A half dozen times I have been tempted to accept your invitation to call, but I haven't because—well, because, although I can stand the gossip, I didn't want any one I cared for—any of my real friends dragged into it. It may have been oversensitiveness—I guess it was—but it is a part of my make-up. I made a fool of myself in that crazy business venture of mine. I ruined hundreds of innocent bystanders, and I was—and am—ashamed of myself. Nevertheless, I dare say I have advertised that shame more than was necessary down here and those who are still friendly may have suffered in consequence. I am going to turn over a new leaf and see what is on the other page. . . . Oh, the decision isn't quite as sudden as it sounds. I have been thinking a lot of late. George and Aunt Susan and Tobias—and you—well, you *are* friends, and I guess the very least I can do is try and please you. I shall be wiping my shoes on your doormat at six to-morrow."

The smile was again in evidence, but still his visitor was not entirely satisfied.

"Oh, dear!" she exclaimed. "I—I don't know what to make of you, Carey Judson."

"Nobody ever did. Father tried to make a banker out of me and see what happened. It is all right, though, Emily. I'm pretty sure you and the rest are right. I have been slinking and hiding altogether too much. Now I shall be openly brazen and display myself in the public places."

"Yes," sarcastically, "I can imagine how brazen you will be. Well, at least you will come to supper. . . . Why," after a glance at her watch, "I must go this minute. I had no idea it was so late."

She rose. He slid from the bench.

"Late!" he protested. "It can't be late."

"It is after five and I have been here over two hours. . . . Why, what—— You're not going with me, are you?"

He had taken his hat from the nail by the door.

"Do you mind if I do?" he asked.

"I? Of course *I* don't mind; but—well," with a little

laugh, "considering what you have said about being seen with me, this is—rather sudden."

"My objection was entirely confined to your being seen with me. You say that is ridiculous. Shall we go?"

They walked through the yard together. A window shade in the Higgins' home moved ever so slightly. They both noticed it. He stroked his chin.

"Poor Phœbe!" he sighed. "This has been a hard afternoon for her. And sewing circle meets to-morrow. . . . Shall we go across the fields or around by the Main Road? The road would be my suggestion. Tobias has a maxim that is not all bad, 'When you've made up your mind to tackle pork,' he says, 'you might as well go the whole hog.' I vote for the Main Road."

Emily told her mother the whole story when she reached home.

"I can't make him out at all," she declared. "He is the *queerest* fellow."

Mrs. Sayles nodded. "Cap'n Jim-Carey was queer, too," she said. "Only a few could make him out. Those who did found it worth while."

# CHAPTER IX

WHEN dinner, next day, was over Carey started as usual for the office. His brother was not with him, having again taken the early train on a business trip to Boston. George's frame of mind during the week just past had been the same curious combination of good spirits and bad which Carey fancied he had noticed of late and which he was inclined to believe dated from his —George's—former short sojourn in the city. At home, except for occasional lapses into absent-mindedness and silence, George was his jolly, joking self, especially when his wife was present, but at the office he was—or so it seemed to Carey—thoughtful, brusque and even gloomy. Instead of loitering in the outer room beside the bookkeeper's desk, chatting, smoking and exchanging badinage with callers, or with Early and his brother, he remained for the most part in his own little room at the back, and Carey, going in there to ask concerning matters of business routine, often found him sitting by the window, an unlighted cigar between his teeth, apparently lost in reveries which, judging by his expression, could not be pleasant. On the way home to dinner, or after closing time, he often suggested walking around by way of the post office and at that office he usually posted a bulky letter. He came to work earlier in the morning, apparently that he might be the first to look over the mail. In fact, he made it a point to see all mail the moment Jabez Drew brought it and Carey more than once saw him extract from the packet envelopes which he pocketed without comment and did not mention afterwards. That he was troubled his brother was now sure, but what that trouble might be Carey had no idea, nor, of course, did he ask.

This Monday morning, after Maggie had served his solitary

breakfast—Cora was suffering from one of the headaches which were likely to follow her husband's departure on a city excursion to which she was not invited—and remained in her room—Carey left the house by the side door, as usual; but, instead of walking directly down to the gate, he turned to the right and hurried around to the back door, that opened from the washroom. Hepsibah was in the washroom, preparing for her Monday forenoon's labor at the tubs. He whistled to attract her attention and then beckoned her to the door. She came, wiping her arms on her apron.

"Well, what is it?" she asked, impatiently. "Don't keep me any longer than you have to. This is wash day and I've got troubles of my own. Yes, and a whole lot that ought to be somebody's else's. I don't know whether you know it or not, but I am supposed to do that Maggie thing's washing nowadays, she bein' too ladified or lazy—I have my own notion which—to do it herself."

This was news to Carey, who smiled at her classification of the second maid. Hepsibah misinterpreted the smile and resented it.

"There's nothing to laugh at," she snapped. "If you could see the amount of ruffled doodads that woman wears you'd think she was the Queen of Sheby instead of hired help. And the way she winds *her*"—meaning Mrs. Judson, of course—"around her finger is enough to turn a decent person's stomach. If she has to do this she'll leave. If she don't have so and so done *for* her she'll leave. But she *don't* leave—no such luck! Well, my patience is wearin' pretty thin and the first thing they know there'll be some real leavin' and it won't be just talk neither. If it wasn't that I've cooked and washed for a Judson ever since I was big enough to earn my livin' and am gettin' too old and sot to like makin' changes I'd walk out of this house and let 'em to starch their own ruffles. . . . Well, what is it you want? Don't bother me any longer than you can help."

"I just wanted to tell you that I shouldn't be here at supper to-night, Hepsy. I thought you might like to know it."

"Humph! Sartin I like to know it. With you and George away there won't be any men folks to cook for, which is a mercy that don't often come my way on a wash day. She and that Maggie will be here, of course, but they can take what I give 'em and be thankful for so much. . . . Where are you goin'? Are those bird playthings of yours so dreadful important you can't leave 'em long enough to eat?"

He shook his head.

"No, not as important as that," he replied. "I—well, I shall probably get supper somewhere else to-night."

"Probably? . . . Humph! I see. I noticed you had your Sunday suit on, but I thought maybe that was because you was too absent-minded to remember that Sunday didn't last all through the week. So you'll probably have supper somewhere else, eh? Well, I hope Desire Sayles is as good a cook as she used to be. If she is you might go further and fare worse."

He stared at her.

"For heaven's sake, Hepsy!" he exclaimed. "How did you know I was going there?"

Hepsibah's mouth was as unsmiling as ever but there was an amused glint in her eye.

"I didn't know," she observed, "but I'm like the boy that stole the green apples—I could guess from the symptoms. Looks as if I guessed right. There, there! It didn't take such a lot of smartness. I heard about you and Emily being out walkin' together yesterday afternoon. No, no; I didn't see you, I had other fish to fry. It happened to be one of that Maggie's afternoons out and she saw you and told me about it. I presume likely she told *her* about it, too," with a jerk of the head in the general direction of the room upstairs. "Half of Wellmouth knows it by this time. If you expected to keep it a secret you and Emily better pick out some other time than Sunday afternoon to do your walkin' in. That's when most folks haven't anything to do except look out of the window."

Carey had no comment to make. Her statement was but

confirmation of his own conviction. He knew that his walk with Miss Sayles along the Main Road had been witnessed by many eager eyes and that it was certain to be the subject of much interested and speculative conversation. More than once since expressing his vow to turn over a new leaf and pay no attention whatever to the gossip of his fellow citizens he had repented of that vow. Having turned that leaf, however, he did not propose to turn it back again—at least not yet.

"There was nothing secret about it, Hepsy," he said, calmly. "Emily had told me she was coming down to the shop to see my birds. Yesterday she came and I walked home with her. Why shouldn't I? I have known the Sayles family all my life."

"No reason in the world why you shouldn't. I'm glad to see you're gettin' spunky enough to do what you please. It's the only way to get along in this town. If you set down to fret about what folks will say you'd never get up, for they're sayin' somethin' most of the time. Do as you want to and let 'em talk. That's my advice and what I told you to do in the beginnin'."

"But how did you know I was going to the Sayles' home for supper?"

"I said I didn't know. I guessed that was it because Desire told me she was goin' to ask you there some of these days. She and I have had lots of talk and we've talked about you along with the rest of this end of creation. Desire Sayles is a fine woman and she and I went to school together when we were girls. *She* hasn't forgot it; there's nothin' stuck up and Lovelandy about *her*. . . . There! I've got to get back to my ruffles. Have a good time, Carey. I shan't tell that Maggie or her where you've gone. Let 'em wonder, if they want to."

Promptly at six that evening Carey knocked at the Sayles' door. Emily herself admitted him. The little hall looked much as he remembered it. He had crossed that threshold many times in his boyhood days. When Lawyer Simeon

Sayles was alive his family and Cap'n Jim-Carey's had been very friendly indeed and Carey and George had eaten many a meal in the big dining room. Emily was a little girl then and the gap of years between her age and that of the older Judson boy was huge. Later, when he came home from college on his vacations, he found the gap greatly diminished, although of course it still existed. Emily was then just beginning her term at the boarding school in Connecticut and Carey remembered well his astonishment at the change that first season away from home had made in her. He found her worshipful adoration of a lordly college sophomore flattering and gratifying. Her interest in his recent Labrador trip was pleasing also and it was during that summer and the one following that he had permitted her to help with his bird mounting and the preparation of his specimens. For girls in general he had no great fancy, nor did they care greatly for the shy, reticent fellow who danced only under compulsion and avoided straw rides and beach picnics whenever possible. They considered him a nice enough boy, but bashful and almost dull. George was the ladies' man always and Carey, even then, was the "queer one" of the family. He tolerated and even liked Emily Sayles because she liked, or pretended to like, things in which he was interested. She was the one girl in Wellmouth he had remembered with sincere pleasure and, after her father's death, when she and her mother moved to New York, he missed seeing her when at home. Also, for some reason which he could not explain, nor attempted to, she had been the one whom he most dreaded meeting after his disgraceful adventure in the banking business.

She welcomed him cordially and made no reference to the fact that he had kept his promise and come to supper. He had doubted the wisdom of that promise many times since making it; and when opening the Sayles gate had fancied that he felt a tingling sensation between his shoulders as if eyes up and down the street were fixed upon that spot. When he took her hand, however, the sensation vanished and with it, for the time, his misgivings. After all, as he had told her at the shop, there were apparently people who wished to be his friends. He had hidden nothing from them. They knew his story, all of it, knew the position he held in Wellmouth— that he was a failure, a man without a future and an object of his brother's charity. They knew all that and yet, apparently, they still were anxious to offer him their friendship, society and even hospitality. Why shouldn't he accept the offer? Except his brother and the Higginses and—yes, Hepsibah, of course—and Emily Sayles and her mother—he had not a real friend left in Wellmouth. He had returned there, knowing that he had forfeited all past friendships and sure that he deserved no new ones. Now he realized that much of this feeling was pretense—make-believe. Honest friendship was what he desired and needed more than anything else. And here, in this house, it was, apparently, waiting for him.

"You are exactly on time," said Emily. "I was sure you would be."

"Why?" he asked.

"Because punctuality was always a strong point with you. Perhaps you have forgotten, but I haven't. On the rare occasions when you deigned to permit me to come to your house and help you—or watch you—stuff those birds of yours you didn't like it at all if I was a minute late. I told mother you would appear precisely at six, and here you are."

"You have a good memory," he said. "Those bird-stuffing days were at least a thousand years ago."

"Not quite, I hope. Mother is in the sitting room and she is very anxious to see you. Go right in. I'm sure you know the way."

He did know the way, but he scarcely knew that sitting room when he entered it. The old furniture was there, most of it, but the hideous old wall paper was covered with a new and cheerful pattern, the marble mantel had lost its lambrequins, the windows were hung with bright curtains instead of the stiff and ugly laces he remembered so well. The changes were all inexpensive, but they were marked. In the old days that room was formality itself, a de luxe edition of fifty Wellmouth sitting rooms. Now, under the transforming touch of the hand of another generation, it was a place where one might not only sit, but sit in comfort. One change he particularly noticed was that the bulky square piano had been replaced by a modern upright.

The big armchair which had been the favorite lounge of Mr. Simeon Sayles was in the place where it used to be, by the center table. It had, however, been reupholstered and Mrs. Desire Sayles was occupying it. She smiled a greeting and extended a hand.

"You'll excuse my not getting up, won't you, Carey," she said. "I can't do as I want to nowadays. Emily has me in charge and she has made me promise to stay in the chair until supper is ready. It is a dreadful thing to have to obey orders from one's own child. I hope you may never reach that stage."

Emily, at the door, shook her head reprovingly. "She has been trotting about the kitchen for three whole hours," she said. "She hasn't the slightest idea of obeying my orders, Carey, and it was only when I threatened to call the doctor that she consented to sit down for a few minutes. She is afraid of the doctor, I am happy to say. He is my sole reinforcement."

Mrs. Sayles smiled. "I am not afraid of my doctor," she declared; "but I don't care for callers who charge for their society. Sit down here beside me, Carey, and talk to me. Emily, if you don't look after those biscuits they will be charcoal and although that is said to aid digestion I don't want mine helped in that way."

"Yes, do sit down and make her behave," begged her daughter. "I must leave you for a few minutes. Supper is almost ready. I shan't be long."

She hastened to the rescue of the biscuits and Carey, drawing a chair beside that of Mrs. Sayles, listened while the latter chatted of local happenings, of the changes which the carpenters and painters and paper hangers had made in the old home and how Emily was responsible for all these changes and had made many others with her own hands.

"She is a remarkably capable girl," declared Desire. "Considering whose daughter she is, very capable indeed. And she manages her mother in a way that makes me feel about ten years old. I remember that your father, Carey, used to say I was too strict with her. He was an indulgent parent, as probably you know better than I."

Carey nodded. "He was indeed," he agreed, soberly.

"Yes, he was, too indulgent in many ways, I'm afraid, and too insistent upon his own way in others. Well, if he sees that daughter of mine ordering me about now, he must feel, I should imagine, that the sins of the parents are visited upon—well, upon those parents themselves, sometimes."

Carey was silent. It occurred to him to wonder how that father of his must feel if aware of the consequences which had followed his stubbornness in the choice of profession for his favorite son.

Mrs. Sayles noticed his silence and turned quickly to look at him. Then she changed the subject and began to speak of Emily's venture with the piano lessons.

"She has—let me see—nine pupils now," she said. "Some of them she seems to think promising, and others—well, not altogether that. That little Elsie Cahoon is her hardest problem. That child is her father all over again. There is one advantage in having lived in a community as long as I lived in this one, it supplies you with reasons for things. I knew Obed Cahoon when he was a boy and of all the pestiferous little imps of Satan that ever lived he was probably the worst. He was a saintly little blue-eyed creature to look at—so is his daughter, for that matter—and the way in which he could lie to the teacher after having run away from school to go swimming was nothing less than a gift. Every one prophesied that he would surely be hanged some day, if he wasn't drowned before he reached the hanging age. Well, he has escaped so far, although some of the prophets haven't given up hope. As for that Elsie— Oh, here is Emily, so I judge that supper must be ready."

It was and they adjourned to the dining room. Carey's bruised conscience received another prod as he noticed how slowly Mrs. Sayles moved, leaning upon his arm, and how feeble was the step which he remembered as so brisk and quick. Those sins of the fathers—surely it should be sufficient to visit them upon the sons, without extending the visitation to innocent sufferers like these.

Desire herself made no reference to her enfeebled condition and chattered gayly all the way to her chair at the table. Emily sat at the foot and Carey was assigned the head. The meal was a simple country supper of the old-fashioned kind, and the conversation accompanying it of a sort calculated to lure the visitor's attention from himself and his own worries to impersonal and therefore more pleasant matters. They spoke further of the alterations in the house, those so far made and the others planned. Emily told of her experiences as a music teacher and was optimistic concerning the future of her experiment.

"I am enjoying it ever so much," she declared. "Just how rapidly my pupils may be learning I'm not sure, but *I* am learning a great deal—how to keep my patience, for one thing. Elsie Cahoon alone is a liberal education along that line."

Mrs. Sayles related more stories of Elsie's father. Some of them Carey remembered having heard before; they were a part of Wellmouth history. He enjoyed hearing them again, smiled, and even laughed aloud at times, and, before the supper was over actually told a story or two of his own. For almost the first time—the hours spent at his beloved bird making excepted—he forgot himself and spoke freely and without self-consciousness. And not once—he was not conscious of this until afterward—was he asked a question about the office of J. C. Judson & Co.

When they rose from the table Desire announced that

there was to be no dishwashing, or even clearing away that evening.

"Leave everything just as it is," she ordered. "I shall have to go to my room pretty soon; the doctor and Emily have entered into a conspiracy to make me keep childish hours and when I rebel I am not permitted to get up until noon next day, so it is easier to do as I am told in the first place. I am put to bed every night at eight, so I don't propose to waste the three quarters of an hour I have left. We will all go into the other room and talk until the clock strikes. Carey, I don't suppose you realize it, but you are the only guest—only table guest, I mean—that Emily and I have had the honor of entertaining since we came back here to live. I, for one, am going to make the most of you."

Carey was surprised to hear this. The home of Lawyer Simeon Sayles was, during his boyhood and college days, a center of social activity. The hospitality there was proverbial. Whenever a famous lecturer or a state senator—or, on rare occasions, a governor—came to Wellmouth, it was usually the Sayleses who entertained him.

Emily, perhaps, guessed his surprise, for she said: "That is true, mother, but we mustn't let Carey imagine we have been entirely neglected. Ever and ever so many people have called and have been nice to us. Nellie Loveland dropped in the very day of our arrival."

Her mother nodded. "She did," she agreed. "And sat in the midst of trunks and boxes and told us all about her art studies and the wonderful people she had met in Boston and retailed every item of gossip that had accumulated in town here for three whole years. And, therefore, we couldn't unpack as much as our nightgowns until it was time to put them on. Oh, yes! We have had callers."

"We haven't invited people here," Emily went on to explain, "because we weren't ready for them yet. And we haven't accepted invitations because the doctor thinks mother should rest and not go out at night. We did go to your aunt's reception, Carey, because—"

"Because Susan Dain used to be one of my best friends," put in Desire, "and I wanted to see her again. I had a good time, too, even if I did have to stay in bed all the next day to pay for it. But the fact remains, Carey, that you are the first person who has taken a meal with us since we came."

Carey said that he appreciated the honor, but that he did not exactly see why he was selected as its recipient. Mrs. Sayles smiled.

"You are Cap'n Jim-Carey's son," she said. "And if your father had been living he would have come without an invitation. Cap'n Jim never stood on ceremony with us. We shall ask George and his wife before long, of course, but—well, Emily seemed to think you might enjoy it more if you came by yourself. *Now* we will go into the sitting room."

The conversation there was quite as general in scope as had been that about the supper table. Not once were Carey's personal affairs, past or present, mentioned. It seemed odd to him. He had been expecting Emily to ask concerning his call upon Professor Knight at the hotel the previous evening. She had appeared greatly interested in the professor and his proposed expedition, during their talk in the Higgins' shop. As for him he had thought of little else. He wondered if her professed interest was so perfunctory that she had forgotten it already.

When the grandfather's clock in the hall boomed eight Mrs. Sayles rose from the armchair. "Bedtime for old folks and children," she announced. "Good night, Carey. We have enjoyed having you here and, of course, you will come again and often. Oh, no! You are not going home yet. Emily will tuck me in and then she will be with you. You must wait. Come, Emily."

She left the room, on her daughter's arm, and they moved slowly up the stairs together. Carey, alone in the sitting room, sat smoking—for they had insisted upon his doing so—his thoughts drifting back to the days when, as a boy, their house had been so familiar to him. As he had told Emily, that time seemed at least a thousand years before, in another and far happier age.

He heard Emily's step on the stairs. She came into the room, her eyes shining with excitement.

"There!" she exclaimed, pulling a chair near his and sitting down. *"Now!* Now tell me about it. I haven't said a word to mother because I thought perhaps I shouldn't until you had seen him again. You *did* see him, of course. What did he say? When is he going? Did he ask you to go with him? Tell me everything. I can't wait another minute."

So she had not forgotten. It pleased him to know that she had not. She was genuinely interested, after all. He smiled and drew the lock of hair down over his nose.

"Why . . . yes," he said, slowly.

"Yes? Yes to what—to which?"

"To everything. I saw him—Professor Knight, of course you mean—at his room in the hotel after supper last night. He is planning an expedition in South America—up the Amazon and then, perhaps, a little way into the interior if he can make it. There will be four others in the party. He asked me to be one of the four."

She clapped her hands delightedly. "Good!" she exclaimed. "I knew he would. I was sure that is what he really came here for."

He shook his head. "I am not so sure," he said, "but he did ask me to go with him. I wish I could have said yes; it would have been a wonderful experience."

She leaned back in her chair. *"Didn't* you say yes?" she demanded. "Carey Judson, don't tell me you told him you wouldn't go."

"I told him I couldn't. I appreciated the honor, for it was one, and I tried to make him understand that I did; but of course my going was out of the question."

"Why?"

He smiled. "For a dozen reasons," he said. "In the first

place I didn't feel that it would be right for me to leave George."

"Nonsense! George would be the first one to tell you to go. Do you suppose he would stand in the way of such a glorious opportunity for you as that is? Of course he wouldn't! He can get another bookkeeper easily enough; bookkeepers are plentiful. Oh, let me talk to him! If *that* is your only reason—"

"It isn't. There are others. And just one of them is sufficient. I haven't the money."

"Money? Do you mean you would have to furnish money of your own?"

"Somebody will have to furnish a lot of money before that expedition starts. Big Jack—the professor, I mean—feels pretty certain that Moore and his crowd will back him to an extent, but he, himself, will pay his own way and so must each one of the party. The other chaps are lucky enough to be sons of rich men. I am not."

"But—oh, dear! Will it cost a great deal?"

"About fifteen or twenty thousand each, probably. Outfit, Indian guides, porters, motor launches, canoes—oh, this isn't going to be any casual picnic. Knight means to go a long way and stay for months. . . . So, you see—"

He waved the proposition away, smiling still. She recognized the torturing disappointment behind the smile.

"Oh, dear!" she sighed. "Fifteen thousand dollars! That *is* a great deal."

"It might as well be a million, so far as I am concerned. Now let me tell you more about their plans. By Jove!" enthusiastically, "it will be a trip! They are planning to go first to the islands on the Pacific side of Central America. They are scarcely known at all, some of them, and the bird life there is—"

He went on to rhapsodize over the prospect of weeks spent in that paradise.

"From there," he continued, "they will come back to the Atlantic and down to the Amazon. Then, after the new outfit, all the boats and crews and the rest of it, are ready they will go up the river—away up. Then perhaps up some of the tributaries. Oh, there are more Rivers of Doubt than one in that neighborhood. Think of it! Places where *no* one, no white man, has ever been before! There may be birds there that haven't even been classified yet. If I could go there— But—oh, well!" with a short laugh, "it is something to have been asked."

The fire and enthusiasm died from his eyes and he brushed the lock of hair away from his nose and turned to her, smiling.

"I'm mighty glad the others are going," he said. "I shall be with them in spirit, at all events."

Her sympathy for him was so keen that she found it hard to face the inevitable as patiently as he was doing. She frowned and bit her lip.

"It is a perfect shame that you can't go," she vowed. "Oh, Carey, isn't there any way for you to get that money? If you told your brother, wouldn't he—"

He raised a protesting hand. "I shan't tell him," he said. "George has done quite enough for me already. Too much!"

"But he is—every one says he is—a rich man. If he could advance the money—"

"No."

"Oh, dear! When you say no that way I know you mean it. But isn't there some one? Your aunt—Mrs. Dain; she is well-to-do. And she is *very* much interested in you. She told mother—"

Again he interrupted. "I have been intrusted with some of Aunt Susan's money before," he said, quietly. "Just as I have with yours—and hundreds of others. No, thank you." Then with a sudden burst which revealed to her a little of his real feeling, he added: "Emily, if that twenty thousand were raised by public subscription and offered to me I shouldn't accept a cent. Good heavens! what do you think I am? . . . There! Now we'll talk of something else. I have some news for you. I had a letter from Ed Moore this morning.

He seems to like those beetle-heads as well as Knight said he did. He wrote a whole lot of nonsense about them and, which is more to the purpose, he sent, not only the check for the hundred and twenty dollars, but added another hundred and fifty, for the black duck I am making now. Seemed to be afraid some one else might get them if he didn't pay in advance. Pshaw!" with a puzzled shake of the head, "I don't see why he did that. For a financier he appears to be a trustful person. Not a word about my sending a receipt."

To her just then anything connected with his making of wooden birds seemed a pitiful anticlimax, but she tried to pretend interest.

"That is nice—your getting the check," she said. "You can pay for your new lathe now, can't you?"

"I shall pay Tobias a part of the price. He advanced the money for the lathe, you know. I shan't pay the whole yet— that is, I doubt if I do. I had intended using the money for something else and somehow I can't give up the idea. . . . I suppose you are wondering what I mean. I told Aunt Susan before she left, but I haven't told any one else, not even George. I don't mind telling you though. That is, if you care to hear it."

"Of course I care. What is it?"

"Well," doubtfully, "all right; if you are sure it won't bore you."

"Nonsense! Tell me."

He reached again for the persecuted forelock.

"It will sound foolish, I warn you," he stammered, hesitatingly. "It always sounds foolish to me when I say it aloud. I . . . humph! . . . Well, I want to pay some of my debts with it. You are surprised, aren't you? I don't wonder."

He began to disclose his cherished plan for making good to the most needy of his creditors in Wellmouth the money they had lost through the failure of his firm. As he talked he became more earnest and she, listening intently, gained a little knowledge of how this scheme, or hope, had been an obsession with him ever since his return to the village, had, in fact, been the one compelling reason which had forced the decision to return.

"It must sound pretty picayune to you, I know," he faltered, pulling up with a jerk in the midst of his torrent of self-disclosure. "It does to me when I permit myself to think of it in a common-sense way. When I think of— of you and your mother, and George and Cora, and Cap'n Higgins, and Snow and Loveland and—oh, all the others right here at home who have been defrauded through me, I— well, I feel like what I am, and that is something too mean to mention. . . . Emily, when I first met you, that night of the reception, I tried to tell you a little of my feelings when I learned that your mother and you had lost so much. You wouldn't let me talk about it. You may find this hard to believe, but it is the truth; I didn't really know that your mother had so much of her money in—in our care. I didn't know it until—until after the smash. Oh, I should have known! It was my business to know. That is what I was there for. I just left everything to Osborne and— Oh, good God, what a mess I made of it all! What a horrible, unforgivable mess!"

For the first time she caught a clear glimpse of his tormented self under the mask of shy reticence and "queerness" that he usually wore. He put his hand to his face and groaned and the misery expressed by the action touched her heart with a pity beyond words. Tears sprang to her eyes. She put her hand upon his arm.

"Don't, Carey, don't!" she begged. "Please don't."

He looked up, drew a long breath, and the mask slipped again before his face. He smiled.

"Excuse the hysterics," he said. "I try not to wail over my sins in public, as a usual thing. . . . Well," more briskly, "what I am trying to say is that, although I can't attempt paying all my Wellmouth creditors, I can, perhaps, pay a few of the smaller ones, and they need it most. Now that I have a little cash in hand, some that I have saved from my salary and the larger part of Moore's check, I am going to begin the payments. What do you think of the idea? As insane as most of mine, is it?"

She was genuinely interested now. Her eyes flashed.

"It is splendid!" she cried. "And just like you, besides. No one else would have thought of doing such a thing."

"No one else would have neglected the care of his friends' money as I did. And some one else did think of it. It was George's suggestion in the beginning. He suggested it to me before I left the hospital. We haven't talked about it since, probably he has forgotten it and believes I have. I haven't mentioned my plan to him, nor to any one else except Aunt Susan—and now you. You won't mention it either, will you? You see, I had rather it wasn't known. I—I am a little ashamed of it, as a matter of fact."

"Ashamed! The idea! Why?"

"Oh, I don't know. It sounds so—so small, as if I were trying to buy people's good opinion or—or buy off a little of the bad. I am not. I hope you understand that."

"I do. So will any one else with brains enough to understand anything. And of course I shan't mention it, if you don't wish me to. But how about those you pay? Won't they tell others?"

He rubbed his chin in a troubled fashion.

"That is the question," he admitted. "That is the most perplexing thing about it. I shall ask them not to, of course, but here in Wellmouth it seems hard to keep a secret. Tobias is always boasting about everything on the Cape being wide open and public and free. It would seem as if that applies to—er—speech and people's personal affairs; don't you think so?"

She laughed and was glad of the excuse for so doing. The shyness and almost timid apology with which he revealed the project which had evidently been sustaining hope for months was far from humorous. She laughed, but she felt more like crying.

"Indeed I do think so," she agreed. "Although I guess

Wellmouth is no different in that respect from any other place where every one knows every one else. I think you will have to make those you pay promise not to tell and—well, trust in Providence. But who are those first ones to be? You have decided that, I suppose?"

He nodded. "Yes," he said. "I have, in a way, but I should like your advice, if you don't mind giving it. I want to pay Mrs. Samantha Bangs something on account. I can't pay her all, I only wish I could, but I thought I would give her a hundred as a beginning. You see, her husband, Erastus—'Ratty' we boys used to call him—worked for father all his life. Practically all she had when he died was a small insurance and—" he shifted in his chair and picked nervously at a wrinkle in his trousers—"she invested it through me because—well, I suppose—yes, I know—because I was a Judson. She is—Hepsibah told me—sewing for Anne Smalley, the dressmaker. I thought even a hundred might help her a little. Don't you think it might?"

"Yes. I know it would. And she is a dear old soul. Who else?"

"Well, there is Miss Letitia Cahoon, Cap'n Obed's second cousin I believe she is. I—I scarcely know why I picked her out. Perhaps it was self-protection, or—or cowardice or something. She is poor and I thought I might give her *all* she lost. It wasn't but a hundred and fifteen dollars, but—" he smiled, ruefully. "I honestly believe she has talked more about it than any other of my—er—victims in town. She doesn't speak to me when we meet. If she were paid now, the very first one, I thought, perhaps, she might be prevented from doing more talking of the same kind if—or when—she learned that others had been paid. Oh, yes! it is just cowardice. I have tried to make myself believe that it wasn't, but there is no use trying to make you believe it."

Her laugh was genuine and whole-hearted this time.

"It isn't cowardice at all," she declared. "And paying her is a very sensible thing to do. Goodness knows she needs every cent. It seems to me you have chosen remarkably

well, Carey. . . . Of course I am not certain that you ought
to feel you must pay any one. The receivers—or executors
—or whatever they call them, have made a settlement of
your firm's debts, as generous a settlement as could be made,
I am sure, and for you to deprive yourself of money you
have earned—and must need—is—well, I doubt if some
people would not think you foolishly sentimental to do anything of the kind. Although," she added, earnestly, "I am
awfully glad you are going to do it."

He had not, apparently, heard the latter part of this speech.
He was fumbling in an inner pocket and from a bundle of
papers of all sorts, he drew a long envelope and extracted
therefrom a folded sheet of paper, a bill form with the name
of J. C. Judson & Co. printed at its head. He spread it
out upon the center table.

"Here is a list of my creditors here in Wellmouth," he
said. "I got it from George. I made him give it to me
when I first came back. It is an awful list, like—like a
death warrant, isn't it? I never saw a death warrant, of
course, but when George handed me this I felt the way I
should imagine a condemned man must feel. All hope
abandon ye who are entered here, you know. I wish, if
it wouldn't trouble you too much, that you would look it
over, Emily. There may be people whom you think it would
be better to pay now instead of Mrs. Bangs and Tish Cahoon.
Jabez—our wharf man—never calls her anything but 'Tish.'
That is to say, nothing more complimentary."

Emily bent her head above the list. She noticed that the
paper was much worn in the folds, as if it had been opened
and reopened many times. Against certain names were
pencil checkings, and written notes, such as: "All they had,"
"*Must* pay a little," or "Among the first." Some of these
notes had had lines drawn through them, as if the person
writing them had changed his mind on reflection. Her
mother's name was there and something had been written opposite it, but the pencil had blackened this to an indecipher-
able smudge. Her first thought was of the hours and hours

of despairing consideration which the poor fellow beside her
must have given to this list. She was glad she was sitting
with her profile toward him and that the shadow of the
lampshade prevented his seeing her face distinctly.

He was watching her intently, however, and in spite of
his absorbing interest in the subject they were discussing,
he found himself thinking what an attractive picture she made
as she bent over that list. The lamplight edged her hair with
a halo of yellow fire and the outline of her young face was as
clean-cut as an old-fashioned portrait in silhouette. He
watched her lips move as she read the names, and the rise
and fall of her long lashes. Strange thoughts were in his
mind, very strange indeed to the mind of Carey Judson. He
did not, himself, realize that they were there, but, when she
looked up from her reading and turned toward him, he
started as if awakened from an unwonted and not unpleasant
dream. He blinked and rubbed his eyes.

She laughed gayly. "Good gracious!" she exclaimed. "I
do believe you have been taking a nap. You look as if
you had."

He blinked again. Then he shook his head. "I have been
thinking, I guess," he said. "I usually look queer when I
do that."

"I don't know any one who thinks more than you do. If
that were the reason I should expect you to look queer most
of the time."

His characteristic slow smile was in evidence again. "I
have been given to understand that that was my usual appearance," he said. "I believe my newest pet name is 'Queer
Judson.' It distinguishes me from my brother, you know."

She had heard the name applied to him and more than once,
but it irritated her to find that he was aware of the local
habit.

"Ridiculous!" she cried. "Who calls you that?"

"Almost every one now. I was called something like it
in college."

"Who told you you were called that here in Wellmouth?"

"Eh? Oh, several people. My sister-in-law told me first, I believe. She was objecting—quite reasonably—to some of my queerness in the matter of the care of my room and she told me."

"Dear me! That was kind of her, I must say."

"Oh, she was excusable. She objected to my leaving my rubber boots on top of the bureau. I was thinking of something else when I took them off and I put them in the nearest place. They might quite as likely have been under the pillow; I shouldn't have been surprised to find them there—although, usually, I am surprised when I am able to find them at all. . . . Well, you have looked over the list of the condemned. Appalling, isn't it?"

It had been, rather, but she had no idea of allowing him to guess that fact.

"It seems to me you have chosen exactly the right pair to pay first," she said. "When are you going to see them?"

"To-morrow evening, I think. I ought to be at work on my ducks, but I shall probably call on Samantha and Letitia instead. It will be an ordeal—especially Tish's part."

"Why? They should be very grateful to you."

"They won't be, if I can help it. And—" he was twisting the lock of hair again, "I shan't know how to tell them what I have come for. I shan't know how to begin, you see."

"I don't see at all. If I were you I should—"

He lifted his hand quickly. "You couldn't be," he interrupted. "That is just it. I am myself, worse luck. Well, I suppose I shall get through with it somehow."

She reflected. "I am dying to know what they say when you give them the money," she declared. "Miss Cahoon particularly. She will be great fun. I—I suppose you wouldn't care to have me go with you?"

For an instant his face lighted eagerly and she thought he was about to accept the suggestion. He did not, however. The light faded and he shook his head.

"No," he said, with decision. "Thanks, but it wouldn't do. If they talk—and I am afraid they will—they must talk about me and no one else. My friends mustn't be mixed up in it."

"But I don't care in the least."

"No. It is my funeral—or partial resurrection—or something. I'll have to perform the ceremony. . . . There!" rising, "I must go now. I have had a wonderful evening. I wish I could make you understand how wonderful. It is the second in sequence. Last evening, with Big Jack, was wonderful, too."

"It is too bad that you can't go with him on that South American trip. I am *so* sorry."

"So am I, or I would be if it were even thinkable. And I own that I am a good deal set up with the vainglory of having been invited to go. Apparently," he rubbed his chin, "queerness isn't so noticeable up the Amazon. . . . Well, good night. Thank your mother for me, won't you? I shan't try to thank you for your patience and interest in— in my debts."

At the door, as they shook hands, she said:

"Carey, you will tell me all about your calls on Mrs. Bangs and Letitia, won't you? Tell me just as soon as you can. I am tremendously interested."

He seemed to find it hard to believe. "Are you?" he asked. "Yes. I—I really think you are. If only I could pay your mother—"

"Hush! Never mind that. And this is only the beginning, you know. Why, perhaps you can pay every one in Wellmouth some day."

He laughed, but the laugh was short. "Perhaps Ben Early may die in the gutter, like Simon Martin," he observed. "It seems unlikely at present. . . . Well, I'll report on Samantha and Tish, if I survive. . . . Good night."

The door closed behind him and he swung into his long-legged stride through the darkness to the gate. Across the road, where a dim light burned in a sitting room window a shade moved ever so little. He did not see it move. His thoughts were otherwise engaged.

## CHAPTER X

MRS. SAMANTHA BANGS—widow of the late Captain Erastus, irreverently called "Ratty"—lived in a small, story and a half, white-clapboarded and green-shuttered house of the usual Cape Cod type which was situated on the Lookout Hill Road, but at the other side of the slope, a full half mile beyond the aristocratic section. She and her husband had bought that house five years after their marriage, and "keeping the place up"—that is, seeing that it was freshly whitewashed each spring, that no pickets should be missing from the fence, nor weeds permitted to flourish amid the grass of the tiny front lawn—had been their care and pride during Erastus' life. Since his death his widow had continued to live there alone, because, as she said, there was nowhere else to go and she should not feel "to home anywheres else" if there were. It was quite obvious, however, to her acquaintances in town, that the upkeep, even of as small an establishment as this, was a burden which her scanty financial resources could not carry many years. Captain Erastus had managed to save a few hundred dollars from the wage paid him by J. C. Judson & Co., and his life had been insured for a thousand dollars. The thousand Samantha had intrusted to Osborne and Judson for investment. From that investment she had been notified that she would probably get back one hundred and fifty. Each day, Sundays excepted, she trudged down to the two rooms over the post office where Miss Anne Smalley carried on a dressmaking business, and there she did plain sewing from eight in the morning to five at night. Miss Smalley's temper was a variable quantity, according to the state of custom, and as midsummer was a slack season her employee earned every cent paid for her services and was made to feel that she did.

On this particular Tuesday evening Samantha had come home late and more than usually weary. Her supper was a perfunctory affair, hot tea, and baked beans warmed over from Saturday night and Sunday morning. She warmed over the beans for the second time, not because they appealed to the taste, but purely from motives of economy. "I've got to get rid of them everlastin' beans, somehow," soliloquized Samantha, who, like most individuals in solitary confinement, talked to herself. "I can't afford to heave 'em away. Somebody's got to eat 'em, and the last time I set 'em in front of the cat he turned up his nose and hollered to be let out door."

So she ate a few herself and drank two cups of tea. Then, too tired to wash dishes immediately, she remained at the table, absently stirring the grounds in the bottom of her cup and thinking, as she so often thought, of how different the suppers in that room used to be when her husband shared them with her.

A knock at the kitchen door caused her to "jump pretty nigh out of her skin," as she said afterward, and she answered it with foreboding. Callers came to the Bangs house but seldom nowadays and the only person likely to call at that early hour in the evening was a representative of the "Portygee" family next door who had the neighborly habit of borrowing developed to an acute stage.

When, instead of a juvenile Portygee, she saw Carey Judson standing on the back step, she was—to quote her own expression once more—so took up short that she just stood there and gaped like a sculpin. "If I'd seen the Old Harry himself perched on that step I couldn't have been more upset," declared Samantha.

"Why, my good Lord!" was her greeting, which, considering the comparison with the Old Harry, was rather surprising.

"Good evening, Mrs. Bangs," said Carey. "Are you busy—too busy to see me a minute?"

Mrs. Bangs managed to say that she didn't know as she was busy. She didn't guess likely she was. No, of course she wasn't. Wouldn't he come in?

He entered and she preceded him into the little dining room. She had been having supper in the kitchen, but she made it a point never to receive company there. She might have asked him to be seated, but she was still too greatly amazed to see him at all to remember conventionalities. Also, it must be confessed, she was apprehensive. Had he come to tell her that she was not to have even the hundred and fifty dollars?

He did not sit, nor did she. He was holding his straw hat in his hand and twisting it around and around by the brim as did John Alden when he came to see Priscilla in the "Courting of Miles Standish," the series of "Speaking Tableaux" given by the Dramatic Society of the Universalist Church.

"Mrs. Bangs," he faltered, "I—I—well, I've come to talk with you about—er—er—money."

She gasped. It must be what she feared. He *had* come to say she could not have the hundred and fifty.

"Money?" she repeated. "Oh, my soul! . . . Oh, dear!"

He looked as if he would like to echo the "Oh, dear." He put the hat on the table and reached into his pocket.

"I have—er—brought you a hundred dollars," he said. "I—I hope you—you can use it."

She stared at him as he produced a pocketbook and opened it.

"I wish it were more," he went on, in the same confused and embarrassed manner. "Perhaps there may be more by and by. You see, I—well, Cap'n Erastus, your husband, was —was—I liked him and he worked for father so many years, I. . . . Well, here is the hundred. You will take it, won't you?"

He was counting the bills upon the table. Her fear was a

certainty by this time and she stretched out a protesting hand.

"A hundred!" she cried. "Mercy on me! What *will* I do? They said—Mr. George himself told me I'd get a hundred and fifty anyhow. I was countin' on it. I don't see how I *can* do with less."

He looked up. "I beg your pardon?" he said.

"Eh? . . . Oh, you don't have to do that, Mr. Carey. You don't have to beg my pardon, if you'll only give me the other fifty. I shouldn't ask it if I didn't need it so, truly I wouldn't. You see, it's the hens I'm thinkin' about most. Afore Rastus died he said much as a dozen times: 'If I don't get the shingles pretty soon, S'manthy, it'll be too late for them hens.' That's what he said, and 'twas almost his last words. He was took down with his final sickness and passed away, poor soul, and he never got 'em. Oh, Mr. Carey, if you *could* just— Can't you?"

Her visitor appeared bewildered. He had been absorbed in his counting and had heard practically nothing of the first part of this involved jumble of jerky sentences. He gazed at her uncomprehendingly.

"I beg your pardon?" he said again. "I don't think I quite understand. What was it your husband wanted?"

She was very much excited and her attempt at explanation was not the most lucid.

"Hey? What?" she asked. "Oh, shingles was what he wanted. If he could only have got the shingles afore he died 'twould have been *such* a comfort to him."

Carey's mental haze was thicker than ever. He had a vague recollection that there was a disease which people called "shingles," but why any one should yearn for it more than any other he could not comprehend.

"I—well, really, Mrs. Bangs," he stammered, "I don't see—er—I thought your husband died of pneumonia. It seems to me George, or some one, told me that he did."

"Yes, he did. That's what he died of, bronicle pneumony. He didn't suffer none to speak of, which was a mercy, but—"

"Er—just a minute, please. If he had pneumonia I can't quite see why— There must be some mistake here somewhere. Why did he want to have—shingles?"

"Why, I've been telling you! He wanted 'em for the hens. For much as a year afore he died—passed on, I should say—that henhouse roof has leaked somethin' terrible every time it rains. The last promise I made to him was that I'd have it fixed soon's ever I could and—and I've been countin' on usin' a little mite of the hundred and fifty Mr. George said I was to get back from the insurance money to put new shingles on the leaky places. Lord knows I can't spare an extry cent, but every time I see them poor feathered critters—though some of 'em ain't got as many feathers as they'd ought to have; moultin' in the wrong season, seems so—when I see 'em settin' all hunched up and resigned, as you might say, on them roosts, with the rain a-pourin' down onto 'em like Noah's flood I—well, seems as if I *couldn't* stand it! And now if I ain't to have but a *hundred*, I—well, they'll have to drown, that's all there is to it."

Carey's mind was relieved concerning her sanity and his. He hastened to offer more relief. He explained that she was to have, not only the one hundred and fifty dollars which was to be her share of the settlement in bankruptcy, but an additional hundred paid by him from his own savings. At first she did not seem to understand, then not to believe, but, at last, when she both understood and believed, her joy and gratitude were the cause of verbal outpourings which threatened to drown him as the rain had promised to drown the patiently resigned fowl.

"My goodness gracious!" she cried. "My goodness sakes alive! How can I thank you, Mr. Carey? If you knew what this means to me—and them hens! It's awful good of you. I'll never forget it. I managed to scratch along on what Annie pays me for sewin', but it's hard scratchin'. And you're goin' to give me this? Just *give* it to me?"

She had, by this time, insisted upon his sitting down and he patiently explained and re-explained his reasons for paying her this small portion of his debt and hinted at the vague hope of other small payments which might come in the distant future.

"Of course I can't promise that," he said. "If I were able I should pay every cent I owe, and the Wellmouth people first of all. I can't do that, but I am going to try and pay a little, here and there, to those, like yourself, who—er—may need it, you know. I wish I could make you understand how badly I feel about your husband's insurance money having been lost through our firm. It has troubled me. . . . Oh, well! We won't talk about that. Cap'n Erastus was kind to me in a hundred ways when I was a boy and. . . . Well, good night, Mrs. Bangs. . . . Oh, by the way, I want you to promise me not to tell a soul about your getting this money. That is part of the bargain; I shall have to ask that."

She was obviously disappointed. "Can't I tell *nobody?*" she pleaded. "Not even Lemuel Baker when he comes to put on them shingles?"

"No. Lemuel, nor any one else."

"Not even Annie Smalley when she learns about it and preaches to me about bein' extravagant and wastin' my money on henhouses? She's always talkin' about the high wages she has to pay for sewin'. She'll cal'late they're higher than ever now."

"I am afraid you mustn't tell any one. I'm sorry, but it wouldn't do."

"No," with a sigh, "I presume likely 'twouldn't. They'd *all* expect to be paid right off, the whole of 'em. Well, I'll promise. But I'm goin' to say this to you, Carey Judson: When folks 'round here used to call you a thief and a cheat and all kinds of names—that was when we first heard of it, you know—*I* always stuck up for you. 'He may be a thief, in one way,' I says, 'but if he is it is because he don't know any better. He never stole money deliberate, you can't make me believe he did. He may be absent-minded and—and kind of cracked about birds and critters, but that's a failin', not a

crime. You wouldn't be for puttin' a feeble-minded person
in jail, would you? No, you wouldn't. You'd say he wan't
accountable. Well, Carey Judson never was accountable
where money was concerned.' That's what I said, and I
meant it, too."

With which frank item of intended consolation and a final
"Good night, now *do* come and see me, Mr. Carey," she
closed the kitchen door and went back to count for herself
the little heap of bank notes upon the dining-room table.

Carey's reception at the house of Miss Letitia Cahoon was
very different from that accorded him at the Bangs cottage.
Letitia occupied two rooms over the bake shop on the Main
Road. The furniture of these rooms was as stiff and hard
and uncompromising as was Miss Cahoon herself. She was
a staunch, even militant, member of the church led by the
Reverend Mr. Bagness, and often said that the only fault she
had to find with the latter's preaching was that he was altogether too soft-soapy when it came to speaking right out
about folks who pretended to call themselves God-fearing
Christians and yet went to ride in their buggies on the Sabbath Day, and swelled around in their purple and fine linen
making their brags that they didn't believe in hell.

"You can call yourself a Universalist or a Unitarian, if
you've a mind to," declared Miss Cahoon, in Friday night
prayer meetings, "and you can send your children to learn
piano playin' and to picture paintin' schools and such
abominations all you want to, but what does it say in Holy
Writ? 'It is a consider'ble sight easier for a camel to get
through a needle than it is for a rich man to get to heaven.'
That's what it says; it's there to be read by those that's got
eyes to see with. All right. If they ain't goin' to heaven,
where *are* they goin'? They're goin' to the place that they
say *ain't* a place, that's where they're goin'. And it is our
duty to tell 'em so. If they don't take the warnin', that's
their lookout."

Her favorite hymn was that which asked the question:
"Is your name written there?" She derived much satisfac-

tion from the conviction that many names of those whose paths in this life were smoother than her own were not there written. When the news of Carey Judson's downfall came to Wellmouth she made little complaint concerning her own loss, although the hundred and odd dollars represented more self-denial by far than did the thousands of some of her prosperous neighbors. She grimly accepted it as a punishment from Providence for some remissness on her part.

"I've been slack in my duty somewhere," she said, "and the Lord's makin' me pay for it. He'll take his pay later on out of the wicked ones that are responsible, maybe not in this world, but in the next. And a true believer, such as I *hope* I am, can find comfort in knowin' that's so."

She had not spoken to Carey Judson since his return to Wellmouth. And when, in answer to his knock, she opened the door and saw him standing in the hall, her greeting could scarcely be called a speech.

"Humph!" she grunted.

Carey, who had expected about such a measure of cordiality and had braced himself for the ordeal, bade her a polite good evening and announced that he had come to see her on a matter of business. "It won't take but a moment," he added. "May I come in?"

She hesitated. "I suppose likely you can," she said, after a moment. "I was thinkin' of goin' to bed, but I can wait. You needn't shut the door. Leave it open. *I* haven't got anything to hide. What is this business you've come to see me about?"

When he told her, with the same hesitancy and confusion he had shown in the interview with Mrs. Bangs, that he had come to repay in full the sum she had lost by her unfortunate investment through Osborne and Judson, she was evidently as greatly surprised as Samantha had been, but unlike the latter, she made no outcry and expressed no gratitude. Instead she regarded him with marked suspicion.

"Do you mean to tell me," she demanded, "that you are

goin' to give me back the money that you and that dissipated partner of yours took away from me?"

He nodded. "Yes," he said, "that is what I should like to do, if you will accept it, Miss Cahoon."

"Humph! . . . Of course I'll accept it. Why shouldn't I? It was mine in the first place. But wait a minute; there's some things I want to know first. Where did you get the money to pay it with?"

He explained that he had saved a little from his salary and also that he had been paid for some work he had done outside the office.

"Work?" she asked. "What sort of work? I never heard you was doin' any work, except whittlin' out those bird dolls down in Tobias Higgins' woodshed, or whatever he calls it. You don't get pay for *that*, do you?"

He explained that, ridiculous as it might seem, he was paid for the wooden birds.

"My soul!" was her comment. "Well, a fool and his money's soon parted, that's all I've got to say. You make those things on Sundays, I hear. Is that true?"

"Why—yes, I suppose it is. I work at them evenings, but I do some work on Sunday afternoons."

"Humph! Well, bad as I need money, I don't take any that's got by workin' on the Lord's Day. If that's where it comes from you can take it right away again."

He strained the truth to the extent of telling her that the money he intended giving her was derived entirely from his wages with J. C. Judson & Co. He expected her to be satisfied with the explanation, but she was, apparently, only partially so.

"Sit down," she said, shortly. "Yes, you might as well. There's some more things I want to be sure of before I take any money from you, Mr. Carey Judson. What are you payin' it for, anyway? Are you cal'latin' to pay everybody you owe? If you are you've got a job, if what I hear's true."

He assured her that, much as he would like to, he could not hope to pay all his creditors.

"Then what did you pick me out for?" she demanded.

The answer to this required all the diplomacy at his limited command. He stammered, twisted his forelock, crossed and recrossed his knees, and then somewhat incoherently explained that he had planned to begin repaying those in Wellmouth to whom he owed the least; and that she was one of these.

"Well," she said, after more reflection, "then I don't know as there's any good reason why I shouldn't take my own. If I supposed for a minute you thought you was doin' me a special favor or that there was any charity about it I shouldn't take it, you can be sure of that. I may be poor, but I ain't on the town yet, I'd have you to know. . . . I suppose you want a receipt, don't you? I shall give you one anyhow."

She insisted on doing so, although anything as businesslike as a receipt had been far from his thought. When he insisted upon her keeping the payment a secret he had to undergo another cross examination.

"Well," she said, at last, "I won't tell. And when I say I won't I won't. I can understand why you don't want everybody to know, of course. Some of 'em here in this town would be sittin' on your doorstep from mornin' till night if they heard of it. And they'd sit there Sundays as well as week days, you can make up your mind to that. And there's one thing more: When I get—or if I get—the little mite that your brother told me those receivers or administers, or whatever they call 'em, might pay me as my share of what was left after the stealin', I'll hand it right back to you. I want what lawfully belongs to me, but I don't want any more. . . . There! Is that all?"

Her caller rose. He was glad of the opportunity to escape.

"That is all, Miss Cahoon," he said. "Thank you for taking the money. And—and I do want to say how sorry I am that you were put to so much trouble and worry through me. I *am* sorry. Please believe it."

She was standing by the door, which had remained wide open during the interview.

"Yes," she said, slowly, "I shouldn't wonder if you was. I guess you are the kind that would be. 'The way of the transgressor is hard,' so we read, 'and the wages of sin is death.' Though I will say," she added, "that some of the sinners take a long time collectin' their salary. . . . Well, considerin' everything, I'm much obliged to you, Mr. Judson. I'll keep still about it. . . . Good night."

Before he reached the door she spoke again.

"Wait a minute," she commanded. "There's somethin' I want you to take along with you."

She went into the adjoining room and returned, bringing two printed leaflets.

"You look these over when you get a chance," she said. "They may set you to thinkin'—I hope so, anyhow."

The door closed behind him. He groped his way down the stairs in the darkness. Outside, on the platform of the bake shop, he pushed back his hat, drew a hand across his forehead and sighed in relief.

"Whew!" he exclaimed, feelingly. At home in the solitude of his own room he inspected the leaflets. The title of one was "Remember the Sabbath Day," and the other "Can the Merely Moral Hope for Salvation?" He read the "Merely Moral" tract before retiring. Its pages were slightly tinged with yellow, either from age or brimstone, he was inclined to think the latter.

George Judson had expected to return from Boston that evening, but he did not appear for another twenty-four hours. At supper he seemed to be in high spirits, although his wife's welcome was not of the sort to encourage hilarity.

"Well," was her remark as they sat down at the table, "you did decide to come home, after all, didn't you? I was beginning to think you were going to stay up there for the rest of the summer."

George explained that he had been detained by one or two business matters.

"You can't always count on getting through with things like that in a hurry," he said. "You make an appointment for one day and, for some reason or other, it has to be put off till to-morrow. That's so, isn't it, Carey?"

Cora T. sniffed. "Oh, yes!" she observed, caustically. "Carey knows all about it, of course. He's such a business man, himself, that he would, naturally. I notice, when you take *me* to Boston, it is always you who are in a hurry to get back home again. The pressing business is always at this end of the line then."

Later on she mentioned that a letter had been received from Mrs. Dain that morning. Her husband, who had been silent for some minutes and whose before supper announcement of prodigious appetite was not borne out by his performance at table, looked up with interest.

"Oh, she wrote you, did she?" he asked. "How is the old girl?"

Mrs. Judson ignored the question.

"She wrote *you*," she said. "She never seems to think it is worth while to address any of her letters to me, for some reason or other. When she was here she didn't hesitate to ask me for everything she wanted, and goodness knows she wanted enough; but when it comes to writing it has to be to a Judson. Some people have 'family' on the brain. I'm glad I haven't."

"What did she say?" asked George, again. "You read the letter, of course."

"Certainly I read it. If you are expecting letters you don't want your wife to read you'd better have them sent to the office. Of course," she added, cheerfully, "I don't know how many of that kind you do have sent there."

Carey put in a word. "I had a letter from Aunt Susan, myself," he said. "She is full of trouble with the house and the servants, as usual. And," he added, doubtfully, "I am afraid she isn't very well. She hinted at having more of those pains of hers and I judge she has had to call in the doctor more than once. I don't like those pains. She had an attack that evening after she had been—"

He paused and did not finish the sentence. Aunt Susan's call at the Higgins' shop had been, so far as he was aware, kept a secret and he thought it well that it should remain so. Fortunately his sister-in-law was not paying strict attention. She began catechizing her husband concerning the "business" which had detained him in the city. George's answers were not very specific. "Oh, more fish, that's all," was his summing up.

That evening Carey did what was, for him, a remarkable thing. For the third successive evening he remained away from his black duck. He started, as usual, for the shop, but instead turned back and walked to the Sayles house. He had promised Emily that she should hear how he had fared in his financial transactions with Mrs. Bangs and Letitia Cahoon and it seemed to him that now was as good a time as any to tell her of his experience.

It was after eight when he arrived and Mrs. Sayles had already retired. Emily invited him into the sitting room and did not seem surprised at seeing him there again so soon. It was he who expressed the astonishment at his behavior.

"I can't seem to get my bearings, as Cap'n Tobias would say," he declared, naïvely. "I know I promised you that I was through paying attention to what people might say about me, and that hereafter I should do what I liked and go where I pleased, but, even then, I wasn't sure I could keep the promise absolutely. I had such a pleasant time here Monday evening—you and your mother were so kind, and it seemed so good to talk about—about whatever I wanted to talk about, that—well, I am like Simon Martin once more. He took one drink and after that he seldom did anything else. I don't want to be a nuisance though, and I shan't be. I won't die in your gutter, Emily."

She laughed. "I hope coming here isn't likely to kill you," she said. "And I know what you have come for. I should have been ever so disappointed if you hadn't come. Now tell me all about Samantha and Tish."

He described the two interviews in detail. He had, in his rare moments of self-forgetfulness, a habit of quiet humor and she laughed until he was obliged to laugh with her.

"Oh, dear,!" she gasped, when he had finished a summing up of the contents of Miss Cahoon's tracts; "that is perfectly lovely. How I wish I could have been there!"

He shook his head. "I am glad you weren't," he declared, with emphasis. "Although I suppose the presence of a third party might have eased the strain on the proprieties, so far as Letitia was concerned. I told you she insisted on keeping the door open while I was in her apartment, didn't I?"

"And now," she asked, a few minutes afterward, "who will be the next on the list? Whom are you planning to pay next?"

He had scarcely planned so far, he told her. When he reached that point he should again ask her advice.

"I had another letter from Moore this morning," he added. "He is insane, I'm afraid. Actually sent me an order for another dozen beetle-heads, a dozen plover and a dozen 'yellow legs.' More shore birds, all of them. He wants the beetle-heads before I finish the duck. They are for friends of his, he says. He doesn't care what happens to his friendships, does he?"

She was delighted with the news. "Why, you are building up a real business, aren't you, Carey!" she exclaimed. "Paying off your—the people you want to pay here in Wellmouth doesn't seem so tremendously impossible, after all—the little ones, I mean."

He smiled. "You forget I am past thirty," he said. "By the time I am ninety I may get through the first twenty-five. After that—well, after that I shall probably begin payment in a different way—and climate. For particulars, inquire of Miss Cahoon."

She came to the door with him to say good night. He saw her glance at the window across the road.

"It has begun," he said, reading her thought. "This Simon Martin habit must not develop. We are attracting attention already. I shan't come again, for a while, at least. The gutter is my own private resting place. My friends are not invited to hear my last—hiccough."

The speech seemed to worry her—either it or the lighted window, or both.

"Whether you come here or not I shall come to watch you work," she declared. "And, some pleasant Sunday, I shall be extravagant enough to hire what they call a hoss'n' team, meaning a horse and buggy, from the livery stable, and bring mother. She is as much interested in your— What-are-they?—beetle-heads, as I am."

"You mustn't do any such thing. What do you think Tobias and his Chippy will say if I begin holding receptions in their boat shop?"

"I hope they will say, 'How do you do?' at least. Mother has been wanting to call on them ever since we came back here."

She kept her promise the very next Sunday. Mrs. Sayles' exclamations of astonishment at sight of the beetle-head and the ducks and her praise of his work were gratifying. Tobias and Phœbe joined them in the workshop and the Higgins' comments were characteristic and amusing.

"I'm cal'latin'," declared the captain, "to get rich myself out of this bird factory. Goin' to print up some stock certificates by and by and peddle 'em out at a hundred dollars a piece. 'The Judson and Higgins Beetle-Head Roost Preferred' or somethin' like that. We shan't declare any dividends, though. That ain't fashionable these days; anyhow it ain't with most of the other stock I've put my money into. Maybe we'd better call it one of them 'Limited' concerns, Carey; meanin' that the profits in it will be limited to you and me. Eh?"

He laughed uproariously at his joke. Carey smiled. "That part would be taken for granted by most of the investors, I imagine, Cap'n," he said.

When the visitors emerged into the yard, leaving him still carving the beetle-head, Phœbe took her husband to task.

"What in the world, Tobias Higgins," she demanded, "do you have to rake up any talk about investin' money for? Of all things in the world to say to him! Desire," she added, turning to Mrs. Sayles, "I wish I could make you folks understand how much we've come to pity that poor soul in there. When he first came back here I was as down on him as anybody else who had lost money through him and that Osborne. But now I've come to believe he wasn't any more to blame than a ten-year-old child. *Anybody* could steal from him and he'd never know it. He *is* a child in most ways, and that's a fact."

Emily put in a word.

"There is nothing childish about his knowledge of birds and such things," she declared, crisply. "And some of these days people are going to realize how brilliant he is, in his own way."

Phœbe did not answer. The tone of speech caused her to glance quickly at the young lady and then at her husband. The latter, however, did not catch the meaning in her look. He was solemnly inspecting one of his mammoth boots.

"Now ain't it amazin'?" he demanded. "Look at that hoof of mine. Number eleven and broad in the beam as a coal barge. You'd think nothin' smaller than a ship's main hatch would be liable to catch that, wouldn't you? But it ain't so. Let me see the least little mite of a hole and I have to run and shove my foot into it. I hadn't no business to make that fool joke about investin' money. It slipped out afore I realized. Sho! It's too bad. Carey 'll mope over it for the rest of the afternoon. Tut, tut! A fellow has to learn to skate on thin ice when he talks to him. He's the most sensitive critter ever *I* see. Don't you think so, Emily?"

Emily did not answer.

As the horse and buggy drove away from their gate Mrs. Higgins watched it go and then turned to her husband with a slow shake of the head.

"That's the third or fourth time she's been here to see him, Tobias," she observed. "And he's been up to their house twice inside of a week. And did you see how short she took you up when you said he was sensitive and all like that? . . . Hum! . . . I wonder."

The captain grinned. "How do you know he was up to see her twice?" he asked. "Who told you she was, Chip?"

"Oh, I heard it. Hannah Beasley lives right across the road and she saw him when he came and when he went, both times."

Tobias snorted. "I'll bet she did!" he agreed. "That woman would make a fust-rate for'ard lookout aboard a vessel. There wouldn't any whales keep out of her sight— not if they was he ones, they wouldn't."

"Well, I don't know about that. Hannah saw him there, anyhow. And Emily keeps comin' to see him. Folks'll begin to talk if it goes on."

"They'll talk, anyhow. Most of 'em talk in their sleep. Why shouldn't they go to see each other, if they want to? Her folks and his were chummy all their lives. Godfreys mighty! Can't a body go to see *any*body without all the women h'istin' distress signals? He went to see Tish Cahoon the other evenin', I understand. Don't cal'late he's gettin' sweet on *her,* do you? If he is I'll kill him, myself, and put him out of his misery."

Phœbe was very much interested.

"Went to see Letitia Cahoon!" she repeated. "Carey Judson did? Who said so? What did he go to see her for, for mercy sakes!"

"I don't know. Somebody said he did, that's all I know. Probably he and she were havin' a little game of seven-up, cent a point, or somethin' like that. No, no! Tish didn't tell about it. She's been asked, of course, but she wouldn't say yes or no. That's one good thing about that clam-shell mouth of hers. It can keep shut when she wants it to."

Other Wellmouth mouths were not so tightly closed. Emily's calls at the bird shop on Sunday afternoons were quite regular now. She was very much interested in Carey's bird making and her Sunday walks were almost always in that direction. His conscience still troubled him, and he more than once hinted that she should not visit him there, but she refused to accept the hints and he ceased to offer them. Occasionally he called at the Sayles' home. It had become for him a port of refuge when his sister-in-law's innuendoes and sarcasms were too annoying or Mr. Early's condescensions and serene pointing out of his errors in book-keeping too humiliating and trying to the patience. Mrs. Sayles and Emily never spoke of his troubles, there was no condescension or even implied pity in their manner toward him. It was the one spot in the village which, in essentials, remained to him as it used to be in the old, happy, self-respecting days. He heard none of the whisperings which were going about, nor, for that matter, did Emily. As is usual in such cases the said whisperings were not breathed in the ears of the parties most interested.

Cora T. heard them, you may be sure, and repeated them to her husband, with sharp-edged embroideries. George, his odd glumness now apparent even at home, paid little attention.

"Oh, bosh, Cora!" he protested. "What if he and she do see each other once in a while? They are old friends. Carey hasn't many friends left, the Lord knows. Let the poor devil enjoy those he has, can't you?"

Mrs. Judson sniffed. "Oh, yes, you'll stick up for him, of course," she sneered. "He's your brother and anything he does is exactly right. Well, you are to blame for bringing him back here and if anything comes of all this that people are talking about it will be your responsibility and nobody else's. My hands are clean and I take pains to tell everybody so."

He turned to look at her.

"What do you mean by anything coming of it?" he demanded. "If you are hinting that Emily Sayles isn't as fine a girl as ever lived you—well, you ought to be ashamed of yourself, Cora."

She tossed her head. "Oh, I suppose so!" she retorted. "Well, I haven't hinted any such thing, that I know of. I wonder sometimes if you are as prompt to fly up in the air when people say mean things about me, your own wife, as you are when they talk about your father's friends—yes, or that good for nothing brother of yours. I wonder."

"I should be if they ever said them before me. As for Carey and that girl being anything more than friendly, that's nonsense."

"Humph! Well, all I can say is that there is a whole lot of that kind of nonsense in the world. If—mind you I say if— Carey is silly enough to even think of getting married and if Emily Sayles is soft-headed enough to marry him, it will be you they'll turn to for money enough to live on. He hasn't got a cent—nor ever will have—and she hasn't got much more, thanks to him and his partner. George Judson, if he ever dares to hint that he's thinking of doing such a crazy thing you tell him if he does you're through with him forever. If you don't—well, if you don't tell him just that I'll walk out of this house and *never* set foot in it again."

Captain Tobias Higgins could have answered this ultimatum as it should have been answered; would, in fact, have been delighted at the opportunity. So, too, could and would Hepsibah Ellis, or others whose opinion of Mrs. Judson was decided and coincidal. But George was a devoted husband. His reply was of another kind. The speech seemed to agitate him greatly and he put his arm about her waist.

"Don't, Cora," he begged. "Please don't talk like that. You—you don't know what you're saying. I like to think— I want to know that you would stand by me whatever happened. If you didn't—I—I—"

She moved from the embrace and turned to look at him.

"Now what on earth is all that for?" she asked. "What does 'whatever happened' mean? You have been acting queer enough lately, and— What are you talking about?"

For just an instant he hesitated. Then he smiled, or attempted to do so.

"Nothing," he assured her. "Nothing at all, of course. But as for Carey's dreaming of ever marrying Emily Sayles, that is too foolish to waste a breath on."

"Maybe. But if he comes to you for money—more money —don't you let him have it, ever. You promise me that, or— well, remember what I just said to you."

He sighed and turned away. "He won't ask me," he said. "If he ever should, I—"

"Well? What?"

"I should say no. I couldn't say anything else."

"I should hope you couldn't. There, there! Kiss me, if you want to, and run along to your old office. I've got things to attend to this morning and I suppose you have."

Carey noticed his brother's odd manner, had been the first to mark it and to be troubled by it. He could not help but feel certain that George was worried about something and he wondered what it might be. Several times he had dropped hints and once, when they were walking home together after office hours, he asked bluntly if anything had gone wrong in connection with business, or elsewhere. George's denial was prompt and almost resentful.

"Of course there hasn't," he declared. "What made you ask that? I'm tired, and I've got a lot of detail on my mind. It gets on my nerves sometimes. I guess I need a vacation."

They walked on for a little way and then he added: "Carey, do you suppose you and Ben could run the place for a week or so if I went away on—well, on some sort of a trip?"

Carey was surprised, but he nodded.

"I am sure Ben could run it," he said. "He thinks he owns it now. And I would do my best to obey his orders. I guess we could keep afloat till you got back. I'm glad to hear you talk about taking a vacation, George. I'm sure it would do you good. Where were you thinking of going?"

"Oh, I don't know. It occurred to me that I might take Cora and go out to Cleveland and visit Aunt Susan for a few days. She would be glad to see us, I guess. She has invited us times enough. . . . Don't say anything about it before Cora yet," he added. "I haven't made up my mind to go."

Nor did he make it up, apparently. At all events he did not mention the subject again. Carey did not urge him, although he might have done so had it not been that he was doubtful whether or not their aunt was well enough just then to entertain visitors. His weekly letters from the old lady—letters which he answered with a regularity surprising in one of his careless habits—were bright and sprightly enough, but in each was a reference to the "plaguy pains" which, it seemed, continued to trouble her. "If the doctor had his way," she wrote, "I guess he would be for keeping me in bed. Well, he doesn't have it; I have mine and intend to have it as long as I'm able to put my foot down."

The summer had passed and it was now September, a beautiful month on the Cape. The comparatively few sojourners and boarders from the city—few, that is, in comparison with the crowds of to-day—had gone back to town, then, as now, the opening of schools and colleges furnishing excuse for the exodus. Carey's bird making was an old story by this time and his evenings and Sunday labors at the Higgins' shop were interrupted by few callers. Phœbe and Tobias could afford to relax their watchfulness. Emily came often, and occasionally, when they felt they could afford the luxury of a "hoss'n' team," Mrs. Sayles accompanied her. Once a week Carey took supper with them at their home. The "talk" was as prevalent in the village as ever, perhaps more so, but it did not reach their ears. Desire was the one upon whom the gossipers settled the bulk of the blame. She was a dreadful silly to let that no-account Queer Judson hang around her daughter the way he did. Nothing could come of it, for he was a pauper and a bankrupt and why she let the girl waste her time that way was not understandable. The effects of the paralytic shock was usually offered as the excuse. Desire must be "feeble in the mind."

Carey finished the dozen beetle-heads, also the dozen black

duck and shipped them to his friend Moore. He and Emily between them had selected the next three individuals upon the list of creditors who were to receive payments when the check came. Only once had he heard from his friend Knight. In a brief note the professor wrote that he was having difficulty in financing the South American expedition. "Money is tight, whatever that means," he wrote. "If I don't have better luck than I have so far the trip may have to go over for another year. By that time you may be able to come along, Judson. Don't *you* get 'tight' on the prospect," he added.

There was little probability of Carey's doing so because of any such prospects as his were likely to be. On the evening of the day when he received the letter he took it up to the Sayles house to show Emily. He knew she would be as interested as he had been.

It was nearly eleven when, after his tramp home, he entered the yard of the Cap'n Jim-Carey place and strode up the walk to the side door. Except on occasions when his brother and Cora T. were entertaining or had gone out for entertainment elsewhere, they retired early and by ten the only light burning was the hand lamp upon the table in the dining room, where Hepsy always placed it for Carey's use when he came in. To-night, however, he was surprised to find the house illumined from second floor to kitchen.

As he entered he heard a babble of voices in the kitchen and, from somewhere above stairs, the sound of hysterical wails and sobbings. As he closed the door from the entry Maggie came running into the dining room.

"Oh, it's you, is it, Mr. Carey!" she exclaimed excitedly. "My, but Mr. George 'll be glad to see you! He's havin' an awful time with her up there. He's been down here two or three times askin' for you. I think he'll be wantin' the doctor soon. He's all upset, himself, poor man, and—"

Carey interrupted. "What's the trouble?" he demanded. "Is Cora sick? . . . Where is Hepsy?"

As her name was uttered Hepsibah came in from the

kitchen. She was very solemn and less calm than he had ever seen her.

"Carey," she said, "I've got dreadful bad news for you. The telegram came about half an hour ago. Carey, I know you'll feel worse than any of 'em, but you'll have to hear it sometime and it might as well be now. Your Aunt Susan is dead."

# CHAPTER XI

THAT was all the telegram told them. "Mrs. Dain died suddenly at two-o'clock to-day. Funeral Friday." That was all. It was signed by one E. W. Phillips, and George vaguely remembered the name as that of their aunt's attorney and general business consultant there in Cleveland.

Carey was at first too shocked by the staggering news to speak or question. Then, recovering somewhat, he asked Hepsibah for particulars. Other than the contents of the telegram she had none to give him. She, herself, was grief-stricken.

"An awful good woman your Aunt Susie was, Carey," she said. "I thought a sight of her."

George, she told him, was with his wife in their room upstairs. "He's havin' one time with her, now I tell you," she added, with a flash of indignation. "Considerin' some of the things I've heard her say when your aunt was visitin' here I should think she *might* feel a little mite upsot and conscience-struck. I guess likely she does. Anyhow, she's behavin' like a young-one and, if I was married to her, I'd treat her like one."

Carey went up to the door of his brother's room and knocked. George opened the door and came out. He was very solemn, of course, but his face was flushed and in his manner, or so it seemed to his brother, there was a curious something which the latter had not expected nor could define. He took Carey's hand and his own hand was trembling. His greeting, however, was conventional enough.

"Pretty tough, eh, old man?" he said, sadly.

Carey nodded. "Yes," he agreed.

"Tough enough. Cora and I feel as if we had lost the best friend we had. She is taking it hard, poor girl."

It sounded as if she were. From behind the closed door came sobs and hysterical moans and outcries. Even Carey, the most unsuspicious of men, could not help feeling a little surprise at the depth of his sister-in-law's sorrow. His own was, however, too overwhelming to permit of the feeling being more than momentary.

"Hepsibah says the telegram gave no particulars at all," he said.

"No. It must have been very sudden. I suppose we shall hear more to-morrow. Well, we've all got to go sometime or other, but I had no idea her time would come so soon. There must have been more to those 'pains' of hers than we thought—or she did either, I guess."

Carey doubted this. He believed his aunt to have been quite aware that her condition was serious.

"Well," he began, dully. "I—" and then paused. Why talk of it now? Instead he asked: "Is there anything I can do to help you, George? Anything you and Cora want done to-night?"

"No, I guess not. She and I will have to go to Cleveland, of course. We shall take the early train—that is, if she is in condition to take it. I wish you might go, too, but I'm afraid Ben will need you at the office."

From the closed room came an agonized call. "George! George!" wailed Cora. "Where are you? How can you go away and leave me like this? . . . *George!*"

George turned the knob. "I mustn't leave her another minute," he protested. "She—well, this is a terrible blow to her, Carey. She thought as much of Aunt Susan as I did. I'll see you in the morning. . . . Eh? Oh, yes, I'll call you if I need you. Good night."

He entered the room. As he did so Carey heard another wail of "George, why *don't* you come?"

He wandered down to the kitchen again, told Hepsibah and Maggie that his brother and sister-in-law would take the

morning train and would therefore require an early breakfast, and then sought his own room. Face to face with the
truth, he found it hard to realize. Yet he had vaguely
feared something like it and now tried to tell himself that
he should have expected it. His aunt's seizure that evening on the way home from the bird shop, the hint she had
dropped during their conversation at the railway station, the
references in her letters to the "pains"—all these showed that
she had been prepared for a fatal, and perhaps not far distant termination to her trouble. And, doubtless, he, too,
should have anticipated it. But he had not; he had been
worried, but he had not dreamed she might die so soon.
Now she was dead, the last of his father's and mother's
generation and, except for his brother, the last of his blood
who had known him as a boy. Ever since he was a baby
his Aunt Susan had had an influence upon his life. Between them had always been an everpresent interest, hers
in him and, in the more careless thought of a child and
youth, his in her. She never forgot his birthday; her
Christmas present for him always arrived on time. And
when his high dreams of a bright future smashed with
the failure of his ridiculous banking venture it was she
whom he had dreaded to face quite as much as any of the
other sufferers from his folly. She could afford to lose
the money invested through him, but he could not afford
to lose—as he had lost—her respect and trust.

Her frank expression, in their first conversation, of the
loss of that trust had hurt. She was always sharp-tongued
and blunt, but she never dissembled and he was sure she had
never said to others more than she said to him. Her erasure
of his name from her will was a relief, in a way. It was what
she should do and, if she had asked his opinion, he would have
urged her to do that very thing. Yet she had not entirely
thrown him over. She was convinced that he was not fit
to be trusted with money, but his attempt at paying a small
part of his Wellmouth debts had pleased her—he was certain
of that. He was very glad he had not neglected their cor-

respondence. Once a week, as he had promised, a letter had gone to her from him, and hers in return had been welcome indeed. Now that he thought of it, she was the only one, Moore and Knight excepted, from whom he had received letters since his return to Wellmouth, and those of the last two were more of a business nature. He was glad to think that his aunt knew of his payments to Samantha Bangs and Letitia Cahoon, that tidings of those payments reached her before she died. At least she had understood that he was seriously in earnest. If she could only have lived a little longer he might have been able to show her more proof. With her departure from this world his small list of friendships had shrunk once more. Friends? Whom might he count as close friends? George, of course—and Hepsibah—and—well, it might be—Emily Sayles. Emily and her mother would be greatly shocked at the news. They both were very fond of Mrs. Dain.

He sat there, by the window, until the small hours of the morning, thinking such thoughts as these. Some of the thoughts were peculiar in their triviality. One was that the "heirloom," the painting of the *Glory of the Wave,* would now be his again. Aunt Susan had said that it should come back to him when she was "through with it." He determined to hang it where it used to hang, in that very room, and Cora's objections should count for nothing. It was his, and, for Aunt Susan's sake if for no other reason, it should remain there undisturbed. Another thought—and one which hurt—was that he could not attend the funeral; he, the oldest Judson, and called, in the old days, "Aunt Susie's favorite." George and Cora must go to Cleveland, of course, and he could not be spared from the office. Nevertheless. . . . Oh well! it was a part of his punishment and he had brought it on himself.

He carefully repressed this feeling at breakfast, where his brother, in his so seldom worn black suit, and Cora T. in hastily improvised mourning, were solemn reminders of a sad occasion. Cora's grief was less hysterical now, but she professed that she couldn't bear to eat a thing, the sight of poor dear Aunty's face, right there where she always used to sit, was before her every minute. She broke down again when the carriage drove up to the door, and her husband and Carey and Maggie—the latter, to quote Hepsibah, a "little mite more human than usual"—were all called into service to help her out and into the vehicle. Hepsibah was present, but she did not offer assistance. Her facial expression was worth notice and her sole utterance as the door closed behind Mrs. Judson was a mighty "Umph!"

George bade his brother farewell at the step. Behind the gravity of his countenance was, or so Carey could not help thinking, that same queer evidence of repressed excitement. Everything he said was conventionally fitting the occasion and he never smiled, but to Carey—who had known him since the day he was born and was accustomed to reading his every mood—there seemed a quality in his manner which nothing explained satisfactorily. He seemed—yes, he seemed, not only excited, but pleasantly so, and that was impossible, for George's affection for his aunt had been as strong as Carey's.

He gave his brother a few hasty directions concerning the office work, messages of explanation to Early, promised to write particulars as soon as he reached Cleveland and to return at the first minute possible.

"Oh, while I think of it," he said. "You better let all my personal mail lie on my desk till I come back. Ben will attend to the business mail, but he needn't touch the rest. I'll see to that myself. There will be nothing important in it, anyway. So long, old man. See you later."

Carey detained him momentarily. "George," he said, hesitatingly, "if it isn't too much trouble I wish you would buy—well, just a few flowers, or—or something, you know, for the funeral—for me. I'll pay you for them when you come back."

"Sure! Sure! Of course I will, old boy. Well, good-by."

They drove off, a distant whistle from the train at the East Trumet station five miles away, hurrying their departure.

Carey went slowly back into the dining room. Hepsy was there, awaiting him. To his surprise her first speech touched directly upon his own thought.

"I declare," she observed, "if it don't look as if George needed a death in the family, or somethin' like it, to shake him out of the dumb fit he's been in for the last month. He's been livelier last night and to-day—yes, and better spirited, if 'twould be sensible to use such a word, than I've seen him afore for a good while. Seems funny, don't it, but I swan it's so."

During the week following the death Carey labored hard at the books of J. C. Judson & Co., enduring resignedly the overbearing nagging of Mr. Early, whose elevation to superior authority had, as Jabez Drew expressed it, "gone to his head, same as rum." The manager's intoxication took the form of petty fault-finding and irritating peerings over the bookkeeper's shoulder, with more than the usual numbers of references to the use of the "scratcher." Also he was extremely particular concerning the hours of arrival and departure and his expression as he pored over the daily mail was a study of importance and responsibility. He did not venture to disregard instructions in regard to the "personals," however. But two letters addressed to "Mr. George Judson. Private," came to the office and these were permitted to remain unopened upon the desk in the inner room. Each of these, Carey noticed, bore the number of a post-office box in Portland, Maine, in their upper left-hand corner.

Carey, himself, received but two letters that week and each of those came from Cleveland. The first came the morning following that of his brother's departure. The handwriting upon the envelope he recognized at once, and with the shock which always accompanies recognition of the writing of a hand since stilled forever. It was from his Aunt Susan and she had written and posted it the evening before her death. It was a long, cheerful, newsy letter. She had been very busy, the servants were at last settling down to what she supposed might be called a sort of armed neutrality; at any rate, they had agreed not to leave: "Which was what each of them vowed they were going to do the minute I set foot in the house and have been vowing ever since." There were a lot of repairs to be made and they were under way. "I can begin to see daylight at last, Carey, and if the doctor *can* tinker up my various ailments so that those pains of mine don't happen around about every other twenty-four hours, which they have developed a miserable habit of doing ever since I landed here from Wellmouth, I shall think there is Balm in Gilead, after all." At the bottom of the fifth page she wrote: "I must tell you how pleased I was to have you write me of your calls on Erastus Bangs' widow and that other woman. I laughed over your story of her and her tracts until I began to be afraid I should have a pain in a new place, and that would be what my cook would call 'super-*floo*us.' I must say, Carey, that your grit in carrying the thing through and, more than all, writing me that you intend to go on with it, pleased me very, very much. I am beginning to change my mind about you, Carey. Yes, and I *have* changed it decidedly in another respect, and, as you may learn some day just as I have, about some other people. There must be considerable Judson in you, after all, even if there is precious little 'banker.'"

He read the less intimate portion of this letter to Emily that evening, when he called at the Sayles' house. Emily and her mother, the latter especially, felt Mrs. Dain's death keenly. Desire and Susan were girlhood friends and had kept up the friendship ever since. Carey learned, and was surprised to learn, that his aunt had written Mrs. Sayles several times since her return to Cleveland.

"There was a good deal about you in those letters, Carey," confided Desire. "Nothing that you would be ashamed to read, either."

Emily, it appeared, had not read the letters herself. "Mother read me parts of them," declared the young lady, "but, for some reason or other she never let me read them nor her own replies. I am beginning to think I am discussed in those letters just as you are, Carey. Mother, of course, is a hen with one chicken and it looks as if you were the closest to a chick which Mrs. Dain had under her wing. So they talked us over between them. Old people are like that, I suppose. Not that mother is really old, of course."

The second letter, which arrived late in the week, was from George. It supplied the hitherto missing details of Aunt Susan's death. "Angina pectoris," wrote George, "just as you and I suspected. Her heart had been in shaky condition for a long while, and she must have suffered a great deal. She was plucky and never talked about it. She always reminded me of father, in so many ways; I have heard you say the same thing. She had a streak of stubbornness in her make-up. That would account for her turning against you as she did after your hard luck. I am awfully sorry about that, old boy, but you can always count on me to see that you have an easy berth. You know it, don't you? And I think you may ease your mind with the thought that the old lady softened towards you a little bit toward the end. She said, for her, some pretty decent things about you before she left us to come out here."

There were particulars of the funeral, which was a large one, and then some rather irritable comment concerning delay in the settlement of the estate.

"Phillips, her lawyer," wrote George, "is sick. He had been under the weather for weeks, and the shock of Aunt Susie's death knocked him out completely. He managed to send us that telegram and then collapsed. Couldn't even come to the funeral. Cora and I hoped that the will might be probated and a general settlement at least started while we were here, but it looks as if it couldn't be. We shall have to come home in a day or two, I guess, and wait until Phillips is up and about again before attending to the rest of it. Then I shall probably have to make another trip. It is too bad, and a confounded nuisance. I suppose things are going well at the office. I get daily bulletins from Ben. He hasn't opened my personal mail, has he? Of course there may not be any, but, if there is, see that he keeps his paws off. Cora, poor woman, is still pretty badly shaken. Her nerves are on the tremolo most of the time and I have my hands full with her."

On Saturday came another telegram announcing that the Judsons would arrive in Wellmouth on Monday. They did so and Carey stole sufficient time from the office to meet them at the station. Cora T.'s outfit of deep mourning was brand-new and complete by this time. George, also, was still in black. The somber shadow cast by Mrs. Judson had the effect of making her brother-in-law, in his ancient gray suit and now out of season straw hat, feel a consciousness of unbecoming irreverence. He had not bought new clothes because of the expense. Then, too, he remembered some observations of his aunt's concerning the trappings of grief.

George went directly to the office after dinner. The first thing he did upon arriving there, so Carey noticed, was to go into the inner room and open and read the two letters upon his desk. Whatever their contents they did not seem to depress him greatly. In fact his manner was surprisingly brisk and his interest in all business details keen. His step was as quick and his method of questioning Mr. Early as bright and to the point as Carey remembered them when he first came from the hospital to take up his dreaded duties as bookkeeper there. The glum taciturnity—noted not only by him, Carey, but remarked by Hepsibah—had vanished. The cloud, either imagined or real, which had hung over him for weeks had lifted, apparently. What had caused it to gather, or what fair wind had blown it away, were beyond his brother's surmise.

The second Sunday after George's return was one of those glorious early fall days to which Wellmouth was occasionally treated at that season of the year. Carey went down to the Higgins' shed immediately after dinner. Captain Tobias saw him enter the yard and came out to join him. The captain had a message to deliver.

"I've got a letter for you, Carey," he announced. "I was up to the post office last night and Sam Griggs give it to me. Said it come on the evenin' train and, bein' as 'twas marked 'Important' and Jabez wouldn't call for the store mail until Monday, maybe I'd take it along and hand it to you when I see you to-day. Here 'tis. Come from Cleveland, I notice. Name of Phillips printed on the envelope. Somethin' to do with your aunt's affairs out there, I shouldn't wonder, eh?"

Carey thanked him and took the letter. Ordinarily he would have opened it immediately, but this time he did not. To tell the truth, the captain's curiosity was a little too obvious. He was so very eager to find out what the letter contained that Carey felt inclined not to gratify the desire. He put the envelope, unopened, in his pocket, and spoke concerning the weather. Tobias hung about for a little while and then went into the house to prepare for a drive which he and Mrs. Higgins were to take that afternoon. Carey set to work upon one of the black ducks and soon the letter was forgotten entirely.

An hour or so later Emily opened the shop door. She had come, she announced, to ask him to go for a walk with her along the beach.

"It is such a glorious day!" she exclaimed. "Leave those wooden birds of yours for a little while and come out of doors and see the real ones. I feel like walking miles and I don't want to walk them alone. Please come. The exercise will do you good."

He protested that he ought to work, the bird making had been rather neglected of late, and he ought to catch up. She would not listen to his argument and, at last, he yielded. They walked together up the shore, under a sky deeper blue than any August had shown, beside a sea bluer still and ridged with flashing lines of white. The breeze blew freshly in their faces, the gulls and sandpipers screamed or whistled, the hard yellow sand creaked beneath their feet, the pines tossed green plumes above the hilltops. They talked of an endless variety of matters, none of them important, but none saddening or disheartening.

They walked almost to the lighthouse at West End, then they turned and climbed the hill to the right—Sewaucus' Hill was its name, so called because, a hundred years or more before, an old Indian named "Sewaucus," or Quaukus, had had his dwelling upon it. Old Sewaucus, apparently, had been sufficiently civilized to appreciate a view. From the top of that hill the entire semicircle of Cape Cod Bay was visible, the distant roundings of the Ostable hills lying low to the south and the high summit of Manomet lifting from the water far away to the west. In a secluded gully just below the ridge, where they were sheltered from the wind, they sat down to rest.

Carey was in an oddly uplifted mood that afternoon. He talked a good deal, for him, and most of his sentences were not only begun but finished, instead of being allowed to fade away in the middle as he relapsed into absent-minded silence. A part of this was due to Emily's light spirits. She drew him out of himself and made him forget the burden of his local pariahdom. She chatted and laughed and he followed her example. He was always, although he scarcely realized it, happier when with her than at any other time, and this afternoon he was very like the whimsical, dryly humorous, lovable Carey Judson she used to know.

She sat in the shadow of a gnarled and wind-twisted pine and he pushed the sand down from the bank behind her to form a support for her back. Then he curled his long legs into what looked as if it might be a most uncomfortable knot, and clasped his knees with his hands.

"There!" Emily exclaimed, with a sigh of satisfaction. "Isn't this the most beautiful spot on earth? Or on this part of the earth, at any rate?"

He nodded. His reply was, for him, prompt and emphatic.

"It is—just now," he agreed. "There is no doubt about it. . . . Even the upper Amazon would have to take a back seat."

She turned to look at him, and a wave of the pity she always felt for him swept over her. She laid a hand upon his.

"Oh, Carey!" she cried. "I am *so* sorry you can't go on that expedition. If you could only get that money! Isn't there *any* way you can get it?"

He smiled. "If I had it in hand," he said, "I could not spend it in that way. I have other uses for it, as you know."

"Yes—yes, of course. I understand. I doubt if many others would feel that way, but—well, I am glad you do. When are you going to play Lady—I should say Lord—Bountiful again?"

He looked at her.

"Meaning?" he asked.

"Oh, you know what I mean. When are you going to visit the next assortment of—of—"

"Of my creditors? Just as soon as I get another check from Moore. And that won't be until I ship those ducks. Upon which, by the way, I should be working this minute."

She did not speak for a brief interval. Then she said: "Carey, what would you do if you had all the money you wanted? Oh, I know you would pay everybody you owe, or think you owe, and a whole lot of others you would be afraid you might owe and had forgotten. I know that. But suppose they were all paid, with interest if you like, and you had—oh, a lot of money left—what would you do then?"

He smiled once more and pulled at the lock of hair above his eyes. "That is a conundrum I never have attempted guessing," he said. "It scarcely seems worth the trouble, does it? I don't know what I should do. Proceed to lose the money as fast as possible, I suppose."

"Of course you wouldn't. You didn't lose it this time; some one else, some one you trusted as you always trust everybody, lost it for you. You wouldn't ever go into the banking business again."

"No, no, I shouldn't do that."

"Then what would you do? Go with Professor Knight first of all, naturally."

"I don't know. I might do that—first of all."

"Certainly you would! But haven't you any other—oh, dreams—hidden away in the back of that queer head of yours? . . . Oh, I beg your pardon! Why did I use that word? I hate it!"

"It is a good word. My head is queer, like the rest of me. . . . Yes, I suppose I dream sometimes, without realizing it. Whenever I do realize it I make it a point to wake up."

"Why? Aren't yours pleasant dreams?"

"Altogether too pleasant. It is the waking which is disagreeable."

"Tell me some of your dreams—the nicest one first."

He shook his head. "No," he said.

"Why?"

"Because—well, because you would not think it pleasant."

"Of course I should," indignantly. "If it is pleasant to you why shouldn't it be to me?"

"Because it is insane and, even when a lunatic is happy in his insanity, his friends aren't likely to enjoy his ravings."

"Oh, *don't* talk that way about yourself! . . . I wish you wouldn't."

"Very well, I won't. Suppose we don't talk about me any longer. Or about dreams. There are realities enough."

"But I don't feel like talking of realities—now. Dreams are ever so much nicer. It is going to rain to-morrow, at least the milkman told me so when he came this morning. He said to-day was nice enough, but it was a 'weather breeder' and that a 'weather breeder' always meant a storm before long. I suppose he is right; to-morrow's storm—and the piano lessons I must give Elsie Cahoon—are realities, and to-day's blue skies and gorgeous irresponsibility the dream. Well, just now I feel like making believe it is a dream that is going to last—always."

He shifted his feet in the sand. "I wish it might," he said, impulsively. Something in his tone caused her to turn and look at him. He was looking at her and again, as on other very rare occasions in their later acquaintanceship, she felt as if the mask had slipped and she were given a glimpse of the spirit behind it. She met his gaze; then she turned away and her next remark had nothing whatever to do with dreams.

"I suppose your brother has heard no more from the lawyer in Cleveland about the settlement of your aunt's estate?" she asked.

"No. He has been ill, the lawyer, I mean. . . . Eh? Why, that reminds me."

He put his hand into his pocket and drew out a mass of envelopes and papers, apparently an accumulation of letters, old and new. He began looking through them in the slow, absent manner in which he did most things. She scarcely noticed what he was doing.

"Carey," she said, "I haven't spoken of it to you before, because—well, because I didn't like to, but—there isn't a chance, is there, that Mrs. Dain's death may make any difference in—in your financial affairs? She must have been well-to-do—every one about here says she was rich. And you and George were her only near relatives."

He looked up from sorting the pocketful of crumpled envelopes and old letters. "If you mean that I may have inherited anything worth while from Aunt Susan," he observed, "the answer is that I haven't. Whatever she had George will have, of course.

"Why, 'of course'? You are her nephew, just as he is."

"But I had my chance and threw it away, and a good sized sum of hers along with it. She was too shrewd and wise a business woman to let me have more to throw after it. She told me so while she was here. She told me that she had cut me out of her will, and I told her she had done precisely the right thing. Which she had. . . . You don't look very much surprised, Emily. Probably she may have told you or your mother of her very sensible intention."

Emily frowned. "She did say something of the sort to

mother," she admitted. "Mother did not mention it to me until the news of her death came. Mrs. Dain shouldn't have done it. I can't see why she did. She should have understood you better. She should have known that you were not to blame at all, really. She should— Oh, how *could* she!"

Carey's smile was without the slightest trace of bitterness. "She did understand me," he said. "She knew, and said frankly, that I was not fit to be trusted with money. George will have it and he should. George is the finest fellow in the world. Able and honest and generous— There is nothing too good for George."

"But he is rich already. He doesn't need it and you do. Carey, think what you could do if all that money were yours. Why, you could do anything—everything you would like to do. That dream of yours—the one you wouldn't tell me— might come true then, just as well as not."

He shook his head.

"Not that one," he said. "Dreams like that one don't come true. . . . Hum! Here it is. I began to think I had lost it."

For the first time she noticed the contents of the pocket. The bulk of it he had dropped upon the sand between his knees. One envelope, a comparatively fresh and uncrumpled one, he was holding in his hand.

"What are all those things?" she asked.

"Eh? Oh, those are a few oddments and remainders that I have been carrying about with me for a month or so. I turn my coat into a wastebasket, always did. When I was a youngster the habit used to worry mother and Hepsibah. I remember Hepsy's remarks when she found a few deceased minnows in my Sunday jacket. I had intended using them for bait the Sunday before. . . . Speaking of Aunt Susan reminded me that Cap'n Tobias gave me a letter just before you came to the shop. He said it was postmarked 'Cleveland.' . . . It is, isn't it. . . . Eh? Why, it must be from Phillips, Aunt Susan's lawyer. There is his name in the corner."

He did not seem in the least excited, or even interested. She was, however, very much so.

"What can he be writing you about, Carey?" she demanded. "What do you suppose it is? Open it! Open it right away!"

Placidly he tore open the envelope, unfolded the type-written enclosure and began to read. He had read but a little way when she heard him gasp.

"What is it?" she cried, eagerly. "What is it, Carey?"

His face had gone white and his hands were trembling. He did not answer, however, but read the letter through to the end. Then the hand holding it fell to his knee and he sat, staring over the bay.

"Carey—" she begged, in alarm.

He handed her the letter. "Read that," he faltered. "Read it. . . . Why, why—good heavens!"

She snatched the letter and read it through. When her own reading was finished her face was as white as his.

"She—she has left you all her money!" she gasped. "All of it! To—to you! . . . Oh, *Carey!*"

He drew a hand across his forehead. Then he laughed, brokenly. "It's a joke, of course," he said. "Some one is having fun with me. This isn't—isn't the first of April, is it?"

She did not answer. She was reading the letter again. "Read it aloud—please," he faltered. "If you don't mind. And—and read it slowly."

She did so. It was rather long. Phillips had, apparently, dictated it to his secretary. The letter referred to the illness which had prevented his attending to business and his regret that the George Judsons had been obliged to leave Cleveland before he could make a move of any kind toward the settlement of the estate. He was on the way to recovery now and he had felt it his duty to write Carey this letter in order that the latter might be at least prepared for the unexpected fortune which was to be his. Mrs. Dain had called him—Phillips—into consultation a fortnight before her death. She informed him that she had changed her mind concerning the disposition of the bulk of her property. Instead of making her younger nephew, George, the heir to her estate, or the greater part of it, she had decided to leave it to Carey. And, with the lawyer's assistance, a codicil to that effect had been added to the will.

I gathered [Phillips had written] that she felt you were in need of the money and that Mr. George Judson had sufficient means of his own. When the tidings and particulars of your unfortunate experience in the banking business came to her knowledge, she was, naturally enough, greatly disturbed and somewhat incensed. She told me that you had convinced her that any considerable sum of money would be a hindrance to your welfare, rather than a help, and it was then that she first changed her will and, with the exception of a small legacy to you, made your brother her heir. Since her visit to Wellmouth, or during that visit—she did not explain her reasons to me fully—her resolution had faltered, she had been led to reconsider, and the codicil mentioned was the result. I cannot, at present, inform you definitely as to the value of your inheritance. Including the house and real property I should roughly estimate your coming into possession of from one hundred thousand to one hundred and twenty thousand dollars. This is, however, only an estimate. I shall attend to the will, etc., very shortly, as soon as my doctor permits my being up and about. I write you this letter, not knowing what your plans may be, nor what effect upon them this, as I presume, unexpected change in your circumstances may have. You are, of course, the only person yet aware of your aunt's disposition of her effects. If I may be permitted to suggest, my suggestion is that you keep the matter a secret until the contents of the will is made public. That, however, is of course for you to decide. I felt it my duty to inform you of your good fortune, for the reasons I have heretofore mentioned. I congratulate you, Mr. Judson, and shall await your instructions.

Emily finished her reading. Then she sat in silence, the typed sheets held between her fingers, her face showing the fight she was making to grasp the unbelievable fact contained in the letter. Carey, too, was silent. His gaze was fixed upon the low hills far across the bay, but he did not see them. He was struggling to comprehend—to believe—to think—

She was the first to awaken from the daze. She drew a long breath and turned to him, her eyes shining.

"Oh, Carey!" she cried. "Oh, *Carey!*"

He started, blinked, and turned to meet her look.

"I—I— Good Lord!" he sighed. "Eh? . . . Oh, good Lord!"

She leaned toward him and took his hand. It lay limply in hers as if he were quite unaware of her touch.

"Mr. Carey Judson, man of affairs, I—I, too, congratulate you," she said, her voice choking between a laugh and a sob.

He blinked again, then he laughed, or attempted to do so.

"It—it is a good joke, isn't it," he stammered. "That is, it—it would be, if—if—"

She interrupted. "A joke!" she exclaimed. "It isn't a joke at all. It is the truth. You are to have all that money, Carey. To do what you want to with. . . . Oh, I'm *so* glad! I—I think I am going to cry. I'm sure I don't know why; I feel like screaming for joy, but—but I am crying. Isn't it ridiculous!"

He sighed again. Then he shook his head. "It is ridiculous enough, there is no doubt of that," he said. "The whole thing, I mean. Of course it is a mistake. Aunt Susan told me—"

"Oh, yes, yes! I know she did! But she changed her mind afterward. He says so, here in the letter. She made a codicil leaving it all to you. Don't you *see?* That is what he says, in so many words, and he was her lawyer. She has left it all to you, just as she ought to have done, of course. . . . Oh, Carey, it means—why, you can go with Professor Knight as well as not now. You can! You can!"

He shook his head, once more. "No," he said. And then with more determination, "No, I can't do that, Emily. Even if this is true and—but I don't believe it is. I think the poor fellow is sick and off his head; he must have been crazy when he wrote this letter. Even if it were true, and he isn't insane, then I should be if I took this money. It doesn't belong to me. It is George's, of course. He expects it."

"But it isn't his. He couldn't have it if he wanted it. It is yours. Besides, he doesn't need it at all; he is a rich man. Every one calls him that. He—"

"Wait, wait, Emily. That doesn't make any difference. I don't deserve it. I had money and I threw it away, not only mine but so much that didn't belong to me. George lost a lot through my carelessness, so did Aunt Susan, so did your mother. Yes, and so did half of Wellmouth. Look how George has stood by me. . . . Where should I be if it hadn't been for him? God only knows, I don't. No, it is his, and he shall have it. It is the least I can do for him."

"But he won't want it. He doesn't need it, I tell you. He will be more glad than any one to know you are to have it. Carey, don't you see what it will mean? You can pay all the people in Wellmouth, all whom you owe, every one of them, in full. And still have a lot left. Don't you *see?*"

Apparently he saw, for the first time. He rose to his feet.

"By Jove!" he gasped. "By Jove, I *could* do that, couldn't I?"

She, too, sprang up and stood beside him.

"Of course you could!" she agreed eagerly. "The Wellmouth debts aren't so very much. How much did you say they were altogether?"

He tried to think. "I—I can't seem to remember anything very distinctly," he confessed. "It seems to me they amount to—oh, well, forty thousand, or something like that."

"Yes. Yes, I am sure that is it. Only forty thousand, and you are to have more than one hundred and ten thousand! Why, you can pay those debts, all of them, and go on the South American expedition and—and have a great deal left. . . . Oh, Carey, I *must* cry! I must! You don't mind, do you? It—it is just because I am so happy—for you."

She laughed and cried together, dabbing at her eyes with her handkerchief.

"I know I am as silly as I can be," she confessed, hysterically, "but—but I have been so sorry for you, and I have been wishing and wishing there was some way I might help you— and now this has come.  And I am so glad—*so* glad!"

She laughed and choked and wept together.  He was standing close beside her, looking at her with a rapidly changing expression, an expression of utter amazement and then of growing hope—belief—almost of conviction.

"By Jove!" he gasped, under his breath.  "Emily, I— Are you—are you really so glad—so happy, just because I— I—"

"Because you are going to be happy at last?  Of course I am!"

His long arms seemed to move of their own accord, without conscious effort of will.  For an instant they hovered about her.  Then they clasped her tight and crushed her to him.

"Oh, by Jove!" he said again.  "I—I— Oh, my dear! . . . I—I— O-oh," with a long, rapturous sigh, "I *know* I am crazy now."

She lifted her head to look up at him.

"Perhaps we both are," she whispered, "but I don't mind, do you?"

Then followed one of those intervals usual in such cases. It was not entirely a silent interval.  Much was said on both sides, but nothing of marked originality; millions of humans have said the same things, and will, if the race is to continue, say them through the ages.  When, at last, they sat down once more in the shadow of the dune, he put his hands before his face and, to her astonishment, began to laugh, quietly, but almost like one whose nerves were unstrung.

She was alarmed.

"Don't, dear," she begged.  "Don't!  You frighten me. What is it?"

He dropped his hands.  "Emily," he said, "tell me: I *am* awake, aren't I?  I'm not asleep or—or dead—or anything like that?  I'm not?"

She was still frightened. The question was so impossible yet asked with such earnestness.

"Don't say such things, please," she pleaded. "What *do* you mean?"

He smiled. "Oh, it is all right," he said. "Only it just seems as if I must be asleep, that's all. If I am I never want to wake up, of course, but—well, you see, this—something like this—was my dream; the one I couldn't tell you."

# CHAPTER XII

THE shadows of the beach plum bushes and pines were long and the chill of the September evening was upon them before they rose from the hollow behind the dune and began their walk back to the village. It was Emily, of course, who first remembered that the scheme of creation contained such an element as time. Carey had forgotten it altogether. His state of mind was far removed from all practical considerations. He was still, apparently, not quite certain that his sudden transition from the depths to the heights was actual and not imaginary and he broke off in the middle of more than one flight into the rainbowed future to announce that it just couldn't be, happiness like this belonged to the other fellow, not to him.

"You see," he said, apologetically, "I have been dodging brickbats so long that I—well, I guess I duck my head as a matter of habit. You are sure, Emily, that—that you really do care enough for me to—to—by Jove, I don't see how you can! You shouldn't, of course."

"I think I should. And I know I do."

"You are throwing yourself away, that is what they will all say. Great Scott, what *won't* they say!"

She laughed, happily. "You and I agreed, long ago," she told him, "that we didn't care in the least what was said. And truly, Carey, do you think they are going to be tremendously surprised? I have heard—rumors have come to my ears which lead me to imagine that Wellmouth is expecting something very like this."

"You don't mean it!"

"I do. Mother has been—well, warned by sympathetic friends that unless she were more careful of my behavior and associates I might come to some such dreadful end."

"Dear me! Oh dear! What will your mother say when you tell her?"

"She will be pleased. She is fond of you, and respects you and believes in you. She knows, she must know I have been falling in love with you from the first time we met, there at your aunt's reception. Yes, and long before that. I used to think I was desperately in love with you when I was a girl home from school and you used to condescend to let me help you with your bird mounting. You weren't in the least aware of my devotion; you were far too lofty and superior in those days."

He shook his head. "You!" he exclaimed. "And—and an impractical, moony failure like me! Well," with a determined outthrust of the chin, "if I fail again it won't be for lack of trying to succeed. But I know what will be said. They will say I am after your money and that you have taken me to support."

She smiled and pressed his arm. "You forget, dear," she said. "That is exactly what they won't say. You are the one with money and I am the dependent. You are worth a hundred and twenty thousand dollars, Carey Judson."

He drew a long breath. "Humph!" he mused. "I keep forgetting that, don't I? Yes—yes, I suppose it must be true, if that man Phillips isn't off his head. But, my girl, I'm afraid there won't be much left after my debts are paid. . . . I must pay them."

"I want you to pay them. And there will be a good deal left. And even if there weren't it would make no difference. You and I could get along somehow. And you are going to succeed. I am sure of it. We shall have to wait, of course, but when you come back from South America Professor Knight will find something for you to do; I know he will. By that time you will have shown him what a wonderful naturalist you are and he will never let you leave him. Wait and see."

There was more of this, much more, with occasional lapses into the reality of the immediate future and its problems. Ever looming large in Carey's mind was the disappointment in store for George when he should learn that his older brother, and not he, was to inherit the Dain thousands.

"I am afraid George may feel hard toward me," he said. "He has expected that money and he may feel that I am to blame in some way, that I influenced Aunt Susan against him. I wish she had, at least, shared equally between us."

"No, indeed," she protested, stoutly. "George has plenty of money, he doesn't need this. He cares so much for you and he is almost as unselfish as you are; not quite, no one could be that. He will be surprised, of course, but, after the first surprise is over, he will be delighted. He is a good man and a good brother."

"There never was a better. Well—yes, I think possibly George may be glad, for my sake. But Cora—her joy won't be overwhelming. Whew! I dread meeting her after that will is made public."

Emily frowned. "I *hope* you won't mind what *she* says," she declared. "I don't like her at all. Neither does mother. And there are very few who do. Your Aunt Susan had decided opinions concerning that woman, and I have heard her express them."

Among the few matter-of-fact items discussed during that slow walk in the gathering shadows was the question as to whether or not Carey should tell his brother of the letter from Phillips. It was decided to tell no one for the present. Nothing was to be gained by premature disclosures; wait until the will was opened, counseled Emily. Carey agreed that this was best.

"I guess I am a coward," he said, "but, dearest, I think I should like to put off the storm as long as possible. Even if this—this clear sky of ours is what your milkman said to-day's sunshine was, a 'weather breeder,' I want to make it last as long as it will. It is decidedly unusual for me and—and I keep reaching for an umbrella. My Wellmouth debts paid, and a stake in the bank—and you to work for! Whew! What was it the old woman in the Mother Goose verse said: 'Mercy me! Can this be I?' Something to that effect."

It was long after supper time when he entered the sitting room of the Cap'n Jim-Carey place. George and Cora were there, the former smoking his after-supper cigar and his wife reading a romance by E. P. Roe. She looked up from the page and her greeting was strongly flavored with sarcasm.

"Well!" she observed, with an air of surprise. "You've come home, haven't you? And so early! We began to think you were taking another night out. We had counted on your eating supper with us; I don't remember your saying anything about being invited somewhere else. But of course you shouldn't be expected to take that trouble on our account. Who were the lucky ones this time; the Higginses?"

Carey, who had only that minute remembered that supper was supposed to be a part of the average daily routine, was conscience-stricken.

"I—I—" he faltered. "I am awfully sorry, Cora. You see—"

His sister-in-law interrupted.

"It was the Higginses, wasn't it?" she asked again. "Phœbe must be planning to take boarders next summer. I suppose she wants to get used to having company at table."

Carey shook his head. "Why no," he confessed. "I did not have supper with the Higginses. They were away. As a matter of fact, I—"

Once more Mrs. Judson broke in upon the unfinished sentence.

"*What!*" she exclaimed. "Why, good gracious me! Was it the Sayleses *again?* Well, well! George," with a significant glance at her husband, "this is getting serious. No wonder people are saying. . . . Hum! well, no wonder."

This was so close to the truth, although in one way far from it, that Carey reddened, became more confused and appeared quite as guilty as he felt.

"I haven't had supper at all," he blurted, desperately. "I—I forgot all about it. I am dreadfully sorry. It is all right, though; I am not a bit hungry."

Cora T. straightened in her chair. "O-oh!" she said. "Oh, I see! Well, in that case, if you didn't care enough about it to remember it, I suppose it doesn't make any difference—except perhaps to those who took the trouble to get it ready for you. *They* might be a little put out, but that doesn't matter, of course."

George, who had been fidgeting and puffing nervously at his cigar, put in a word.

"There, there, Cora!" he said. "Of course it doesn't matter. Hepsy's kept your supper for you, Carey. Go out and see her; she'll fix you up."

Carey thankfully departed to the kitchen, the sound of Mrs. Judson's prodigious sniff accompanying him to the door. After his exit the lady turned to her husband.

"He *has* been with that Sayles girl, even if he didn't stay for supper," she announced. "Did you see how red he got and how foolish he looked when I mentioned her name? Well, whatever happens there you can't say I didn't warn you, George Judson. The whole town is chattering about it. I should *think* Desire Sayles would have more sense than to let it go on, even if her daughter *is* weak in the head."

Carey, although conscious of a tremendous pull in the direction of the Sayles' dwelling, fought against it and remained at home that evening, going to his own room very soon after finishing the supper Hepsibah had kept warm for him. Knowing what he knew and that George and Cora did not yet know, he could not remain with them. Each time that his brother's eye met his he felt as if the secret—or pair of secrets—must be written plain upon his face. He went to bed shortly after nine, but his brain was in too great a whirl for sleep. The amazing revolution in his life—the complete overturn in all his plans for the future—more than all, the paralyzing fact that Emily Sayles really loved him, was willing to marry him, and that that marriage was now a sane, human possibility—why, yes, a certainty—all these were miracles. They could not be true—but they were. He could pay every debt he owed in Wellmouth. He could—there was a chance that he might give up bookkeeping and work openly and whole-heartedly at his birds or something like that. He could be a free, respected and self-respecting member of society once more. He—*he*, queer Carey Judson, could marry the most wonderful girl in the world, marry and, perhaps, have children of his own—live and be like other men. *He* could! And Emily had said—he repeated every word she had said to him during those glorious hours behind the sand dune. Then he sprang out of bed and paced up and down the room, trying to grasp it all, to comprehend.

Only the thought that his brother might consider himself unfairly treated kept drifting in to mar his ecstasy.

At the office next day his use of the scratcher became so frequent that Mr. Early's remonstrance was more than a hint. The perturbed Benjamin crept up behind him during one furious scratching and Carey was made aware of his presence by a hissing intake of breath close to his ear.

"That isn't—isn't *another* mistake, is it, Carey?" queried the manager, in agonized entreaty. "I—I hope not."

Carey turned his head. "Eh?" he asked. "Oh, no! It is the same one, Ben. I have made it again, that's all. I'll get it right eventually, if the paper is thick enough."

Mr. Early's irritation got the better of his usual diplomatic heed to the fact that the bookkeeper was his employer's brother.

"We shall have to buy you another one of those things, I guess," he observed, tartly, referring to the scratcher. "That one must be worn out by this time."

Carey's reply was as serene as the weather of the day before.

"Not a bad idea, Ben," he agreed heartily. "Sometimes I make two mistakes at once and it might save time if I could dig with both hands."

That evening, after supper, he went straight to the Sayles' homestead. The hour was earlier than that of his usual calls and he was quite aware that his progress was observed from many neighboring watch towers. He did not care in the least. The time was approaching when he would set the beacons burning from one end of Wellmouth to the other. *How* they would talk when they knew—all! He laughed aloud as he strode up the walk, and the smile was still upon his lips when Emily opened the door to admit him.

In the little hall she whispered—after more important whisperings on both sides—that she had not yet told her mother their great secret. "And I haven't told her of your aunt's leaving you the money, Carey," she added. "I thought, perhaps, it might be as well to wait until the will was made public. Then we can tell the whole story and mother can hear all the good news at once. She must be told first of all, of course."

After Mrs. Sayles had retired they sat together upon the sofa in the sitting room talking of the future, of his debts and their payment, of the probability of his joining the South American expedition—Emily insisted that it was a certainty and would not listen to any doubts or misgivings on his part—of possibilities of employment afterward, work which was to be of the sort he loved and for which he was fitted. "With Professor Knight somewhere," she said. "He will find it for you, Carey; I know he will." The subject of marriage was touched upon but vaguely, for, first of all, so she declared, he must think of his career and the success, which would come when he was once established in his profession. "We must wait until you find the opportunity you are sure to find, dear," she counseled. "Then—well, then we can be together. There is so much to be thought of before that. Even if everything else were settled and assured I could not leave mother now. Perhaps, by and by, she may be well and strong enough to go with us, wherever we may go—to live, you know, but at present that is out of the question. We must be patient and wait. Perhaps the waiting won't be so very long."

Once he expressed the dread which was always in his mind, the fear that his brother might consider himself illused and that the affection which had always existed between them might be shattered, or at least impaired.

"I don't feel right about taking all that money, Emily," he confessed. "I try to see it as you do, and I suppose that George is well-to-do and doesn't need Aunt Susan's hundred thousand, but—well, I know he has expected it, and that every one will feel that he should have it. He has always been so straight and honest and capable. He hasn't wasted his substance in—in riotous banking. Father always gave me the best of everything—yes, and a larger share than he ever gave George. I know that and so does every one else, I was the spoiled favorite. Oh, I know it! I have heard it said often enough. And it is true. Now—"

She interrupted. "Don't!" she protested. "You mustn't talk so. George will be the gladdest of all when he knows that, after all your trouble, at last you are to have a bit of good fortune. He will; but even if he shouldn't be, if at first he may be—well, just a little disappointed, you must not allow that to influence you. It is right, absolutely right that you should have your aunt's money. She wanted you to have it, she took care—as ill as she must have been—to make sure that you were to have it. It means practically nothing to your brother and everything in the world to you. Carey, dear, I want you to promise me this: You will not permit anything—anything or anybody—to persuade you against accepting Mrs. Dain's legacy. This isn't for my sake. For myself I don't care at all. If you were as poor as poverty I should still be just as happy as I am this minute. It is you I want. But for your own sake you must take the chance which has come to you. Promise me you will take it and never think of doing anything else. Promise."

He sighed, but he promised. "I will—because you want me to," he said.

"Give me your word of honor that nothing George, or his wife, may say or do will make you change your mind."

He hesitated. "My word of honor, then," he said, gravely, after a moment. "It is going to be hard, but—I suppose you are right. It does seem as if that was what Aunt Susan wanted. . . . Very well, it is settled. Now let's talk about something pleasant."

There was much that was pleasant—very much—and they talked of it until eleven o'clock. At the door Emily whispered:

"Carey, there is just one thing I want you to tell me you are sure of. I have made you promise to accept this inheritance from your aunt. I have insisted upon it. Tell me that you don't think—tell me, you *know* I am not in the least interested in the money for its own sake. I am not! Oh, I am not! It is just for you and what it means for you. Tell me you are sure of that."

He did tell her, of course, and tried to make the telling convincing.

"It seems a little superfluous, all this, doesn't it, dearest?" he asked, with a happy laugh. "By the time those Wellmouth debts are paid, and if I do go with Big Jack, there won't be enough of Aunt Susan's money left to worry about. Some, perhaps, but not much."

"I hope there won't be. I do truly hope so. Carey, I— I want you to believe this: If you had asked me to marry you that every first evening when we met at the reception, I think—I think I should have said yes. And if you had asked me after I heard, from others, the news of your being a wealthy man I—I doubt if I should have said it. I might—perhaps I couldn't have helped saying it—but I should have tried to say no. I should have been ashamed to say anything else. You see—well, you see, when you did ask me, I—I was so happy for your sake, that—oh, it just happened, didn't it?"

He held her close. "That was my lucky day," he vowed. "I don't remember that I did ask you, so far as that goes. I certainly shouldn't have dared do such a wildly outrageous thing if I had remembered what I was doing or—or who I was—or what you were, I guess, as you say, it just happened. You are sure you are not sorry that it did?"

Well . . . it was half past eleven when the Sayles' gate swung shut behind him.

The next morning he and his brother walked together, as usual, down to the office of J. C. Judson & Co. George was, as he had been of late, in good humor and he chatted of this and that. It was Carey who had little to say. The storm, foretold by the milkman, seemed still far removed; the sky was as clear and the sunshine as bright as on the Sunday which had been tagged a "weather breeder." George commented upon the fact.

"Gorgeous weather, isn't it?" he observed. "All the old salts have been prophesying that we are going to pay for it pretty soon. Jabez Drew has been issuing bulletins for a week and the better the day the blacker his prophecies. Jabez vows he never saw a stretch of weather like this at this time of the year without a hurricane or a typhoon, or some other upset following in its wake. He says the 'equinoctial gale' is about due and that we can expect it to heave in sight at any minute. That 'equinoctial' is the shiftiest storm on record, it seems to me, but all the old-timers swear by it. It never shows up according to schedule, but that doesn't shake their faith in the least. If it doesn't come one week they wait until the next and if it doesn't come then they wait until it does and then declare they prophesied it just the same. Father used to be always on the lookout for the equinoctial; don't you remember?"

Carey absently agreed that he did remember. His brother nodded.

"Of course you do," he said. "It comes from the deep sea training, I suppose. When a sea captain has a stretch of fair wind and blue water he is certain that it is too good to last and is on the lookout for squalls ahead. Father used to say that he was always suspicious when there was nothing but smooth sea under his bows for more than three days running. 'When the glass is high that's the time to watch it,' was his pet word. That is true enough, maybe, but it works the other way sometimes. I've seen all creation as black as the devil and then have it clear away just when I was ready to give up hope. . . . Indeed I have!"

The concluding sentence was emphatic and accompanied with a long drawn breath expressive of what seemed to be relief. Carey looked at him in surprise. George caught the look and slapped him on the back.

"So don't you get to worrying about the 'equinoctial,' old man," he said. "I've come to believe that there is just as much truth in that other motto, that about its being darkest just before sunrise, or whatever it is. . . . Well, here we are. Wonder if we beat Ben again this morning."

They had not. Mr. Early was already behind the bookkeeper's desk, looking over and assorting the mail which Jabez Drew, always the earliest of the early birds, had brought down from the post office. Jabez was outside by the door, and George lingered to speak with him concerning a shipment of fish which was scheduled to leave for Boston that day. Carey entered alone, and after hanging his hat on the rack joined the manager behind the desk.

"Well, Benjamin," he observed, "glad to see you so serene and smiling after last evening's dissipation. Anything important from Uncle Sam?"

The "dissipation" had been a sociable at Mr. Bagness' church. Mr. Early looked annoyed. The flippancy of the greeting and question was a shock to his dignity, a dignity which, to be honest, the bookkeeper was in the habit of shocking rather frequently.

"Oh—ah—good morning, Carey," he said, shortly; adding, "No, I never let *my* dissipations, as you call them, keep me from getting to work on time. Never. Of course *I* don't happen to be a relation of the firm, though. . . . Humph! *Is* our clock here a little mite fast? According to that it is pretty near quarter past eight."

Carey did not answer. He had picked up the smaller heap of letters upon the desk and was looking at the upper one. His expression was odd. Early did not notice the expression but he did notice what his subordinate was doing. He took the packet of letters from the latter's hand.

"*That* happens to be Mr. George's private personal mail," he announced, sharply. "Of course you've forgot that nobody else is supposed to handle that."

Again Carey made no response, nor did he attempt to retain the letter. In the upper left-hand corner of the envelope on the top of the little heap he had seen a printed name and address. The name was E. W. Phillips, and the address a number in a street in Cleveland, Ohio. He knew, as well as if he had read the envelope's contents what that contents was. It was the announcement, already made to him and now made to his brother, that Mrs. Susan Dain had left her worldly goods to Carey Judson. And in a few minutes George would read and know.

Mr. Early, surprised by his silence, had turned and was looking at him. Now he spoke.

"Why, what is the matter?" he demanded. "Are—are you sick or something?"

Carey might have answered this time, he was struggling to do so, to say that nothing was the matter, that he was all right; but just then his brother, having concluded his instructions to the wharf boss, came into the office. Early promptly forgot the bookkeeper and his questions concerning the latter's strange look and behavior, and greeted his employer with unction.

"Good morning, Mr. Judson," he said. "Another fine morning. Yes, indeed. Ahem! A good deal of mail this morning. I haven't had a chance to look it over yet. There are some personal letters for you and," with a glance at his companion behind the desk, "I have, of course, laid 'em to one side. Here they are."

George took the half dozen letters and idly shuffled them. Carey, anxiously watching, saw him pause and stare at one of the envelopes. Then he put them in his pocket.

"I see," he said. "Well, I've got a few matters to attend to and I'm going into my room for a little while. I'll talk with you about the mail later, Ben."

He went into the private office, closing the door behind him. Carey longed to go with him, to be there when he opened the letter from the lawyer, to explain, then and at once, his own feeling of amazement at Aunt Susan's change of mind, his conviction that she had made a mistake, his knowledge that he was not deserving of such a benefaction. He would have liked to ask his brother's pardon—for what he could not be certain, but he would have asked it. More than all he would have liked to make sure that, as Emily was sure, George's disappointment was not keen, and that, as she declared, he was happy in his, Carey's, good fortune.

The door, however, remained shut and George did not call for him. With a deep sigh he turned to open the safe, take out the ledger, the journal and the rest of the books, and square his elbows for the day's grind.

It was a grind, even more so than usual. Mr. Early methodically and importantly opened the letters remaining upon the desk, assorted the bills and checks, and grudgingly delivered to his assistant such enclosures as required attention. Carey, striving hard to fix his thoughts upon affairs in that outer office and drag it from those in the room where his brother sat, entered and posted somehow, he realized and cared little how. As the minutes were ticked off by the ancient clock and still no call for him came from his brother, as still the latter's door remained closed, his own agitation grew and grew.

It was after ten when the door did open and George Judson appeared. Carey, looking anxiously at his face, saw that it was flushed, that his eyes were congested and—or perhaps it was fancy born of a guilty conscience—it seemed that his hand as he took it from the knob was shaking. Carey tried to catch his eye, hoped that he might speak, but George did not look in his brother's direction nor did he utter his name. Early, who had been nervously awaiting the opportunity to confer upon matters of the daily routine, stepped forward with an apologetic cough.

"Ahem!" he began. "Mr. Judson, now if you're ready, there are one or two little things that—that perhaps you'd like to go over with me. If you ain't too busy, of course."

George brushed by him as if he had not heard. He took his hat from the rack.

"I—I can't talk with you now, Ben," he said, with an apparent effort. "I'm going out for a while. Go ahead and use your own judgment. . . . No, don't bother me."

The last was a command given in a tone which caused the manager to stare.

"Oh—er—well—all right, all right, Mr. Judson," he stammered. "Just as you say. I don't know as there's anything so very important. I just—that is—"

His employer appeared to realize that his manner may have seemed oddly abrupt. He stopped and spoke, but without turning his head.

"All right, Ben," he said, more quietly. "Don't mind me. I've got a bad headache and—and I'm going to try and walk it off. I'll be back by and by, probably. If I don't—why, don't worry. . . . I shall, though. Yes, I'll be back."

After his departure Early turned a puzzled face to the bookkeeper.

"A headache!" he repeated. "I never knew he was subject to headaches. Can't remember his ever having one before. It must have come on mighty sudden and he certainly looked as if he had *some*thing. Seemed to be all right when he came down this morning. Did he say anything to you about feeling sick, Carey?"

Carey shook his head. "No," he said, and was silent while the manager continued to comment and surmise concerning the sudden indisposition. He was profoundly thankful when outside duties called Early from the office. He knew—or felt certain that he knew only too well—the cause of his brother's "headache." Above all things he dreaded the coming of the dinner hour and the family session awaiting him at the Cap'n Jim-Carey place.

His forebodings, however, were not realized. George was not at home when he entered the dining room. He had gone over to the bank at Bayport, for some reason or other, so Cora T. announced, and had sent her word to that effect by Jabez.

"What in the world he went there for I'm sure I don't know," she snapped. "It isn't the day for directors' meeting. I suppose likely he told you, though. He generally tells everybody but his wife. Seems to think I won't be interested in his doings. Do you know what he went to Bayport for?"

Carey was obliged to admit that he did not know; George had said nothing to him of his intention. Mrs. Judson seemed to think it rather queer.

"Didn't he say a word?" she persisted. "To you or to Ben Early or anybody? Didn't he say *anything?*"

"No. . . . Well, he said he had a headache, and that he was going out to walk it off. That is all he said."

This admission, made on the impulse of the moment and without forethought, was a mistake. Cora T. leaned back in her chair.

"A headache!" she repeated. "Well, that's something brand-new. I never knew him to have a headache in all his life. I'm the one that has the headaches for the family. He didn't tell me there was anything the matter with his head when he went out of this house after breakfast. And there wasn't anything wrong with his appetite *at* breakfast, either. You went down with him to the office. Did he tell you then that his head bothered him?"

"No. No, not that I remember."

"I guess you would have remembered if he had told you. He went out to walk the headache off? That was it, was it?"

"Yes. That is what he said."

"Well! And the next thing we hear he's gone to Bayport. He didn't walk *there,* I guess. Humph! there's something pretty funny about all this, I must say. . . . And what has become of *your* appetite? You haven't eaten a thing so far. *You* haven't got one of those all-of-a-sudden headaches, have you? If you have they must be catching."

Carey tried to eat and did eat a little, but every mouthful was a struggle. His answers to his sister-in-law's questions were vague and absently given and he volunteered no remarks of his own. Cora declared the dinner to be about as unsociable a meal as she had ever sat down to and her suspicions at its conclusion were evidently quite as keen as they had been at the beginning.

George did not return to the office that afternoon and his brother spent a wretched session at the books. He tried to satisfy Early's curiosity by telling the latter of their employer's sudden call to Bayport, but Benjamin could not imagine what had sent him there and his speculations were quite as annoying as his former worry concerning the headache.

Carey Judson went home to supper with a dread even greater than that which had accompanied his walk to dinner. And again that dread appeared to have been unwarranted. He found George in the sitting room. He looked pale and jaded, but he explained that this was the after-effect of the headache, which had stricken him without warning. He went on to say that he had walked up and down the beach for an hour or so and then, his suffering much relieved, remembered that he had an errand at the bank in Bayport and had taken the noon train to that town.

"I wanted to look up that note of Sam Hawley's, Carey,"

he added. "That is due pretty soon and, as I told you, I am a little worried about it."

Carey had no recollection of his brother's expressing apprehension concerning the Hawley note. The sum involved was not a large one and, so far as he knew, Sam was perfectly good for the amount. He caught George's glance, however, and, reading in it anxiety and what appeared to be a desire for agreement, nodded and said "Yes." Just then Maggie called them to supper and unpleasant questioning by the still suspicious Mrs. Judson was avoided—or at least postponed.

Supper, as dinner had been, was an unsociable meal. Carey, covertly watching George, found in the latter's manner and appearance no solace for his apprehensions. George was very nervous and he ate almost nothing. Cora T. did the most of the eating and of the talking also. A few moments after they rose from the table Carey took his hat and went out. He was going down to the shop for a while, he said.

And to the shop he went. He was strongly tempted to call upon Emily, but he resisted the temptation for two reasons. The first was that work upon his birds had been very much neglected of late; the second was his anxiety concerning George. He was sure that the letter from Phillips conveyed the news of Aunt Susan's codicil to her will and he was now equally certain that that news had come as a tremendous shock to his brother. There was more than disappointment in George's look and bearing. He had aged years since morning. Even Cora had declared that her husband looked as if he had had typhoid fever instead of just a headache. And Carey had known George, had shared his joys and troubles since childhood. They were far closer than brothers usually are. No, George was hard hit, and Carey knew it. He could not understand why, but it was so. And, for some unguessable reason, he had not yet told his wife of their aunt's change of mind, in the disposition of her property. Cora's attitude toward her brother-in-law proved that. Carey had expected scenes and reproaches and bitter recriminations from her. No matter how complacently and cheerfully George might have accepted the tidings of his slighting in Carey's favor she would have been angry and envious and savagely resentful. Carey, when he entered the sitting room and found his brother there before him had braced himself for the storm; but there was no storm. Mrs. Judson was sarcastic and tartly ironic, but she was always that. No, her husband had not told her the news. He had kept it a secret, even from her, and so far as Carey knew, this was absolutely unprecedented. She might be capable of keeping a secret from her husband, but George had never before been known to hide anything from his wife. The fact that he had done so in this instance was the most disturbing element in the affair.

Carey's work upon the black duck was not at all satisfactory that evening. He gave up trying after a while and sat there upon his packing box brooding and downcast. The dazzling sunshine of his own great happiness was now shadowed by the cloud which apparently had settled upon his brother, the brother who had stood by him through his trouble, who had pulled him to land when he was drifting—where? To suicide, perhaps. If George had not been to him more than a brother, if he had not offered him a home, an opportunity, had not suggested his attempt at paying some of the Wellmouth debts—if George had not done all this—? Why, if it had not been for George he might never have come back to Wellmouth. And, if he had not come, he might never have met Emily. He owed everything to George—everything!

He left the Higgins' yard shortly after nine o'clock and walked toward home. Again he was tempted, late as it was, to visit the Sayles' home and tell Emily of George's strange behavior and of his own distress of mind, and ask her advice. He did not go there, however, and for the same reason which had kept him away at first. If he told her she would be as troubled as he was. Perhaps—he did not dare believe it, but perhaps—it was not the loss of Aunt Susan's money which was disturbing his brother. It might be something else, and until he knew what it was, learned it from George himself, why distress Emily? No, he would wait. He would find an opportunity the very next day and have a heart-to-heart, frank and open talk with George. That is what he would do.

He reached this conclusion on his way home. Instead of crossing the fields as he usually did after leaving the workshop, he walked along the shore until he reached the upper end of the wharf fronting the office and warehouse of J. C. Judson & Co. As he came up to the road he was surprised to see a light in the office window. He could not imagine who might be there at that time of night and tiptoeing to the window, the shade of which was still in the condition in which it had been on the evening when Emily saw him struggling with the trial balance, looked in.

A man was standing behind the tall desk, his own desk, looking over the books which were spread before him. At first, his eyes dazzled by the light, Carey guessed the man to be Early. A moment later, however, he saw that it was not Early, but George Judson. And just then George looked up and Carey saw the expression upon his face.

He waited no longer. Striding from the window to the door he opened it and entered the office.

# CHAPTER XIII

THE door opened quietly, but the sound of Carey's step and the rush of air accompanying his entrance caused George, whose head was again bent over the books and papers upon the desk, to look up with a start. He caught his breath with a gasp and his hand shot forward as if to hide one of those papers. He was pale, his eyes were bloodshot, and upon his face was that same expression which Carey had noticed there when he peeped beneath the window shade. He stared for an instant and then, the tension of his attitude relaxed as he recognized his brother.

"Oh!" he exclaimed, in evident relief. "It's you, eh?"

Carey crossed the room and stepped behind the desk.

"George," he asked, "what are you doing here?"

George's hand drew the paper which it partially concealed nearer to him and farther away from the side upon which Carey was standing. Carey caught a momentary glimpse of it as he did so and saw that it was a large sheet covered with lines of figures, figures which meant nothing to him. He paid no attention to it, however. His eyes were fixed upon his brother's face.

"George," he persisted, "what is it? What is the matter? What are you doing down here at this time of night?"

George, the sheet of paper now hidden by his right arm, tried to smile and to appear at ease, but the attempt was ghastly.

"Why, nothing, nothing," he said, hurriedly. "I—I wanted to do a little figuring, that's all and—and I couldn't do it to-day—that headache, you know—and—and so I thought I would—I would—"

He left the attempt at explanation unfinished. Carey's gaze was still fixed upon his face and he turned away.

"What are you staring at me like that for?" he demanded, irritably. "And what are you doing here, yourself? . . . Eh?" with sudden anxiety. "Cora didn't send you, did she? She doesn't know where I am?"

"No. At least she doesn't know it from me. I haven't seen her since supper time."

"Then who sent you down here after me? Who told you I was here?"

"No one told me. I have been down at Cap'n Higgins', working on my birds, and I walked home the long way, that's all. I saw you here alone—that window shade is only partly down—and I came in. That is why I happen to be here."

George drew his left hand across his forehead. "Oh— oh, I see!" he muttered. "Well—well, all right. I'm tired and nervous, I guess, and— Oh, clear out and don't bother me, Carey. I'll be home pretty soon. Don't tell Cora you saw me here. She'll ask a lot of questions and—what's the use? Go away, will you, like a good fellow."

Carey did not move. Instead he remained where he was, looking his brother straight in the eye. George attempted to meet the look for a moment, but again he could not do so.

"Stop staring at me, will you?" he exclaimed, turning once more and picking up a pen. "Can't you see I want to be by myself? For heaven's sake go away and let me alone!"

Carey laid a hand upon his shoulder.

"George, old boy," he said, quietly, "don't go up in the air like that. You and I have pulled together long enough to know each other's ways by this time. Something has gone wrong and I know it. Pretty far wrong, too, I'm afraid. I haven't the slightest idea of clearing out till you tell me what it is. Come on; out with it. I may be able to help you, you can't tell."

George seemed to lose control of the feelings he had been struggling so hard to suppress. He whirled about, the papers beneath his elbow fluttering to the floor.

"You help me!" he retorted, in a savage sneer. *"You!* . . . Oh, shut up and get out! Get *out,* before I say something you won't like to hear."

He tried to throw off the hand upon his shoulder, but its grip merely tightened.

"No," declared Carey, "I won't. Now then, George, you're in trouble. All right, I've been in trouble myself and not so long ago and you stood behind me like a brick. Do you think I am likely to forget it? Maybe I *can* help you. Maybe I know what the trouble is—or part of it."

George faced him now, staring at him in a sudden panic of intentness which his brother had not expected nor could understand.

"What! What!" he cried. "What's that? You know— you can't know! Who told you? Have you been reading my letters? Have you and that damned Early been spying on me? Good heavens, it hasn't got into the papers, has it? . . . What do you mean? What are you talking about? . . . Speak up! Don't stand there with your mouth open. *What* do you know?"

Carey's mouth was open and his eyes as well. The fierceness of this outburst made him speechless for the moment. He had believed that he knew the cause of George's trouble, but now his conviction was shaken. Perhaps he did not really know at all. Apparently there was something more, something far worse.

"Why, George," he pleaded. "I— What *is* it?"

George ignored the question. "Answer me, will you!" he demanded. "What are you talking about? What do you mean by saying you know? Does any one else know? Does —good heavens! does she— Does Cora know?"

"Of course she doesn't. She, nor any one, except you and me, knows it yet—that is, if we are talking about the same thing, George. I had a letter from that lawyer, Phillips. It came on Sunday. He wrote me about—about Aunt Susan's leaving me her money."

He paused, expecting his brother to express surprise, to

make some comment; but he did not. He did not speak, and after a moment, Carey went on.

"So I know it, you see," he said. "In the letter Phillips asked me not to tell you or the family until—well, until the will was made public. I wanted to tell you, old man, indeed I did. I am glad to get all that money, George. I can use it all right; but I did feel—yes, and I do feel badly to think you aren't to have it. You should have it, you deserve it, you know. And, honestly, I can't understand—"

George interrupted. He seized his brother's arm and, leaning forward until his face was close to Carey's, peered into the latter's eyes.

"Wait! Wait!" he commanded, hoarsely. "Is that—that about—about her will—what you meant when you said you knew?"

"Why, yes. Yes, of course. I—"

"Wait! Is that *all* you know?"

"All! It's enough, isn't it? I tell you, George, I have felt as guilty as a crook ever since I got that letter. Of course, as I say, I am glad to get the money. The Lord knows I need it, but I didn't expect it. I caught a glimpse of the envelope with Phillips' name, the one you got this morning, and so I guessed that he must have written you what he wrote me. I have been hoping you might not feel too bitter against me, but of course—"

Again George broke in. If he had heard and understood the greater part of this halting explanation and apology he did not refer to it. Instead his speech was a repetition of the command to wait.

"Hush! hush! hold on!" he ordered. "Don't say anything more to me for—for a minute. I—I want to think."

Carey was silent. George left the enclosure behind the bookkeeper's desk and, his head bent and his hands in his pockets, strode over to the door, opened it, and stood there, looking out into the quiet night. His brother watched him anxiously. For much more than the promised minute he remained there; then he seemed to make up his mind. He shut the door, locked it carefully, and came back to the desk.

"Carey," he said, more calmly, "come into the private office with me. I'm going to make a clean breast of the whole business. I should have done it pretty soon, anyway. All day long I have been trying to see my way through the fog, and you were the only light in sight. I intended to have a talk with you to-morrow, but it might as well be now. You said perhaps you would help me. Well, I guess you can, if you will. If you don't nobody can. And if nobody does I'm gone, that's all. . . . Come on! Let's get it over."

He threw open the door to the inner room and led the way into that small apartment. Carey, his brain filled with a dread of he knew not what, followed him. George's roll-top desk stood by the wall, a revolving chair before it. He threw himself into the chair and opened the desk. Then he turned.

"Sit down," he ordered. "Wait a minute. Light that lamp first. I'm going out to get a paper or two. You stay here."

He rose and went again to the outer office. When he returned his brother had lighted the hanging lamp and was sitting in another chair beside the desk. George sat down. In his hand was the sheet of figure-covered paper upon which he had been at work when Carey first came upon him. He looked at it, turned it over and over, and then spoke.

"Carey," he said. "I've been a fool. I've behaved like a fool and now I'm paying for it. Of course you don't know what I mean by that. Well, I am going to tell you. . . . It isn't so easy to tell. . . . I'll begin with the worst, so you may know just where I stand. I am right on the edge of smash, failure, bankruptcy. Unless I can get money—and a lot of money—inside of the next month I'm going to smash and the old firm is going with me. That's

the plain truth. There! Now you know it. Nobody else
does—yet."

Carey could not believe it. His brother's reputation as
a wealthy man and a shrewd, cautious, farseeing man of
business was so firmly fixed in his mind that even his
confession, made with the deliberate earnestness of despair,
failed to carry conviction. He stared, breathed heavily, and
then slowly shook his head.

"Nonsense, George!" he protested. "Don't exaggerate.
You don't mean it. *You* fail! Oh, come now! It isn't
as bad as that."

George shrugged. "I am trying to tell you just the plain
truth," he declared. "If you don't believe me wait until
the month is up and there'll be proof enough. Yes, I'm
on the rocks and the firm is there with me. The Judsons
are going to get into the papers again and in pretty much
the way they did before. A family trait, eh? Lord! It
would be funny—if it wasn't a long way from fun for
me."

Carey was beginning to believe, in spite of himself. And
yet—and yet it seemed so impossible. He was no business
man, nor did business interest him, but his acquaintance
with the accounts of J. C. Judson & Co. was sufficiently
intimate to show him, or so he thought, that the house was
doing well. Ever since his return to Wellmouth his brother's
praises as one of the town's influential solid men of affairs had been poured into his ears. The old sea captains
spoke of George Judson as a financial Rock of Gibraltar
and the failure of one was no more to be expected than
the collapse of the other. Yet George must know what he
was talking about. His tone, his manner, his haggard pallor
—quite as much as his words—these were guarantees that
he was in deadly earnest. And suddenly Carey remembered
his own suspicions of a few weeks before, suspicions that
something was seriously troubling his brother. Since Aunt
Susan's death it had seemed to him that George's trouble,
whatever it was, had vanished. He had wondered why.

And now—now he thought he began to comprehend, to catch a glimmer of the truth.

"Go on, George," he faltered. "I can hardly believe it, of course; but if you say so, why— Go on; I won't interrupt."

George nodded. "Don't interrupt, then," he said, grimly. "The more interruptions the longer it will take me to tell the thing. It isn't a pretty story and I want to get it out of my system. When a man has made a jackass of himself he—well, he doesn't enjoy talking about it. It isn't pleasant to boast of being a fool."

Carey stirred, uneasily. "This jackass can understand that much," he said.

George was too deeply engrossed in his own humiliation and anguish of spirit to heed. He groaned and then continued.

"Yes, I have been a fool," he repeated. "And yet—yet, by Jove, it didn't look like a foolish deal when I went into it. Looked like a sure thing. I believe yet it would be a sure thing if I could hang on and wait. It hadn't anything to do with the business here—in the beginning. That is the worst part of it; that is what people won't understand. They will say I used the firm's money for private speculation. Well, I did, in the end, but I didn't mean to. By the Lord, Carey, I didn't! I swear I didn't. It—it got me, you know. It just got me."

Carey raised a hand. "Hush, hush, George!" he urged. "I know you well enough to be sure you haven't done anything wrong. Tell me what you did do. And pull yourself together, old boy. Come!"

George tried his best to be calm. He did not succeed, of course, but he managed to tell his story in a fairly connected and coherent way. It took a long time, as he told it, but, briefly put, it amounted to this: A Boston business acquaintance of his, "One of the big men up there, Carey; one of the biggest, I give you my word," had spoken with him concerning an interest he had taken in a shipbuilding company in a Maine seaport city. The present company was a long-established, conservative corporation which had built ships and steamers, wood, iron and steel, for years; the wooden ones for two thirds of a century, the iron and steel more recently. The Boston financier— Carey recognized his name; he had been a friend of Cap'n Jim-Carey's—confided to George that this firm had acquired the sole rights to a new form of marine engine which, they believed, would revolutionize the steamships of the future. They had formed a subsidiary company to develop that engine and, later on, to market it. The Boston man had invested a large sum in the new project. He offered George Judson, as his friend, the opportunity to come in with him and his associates "on the ground floor."

"It looked like a chance for a million, Carey," vowed George. "I swear it did. Yes, and does yet, if I could wait. Of course I didn't figure on having to wait more than—well, a year—for my first returns. I put all I could scrape together into it. I took a good-sized block of stock. It pinched me to get the ready money, but I considered myself pretty well fixed, my credit was good at the banks and everywhere else, the firm here was doing well and—well, I plunged. Oh, yes! I was a fool! . . . But I guess you, or anybody else, would have been as big a fool if the chance had come your way. I'll bet you would!"

Carey, hunched in the chair, his long legs crossed in their customary awkward knot, his fingers playing with the lock of hair in the middle of his forehead, nodded gloomily.

"I never missed an opportunity of making a fool of myself yet, George," he observed. "You would probably win your bet. Go ahead."

George went on. For a month or two everything connected with his venture went well. Then new and unforeseen complications developed. A rival inventor claimed infringement on patents of his own. The claim, upon investigation, proved genuine. To avoid lawsuits and the publicity which was not desired as yet, it was decided to buy off the claim. A large sum of money was necessary and the first assessment was levied upon the stockholders. The demand caught George Judson unprepared, but, through the sale of securities and pledges of personal credit, he managed to meet it. Others, however, followed. The manufacture of the new engines entailed more outlay than had been anticipated and there was a second assessment. It was here that George, in desperation, drew upon the credit of his firm, J. C. Judson & Co.

"I had to pay that assessment," he said. "Had to, or lose all I had put in, and I couldn't do that. They were certain—the men behind the thing, you know—that everything would be all right in the end and that this would be the last payment I should have to make. So I gave the firm's notes. People who knew me up there in Boston, and who had known father, were willing to take my paper and they did. It looked as if I were going to pull through and keep afloat. For a month or so I felt pretty safe. Then there was a third assessment."

Carey, listening anxiously, could not repress an exclamation of dismay. His brother heard it and groaned.

"Yes," he said. "I know. It was like a fist between the eyes for me. I was beginning to catch my breath again and see a little daylight, when it landed. Carey, I don't know how I have looked and acted for the last few weeks; I have done my best to keep up appearances at home and around this office, but I felt all the time as if everybody that saw me must be watching me and suspecting. Cora doesn't know, of course. I couldn't tell her. I *can't* tell her. She wouldn't understand and—and. . . . Oh, good heavens!"

He put his elbows on the desk and covered his face with his hands. Carey, bewildered and aghast, leaned forward.

"Yes, yes, I know, George," he murmured. "Well, she doesn't know, you say?"

"No, not yet. But she will have to know pretty soon;

everybody will know, unless—but there, let me tell you the rest."

Faced with this new and staggering complication he had endeavored to meet it, somehow. He had gone at once to the holders of the notes in Boston and asked for an extension of time. In two instances he was successful, in the third he was not. The holder of that note—the largest —was himself facing an unexpected demand for money and had counted upon payment of the Judson note to meet the demand. That note must be paid when it fell due.

"If I don't pay the assessment,'" George explained, "I might possibly pay the note; but if I let that assessment go all I have put into that miserable engine company will be lost, every cent of it—and that means smash—smash and nothing else. It will clean me out, Carey. And—and I *can't* let it go. This *will* be the final assessment. The Boston people tell me that much is certain. The company is ready to do business, the factory is built, prospects are first rate. This payment is needed just to clear off the debt and start fair. And—and now—*now,* just when I could begin to get back what I have put in, when I honestly believe I might be on my way to making that million I hoped to make, I—I. . . . Oh, it is *too* hard! It can't be. I can't face it. . . . I won't. You are my only chance, Carey. Unless you are willing to help me out of this mess I'll— well, I can't swear what I may not do."

Carey did not speak immediately. Gradually, during this revelation of his brother's agony he had been dimly conscious of the appeal behind it, was growing more and more certain what that appeal would be. And, as the certainty grew, with it grew a benumbing consciousness of what it meant to him, of the answer he must make, of what that answer must be.

He sighed. "Well, go on, George," he urged. "We can't let you do anything desperate, you know; and you're not going to do it. Go on. Tell me the rest."

George went on to tell of his desperate effort to save his

own fortunes and those of the firm. Times were not bad exactly, but they were not good. Business was fair, but collections were slow, and any such sum as he was in need of impossible to raise.

"At last," he said, "I thought of Aunt Susan. She was well fixed and I knew—or thought I knew—that she was going to leave me the bulk of her property when she died. I made up my mind to go to Cleveland, tell the whole thing, lay my cards on the table, and see if she would either lend me the eighty or ninety thousand I had to have or borrow it for me out there. I hated to do it—you can guess how I dreaded it—but I had made up my mind to do it. And then she died. . . . Carey, I don't know what you will think of me, but I swear I—I was almost glad when I got the news. As fond as I was of her, I—I was almost happy that night. It is an awful thing to say—to tell you —but it is the truth. I went to bed that night thinking: 'This will save me and the old firm.' In one way I was sorry, as sorry as you were. And in another—well, I wasn't."

He groaned again and turned away, as if fearful of meeting his brother's look. If he had met it he would have found it one of pity only. This last revelation was not unexpected. Carey—yes, and Hepsibah—had noticed the strange air of elation, of relief, in George Judson's manner that night, the next morning and ever since his return from the funeral at Cleveland. Hepsibah had spoken of it.

Another moment of silence followed. Carey said nothing; he could not. His own thoughts were far away from that office and his brother. They were busy with the shadow that was darkening about him, with the overthrow of all his dreams—of Emily. George raised his head.

"Well," he said, recklessly, "that is the truth, anyway. I don't wonder you won't speak to me. I am as ashamed of myself as you can be; but it is the truth. That is how I felt. And maybe if you had been in my place--if you were in the hell I was in—you would have felt pretty much the same. It is easy to be decent when you haven't any reason not to be."

Still Carey did not speak. George shrugged, and continued.

"Then, this morning," he said, "I got the letter from Phillips, telling me that she had left everything to you. To *you!* God knows why she did it! She gave me to understand that she had cut you out altogether. You may not believe it, but I was sorry when she told me that. I tried to make her change her mind, to leave you a little, anyway. . . . Humph! I needn't have troubled myself. She was playing a little joke on me, that's all. She always liked you better than she did me, and, for some reason or other—one of her cranky notions, I suppose—she never had any use for Cora. Well, she's dead, so there is no use calling her names, but. . . ."

Carey broke in. "There, there, George!" he protested. "She is dead; and she was good to you and me."

"Good to *you;* there's no doubt of that. And I was as fond of her as you ever were. Yes, and did my best to show her that I was. Lord! it seems sometimes as if it didn't pay to keep your nose to the grindstone as I've done all my life, to be honest and work hard and try to do the right thing. What's the use? When father lived I was always the one who paid the fiddler while—while other people danced. Do you suppose *I* didn't want to go to college? Do you suppose *I* wanted to be stuck down here and plug along in the rut, without a chance to make good up in the city like—well, like you? And *I* could have made good there. I could—I know it. . . . Oh, well! never mind. I'm not holding it against you, Carey; don't think I am. And I'm saying a lot of things I shouldn't, of course. I'm sore, that's all. Sore and sick and—and about crazy. . . . And as for making good," with a savage sneer, "I'm a fine one to talk about that just now. People will say the Judsons are all either fools or crooks, and maybe they won't be far wrong. I can stand it myself, I suppose, but when I think of—of Cora, I—I—"

The tears came to his eyes and he turned away again, staring at the wall behind the desk. Carey bent forward and put a hand on the back of his chair.

"George," he said, quietly, "you are hauling down the flag a whole lot too soon, it seems to me. How much do you need to square that note and pay your assessment to that engine company? Eighty or ninety thousand you were going to ask Aunt Susan for, you said. Would that have kept you and the firm out of trouble?"

George nodded. "Yes, it would," he said.

"So you could stay out—for keeps?"

"Yes, I guess so. There won't be any more assessments, that much I know."

"All right. Phillips says Aunt Susan's estate will amount to over a hundred thousand, so you're all right, aren't you?"

George whirled about in the chair. His hands tightened upon the arms and the blood rushed to his face.

"What!" he cried. "What's that? Do you mean—do you mean that you—"

"I mean that with this money of Aunt Susan's you can pay your note and the assessment. Then you will be out of the woods."

"You—you mean you will let me have that money? You will?"

"Of course. Why not? That is what you were going to ask me to do, wasn't it?"

George's eyes closed. He turned and then, to his brother's consternation, dropped his head upon his arms on the desk, and began to cry like a child. Carey sprang to his feet and bent over him.

"Here, here!" he exclaimed. "Good Lord, George, don't do that! What is it? It's all right now, isn't it? There isn't anything more? There isn't— Don't, I tell you! Stop! Take it easy, old boy. Come! I can't stand this."

George raised his head. Slowly he leaned back in the chair and drew a long breath.

"All right, Carey. All right," he said, with an effort. "Don't mind my playing crybaby. I'm—I'm pretty well shaken these days and—and this— Humph! Well, you knocked me over, that's all. . . . You mean it? You will let me have that money?"

Carey nodded. "Certainly," he said. "Come now; you didn't think I wouldn't."

"I didn't know what to think. There isn't any real reason why you should. It is yours; she left it to you. They are mighty few that would, in your place. . . . And," with a sharp lift of anxiety in his tone, "you said—you told me just now you were glad to get it. You said you needed it. You did! That is what you said."

Carey smiled. "Sshh!" he ordered. "Yes, I did say so. Well, I thought I did need it. But I guess—well, George, I don't need it as much as you do. At any rate, it is yours. Take it and don't talk any more about it."

"Of course I shall talk about it. Good heavens, do you think I'll let you do this thing for me and keep my mouth shut, as if it was nothing? . . . Why—why, Carey, you've saved my life, that's what you've done. I was going to ask you—yes, I was—but you can't imagine how I hated to do it. I suppose you've planned all sorts of things you were going to do with this money."

Carey rose to his feet. "Oh, never mind that, George," he protested, nervously. "It's all settled, isn't it? Come on! Let's go home."

George seized his arm. "Indeed we won't go home," he cried. "Why, we've only begun to talk. I want to show you some figures. I want you to understand just what shape the firm is in. You aren't *giving* me this money, Carey. You're lending it to me, that's all. In two years —maybe in a year—I can begin to pay you back. I'm going to pay you, you know."

"Oh, all right, all right, George. I'll take your word for it."

"I don't want you to take my word. I've got the figures right here. I was going over them when you came. J. C. Judson & Co. isn't in so far that it can't pull out, now that you've given it the chance. Let me show you these figures."

Carey's face was now as pale and haggard as his brother's had been, and his attempt at a smile as great a failure.

"George," he said, wearily, "what is the use of showing figures to me? I'll take your word for them without looking. And I never found any one who would take mine after I had looked. Come!"

"No, I shan't come and don't want you to go. Sit down here again. Carey, I don't like this. You don't act like yourself. See here, boy, this giving up the money—for a little while—isn't going to hit you too hard, is it? What were those plans of yours?"

"Oh, nothing, nothing. That is what most of my plans amount to—nothing. Don't talk about them."

"I shall talk about them. And when you speak and act that way I know they ought to be talked about. What were they? Tell me."

"No. They aren't worth telling. For heaven's sake, George, forget them, will you?"

George looked at him intently. His brows drew together.

"Carey," he said, slowly, "what is it? I want to know what you meant to do. Give up bookkeeping, I suppose, and go off somewhere and settle down with your birds and natural history stuff? Something like that, was it?"

"Yes. Yes, something like that. But it doesn't make any difference."

"If that is all, then you can call it just a postponement. In two years at the outside you will be able to do that, or anything else in reason. But is that all there was? I'm in a bad hole, about as deep a hole as a man can be in, but I'm not going to lift myself out by shoving you down.

*You* aren't in any money trouble, are you? Any more, I mean?"

Carey shook his head. "No," he said, with a short laugh. "I'm not. Make your mind easy on that."

"I didn't see how you could be. Then you are just disappointed at not being able to give up your job at the office—oh, I know you don't like it—and play at being a naturalist. Is that it?"

Carey lied bravely. "That's it, George," he said. "I'm a kid, you know. I'll never grow up. I am a little disappointed, but I'll get over it."

"You're sure that's all? Well, I hate to disappoint you. And I hate to ask you to postpone your fun, but—"

His brother interrupted. "That will do, George," he said, firmly. "You know what you've done for me. I know it, if you've forgotten it. Now it is my turn and it is all right. . . . Well, are we going home?"

They did not go home—then, nor for another hour. George, insisted upon showing the financial statement, explaining it, and pointing out his reasons for optimism concerning the future. Carey, coaxed back again to the chair, pretended to listen and to express understanding, but it was all pretense. His thoughts were also of the future, but there was no optimism in them.

At last George folded the paper and put it in a pigeon-hole of the desk. Then he turned toward his brother and again there was a hesitancy, an embarrassment, in his manner and tone.

"Carey," he said, "I—I have asked favors enough of you to-night, but I am going to ask one more. I must ask it and you've got to say yes. If you don't—if you don't I shall be in—well, not as great a trouble as I was before you said I could borrow the money, but in one that is bad enough. One I haven't got the nerve to face, and that's a fact. It won't mean much to you—at least I can't see why it should —but it will mean the difference between peace and perdition to me."

He picked up a penholder and began tapping the desk with it. Carey, not understanding what this new favor might be, nor caring greatly, anxious only to get away, to be alone, tried to hurry him on.

"All right, George," he said. "I'll say yes before you ask it. You can consider it said already, if you want to. What is it?"

"It is just that—well, it is just that you won't tell a soul about what I have told you to-night. If it came to be known that I had been making a fool of myself as I have it would shake everybody's confidence, my credit and the firm's would be down to zero, my other creditors might crowd me and there would be the deuce to pay. We've got to keep it a dead secret, you and I. We have, there is no other way out of it."

"All right. I understand."

"Perhaps you don't understand, exactly. You mustn't tell *any* one. No one must know that you have let me have this money—no, or that Aunt Susan left it to you. Even that must be kept to ourselves—for the present, anyway. It must."

Carey was amazed. Even to his unbusinesslike mind this new demand seemed ridiculously impossible. Yet it was made, in earnest. He twisted his forelock, shifted in his chair, and then shook his head.

"I suppose you know better about such things than I do, George," he observed, "but—well, I don't see how we can keep that to ourselves. Wills are public property, aren't they? They print them in the papers for everybody to read. I have seen them there."

"Yes. Yes, they do sometimes. And this one may be printed, perhaps. I shall try to get Phillips to keep it out of print, if he can. If he can't—well, if it gets to be known about here, you and I must say it is all a mistake. There was a codicil, you know; Aunt Susan changed her mind. She did, that is the truth, but we must let them think that the change was the other way about. She intended to leave her property to you, but she didn't—she left it to me instead. The announcement in the papers was wrong. That is what they must think, all of them."

Carey's bewilderment was greater than ever.

"Why?" he stammered. "I can't see— Why, George? What difference will it make? It is my money. I can do what I like with it, can't I? If I choose to turn it over to you what—"

George broke in. His manner was an odd combination of eagerness, anxiety, and shamed embarrassment. He laid a hand upon his brother's knee.

"Wait a minute, Carey," he begged, "I'm going to tell you why. I—I've got myself into another mess—at home this time. I haven't told Cora a word about—about that engine company or how close I am to losing every cent she and I have in the world. Oh, she knows I took that stock. She knows that, but she doesn't know that I have been ruining myself paying those assessments. She thinks everything is all right and that—well, that I am on my way to being a millionaire. I ought to have told her at first, I suppose. I wish now I had; but I didn't. I didn't want to worry her, and I thought everything would come out right, pretty soon. She is proud and—and high strung—and, by the Almighty, Carey, I don't know what she might not do if she learned I was close to smash and—and had kept it from her, been lying to her and—and all that. You see, don't you, old man? You know her. Why—why, she might kill herself. She might; her nerves are—well, you know what they are. She might leave me. She—she never would forgive me, I know that. You've got to go the whole length with me, Carey. Don't you see? You've *got* to."

Carey saw, at last. As his brother said, he knew Cora Judson. That she would commit suicide was wildly ridiculous. Nor would she ever leave her husband unless perhaps when convinced that the latter was utterly and irretrievably ruined. It was absurd—all this; but it was not absurd to George. He believed it; his worship of his wife was a very real and true thing, the greatest influence in his life. Blind to all her faults; patient and excusing under her domineering nagging—he loved and admired her and indulged her every whim. *He* believed she might do these things. And he was afraid. Carey saw now that it was the fear of her, much more than the fear of bankruptcy and disgrace for himself, which had been tormenting him to desperation the past months. He saw it—but what he could not see was his own way out.

George, anxiously watching him, gripped his knee tighter. Carey felt the hand tremble. Yes, it was real to George Judson—tremendously, agonizingly real.

"It will be easy enough, Carey," he insisted. "Perhaps—yes, probably, no one here in Wellmouth will ever know what is in that will. I shall go, myself, to Cleveland. I think I shall. The people here expect the property to come to me. Cora expects it, of course. She—"

And now Carey, groping for that way out, broke in upon him.

"Wait, wait, George," he urged. "I—I don't see. Why shouldn't Cora know that Aunt Susan's money came to me and that I let you have it? We—we could fix up some sort of explanation, couldn't we? I invested the money with you—say? I let you have it to—to buy fish with, or something. Wouldn't that do?"

"No. No, it wouldn't. Don't you see? No one must know. There would be all sorts of talk. And Cora would ask questions; she has been asking them for weeks. She suspects that I am hiding something from her. If she knew that you were Aunt Susan's heir she would be—well, she would feel pretty hard about it. I don't know what she might not say to you. She thinks—er—naturally, that I ought to have that money. If she learned you had it she—she would say things to you—and to everybody else—and—and some one would find out the truth. Then those Boston fellows—the ones with the notes—would be worried

and—Carey, we've *got* to lie about it. You don't want to
see father's firm go under. You don't want to see me
ruined, my home broken up. . . . Come! for God's sake! it
isn't so much to ask, is it? Haven't I—well, you have told
me over and over that if ever there came a time when you
could get square for—for my helping you when you were
down and out, you would—"

It was the final straw, the one appeal that could not be
resisted. Carey rose.

"All right, all right, George," he broke in. "I'll keep
my mouth shut. I'll try to. . . . I am going now. I don't
want to talk any more. Don't ask me to."

"I won't. I'm sorry it had to be this way. I can see
there is something I don't understand. But—"

Carey's long tortured nerves gave way.

"You don't have to understand, do you?" he demanded.
"I'll do what you ask—if I can. And I suppose I can. That's
enough, isn't it?"

He hurried to the door. George called to him to wait,
that he would walk home with him; but he did not wait.
He strode through the outer office and out into the night,
a night now as black and lowering as his own thoughts, as
threatening and prophetic of storm and disaster as his
future.

# CHAPTER XIV

"WELL!" observed Cora T., as she and her husband came downstairs the next morning, "I will say that, for a man who was as used up as you were yesterday, you do seem remarkably lively, not to say chipper, George Judson. Yesterday I began to think it was hardly worth while fretting myself sick planning meals for you and that brother of yours. And you were scarcely out of bed this morning before you began to wonder what we would have for breakfast. It must do you good to have headaches."

George laughed. "Perhaps it does," he replied. "I certainly feel a whole lot better than I did yesterday, that's a fact. Where is Carey? He is usually down ahead of us."

"*I* don't know where he is. I don't know where he was last night, either. It was late enough, goodness knows, when *you* got in. Seems to me you might at least forget your old fish store when it gets dark, even if you have to hang around it all day. Other business men take a day off once in a while, but not you. You'll take to working Sundays pretty soon, I suppose, like Carey. · Everybody talks about his never going to church and spending his Sundays whittling and loafing down there at Tobe Higgins', I get so ashamed of listening to hints about his doing that, and about his chasing after Emily Sayles, that I hardly dare look people in the face. Why, the last time I met Nellie Loveland she—"

Her husband hastily broke in to ask if breakfast was ready. Just then Maggie appeared to announce that it was.

"Is Mr. Carey down yet?" inquired George.

"No, sir. I ain't seen him."

"All right. He will be in a minute, I guess. We'll come right out, Maggie. Humph!" he added, turning to his wife, after the maid's departure, "that's funny about Carey. He is always up by seven. Don't suppose he is sick, do you?"

"Sick? No! He doesn't work hard enough to make himself sick. If a person stays up all hours you can't expect him to jump out of bed at the crack of dawn. Do you know what time he came into this house last night? Well, I don't either, but I know it was after eleven when *you* came upstairs and he hadn't come in then."

George nodded. "So you said," he admitted, rubbing his chin. "That is funny, too. I don't see where he went after—"

"After? After what?"

"Eh? Oh, after he left the Higgins' place. I hope he didn't get wet. It was beginning to rain when I came into the yard."

"Well, if he did it was his own fault. And, if you asked me to guess, I should guess that Sayles girl might know where he was. I don't know what time he came home, but I woke up and heard the clock strike three, and I could hear him stirring around in his room then. If *I* was Desire Sayles and Emily was my daughter, I'd—"

George motioned her to silence. "Sshh!" he ordered. "Here he is."

Carey entered the sitting room. His appearance startled his brother and, for the moment, caused even Cora T.'s impatience at his tardiness to be forgotten. Her inference that he had not retired until after three seemed to be warranted. He looked as if he had been awake all night— yes, and several nights. He bade the pair good morning.

Mrs. Judson was the first to acknowledge the greeting and her remark could be scarcely called an acknowledgment.

"Well, for mercy's sake!" she exclaimed. "What *is* the matter with you, Carey Judson?"

Carey regarded her, apparently with surprise.

"Matter with me?" he repeated. "Why—why, is there anything the matter?"

His collar was rumpled and soiled, evidently the one he wore in the rain of the previous night. He was pale and his eyes were heavy and sunken. His hair was tumbled and his chin unshaven. George frowned anxiously.

"Are you sick, Carey?" he asked.

Carey shook his head. He tried to smile. "No," he said. "No, I'm not sick; not sick, George, no. Why should you think I was?"

Cora answered the question.

"Because you *look* as if you were sick—or asleep—or half dead, or something," she declared. "Look at yourself! Look at your hair! What have you done to it?"

Carey put a hand to his hair, felt it, and then moved dazedly to the mirror hanging by the closet door. He peered at his reflection.

"Humph!" he observed, gravely. "Humph! it looks as if I hadn't done anything to it. I must have forgotten to comb it. That is odd."

His sister-in-law sniffed. "I should say it was odd," she declared. "As much as that. And you forgot to shave, too, didn't you?"

Carey rubbed his chin. "I think you are right, Cora," he admitted. "I—I seem to have forgotten a good many things."

George's puzzled and anxious frown was still in evidence.

"What is it, old man?" he asked, quickly. "What has struck you all at once?"

Carey turned from the mirror. "I don't know, George," he answered, with another wan smile. "Perhaps it is that 'equinoctial' you and I were talking about. *That* seems to have struck, judging by the weather outside."

The wind was wailing about the house, rattling the dead leaves of the woodbine over the side door, and driving splashes of rain against the windows. George paid no attention to the weather.

"If you are sick," he said, "you go upstairs again and turn in. We can get along without you at the office to-day. Go ahead now; be sensible."

His brother shook his head. "I'm not sick," he repeated. "I was—well, I had a rather mean night. I didn't sleep very well and—and I guess I'm not quite awake, that's all. You and Cora have your breakfast. I'll go up and finish my toilet—or begin it. Don't wait for me. I'm not very hungry this morning."

He turned, and, crossing the room, climbed the stairs which he had just descended. George and Cora T. watched him until he disappeared and they heard his step on the floor above. Then the former spoke.

"What on earth ails him?" he demanded. "He acts as if —as if he didn't know what he was doing."

Mrs. Judson's sharp voice supplied a reason.

"He acts the way folks are likely to act after they've stayed out till three o'clock," she answered. "Look here! You don't suppose he's beginning to take to drink, do you? He might. It runs in your family, drinking does."

Her husband stared in amazement.

"Runs in our family!" he repeated. "What are you talking about? Who ever drank in our family?"

"Your mother's uncle did, for one. He used to get tipsy every little while when he was on voyages. Oh, I've heard my own grandfather tell about it. He was sober enough when he was aboard his ship, but when he got into foreign ports he—"

"Rubbish!" impatiently. "I doubt if Carey ever drank any more than I ever did—or as much. Don't be foolish, Cora."

"Foolish! Well, from what I hear about colleges, there is drinking and carousing enough going on there most of the time. And what do you mean by saying he never drank as much as you did? I never knew you drank at all. *That* is something new. I seem to be learning all the time. Well! I must say!"

Maggie reappeared with another announcement concerning breakfast. Mr. and Mrs. Judson went into the dining room, the lady still talking. She continued to talk during the entire meal. George said little. He seemed very uneasy and more than once suggested that perhaps he had better run up and see how Carey was getting along. His wife sternly snubbed these suggestions.

"You let him alone," she ordered. "If he doesn't care enough about his breakfast to come and get it then he can go without. If he hasn't been drinking, all I can say is that he acts as if he were going crazy. I shouldn't be surprised at *that*. A grown man who spends his spare time making playthings out of wood hasn't very far to go. The next step ought to be the asylum. . . . Oh, *do* stop fretting about him and talk to me before you go out and leave me alone all day. He's all right, or will be pretty soon. A person who stays out rampaging around until three o'clock in the morning is likely to feel queer when morning comes. Yes, and not want his breakfast, either."

Carey, shaved and combed and clean-collared, joined them just as they were rising from the table. He insisted that his brother should not wait for him.

"Go right along down, George," he said. "I may catch up with you before you get there. Hurry! You are late already."

George, after a glance at the clock, reluctantly departed. His parting words were that, if Carey did not feel fit, he should take the day off. Cora did not deign to remain with her brother-in-law.

"I've got things to do," she declared. "There's a church committee meeting this forenoon, and time means something to me, if it doesn't to other people. You help yourself to what you want. I guess there's enough; there generally is."

She flounced into the sitting room, slamming the door behind her. Carey, left alone, drearily stirred his cup of lukewarm coffee and gazed at the rain as it beat upon the

window. A moment or two later Hepsy appeared from the
kitchen.

"My land of love!" she exclaimed, as he pushed back
his chair. "You ain't through your breakfast already, are
you? Why, you ain't ate enough to keep a sick chicken
goin' till noon time." Then, as she saw his face, she added:
"And you look like a sick chicken, if ever a body did. What
ails you, Carey Judson?"

He moved toward the door. "Nothing, Hepsy," he said.
"I'm all right, I guess."

"You guess! Well, you always was a poor guesser. If
what you've got is nothing, then you'd better see the doctor
and get *somethin'*, quick. . . . Carey, you ain't worried
about *her,* are you? Oh, I heard her tongue goin'! You
could hear it way out in the woodshed. She's always this
way when she's got a missionary meetin' on to bile. I
wish they'd send *her* missionaryin'. The Bible wants to
know what makes the heathen rage. If they had her amongst
'em a spell they wouldn't have a chance to rage; she'd do
it for 'em. Between her and that Maggie I've about got
to the end of my towline. I don't know how much longer
I can stand it. If it wasn't that I've worked for Judsons
all my life I *wouldn't* stand it. Carey, why don't *you* get
married and let me come to work for you? . . . Now what
are you laughin' at? If you can call such a sickly performance laughin'?"

Carey turned, his hand upon the door knob. "Hepsy,"
he said, "why not laugh? 'Laugh and the world laughs with
you. Weep—' and it laughs at you, I guess. I don't wonder.
Well, so long."

All that weary day at the office he fought with the
figures upon the Judson & Co. books. Early's busybody
questions annoyed him less than usual; he paid no attention to them. His brother's solicitude was harder to bear
and to dispel. George, of course, was suspicious. He called
him into the inner office and would have questioned.

"I know there's something dead wrong, Carey," he insisted. "Don't tell me there isn't. Look here," lowering his voice, "is it on account of our talk last night? Is there something on your mind that you haven't told me? Does my borrowing Aunt Susan's money make such a devil of a difference to you? Because if it does—well, you know what it means to me, but I'm not altogether a hog. I'm not—"

Carey motioned him to silence. "Forget that money, will you, George," he commanded, sharply. "That matter is settled, and what is the use of digging it up again? I've forgotten it myself. Now you do the same thing."

George frowned. "Forgotten it, have you?" he repeated. "I don't believe it. And I am beginning to believe—Carey, you didn't deny that you made some plans of your own when Phillips wrote you about the will. What were they? If they were so darned important—important to you—that giving them up is going to make you as sick and half crazy as you look and act to-day, then—"

"Oh, dry up, George, will you! I'm—I'm—I've got one of your headaches, that's all. I had a bad night, and I'm cranky, I suppose. Now let me go. Ben is out there, waiting for me."

"I wish you would tell me what those plans of yours were. Maybe I could help them along a little."

"What plans would I be likely to have? There, there! If I am nervous to-day, do you wonder? What you told me about your affairs last night was enough to make us both nervous, I should say."

George looked relieved. "Oh!" he said. "Yes, it must have been a big shock to you, that's a fact. You needn't worry now, though. You've pulled me up to the wharf, and if ever I get a chance to do as much for you—well, it will be done. That is something *you* mustn't forget. Say, Carey, where did you go last night after you left here? Is it true, as Cora says, that you didn't get home until three o'clock?"

"What? Don't bother me, George. . . . All right, Ben, I'm coming."

The dinner hour was another trying period, although

Cora T.'s absence at her mission meeting helped to make it more endurable. In the afternoon there were few visitors at the office. The wind, by this time, was almost a gale and the rain a steady, driving downpour. Captain Tobias Higgins, oilskinned, sou'westered and rubber-booted, dropped in for a minute or two on his way to the post office. He declared it to be Black Republican weather. "Just what you might expect with a Board of Selectmen same as you and your gang put in last town-meetin', Ben," he added, addressing Mr. Early, whose politics, like his religion, were strictly orthodox.

"What became of you last night, Carey?" he demanded. "When it commenced to rain I went out to the shop to see if I couldn't lend you a slicker, or an umbrella to get home with; but you'd gone already. Wasn't took sick or anything, was you? You look kind of peaked to-day, seems's if you did."

Carey, pretending to be very busy, answered the question with the brief statement that he was all right. He was glad when his friend left the office.

The ordeal of supper he bore somehow. But when, just before eight o'clock, he came down from his room and announced his intention of going out, he was obliged to face a battery of protest.

"Go out again! To-night!" exclaimed George. "In a storm like this! Of course you aren't going to do any such thing. Where are you going?"

"Oh, I don't know. Down to the shop, perhaps. I have got some—some things to do and the rain won't hurt me."

"Won't hurt you! This tornado would drown a fish. . . . Come here! Come back here, Carey!"

The slam of the door shut off the shriek of the gale and the rush of the rain. George Judson turned to his wife.

"Well, for heaven's sake!" he exclaimed, aghast. "I believe he *is* crazy!"

Cora T.'s smile was significant. "He is crazy enough in one way," she observed. "There is only one person that can cure him and unless she is crazy, too, she'd better do it pretty soon. I'm far from being the only one who is saying that very thing."

Her husband stared. "Do you mean you think he has gone up to the Sayles'? A night like this?" he demanded. "Nonsense! And he said he was going to his shop."

"No, he didn't. He said 'perhaps' he was going there. *I* guess he isn't. And 'perhaps' he is going to call on his precious Emily, rain or no rain. You mark my words, George Judson, unless she or her mother—or you—come to their senses pretty soon, you'll have two paupers on your hands to support instead of one. I've said it before and now I say it again. It's my prophecy and you can take it or leave it."

George said "Nonsense" again, but not quite as confidently. He walked to the window and, raising the shade, gazed out anxiously into the huddle of threshing trees and rain-streaked blackness.

Cora was right. Carey Judson, his head bent against the blasts, an unopened umbrella in his hand, and the water pouring from his hat, his shoulders and his face, was even then striding along the road in the direction of the Sayles' homestead. All that day, and for the greater part of the preceding night, his imagination had trodden that road and each trip had ended, in despairing futility, at Emily's door. On the other side of it she would be standing, waiting for him, her face aglow with welcome, radiant with faith in him and their future, eager with new plans for the life they were to live together, confident, trusting, happy. And he—what would she say when he told her? What could he tell her? That was the most horrible feature of it all; he could tell her nothing. The bare fact that their dream was ended, that was all. George's confession and desperate appeal had sealed his lips. He could not tell why he must not accept Aunt Susan's legacy. He could not explain. He could not tell even that the sacrifice was for his brother's sake. *For* that sake he must be silent. She might surmise

—but he had given her his word of honor that nothing George might say or do should shake his resolve to keep and use the money which was to have opened the gate of Eden for him and her. She might—perhaps would—guess that he had yielded, but, if she did, she would know that he had broken his promise to her, had lied to her. Well, he had. As he saw it, he could have done nothing else. George's hand had been the only one to reach down to him when he was in the depths. George's voice was then the only one to whisper comfort in his ear. And now it was George who appealed to him for salvation. He could not have refused.

If he could but tell her the truth she would forgive him. She would understand and forgive—he knew it. He had promised—yes; but who could have expected this? She would forgive the broken promise if she knew why it had to be broken. He was sure of that. If he could explain, could give his reasons; but that he could not do. The slightest whisper—George had said it—might mean his brother's ruin and the sacrifice would have been in vain. He could not explain, nor hint. No—no! He could say nothing in his own extenuation. He could only tell her that . . . that. . . . Oh, what *could* he tell her?

When, the evening before, he had left the office, to go out into the night and face the catastrophe the full enormity of which he then scarcely realized, he had started up the beach, walking and thinking. The rain began to fall and continued to fall. The wind steadily increased. He did not heed. For miles he walked and when, at last, he entered the side door of the Cap'n Jim-Carey place and climbed the stairs to his room, he was quite unaware that he was drenched to the skin. He threw off his soaked garments and lay down upon the bed to think and toss and think again until morning. By that time he knew—knew that his riddle was answerable only by one word—despair.

All that long day he had been stretched upon the rack. More than once he had been tempted to write Emily a note, telling her that their love had been a mistake, that nothing could come of it, that even their friendship must end and she must not ask for explanations or try to see him again. It would have been by far the easier way and the result would be the same. Once he even began to write the letter, but he tore it up. No, he must see her. He must go through with it to the inevitable end. She would think him a liar and a weakling, but she should have no reason to think him a coward.

It was nearly nine when he came up the walk to the Sayles' door. A faint light burned in a room upstairs, Mrs. Sayles' room. The windows of the living room were alight also. Emily was there and her mother had retired. Well, that was what he had hoped. He had to see her alone and to have waited, to listen, to have been forced to take part in a casual conversation, was more than he could have borne that night.

The sound of the knocker as it clattered against its plate on the door was like the tolling of a death bell. The wait which followed seemed interminable. Then he heard her step and the door opened. She saw him standing there, a dripping silhouette against the wild background of the storm.

"Why, Carey!" she cried, in amazement. "Carey Judson! What *are* you doing here—to-night? Why did you try to come in such weather? Come in! Come in this instant! You must be wet through."

She seized his drenched coat sleeve and drew him into the hall. He did not resist, nor did he speak. She was too concerned about his condition to notice his silence or the fact that his greeting was not that of an eager lover.

"Take off that wet coat this very minute," she insisted. "It is soaking. Why, you must be half drowned. Why *did* you come away up here this horrible night? Come right in by the fire. Take off that dripping thing. Hurry!"

She was tugging at the garment as she spoke, but he resisted.

"No, Emily," he said.

"No! Why, what do you mean? Aren't you going to stay, now that you have come?"

"No. Not long. I—I—"

"Carey! What is the matter? Has anything happened? What is it?"

He disengaged his sleeve from her grasp and led the way into the sitting room. She followed him, anxious and alarmed. He stood upon the braided mat by the center table, his drenched hat in his hand, the water dripping from it, from the hem of his coat, his sodden boots, running in rivulets down his face to complete the ruin of his collar and tie.

"Emily—" he faltered, and then stopped. She was gazing at him and her cheeks were losing their color.

"Carey!" she gasped. "Oh, Carey! What is it?"

He breathed heavily. Hard as his renunciation had been in prospect, it was harder now in reality; now that she was there, before him, with all her beauty and appeal, all the love and pity and yearning in her eyes, all that was to have been his—was his even yet. How could he give her up! Oh, he would not! Why should George—

For the instant his resolution faltered. Then it tightened again. He must go through with it.

"Emily," he began, "I—I have come to tell you that—that—"

"Yes, Carey? . . . Oh, my dear, what is it? You frighten me!"

"Emily, I have decided that—that all this—this that has been between us is—is a mistake. You and I can't—can't go on with it. It must end—now. It is a mistake. We —we can't. I came to tell you so. . . . Oh," desperately, "don't make it any harder than it has to be. *Don't* look at me like that!"

She was looking at him and she continued to look. And now she came forward and laid her hand upon his arm.

"Carey, dear," she said, gently, "you mustn't do this.

You frighten me very much. Come and sit down. Please do! You can tell me then. Don't stand there and—and— Oh, *please!*"

He shook his head.

"No," he said, after a struggle, "I can't. I mustn't stay. There is nothing to be gained by my staying and—and it would only be harder—harder." He paused again, and then went on, speaking hurriedly, almost incoherently. "Something has happened—I mean I have been thinking and I have made up my mind. I mean I can't marry you. I must give you up. I—I have come to-night to tell you so and—and to say good-by. . . . That is it, to say good-by. It is all over."

She did not speak. She was now as pale as he, and her eyes were gazing directly into his. His own gaze shifted. He stared wretchedly at the floor.

"That is all, I guess," he muttered. "Yes, it is all. Just good-by. . . . Well, good-by, Emily."

He turned, dropping his hat as he did so. He did not seem aware of it, nor did she. He moved toward the door, leaving the hat where it had fallen. She spoke his name.

"Carey!" she cried.

He did not turn, but he stopped.

"Yes?" he asked, wearily.

"Carey, wait. You can't go this way, of course. You must tell me more than that. You must."

He sighed. "I can't tell you anything," he said. "There isn't anything to tell. I have just been thinking, that's all, and—and I have thought it out. . . . I am sorry. . . . You can't forgive me, I know that. I don't expect you to. . . . Good-by."

"Stop! Carey, you can't go like this. What has happened since you were here last? Tell me."

"Nothing. Nothing has happened. I—I have been thinking and—and— Oh, I told you I had, Emily. Let me go now."

"You told me something had happened. You began to tell me that, and then you changed your mind. What has happened? You must tell me. I have the right to know that, at least."

"Yes—yes, you have. God knows you have! I can't tell you, though. You mustn't ask. Just let me go— please."

"Something has happened, then. Of course I knew it had. And you won't tell me what it is?"

"No. . . . It wasn't anything. I—I— You're well rid of me. You will be thankful by and by."

"Thankful! And it wasn't anything—this happening, whatever it was, that has changed all your life—and mine! Carey, has your brother—"

"No, no!" in agonized entreaty. "He hasn't— Don't ask me about him. Don't ask me anything. Oh, don't!"

"I am sure it was your brother. Carey, you promised me—you gave me your word of honor not to be influenced by anything George or his wife might say or do. You promised me that. Have you broken that promise?"

His eyes closed and he swayed on his feet. "Emily," he pleaded, "if—if you care—if you ever cared—anything for me, anything at all, you won't torture me any longer. I— I can't stand it. Say good-by and—and let me go—and forget me, that's all. Just forget me. I am not worth remembering."

"Carey, tell me this: Are you doing this because you don't love me any longer? Or because you find you never did really love me?"

He turned then, and took a step toward her. His eyes blazed and his arms lifted. Then they fell helplessly back. He groaned, and rushed from the room. She heard the outer door close behind him.

She went back to the table and sank into the rocker. Her feet touched something and she looked down. It was the hat he had forgotten, wet, shapeless and forlorn. She picked it up and held it in her hands. She pictured him, bareheaded, drenched, hopeless, fighting his way through the storm. Then her tears came, but they were not tears of anger or a just resentment; they were tears of pity—overwhelming, heartbreaking pity for him.

# CHAPTER XV

WHEN George Judson finished dressing next morning he stopped at the door of his brother's bedroom on his way to the stairs.

"Carey," he called. "Carey, are you all right?"

There was no answer and, taking it for granted that Carey had already gone down to the sitting room, he was about to turn away. Then he decided to make sure. He opened the door. Carey had not gone down, nor had he risen. He was still in bed and the sight of his flushed face upon the pillow caused George to utter an exclamation and to hasten to his side. He laid a hand upon his forehead and found it blazing with fever. Carey woke and stirred.

"Why—why, hello, old man!" he said, dazedly. "Up already? I am late, I guess. I'll be with you in a shake."

He tried to rise, but got no farther than to prop himself upon one elbow. He blinked, caught his breath, and sank back again.

"I—I seem to be dizzy—or something," he muttered. "Indigestion, I guess. It's all right, though, George. I'll be better in a minute."

George ordered him to stay where he was and hastened downstairs. A few minutes later he was on his way to fetch the doctor and Hepsibah was flying about Carey's room, smoothing the pillows and bedclothes, straightening the window shades, picking up odds and ends, and scolding to herself as she did so. The condition of his garments, thrown helter-skelter about the room just as he had taken them off the night before, caused her to wax eloquent.

"My soul and body!" she exclaimed, lifting a sodden heap of dampness from the floor and shaking it into the wrinkled semblance of a coat. "Look at that jacket! Soakin', soppin'

wet yet! And the pants are worse. And as for the rest of
your things—my heavens and earth! Carey Judson, why—
*why* did you get yourself into such a state? Every rag you
had on is as wet as if it had been in a washtub, and that's
where most of 'em are goin' to go this minute. *What* sent
you out of door such a night as last night was the Lord only
knows, and He won't tell. . . . No, no! And I don't want
*you* to tell, either. You keep right still in that bed till the
doctor comes. If you haven't got your never-get-over it'll be
a mercy. . . . What shall I get you for breakfast? No,
don't you answer me. Don't you try to talk! Oh, where *is*
that doctor? Tut, tut, tut! Well, if it ain't pneumony then
we're lucky. The idea of your cruisin' down to that bird
cage of yours in such a flood! That's where you was, wasn't
it? . . . No, don't tell me! Don't you speak! You keep
still in that bed."

Carey had no intention of telling her, nor had he any
desire to speak. The fever aches in his bones and the throb-
bing pain in his head were of themselves sufficient to prevent
his doing so. Worse than these, however, was the crushing
memory of his parting with Emily and the realization that
that parting was final. He had returned home in benumbed
blank misery. He remembered nothing of the walk nor of
his reaching his room—nothing. His night had been one
confused dream after another and where reality ended and
the dreams began he could not have told. Now, awake, he
wished only that he might never have wakened. Hepsibah
was prophesying pneumonia. Well, he devoutly hoped her a
true prophet. Pneumonia was quick and soon over and often
fatal.

It was not pneumonia, however. A bad cold, so the doctor
said when he came, the result of exposure, tramping the
streets during an equinoctial gale. The patient must stay
in bed for some days at least, must be kept warm, must not
worry about business or anything like that, and must take
liberal doses of bad-tasting medicine, the usual prescriptions
of the old-school physician.

George, anxious and alarmed, questioned him when he left the room.

"It isn't serious, is it, Doctor?" he asked. "He looks bad enough."

Doctor Hamlin combed his long beard with his fingers. In those days whiskers were an essential part of the equipment of a general practitioner.

"No," he declared, "I shouldn't call it serious. He does look bad, that's a fact, but so far as I can make out he's got cold and the fever that goes with it. We'll pull him through all right, but it looks as if we should have to do all the pulling. He doesn't seem to take any interest in the job. Asked me if he was going to die and when I laughed at the idea, he— well, I declare he acted more disappointed than encouraged. Has he had any nervous shock lately; any serious trouble, or anything like that?"

George shook his head. "No-o," he answered, thoughtfully. "No, nothing that—well, you do your best for him, won't you, Doctor?"

Doctor Hamlin did his best, but it was a week before his patient was well enough to leave his room and another before he regained strength sufficient to carry him back to the office of J. C. Judson & Co. George was solicitous and kind; Hepsy waited upon him night and day, cooking for him what she called "sick folks' messes," and trotting up and downstairs to bring them and make sure that he ate them after they were brought. Maggie was cheerful and talkative. Even Cora T. was surprisingly gracious, particularly during the latter part of his illness. She was in high good humor then and tolerant toward the world in general.

For news had come to Wellmouth and Wellmouth was discussing it. It reached the town, as most outside news did, by way of the Boston dailies. A dozen citizens reading those dailies in Griggs' store happened upon the Associated Press dispatch at practically the same time. It—the dispatch—was brief and was headed "Cleveland." It concerned the will of the late Mrs. Dain of that city. She had, so the item stated, left an estate estimated at one hundred and twenty-five thousand dollars and, except for a few trifling legacies to old servants and friends, the property was to go to a nephew whose name was Judson and who resided in Wellmouth, Massachusetts.

That was all, there were no further particulars. It was enough, however, so far as Wellmouth was concerned. "A nephew" was, of course—the town took it for granted—George Judson, and he, already a rich man, was now richer by another hundred thousand. Callers came to the house to congratulate Mr. and Mrs. George Judson. The Lovelands came, and the Halls, and others of the *élite*. Cora T. received them graciously, accepted the congratulations with becoming humility, wept a little when Aunt Susan's name was mentioned and spoke casually of a summer in Europe "some of these days, perhaps. We've been talking about going for ever so long, you know, and now I guess we shall. Not that this extra money makes any real difference, but it will help Mr. Judson feel easier about leaving his business." She spoke, too, of additions and repairs to the Cap'n Jim-Carey place which were to be made in the immediate future.

To the Reverend Mr. Thomas, when he called, she said:

"Yes, of course George and I do feel sorry about poor Carey. We did our best to show Aunt Susan that he wasn't really to blame for not being a practical business man and letting his banking business go to ruin. I said to her—over and over again I said—that Carey couldn't help being just a dreamer and absent-minded and all like that; he was made that way and he couldn't help it. But Aunt Susan was *so* practical herself that she could only see it her way. He wasn't fit to be troubled with money, she said; he had proved it by losing all he had of his own and a lot of other people's. Yours, too, Mr. Thomas. Oh, everybody knows what you lost and what it meant to you. Aunt Susan knew what an able, common-sense—what you call conservative—man my husband is and she knew *he* could be trusted with *any* amount. But we shall look out for Carey, of course. He'll never come to want again. Mr. Judson and I will see to *that*."

Other callers brought their congratulations to the office. Captain Tobias Higgins was one of these. He walked into the inner office without knocking, greatly to the indignation of Mr. Ben Early who, having had the duties of bookkeeper temporarily added to his other weighty cares, was busy at the desk and did not guess his intention until too late to protest. Not that it would have made any material difference if he had.

The captain entered the sanctum, closed the door behind him, and stood beside George Judson's desk, his hands in his trousers pockets—his "beckets," he called them.

"Well, George," he observed. "I see by the papers that you've had another windfall. Some folks are always under the tree when the apples get blowed off. Every time I've ever been under there the only thing that comes down is the rotten ones. I ain't complainin' when the other fellow has better luck, though. You're a good square man and you deserve what's comin' to you. I'm glad for you. So's Chippy."

George smiled, although he seemed a little embarrassed. "Much obliged, Cap'n," he said. "Well, what's up? What can I do for you?"

"Nothin' for me, thank you. I generally manage to make out to do for myself and the apples I get I pay for. I came in to—to—well, to talk about somethin' that ain't any of my business. That ain't as common a habit with me as 'tis with the heft of folks in this town, but I'm goin' to do it now. Can you spare a minute or so?"

George said he could and invited his caller to be seated. Tobias sat, rubbed his knees with his big hands and cleared his throat. *He* seemed embarrassed now.

"I just—well, I just wanted to say a word to you about your brother, about Carey," he began. "George, I might as well be honest and tell you that I was disappointed when I read that in the paper about Susie Dain's will. Now, don't make any mistake about what I mean. You deserve all you can get and I'd be the last one to grudge it to you; but—well, Phœbe and I were kind of hopin' that your aunt wouldn't leave Carey out altogether. When she fust come here to visit you and Cora she was pretty down on him. No wonder—no wonder at all. So was I when I found my seven hundred had gone to pot with that bankin' firm of his. So was everybody else, I guess. But after you fetched Carey back here, and I come to see more of him and know him better, I began to change my mind about him. I began to realize that, of all the gang who suffered from that smash, he was the one that suffered most. I began to see, what I ought to have realized in the beginnin', that he wasn't to blame any more than a child. He *is* a child in a whole lot of ways, and a fine, clean, lovable sort of child at that. I've come to think a sight of your brother, George. Yes, I have."

He paused. George nodded.

"I'm glad you've found that out, Tobias," he said. "I have known it all along. I don't believe—honestly, I don't believe there is a better man in this world than Carey Judson."

"I guess you're right, George. Well, he's always said the same thing about you, fur's that goes. Well, what I was hopin'—yes, and comin' to believe, too—was that your aunt was veerin' 'round to the p'int of the compass herself. From some things she said to me and Chippy afore she went back to Cleveland we'd come to think she was. And—well, we rather guessed that maybe she would look out for him in a money way when she died, if not afore. She hasn't and—well, I think it's kind of too bad. Hope you won't get mad, George, on account of my sayin' this, but it's the way I feel."

He regarded his companion rather anxiously as he made this frank statement. George did not meet the look. Instead he turned over a paper or two upon the desk and was silent for an instant. When he did speak there was no trace of irritation in his tone.

"That's all right, Cap'n," he said, gravely. "I shan't quarrel with you over that. . . . Well?"

"Well," Captain Higgins seemed more embarrassed than ever. "Well," he began again, "that's off my mind and this is what I really came aboard to talk to you about. You see—George, I wonder if you realize what a darned clever fellow that brother of yours is—in his way? I don't cal'late you do. I didn't, myself, for a long spell. Those wooden birds he is makin' down in my shop, the average jackass—and there's a lot of that kind of average in Wellmouth—calls 'em playthings and doll-babies and the Lord knows what. Even the folks with as much brains as the Almighty allowed to a horsefoot crab think what he's makin' are just decoys. They *ain't* just decoys, by thunder! They're birds—that's what they are—birds. When he finishes with one of 'em all it needs is a whistle or a quack. Why, George, listen to me."

He went on to enthuse at length over the miraculous perfection of the beetle-heads and black ducks.

"I ain't the only one that's gone loony over 'em," he declared. "That Moore man, up there to Cambridge, you ought to read some of the letters he writes about 'em. And that fellow that spent Sunday in town here a month or two ago—Knight, his name was; his sister used to live up on the Back Road, you remember. Well, seems he's in the bird business, runs a museum or a bird show or somethin' of the sort out West, I understand he does. He told Sparrow up at the hotel that he'd never seen anything as nigh perfect as those beetle-heads of Carey's. That's what he said. Well, now, George, you see—"

He explained his own interest in the work. He had helped Carey to the extent of advancing money for the purchase of a band saw and a lathe, would have done more if he had been permitted. He had offered to go into partnership with him and back the enterprise to the extent of two thousand dollars if necessary.

"He wouldn't let me," he snorted, indignantly. "And I

could have spared the money just as well as not—or I would have spared it, anyhow. The trouble with Carey is that he's just as big a jackass as the rest of 'em when it comes to realizin' how good those birds really are. He 'pooh-poohs' me when I tell him so. But I'm right. Why, George, there's money in that bird making, a lot of money. That Moore alone would dispose of a thousand of Carey's decoys if he could get 'em. Carey can't turn 'em out, that's what's the matter. He ought to have a factory, a reg'lar little factory with steam power and machinery and the like of that. *Then* —well, then we could build up a business that would hum. Yes, sir-ee! hum like a taut jib sheet in a gale such as we had last week."

He paused, principally for lack of breath. George said nothing. The captain seemed disappointed at his silence, but went on.

"That's what I came to you about," he continued. "I didn't know but what, now that you'd got this extra cash from your aunt, you might be interested enough to go in— well, with me, say—that is, as far as I *could* go in—and back your brother with a chunk of that money. Build him a factory, get him goin', and then set on the quarter deck and let the hands pass aft the dividends. It would be worth your while, I tell you that."

Again he paused, expectantly waiting. George Judson was still toying with the papers on his desk. He asked a question.

"Cap'n," he queried, slowly, "do you think Carey had counted on getting money from Aunt Susan and—well, doing something of the sort—carrying out some such scheme as you have been telling me about?"

"Eh? I don't know. If he has he's never said anything to me about it. Maybe he has, though; 'twouldn't be surprisin'. I've preached it to him enough. Why? What makes you ask?"

"Oh, nothing. . . . If he had had any such plans—if he had had any reason to expect anything from that will—he

would be a good deal disappointed now, wouldn't he? . . .
Yes, he would. . . . Humph! that would explain—"

He did not finish the sentence. Tobias jogged his memory.
"Explain what?" he asked.

"Nothing. . . . Well, Cap'n, I am glad you told me all
this. I'll think over your proposition. I can't do anything
just at present. I—er—well, I need the money for other
things; but I'll think it over and some day—then, perhaps,
we'll see."

Higgins was obviously disappointed. He rose from his
chair.

"Better think about it pretty hard," he grunted. "It's a
good chance for you and it would be the makin' of Carey.
And he deserves all the help he can get. Yes, he does. He
won't ask you for a cent, of course; he wouldn't ask me.
That's him, all over. But if either of us came to him for
help we'd get it—we'd get the last red cent he had in his
pocket. You can think that over, too, George, if you've a
mind to."

He rolled out of the office, righteous indignation and disapproval in the set of his jaw. George leaned back in his
chair. He, too, was disturbed. It troubled him to know
that Captain Higgins considered him overcautious at least—
stingy and self-centered, probably. That opinion, however,
he might be able to change in a year or two, when his own
tangle was straightened. And in one way the interview had
brought relief. He believed he understood now the cause
of Carey's peculiar behavior, his listlessness and dejection.
The "plans" to which Carey had referred had to do with
the expression and development of the latter's bird making.
The letter from the lawyer, that which had brought the news
that the old lady's hundred thousand was his, had opened a
way to the "factory" and all the rest of the air castles for
which Higgins' exuberant fancy had supplied material.
George was not inclined to share Tobias's optimism regarding the fortunes to be made by unlimited supplies of decoys.
He, like the majority of Wellmouthians, estimated his

brother's hobby rather lightly. And the idea of Carey Judson as the head of any important business venture was pathetically funny. The new "bird company" could end only as the firm of Osborne and Judson had ended. He was sorry for Carey, very sorry and very sympathetic; but he could not help feeling relief in the knowledge that the wrecking of the latter's plans was not more seriously disastrous. Carey was down in the mouth now, poor fellow, but he, George, would make it up to him by and by. Indeed he would!

He said nothing to Carey or Cora, or any one else, concerning the talk with Captain Higgins. His manner toward the convalescent was kindness itself. Cora T. was somewhat suspicious of this kindness; she feared it might lead to foolish generosity. She took her husband to task on the subject one evening, when the pair were in their room preparing for bed.

"Look here, George," she demanded. "What were you and Carey holding hands about over in the corner just now? What was he asking you to do? I tried to hear, but you both were whispering and mighty anxious that I shouldn't. What was it?"

George laughed. "We were talking about his going back to work, that's all," he replied. "He was trying to tell me that he was well enough to go now, and I was telling him that he shouldn't do any such thing. That is all we were talking about. There wasn't anything secret about it. Cora, what does make you so suspicious all the time? You can scare up more mare's nests than anybody I ever heard of."

Mrs. Judson's eyes narrowed and her thin lips tightened.

"Maybe I have reasons for being suspicious," she announced. "And as for secrets—why didn't you tell me that Tobe Higgins had been trying to get you to let him and Carey have money to throw away in that crazy wooden bird foolishness? Why didn't you tell me that? . . . Humph! I don't wonder you look ashamed. I should think you would. Well? What have you got to say?"

Her husband found it hard to say anything at the moment.

He might not have looked ashamed exactly, but he certainly did look surprised and rather guilty.

"It—it didn't amount to anything, Cora," he protested. "I didn't think it was worth while bothering you with. I said I couldn't do it, anyway. . . . How in the world did you come to hear about it?"

"Oh, I heard! I hear a good many things you think I'll never hear—and hope I won't, I guess likely. Phœbe Higgins told somebody and that somebody told somebody else and, finally, it got to me. I said a few things when *I* heard it, I can tell you that. George Judson, you didn't give that man the least bit of encouragement, did you?"

"No."

"You're sure? You told him you wouldn't do it, now or at any other time? That is exactly what you told him?"

"Yes."

"Well, if you hadn't I would have gone to him and told him myself. Impertinent, interfering thing! What right has he got to say what you shall do with the money your aunt willed to you? It is yours, isn't it; yours and mine? Poor Aunt Susan wanted us to have it and she took pains to make sure that we got it. *She* knew that Carey wasn't fit to be trusted with a penny; yes, and that he didn't deserve one, either. He was behind that Tobias's impudent talk, of course. *He* was the one that put him up to come begging. Oh, if you ever let him have any of that money I'll— I'll—"

"Oh, be still, Cora, will you? Carey didn't know that Higgins was coming to me. He didn't know a thing about it, the cap'n said so. And I said no, didn't I? What more do you want?"

"I want this much more: I want you to promise me you will never, *never* let him have a dollar of that money, no matter what kind of excuse he puts up. You're so soft-headed you never can say no the way it ought to be said. You promise me that you'll say it now and mean it and stick to it. Will you?"

For a man who could not say no, George said it then with amazing promptness.

"No, I won't," he declared, emphatically.

"What! *What?* You won't promise me—"

"No, I won't. I told Higgins I couldn't spare the money and I should have told Carey the same thing if he had asked —which he wouldn't have done. But I'll be hanged," he added, his voice rising, "if I promise what I'll do the next time, if there ever is one. I don't know what I'll do. Confound it, Cora, how can you go on this way! Aunt Susan thought as much of Carey as she did of me—of us. Yes, and by all that's honest, he has just as much right to her money as we have. Just as much. More, if you want to know."

Cora T. gasped. "More!" she repeated. "More right to— Oh, you're crazy! I never heard such nonsense in my life. George Judson—"

"Be still. Carey's the salt of the earth, that's what he is, and I'm tired of hearing you run him down. Stop it. And stop picking on him. Now you know how I feel. Go to bed and behave yourself."

She did not go to bed, nor did he, for some time. . . . There were the usual tears and agonies and threats of suicide on her part and repentant pettings and fervent protestations of affection on his. The quarrel ended, of course, in his being partially forgiven, provided he never, never, never treated her so cruelly again. But the question of the promise was still unanswered. George did not make that promise, and Cora did not insist upon his making it—then. From experience she had learned just how far, in the matter of relations between the Judson brothers, it was wise to press a point. This did not mean, however, that the point should not be pressed later on. She could wait; but she did not intend to forget.

She expressed sympathy for her brother-in-law, expressed it to him when her husband was absent.

"Of course," she said, "George and I feel terribly—ter-

ribly, Carey—about Aunt Susan's not leaving you anything
in her will. We think she ought to have left you something,
even if it wasn't much. It was natural enough, considering
what a lot of her money you had had already in that banking
business of yours—that she should have given George and
me most of it, but we do think you should have had a few
of her own personal things, if only to remember her by.
Well, you shall have them; George and I will see to that.
There is that ship painting of great-grandfather Judson's;
she thought the world of that. You shall have that picture,
to keep always, Carey, and more besides. And, of *course,*
you can have a good home here with us just as long as you
want it."

Carey thanked her solemnly. After she had left the room
he smiled for the first time in a long while.

Hepsibah's indignation was emphatic.

"I'm ashamed of Susan Dain," she vowed. "I thought
she had more sense. No, I don't want to hear you make
excuses for her. I'm ashamed of her and that's all there
is to it."

There were callers, not many but a few, who came to the
Cap'n Jim-Carey place, to inquire concerning Carey's health
and to see him, if possible. Mrs. Higgins came and Captain
and Mrs. Joshua Bailey and several others. Mrs. Benjamin
Early came on a Sunday afternoon in tow of her husband.
There had been a brief but pointed interview between the
pair at the Early dinner table that noon. Mrs. Early had
ventured one of her very rare protests.

"But, Ben," she said, "I don't see how I can go callin'
this afternoon. I don't truly. I tore my best dress goin'
into meetin' this mornin'. You know I did; you heard it
go. Cap'n Elkanah stepped right on the train of my skirt
and I declare I didn't know but he would pull it right in
two. He *is* such a heavy man! That Simmons boy, the
one that drives the express cart, says the way Cap'n Elkanah
hauls his feet around always makes him think of movin'
trunks. Now it will take me a whole day to fix that dress.

again. How can I go out callin' on Sunday afternoon? I haven't got anything fit to wear."

Her husband snorted. "Then you'll have to wear something that ain't fit," he announced. "We've got to go there, that's all. Carey Judson is a plaguy nuisance, sick or well, but he's the boss's brother and we've got to palaver to him. *I* don't care how he's getting along. If he never was able to get back to his job in the office it would be the best thing for the office and everything in it. Such a set of books *I* never saw! But George asked me yesterday when we were coming up to see him, so we've got to go. Come on! Let's get it over with."

They called, but they did not see Carey. No one, except the doctor and the members of the household had caught a glimpse of him since he was taken ill. He went to his room the moment callers were announced and obstinately refused to come down during the visits. To his brother or Cora, when they urged him to do so, his answer was always the same.

"No, I don't feel up to seeing them yet awhile," he declared. "I want to get well and back to work as soon as I can, and talking seems to make me nervous. Say that I am lying down or something of the sort. Part of that will be true, the 'lying' part, at least."

Cora accepted the excuses complacently enough. She was always quite willing to dispense with her brother-in-law's society. She was much too fond of being the center of attention herself to care for that of a possible rival. Questions concerning Carey's health she answered with the statement that he was getting along real well. "Just a cold, that's all; exactly what you might expect after the soaking he got in that storm. Oh, dear! He doesn't take any more care of himself than a child might, and George and I have to look out for him and think for him as if he was a child. We are glad to do it, of course. George thinks the world of him and so do I, but we realize we shall always have him on our hands to care for as long as we live. Don't tell any one I said that, Mrs. Snow, will you? George wouldn't like it a bit if he knew I said it outside the family, but it is the living truth. All of us have our burdens in this world, don't we?"

George's remonstrances were not as easily quieted.

"You ought to see these people, Carey," he insisted. "They've taken pains to come here to see you and you ought to say 'How d'you do' to them, if nothing more. Why, Desire Sayles and Emily have been here twice to ask about you and once Emily came alone. She was real disappointed when Cora said you couldn't see anybody. The next time she comes you make it a point to see her, will you? I thought you and she were—humph!—well, pretty friendly. The whole town used to say you were, anyhow."

Carey, sprawled in the rocker by the bed, did not look at his brother. "Oh, I guess they don't want to see me, George, really," he said. "They are being polite, that is all. I am much obliged to them, of course, but— Oh, don't bother me any more, that's a good fellow."

"Humph! If you think Emily was only being polite when she came last Sunday, you're mightily mistaken—or I was, one or the other. She wouldn't take no for an answer at first. I had a good mind to come up here and drag you downstairs by the scruff of your obstinate neck. What makes you so pig-headed all at once? What has come over you?"

Carey smiled in a lopsided fashion.

"Oh, nothing in particular, George," he replied. "This cold, or the equinoctial or something, took the ginger out of me, I guess. I don't feel up to talking. . . . Just let me alone. I'll be moderately decent by and by, I hope. I shall try to be."

"Better try pretty soon, then. Here you are fussing because the doctor and I won't let you go back to the office before next Monday and yet you say you haven't got ambition enough to go downstairs and meet some of your best friends. That equinoctial must have been a tough one, I should say. Emily Sayles looks as if she had been out in it, too. I never saw her so white and peaked since I've known her. She says she is all right, but I give you my word she doesn't look or act all right. Now if she comes again you see her, will you?"

Carey, his face still turned away, was absently twisting his forelock.

"Well, perhaps, George," he said. "But don't worry. Probably she won't come again."

He was practically sure she would not. From his bedroom window he had watched her come up the walk to the side door that Sunday afternoon. He had watched but a moment, however. He turned away, fearful that his resolution might falter, that it might not be equal to the strain. He locked the door and when his brother called him, groaned, and vowed that his head was aching and that he couldn't be disturbed. Later on Hepsibah brought him a note.

"Emily left it for you," explained Hepsy. "She came around to the kitchen door after she left here and asked me to hand it to you when I got a chance. Said she was afraid you might not be able to see her and so she wrote this at home afore she started. She looks about as used up as you do, Carey. Vows she isn't sick or anything, but I know somethin' ails her. She's workin' herself to pieces givin' those pesky piano lessons, I shouldn't wonder. That Elsie Cahoon is enough to wear out one healthy set of nerves. Next time I see Desire I'm goin' to tell her what I think about those lessons. . . . Well, there's your note. If there's any answer I'll see that she gets it. And," lowering her voice and glancing cautiously behind her at the closed door, "I'll take care that nobody else sees even the outside of it. No use in stirrin' up more talk around this house than there is, already. *That* would be like stickin' extry bones into a salt herrin'."

Carey read the note after Hepsibah's departure. He did not do it immediately. He turned the envelope, bearing his name in her familiar writing, over and over in his hands, and when he did tear it open it was with a sudden burst of desperation. The note was brief.

Carey, dearest [she had written]. *Won't* you see me? You *must* tell me more than you did the other night. I know you have not told me the real reason for your speaking as you did. And I know that when I hear that reason I shall understand. You and I cannot part this way. You must tell me everything and let me judge what is best for us to do. If something has happened—and I know it has—to make you feel that you and I cannot be together as we planned—if it is only that we must wait, why, that is nothing, dear. Nothing at all. And if you broke your promise to me I know you did it for a reason you thought sufficient. Just tell me what it is, that is all I ask. You will do that for me, won't you? I beg you to.

It was an hour later when he sat down at the table in his room to write his answer, a long, long hour. And another had ended before the reply was written. It was shorter even than her note had been.

Dear Emily [he wrote]. I can't see you. It would not do any good and would only make us both more miserable than we are. I can't tell you anything more than I told the other night. You must not come to see me again and when we do meet, as I suppose we shall if I stay here in Wellmouth, you must not ask me for my reasons. You must forget me as soon as you can.

This was the final result of the hour of writing and rewriting, tearing up what was already written and beginning again. The utter hopelessness of his position overwhelmed him just as it had the night and day following his brother's confession and appeal. For George's sake—for George's sake he must keep silent. If he explained—if he even hinted at an explanation, she would insist that such sacrifice was unnecessary; she might go to George and demand that the latter restore the money which was his only means of salvation.

If she did that the whole affair would almost surely be made public. Then the old firm, the firm their father had founded, would go to ruin, George would be crushed, he would be a pauper—yes, and his domestic happiness would be wrecked also, for he knew Cora, her pride and temper. Compared with such disaster, what else mattered? Nothing, of course. No one accounted him as anything but a failure; a failure he had always been. But George Judson—why, Wellmouth swore by him, just as it had sworn by and boasted of Cap'n Jim-Carey. He could not desert George. This was always the one inevitable conclusion of his tortured self-questioning and desperate struggle. He must do what George had asked him to do. He would.

So his note to Emily was short and cold and decisive. All the longings and heartbreakings of his tormented soul, all the pleas for forgiveness, he wrote them, but he tore them to bits and consigned them to the wastebasket. The briefer, the more brutal, that word to Emily, the more conclusive. She would hate him now; well, if she did she would never try to see him again or ask for the reasons he could not give. It would be better, in the end, for her. She might forget him sooner, and be happier in consequence. Anything which might make her life easier and her future brighter—well, that was what he desired, surely. Yes, he did desire it. So, if she hated him—well, that was as it should be.

He crushed the note into its envelope, hurried down to the kitchen and gave it to Hepsibah. Then he hastened back to his room again to begin once more the fight with his always wavering resolution. He won that fight and Hepsy delivered the note that evening. Emily called no more at the Cap'n Jim-Carey place.

He went back to the office and the books the following Monday, two weeks after his illness began. George and he walked down together. George was in a cheerful mood. Things were looking brighter, much brighter, he told his brother. The items in the papers concerning the will had been read by his Boston creditors and they had helped a great deal.

"That was a lucky mistake, if you can call it a mistake," he said. "That leaving your name out of the piece in the papers, I mean. Everybody takes it for granted that I am the 'nephew' Aunt Susan's money is coming to, and it saves you and me a whole lot of troublesome explanation. I am willing they should think so now, but some of these days— in a year or so, I hope—I shall be in a position when their knowing the truth won't do any harm; then they shall know it. They shall know what you have done for me, old boy. I'll see to that."

Carey's remonstrance was emphatic.

"No, you won't," he declared. "I don't want them to know it. Let them keep on thinking what they think now. It will be better for all hands."

George slapped him on the back. "Don't you believe it!" he exclaimed. "They are going to know, all right. And you are going to have that money, with interest. That was a part of our bargain. I haven't forgotten it, if you have."

"I don't want it, George. What good is money to me? What would I do with it if I had it? Lose it, that's all. I am not fit to have money. Ask any one here that knows me, they'll tell you so—and be glad of the chance."

"No, they won't, for I'll tell my story first. That is the trouble with most people, Carey; they *don't* know you. I do. . . . Oh, well! we'll attend to all that when the time comes. Just now, though, that twisted newspaper yarn has helped a lot. Why, that fellow in Boston, the one that holds the note that was worrying me most of all, writes that he isn't sure that he can't give me a renewal, after all. I know what that means. It means that he has learned that I am sure of an extra hundred thousand and he feels safe. You and I have got to keep our secret for a while, and I tell you again I am mighty thankful it is a secret. It is a mercy you didn't show anybody the letter you got from Phillips. If you had the fat *would* have been in the fire."

Carey did not answer. He had shown that letter to one person and it was his doing so which had lifted him to Paradise and then dropped him into the pit. If that letter had not been in his pocket that Sunday afternoon his lot, hard as it was, would have been so much easier. Emily would never have known of his love for her, and his renunciation would not have been accompanied by the knowledge that she thought him a liar and a brute. She might never have known that he loved her, but at least she would not hate and despise him as now she did. Yet she had loved him then; she had told him so. The memory of her love, even though it was now turned to loathing, was the one bright spot in the blackness.

At George's suggestion he had signed a power of attorney making his brother his representative in all matters pertaining to the settling of the Dain estate, and the collection of the inheritance. "When the settlement is made," said George, "I will turn the money over to you, you can sign a receipt or whatever Phillips thinks necessary for you to sign. Then you can hand the money to me and I will give you my note. That will be the simplest way out, I think."

Carey did not care how it was settled. He did not wish any note. So far as he was concerned he never wished to hear of his Aunt Susan's legacy again.

At the office he did his best to keep his mind upon the rows of figures, the current prices of cod and haddock and halibut, the monotonous routine of the daily grind. So far as accomplishing results was concerned he succeeded surprisingly well. Even the supercritical Early deigned to express a measure of satisfaction.

"I declare, you're getting along pretty well, Carey," he observed. "You don't make as many mistakes as you did there one spell. I guess being sick was what you needed. Maybe it showed you there was something worse than keeping books. Eh? Ha, ha!"

Carey pulled at his pet lock of hair.

"It isn't altogether that, Ben," he replied, solemnly. "I

learned what it meant to be away from you for two whole weeks. I was pining for you, Ben. . . . No, please don't move. Stand right there in the sunshine for a minute longer. I have a hard bit of adding to do and the sight of your face will be an inspiration."

The manager grunted. He was suspicious of levity somewhere. As a matter of fact there was a note of carelessness, almost of reckless bravado as he estimated it, in his subordinate's manner these days which was new and which he neither understood nor liked.

He expressed this feeling to his wife at supper that evening.

"I can't make him out," he declared. "He's different, somehow. He does his work considerable better than he did, though mercy knows that isn't saying a whole lot; but he just seems to take it all as a sort of joke. Yes, and I swear if I wouldn't almost say he took me as a joke, too, if such a thing was possible. When I haul him over the coals for digging holes half through the ledger with that everlasting scratcher he's so handy with, he always stops everything to listen as if he was in church and I was preaching a sermon. He never used to answer me back—except once in a while. Now he always does. What he says is mostly nonsense, but it sounds respectful enough, almost too respectful, if you know what I mean. And when I come to think it over it always seems as if there was a kind of poking fun at me underneath. Nothing you can put your finger on, you know. If he was fresh I'd put my foot down on him, Judson or no Judson. It ain't freshness exactly, it's —it's—well, I don't know what it is. Kind of 'don't care a hang,' that's the only way I can describe it. But coming from moony, sleepy-head Carey Judson it's strange. Yes, he's different. I don't know why he is, but he is."

Mr. Early was not the only one who noticed that difference. Captain Tobias Higgins noticed it when he dropped in at his back-yard shop to watch the bird making. Carey carved the black duck and plover and beetle-heads in his spare time,

just as he had done since his tenancy of the Higgins' out-
building began, but it seemed to the captain that his interest
in the work was not as keen, and that he was less critical
of the output.

"If it was anybody else," Tobias confided to his "Chippy,"
"I'd say he was gettin' sick of the job or careless or somethin'
like that. 'Tain't that the birds he makes ain't good enough.
Godfreys! They're so good that I feel like gettin' my gun
and takin' a shot at every one he turns out. It ain't that,
but—well, it's more that he don't sit and squint at every
feather and pick flaws and shake his head and groan when
it don't suit him. He seems a lot more willin' to let 'em go
as they are, and that ain't natural for him. And he acts
queer other ways. Sometimes when I go out there he won't
say a word scarcely; don't seem to hear me when I talk to
him, and looks so kind of pale and—oh, miserable, you
know. Then the next time he talks a whole lot about nothin',
and makes jokes and tries to sing; and godfreys! when *he*
sings that's sadder than anything else! Well, I don't know
what 'tis, but somethin's gone skewangles with him. I'm
goin' to ask George if he knows. I'm gettin' kind of
worried."

Early in November Cora T. departed on a trip to Washington. The Ladies' Literary Society, of which she was
secretary and a brightly shining light, was going in a body—
not a large body in the aggregate, although as individuals
there were some rather bulky exhibits. The White House,
both branches of Congress, the Supreme Court and Mount
Vernon were to be honored by their attentions and Mrs.
Judson delivered lectures, lectures historical, architectural
and governmental, at breakfast, dinner and supper during the
days preceding the exodus. The excursionists departed on
a Friday morning train and Captain Higgins declared that
all the occasion lacked to make its grandeur complete was a
brass band. "Though," he added, "the depot master tells
me that there was so much tongue-waggin' and clack a-goin'
on the platform that a body couldn't hardly hear the

engine whistle, let alone a bass drum, if they'd had one."

The Judson brothers were left alone in the Cap'n Jim-Carey place, to be cared for by Hepsibah and Maggie.

On the following Sunday afternoon, after Carey had, as usual, gone down to his bird shop, George was reading his Saturday *Evening Transcript* in the sitting room when Hepsibah entered to announce a caller.

"Desire Sayles is here," she said, "and she says it's you she wants to see. She's comin' right in. . . . Yes, here she is now."

# CHAPTER XVI

"WELL, Mrs. Sayles," observed George Judson, after Hepsibah had gone and he and his visitor were alone in the sitting room, "this is something of a surprise. I didn't expect callers here at home, now that Cora is off sight-seeing. I am very glad to see you, though, of course. Take off your things, do. Where is Emily?"

Mrs. Sayles accepted the armchair which he pushed forward; and threw back her cape. She did not, however, remove her bonnet. She was breathing quickly and appeared fatigued.

"First of all, George," she said, "you must let me rest a minute before you expect me to do much talking. This is the longest walk I have taken for almost a year. Oh, why *do* you live on the top of the highest hill in town!"

George looked at her in surprise.

"You didn't walk up Lookout Hill, did you?" he asked. "Of course you didn't!"

"I most certainly did, all the way up. Sylvanus Snow and his wife were going out to ride and they brought me as far as the corner of the Main Road. They would have brought me all the way, I suppose, if I had told them I was coming here, but I didn't tell them. They thought I was going to the Halls' and I let them think so. There is no particular reason why they, or any one else, should know that I was coming here to see you, George—and several why they shouldn't. I walked—or climbed—up from the corner and I am decidedly out of breath."

George rose to his feet. Considering the state of Desire Sayles' health the idea that she should have dreamed of

317

making such an effort was incomprehensible. He was rather alarmed.

"Let me get a—a cup of tea or something," he urged. "Hepsy will make it for you in a jiffy. You shouldn't have done such a thing, Mrs. Sayles. I wonder Emily let you do it. Is she with you?"

"She is not," with emphasis. "No, no, I don't want any tea. I am all right, or I shall be pretty soon. Oh, I do lose patience with myself these days! There was a time, when your mother was living, when I could run back and forth between this house and mine a half dozen times a day and think nothing of it. But now—oh, dear! Be thankful you are young, George Judson. Old age is nothing to be proud of, take my word for it. . . . And sit down, please. I have a great deal to say to you and not much time to say it in."

George sat, rather reluctantly. He made the tritely polite protest which her remark concerning age seemed to invite. Desire accepted the compliment with a tired smile. "Thank you," she said, dryly. "I may not look as old as I feel, but if I don't it is because it is impossible for any one to look as old as I feel just now. . . . There, there! I didn't come here to discuss my age. Where is Carey?"

"He has gone down to his workshop, I suppose. That is where he said he was going and where he usually goes on Sunday afternoons. But I don't understand how Emily happened to let you come alone. She isn't with you, you say?"

"No, she isn't. She hasn't the slightest idea that I have left the house. She has gone up to Obed Cahoon's to talk about that child of his. She seems to feel conscience-stricken because Elsie hasn't made the progress with her music which she expected—Emily expected, I mean—the little imp has made quite as much as *I* expected. I wish *I* could have a talk with Obed. It might not—probably wouldn't—do him or his daughter any good, but it would help me a great deal. However, I didn't come to free my mind concerning Elsie Cahoon either. To do that completely would take more time

than I can spare this afternoon. Well, George, Emily isn't
here and you say Carey isn't. That is precisely what I
hoped, for it is of those two that you and I must talk now.
. . . Is that door shut—and latched?"

Judson, wondering what on earth all this secrecy could
mean and impressed by the earnestness of her tone and manner, walked to the door leading to the dining room, made
sure that it was securely fastened, and returned to his chair.
Mrs. Sayles waited until he was seated and then leaned
forward.

"Now, George," she said, "I want you to listen to me and
not interrupt when I am talking; and answer my questions.
when I ask them. This is an important—very important
matter I have come to see you about. It must be settled—
and I think—I *think* you can help me settle it if you will.
First of all, what is the trouble with your brother? Do you
know?"

George's wonder was now close to bewilderment. There
was no doubt whatever that Desire Sayles was in deadly
earnest and that she had risked her health in order to interview him that afternoon. The important matter she had
come to discuss must have something to do with Emily
Sayles and Carey. What, he could not imagine. His bewilderment showed in his face as he spoke.

"Trouble?" he repeated. "Trouble with Carey? What
do you mean, Mrs. Sayles? So far as I know, he is all right.
He caught cold in that storm last month and was knocked
out for a fortnight, but he is over that now. What sort of
trouble do you mean? I don't understand."

His caller seemed a little doubtful.

"Are you sure you don't?" she asked, slowly. "Well,
perhaps not. Certainly you don't if you can sit there and
tell me there is nothing the matter with him. Of course I
know he has been sick; every one in town knows that. And
I believe the doctor tells people he is all right again. But
that doesn't prevent my knowing quite as well that he is a

very long way from being all right. George Judson, *don't* you know what is the trouble with Carey? Or are you only making believe?"

George's expression should have been answer sufficient. There was surprise in it, and puzzled perturbation, but there was no trace of embarrassment or guilt. He shook his head.

"I certainly don't, Mrs. Sayles," he replied. "And when you say 'trouble' I don't—well, what sort of trouble are you hinting at?"

"I am not hinting, George. There will be no hinting on my part. I am going to be frank enough before I finish, goodness knows. I am asking you if you know of any reason why your brother should have changed absolutely from what he was a few weeks ago. People are saying he doesn't look well and that his sickness has changed his appearance surprisingly, but it isn't that kind of change I mean. George, do you know of any sudden shock, or disappointment—anything of the sort—which has come to Carey of late?"

George's expression had altered. His look of puzzled innocence and surprise was superseded by one quite different. He was thinking hard, groping for the meaning behind her words, and for an instant the alarming suspicion that she or Emily might have learned the truth concerning the contents of his aunt's will flashed to his mind. So far as he knew no one on the Cape was aware of Mrs. Dain's real disposition of her property, no one save Carey and himself. It could not be that. She had used the word "disappointment," however. Then another idea came to him. He remembered Tobias Higgins' conversation that day in the private office of J. C. Judson & Co. It might be that the captain had told others of his proposition that he—George— should back Carey's bird manufacture with the presumed legacy. He might well have done so and Desire and Emily might share Higgins' resentment and fancy that Carey shared it also and was brooding over it. That seemed probable—at least more probable than any other surmise.

He frowned slightly and toyed with his watch chain. Mrs. Sayles' sharp scrutiny did not waver.

"*Do* you know of any such thing?" she persisted. "You look now as if you did. You must answer me, George. I should not ask you these questions if I hadn't a very serious reason for asking. I have told you that I intend to be very outspoken and frank. I hope you will be. I have known you and Carey since the days you were born and I am about as close and old a friend as you two have in the world. Also," she added, with the trace of a smile, "I am not in the least afraid of you, you see."

He met her look then. "Mrs. Sayles," he said, "I don't exactly see what you are driving at, but— Well, I guess Cap'n Tobe Higgins has been talking to you, hasn't he? If he has, and you feel, as he seems to, that I ought to take the money that Aunt Susan left—the money that is coming from her estate—to back his scheme of organizing a company and building a factory for Carey to use in making his decoys on a big scale, I—well, I can only tell you what I told him, that I can't spare that money just now. Yes, and I will tell you more than I told him. If I had the money lying idle I should think a long while before I backed Carey in another business venture. He isn't a business man. He is my brother and I would do anything on earth for him— anything that would help him, I mean—but I don't believe making him the head of a business concern would help him at all. It would only mean another failure; at least that is the way it looks to me now. I am sorry if he is disappointed and troubled about it. I didn't know he was. I didn't even know that Tobias had mentioned the idea to him. Certainly Carey has never spoken to me about it. And I am just as sorry if you and Emily feel—"

She broke in on the sentence. "George Judson," she demanded, "what in the world is all this? What are you talking about? Tobias Higgins hasn't said a word of any such plan to me. I haven't seen him for a month. I didn't know anything about it, and I am sure Emily doesn't."

George's bewilderment returned. "You don't!" he exclaimed. "Well, then, I'm sorry I spoke of it. But when you were so certain that—"

Again she interrupted. "Now we must stop talking in circles," she declared. "It doesn't get us anywhere and I haven't time for it, besides. George," earnestly, "please answer me this question: There will be more, but this is the first one: Didn't you know that your brother and Emily were engaged to marry and that, for some reason—heavens knows what—he came to her that awful night in the rain and gale two weeks ago and broke their engagement without giving her the slightest sane excuse for doing it? Didn't you know that?"

George leaned back in his chair so suddenly that it creaked. "What!" he cried, sharply. "What's that you say, Mrs. Sayles?"

"You didn't know it, then! No, I can see you didn't. Well, it is true. They were engaged and then, the night of the storm, Carey came to our house and broke the engagement. Now can you think of any reason why he should do such a thing?"

George did not answer her question. The statement she had made seemed so incredible that he scarcely believed it.

"Carey and Emily were—were *engaged,* you say?" he repeated. "Really engaged to be married?"

"Yes. And you didn't know even that? Well, I didn't know it myself until a day or two ago. Of course I could see that he and Emily were growing more and more friendly. So far as that goes they have always been friends. And I shouldn't have been greatly surprised to hear that they had concluded to be something more than friends. In fact, I rather expected it. And I was satisfied with the idea. I like Carey Judson. Oh, I know that he isn't precisely what I should call a practical person, and I have learned to my sorrow, and as a good many others have, that as a business man in the ordinary sense he is a decided failure. But in his own particular line, the line the Almighty fitted him for,

I am convinced that he is far from being a failure. I believe that, given the right chance, he is capable of making us all proud of him. And, aside from all that, I like him—I have always liked him. He is as good as gold, and as kind and generous and brave a soul as ever lived. I know how they talk about him, that they call him 'Queer Judson' and make fun of him, but I haven't spent all my days in Wellmouth, thank goodness, and Wellmouth's opinion isn't necessarily law and gospel to me—indeed it isn't! And, besides, I am not the most practical person on earth, myself. I like what money will buy well enough, and I should be quite willing to have more of it than I have now; but there are some things one can't buy with money and some others that I wouldn't sell for all the millions on earth. My daughter's happiness is one of those. I had much rather see her marry a good, poor man than I would a rich bad one. That may be an old-fashioned and sentimental doctrine, but it is mine. If she loved Carey and he loved her, then I was content. I was a poor girl and I married a poor man, and whatever of the world's goods came to us afterwards we earned and enjoyed together. No, if Emily had come to me and said that she and Carey cared for each other and meant to marry, I—well, I probably should have asked her what they expected to live on after they were married, and I might have said, 'Wait a while,' but I shouldn't have objected in the least. There! That's a long speech, but it is only the text of my sermon. You and I must go a great deal further with the matter than that before I leave you this afternoon."

George was listening now; he had heard all that his visitor said, but he seemed to be lost in thought. He shook his head once more and drew a long breath.

"So they were actually engaged," he said again. "Well, well! . . . Of course I have heard—I knew—that he was calling at your house pretty often, and that there was a lot of gossip drifting around, but there is so much of that in a town like this I seldom pay attention to it. I never supposed there was anything serious between Emily and Carey. Great

Scott! Why, I—I guess I should have laughed at the notion.
Carey was—well, I know his circumstances and—and—"

He stopped short, with a sudden catch of the breath. Then
he asked, quickly, and with a sharp change in his tone:

"When did they decide to do this?"

"What do you mean? When did they decide to marry?
Oh, I don't think they had gone so far as to consider the
time of marriage. They were to be married some day, that
was all. At least that is what I gather from what Emily
told me."

"I don't mean that. I mean was—well, was the decision
—the engagement—er—a sudden sort of thing? When did
you hear about it, Mrs. Sayles?"

"I heard about it only a day or two ago. And when I
did hear there was no longer an engagement; Carey, as I
told you, had broken it. Emily didn't tell me this of her
own accord; I am not sure that she would have told me for
ever so long, perhaps never, if I hadn't insisted on being
told. I have, I hope, a moderate amount of common sense
and that shock I had last winter hasn't affected my eyes to
the extent that I can't see what is as plain as a pikestaff.
Emily had been very happy, so happy and in such good
spirits that I began to suspect what might have happened to
make her so. Then, all at once, she was as miserable as she
had been joyful. She was pale and silent and perfectly
wretched and when I asked her if she was sick—which of
course I supposed she must be—she said she was well and
that nothing was the matter. I knew better than *that*, of
course, so I began to look for a reason. Carey had been
dropping in for supper or to spend the evening pretty frequently. Now he didn't come at all. He was sick, himself,
of course, but not very sick; yet when Emily and I came
here to call he wouldn't see us. I put two and two together,
as any one would—any mother, certainly—and when I was
ready I shut Emily up in the sitting room with me and made
her tell me the whole story. She did and there were some
parts of that story, George, that sent me down here to see

you to-day. Emily doesn't know I am here. She had no idea of my coming. She would be perfectly furious if she even guessed it. But that doesn't make any difference. I had to talk to you—and—yes, I guess, George, you will have to talk to me."

George was silent. His brows were drawn together and now there was a strained, haggard look upon his face. He sighed, glanced at her, and then looked away.

"Go on," he said. "Tell me the whole of it, please. All that Emily told you. That is, if you think she would be willing for you to tell. I—I guess I ought to hear it."

Mrs. Sayles nodded, a nod which expressed decisive and absolute agreement with the last statement.

"I *know* you ought to hear it," she declared. "I am as sure of that as I am that Emily wouldn't consent to have me tell you. It is for her sake—and Carey's—yes, and yours, too, I hope, George—that I am going to do that very thing. Now listen."

She told, as Emily had told her, of the latter's walk with Carey on the fateful Sunday afternoon. Then of Carey's sudden recollection of the letter handed him by Captain Higgins on his arrival at the workshop. She described the reading of that letter and its amazing contents, also the entirely unpremeditated and spontaneous avowals of mutual affection which followed. She stopped then, apparently waiting for him to speak, but he did not. So she continued.

"That letter and the news in it were responsible, as you can see," she said, "for the engagement. I don't suppose—being Carey Judson—he would have ever dared to speak of such a thing if it hadn't been for that. But that, of course, changed everything. He was—he thought he was—worth over a hundred thousand dollars and—well, even in these days a person worth that amount can consider marriage. They talked, those two—oh, Emily told me everything— about what he could do, now that he wasn't poor any longer, all about his plans, plans that he had told her about before. . . . I wonder if he ever told you any of those plans, George?"

I doubt it. I think he never told them to any one except Emily. Oh, yes! and Susan Dain. He told them to her when she was here visiting at your house. *Did* he tell them to you?"

George's hands were tightly gripped upon the arms of his chair. His head was bent and she could not see his face.

"I guess not," he muttered. "I—well, you can tell them to me now, if you care to. I should like to hear them."

"You are going to hear them. They are worth hearing. They may give you a little idea of the sort of man your brother is, down underneath his 'queerness.' Did he ever tell you how he had begun to pay some of his debts here in town?"

George looked up then, startled, for the moment, from his restraint.

"Pay his debts!" he repeated. "What debts?"

"He didn't tell you even that? He hasn't told you anything, I see. Well, he wouldn't, I suppose. He would be afraid it might trouble you. He has been scrimping and saving from the salary you pay him as bookkeeper and working night and day at that bird shop of his, to pay some of the poor people in town the money they lost when that rascally Osborne wrecked their banking firm."

She went on to tell of Carey's cherished plan, of his paying Mrs. Bangs and Letitia Cahoon, of the list of Wellmouth creditors and its careful checking. She told also of the offer from Professor Knight, of the expedition to Central and South America.

"It would have been a wonderful opportunity for him," she declared. "You can see that, yourself. The chance of a lifetime. He told Emily of it when the offer was first made and she urged him to accept. She wanted him to go to you, or to Susan Dain, and borrow the money. He wouldn't do that. He considered that he had already squandered and lost enough of his aunt's money, and as for taking another penny from you, asking more favors from the brother who had saved his reason and his life, that is the way he expressed it, he would not listen to such a thing. I wish you might hear some of the things he says about you, George; some he has said to me and more that Emily says he has said to her. If you could hear you might realize that there are such things as devotion and gratitude in this world, in spite of all the cynical stuff we read in books."

She paused again, but George made no comment.

"As for his plans—well, if he had any such plans as Tobias Higgins spoke to you about he has never mentioned them to me or to Emily either. I don't believe he had them. Any scheme with as strong a personal element as that wouldn't have appealed to Carey Judson. His one plan— the one he had set his heart on—was to pay every cent the people in Wellmouth had lost through his wicked carelessness, as he called it. Why, even after that lawyer's letter surprised him into letting Emily see how he felt toward her— even then, she tells me, he insisted that before he could think of marriage, or of going with Knight or anything else, those debts must be paid. . . . And he has never told you a word about it?"

George shook his head. "No," he groaned.

"Well, you know it now, at any rate. And now, George, here is what I really came to talk with you about. Carey and Emily were engaged. They were very happy. Certainly she was and there doesn't seem to be any doubt of his happiness—for a little while. It was on a Sunday afternoon that they had their understanding there on the beach. He came to call the next morning, Monday, and, so she says, was as full of hope and optimism as ever. Of course, even then he seemed to feel uneasy about accepting all of the money his aunt had left him; he said over and over again that he didn't deserve it, and you did, and that he ought to, at least, share it with you. Emily told him—and I must say I think she was right—that you didn't need it. That it would have meant only an extra fortune for you who had one already, whereas it meant all the world to him. She said, too, that she knew you would be more glad than any one else when you learned of his good luck. Well, that was the way that Monday evening session ended. . . . The next time he came it was quite different.

"On Tuesday evening—that was the night when the storm began—he did not come, although she rather expected him. But the next Wednesday he came, and mercy knows she did *not* expect him on such a night as that! She says he was soaked to the skin, he was as white as a sheet, and his look and manner frightened her almost to death before he spoke a word. And when he did speak it was like—well, as if he was in a sort of daze. He scarcely seemed, she says, to know what he was saying. He stayed only a few minutes and all she could get from him was that it was all over between them, their engagement was a mistake, it must end then and there. Even their friendship must end and she must never see him again and forget him as soon as she could. No explanations, no sensible reasons—nothing. When she tried to get him to say more he ran away, out into that howling gale, bareheaded. She hasn't seen him since, though she has tried several times. She has heard from him, though."

She went on to tell of Emily's note of appeal and its uncompromising, almost brutal answer. Through all the long story George Judson sat in the chair, his head bent and his gaze fixed upon the floor at his feet. When she finished he neither looked up nor spoke. She regarded him intently and then continued:

"There, George," she said, "now you know as much about it as I do, or as Emily does. I wonder if you don't know more. On that Monday your brother was sane and happy and full of hopes and glorious expectations. On Wednesday he was in despair and wretched and almost crazy. What happened, between that Monday and Wednesday, to make him that way? I wonder if you don't know—or can guess. Emily is sure that you do, or can, and—well, to be honest, I am almost as sure, myself. *If* you do then you must speak out. You must, George. Carey is your brother and you owe it to him. Emily is my daughter and I don't intend to let her happiness go to wrack and ruin without a fight. If you don't tell me, I shall try and find out in other ways, that is all."

Still he was silent. Her next speech was in a tone less gentle.

"There is no use beating about the bush," she said. "As I told you before, I have some common sense and I can see through a hole as big as a barn door. Carey had a letter—Emily saw it and read it—from Susan Dain's own lawyer, the one who drew her will and was in charge of her affairs, stating as plain as a fact could be stated that she had left him property amounting to a hundred and twenty-five thousand dollars. Last week we learned, through that item in the papers, that she has left it all to 'a nephew' named Judson here in Wellmouth. Every one takes it for granted, of course, that you are that nephew. Even Cora says you are, and, so far as I have ever heard, you have never denied it. Well, are you, George? If you are, why did Mr. Phillips write Carey that letter which came to him? Was there another will? Did they find it after Carey's letter was written? . . . Or," she paused and then added, impressively, "is there something else between you and Carey that no other person knows about, not even your wife?"

George's rigid attitude changed. One of the hands upon the chair arm lifted to his forehead and he leaned heavily upon it.

His caller was relentless. "There is one thing more. I may as well tell you before you answer me," she persisted. "Emily made Carey promise solemnly—she knew him, you see, and she knew there was nothing on earth he would not do for you—she made him give her his word of honor that no one, you and Cora especially, should be permitted to persuade him into giving up that inheritance which had come to him. Emily thinks he broke that promise. She is almost sure of it. I think, in all probability, she is right. Is she, George? You must answer me now. Is she?"

He rose to his feet. The face he turned toward her now

was so unlike that of the good-natured, contented, self-assured George Judson she had always known that she would scarcely have recognized it.

"Why, George!" she exclaimed in alarm. "Why, George, what—"

He raised a hand. "Don't say any more, Mrs. Sayles," he begged. "I—well, I—you have told me things this afternoon that—that—"

"I had to tell them. For Emily's sake—and for Carey's."

"Yes, yes," hurriedly. "I know. I am glad you did. Only don't say any more now, please. If you don't mind I —I should like to be alone and—and think for a while."

"You shall be. I am going this minute. . . . But—well, George, what are you going to do?"

He was walking up and down the floor. He continued to do so for a moment before he spoke. Then he turned.

"Is Emily going to be at home this evening?" he asked.

"Yes. That is, I suppose so. She generally is at home in the evening."

"All right. I shall probably—yes, I will come up to see her then. I will. Good-by, Mrs. Sayles. . . . Oh, I—I must see about getting you home again. Of course I must. Ask Hepsy to tell the man to harness the horse. I would attend to it myself, but—but—"

"You nor Hepsy need do any such thing. I shall walk as far as the Halls'. I was planning to call there anyway; it is my excuse to Emily for leaving the house this afternoon. The Snows will stop for me on their way back from their drive. Don't trouble about me, George. I shall be all right."

He smiled—or tried to.

"Well, if you are sure," he said. "Good afternoon. . . . Oh, and Mrs. Sayles, I don't think you—or Emily—need worry any more."

She hesitated. She wanted to tell him that now her worry would be concerning him. She did not, however; she went out and left him.

When Carey returned from the bird shop he was surprised to learn that his brother had gone out and had left word that he would not be home for supper. As a matter of fact he did not come home until after eleven, and when Carey, awake and, as usual, reading in bed, heard his step in the passage at the head of the stairs and called to him, he did not answer. He went into his own bedroom and closed the door.

The next morning he seemed tired, and he certainly looked so, but he declared himself to be perfectly well and assured Hepsibah that nothing was the matter. When Carey asked concerning his whereabouts the previous night he said that he had been on a business errand and volunteered no particulars.

# CHAPTER XVII

CAREY was a trifle late that Monday evening in reaching the Higgins' premises. He and his brother ate supper together and then George had gone up to his room, saying that he must write a letter to Cora. He had talked little during the meal and seemed, as he had seemed all that day, absent-minded and *distrait*. The tired and worn look which his brother and Hepsibah had noticed and commented upon at breakfast was still upon his face, but he dismissed all questions concerning his health with the statement that nothing was wrong with him and silenced the solicitous inquiries of the housekeeper by the impatient request that she let him alone.

"I am all right, I tell you," he insisted. "I am not hungry, that is all. . . . Well, I suppose you are going down to your bird whittling, as usual, aren't you, Carey?"

Carey was not quite certain whether or not he should go to the shop that evening. He, too, had not been talkative during the meal. The day had seemed particularly long and now the prospect of a few hours of relief with his tools and brushes was not as alluring as usual. He wondered if even that source of forgetfulness was failing. The previous afternoon he had made two calls in the village, had amazed and delighted two more of the Osborne and Judson creditors by paying their small losses in full. From them he had exacted promises that knowledge of the payment should be kept a secret. Their joy and profuse thanks had gratified him and, for the time, acted as a cheerful tonic upon his spirits. Now he was feeling the reaction. He had looked forward to the erasure of those two names from the long list and, when he found his thoughts straying to the hopelessness of his own future, had forced them to return to the pleasant anticipation of that act. Now it was done. Now he must set to work again in preparation for the next payment. And, to his dismay, he found his ambition lagging. He really did not seem to care whether or not he ever made another decoy.

When he answered his brother's questions by expressing uncertainty concerning his occupation that evening, George, for some reason, appeared to find that answer a trifle disturbing. He stopped on his way to the stairs.

"Oh, I guess you'll go," he said. "Why don't you? You might as well be doing that as loafing around here alone. I'm going out, myself, by and by, for a little while. Oh, yes! And you can do me a favor if you want to. You can take Cora's letter to the post office on your way down. I'll finish it in a few minutes; it won't be a long letter."

Carey made his decision. "All right, George," he said. "I'll go, I guess. As you say, I might as well whittle as loaf. I'll take your letter, of course."

George climbed the stairs. Hepsibah, standing in the doorway, sighed. "Well, now, what has come over *him* all at once?" she wanted to know. "Is *he* goin' to be sick? Or is the peace and quiet around this place since she cleared out for Washin'ton so much of a shock that the unnaturalness of it is gettin' on his nerves? Maybe that's it, I shouldn't be surprised. I find myself wonderin' if it really is as quiet as it seems these days, or if I'm gettin' hard of hearin'."

The letter was soon written and George handed it to his brother.

"You will be at Higgins' until nine o'clock, won't you, Carey?" he asked.

The tone of the inquiry seemed more than casual. Carey turned to look at him.

"Yes," he answered. "I shall be there. Why?"

"Oh, nothing, nothing! Don't forget the letter."

After Carey had gone, George turned to Mrs. Ellis.

"Hepsy," he said, "I'm going to drive—er—over to Trumet by and by. It's a nice night. Don't you want to go with me?"

Hepsibah stared. "Why—why, I suppose I could go," she said. "And I haven't been to ride for I don't know when. But what in the world makes you want to take me along?"

"Oh, just for company. You be ready at half-past eight. We shall probably start then."

When Carey reached the post office and dropped the letter to Cora T. in the slot beneath the rack of boxes, Sam Griggs came out from behind that rack with another letter in his hand.

"Here's some mail for you, Carey," he said. "Came on to-night's train. I put it in with the J. C. Judson bunch, but you might just as well have it now, hadn't you?"

Carey accepted the proffered envelope and thrust it unopened into his coat pocket. He was expecting a letter from Moore, his Boston friend, and he took it for granted that this must be from him. He walked out of Griggs' store and strode moodily along the beach until he reached the Higgins' front gate. The latch caught and clicked noisily and, as he passed the house the back door opened and Captain Tobias called to him.

"Ship ahoy, there!" he hailed. "That you, Carey? You're kind of late to-night, ain't you? Come in a minute and pass the time of day with me and Chippy."

Carey did not feel in the least like making a call or listening to Wellmouth gossip as retailed by the voluble Mrs. Higgins. He went in, however, but declined the captain's invitation to take off his hat and coat and come to anchor abaft the stove.

"Can't stop, Cap'n," he said. "I must get to work if I am going to accomplish anything to-night."

Mrs. Higgins spoke her mind. "That's just the trouble with you, Carey Judson," she declared. "Tobias and I were talkin' about you at supper time—yes, and we've talked a whole lot of other times lately. We're kind of worried about you. You work altogether too hard. You slave away at that office every workday, and on Sundays and evenin's you're

down here cuttin' and paintin' and contrivin' every minute
except meal times. You do too much work. It's beginnin'
to show in the way you look. I never see such a change in
anybody as there has been in you these last few weeks."

Carey smiled. "Oh, you mustn't worry, Mrs. Higgins,"
he said. "That cold I picked up last month rather took it
out of me, I guess."

Tobias nodded. "You're right, it did!" he vowed. "And
the way you dig into work night and day is takin' it out of
you, too. What you need is a vacation and you'd ought to
have one. Ask George to let you off for a couple of weeks.
He can do it, as well as not. Godfreys mighty! Ain't he
got Ben Early and ain't Ben capable of handlin' the whole
United States Navy, let alone two or three fishin' schooners
and a set of account books? 'Course he is! He owns up
to it, any time a person asks him. Look here, Carey; me
and Chippy are figurin' on goin' on a little trip and we don't
see why you don't go along with us. Cora T. Judson and
her crew have gone to Washin'ton to give the President a
treat; why can't the rest of us fo'mast hands go, too?
'Course," he added, with sarcasm, "my wife may not be
high-toned enough to ship aboard a Ladies' Lit'rary Society,
but that ain't any reason why we can't navigate a dory of
our own. We're goin' to go, some time between now and
Thanksgivin'. Why don't you come along with us?"

"Yes, do, Carey," urged Mrs. Higgins. "We'd just love
to have you."

Carey thanked them and said he would consider the proposition. It seemed the simplest way to avoid argument and
hasten his escape. Phœbe returned to the subject of his
cold, spoke of the prevalence of colds and minor ailments
in town and expressed gratitude that she and her husband
had so far escaped contagion.

"You ain't the only one that's lookin' peaked and pulin'
these fall days," she said. "Indeed you ain't. Why, Tobias
says he sees the doctor's buggy flyin' around, up and down
the road, every time he goes to the village. Caroline Snow

is laid up, and the Bassett boy and—oh, I don't know how many more. And Emily Sayles is sick, too. Did you know it?"

This statement and question, spoken with guileful innocence, had an effect which was noted—as, perhaps, it had been expected—by both Tobias and his wife. Carey, whose hand was upon the doorknob, turned back.

"What?" he asked, sharply. "She—Emily Sayles is sick, you say?"

Phœbe nodded.

"Yes," she said. "I understand she is. She's real poorly, anyhow."

Her husband, who was watching their caller intently, laid a hand on her knee.

"Now, heave to, Chip," he ordered. "You hadn't ought to say she is sick. You've heard folks say she must be sick, or that somethin' ails her, that's all. I guess likely she ain't real sick, Carey. She's up and out and givin' her piano lessons, same as ever."

"But she looks right down miserable," declared his wife. "I know that myself. I met her at Griggs's only a day or two ago and, I snum, I was real shocked to see how white and used-up she did look. She told me she was feelin' pretty well, but I didn't believe it. And her mother is worried about her, I know that. . . . We thought, Tobias and I, that you might have heard some particulars, Carey."

Carey shook his head. "No," he said. And added, "Well, I must be getting to work. Good night, Cap'n. Good night, Mrs. Higgins."

After the door had shut, Phœbe turned, in triumph, to her husband.

"Ah, ha!" she crowed. "You see now, don't you, Tobias? You noticed how he looked when I said she was sick. That's what's the matter. The same thing ails her that ails him. There's been some trouble between those two and they're both upset about it."

The captain was inclined to believe she was right, but he made it a point never to agree too completely.

"Oh, bosh!" he snorted. "That's woman's talk, that is. You and all the rest of the sewin' circle gasworks have been so sot on the idea that she and Carey were keepin' comp'ny that you can't get it out of your heads. Maybe they weren't at all."

"Yes, and maybe they were, and maybe they've had some sort of quarrel and it has broke 'em all up. It don't take much to make trouble between young folks that are goin' 'round together. You remember that time when we went to that strawberry festival in Bayport and that young minister they had there then told my fortune with tea leaves and said I was goin' to marry a tall, thin man who loved books and nature and could understand a girl with refined instincts like mine. I remember how you talked to me all the time we was drivin' home. We didn't speak to each other for a week and I cried myself to sleep every night. Oh, I shouldn't do it now! Indeed, I wouldn't! I'd have a few things to say, myself. But I did it then and was just about half sick; and, after we made it up, you told me you'd been as miserable as I had. *You* may have forgotten it, but I haven't."

The workshop, when Carey entered it, was cold and dark and uninviting. He lit the bracket lamp above the bench and gazed listlessly at the partially finished decoy and the tools laid beside it. They did not interest him at all. He turned to kindle the fire in the stove and, as he did so, the letter in his overcoat pocket brushed against his arm with a crackling sound. He drew it forth and held it beneath the lamp. The name printed in the corner of the envelope was not Moore, as he had expected, but one quite different. The letter was from his old friend, Professor Knight.

He threw off his coat and hat and sat down upon the packing box by the bench, tore open the envelope and read the inclosure. Knight, it seemed, was back again at his museum in the midwestern city. The proposed expedition was off for the present. The difficulties in its financing, those mentioned in the former letter to Carey, had proved too formidable to overcome that year, and perhaps for a longer period.

This doesn't mean that I have given up the idea [wrote the professor]. I am just as keen for it as I ever was and some of these days I shall carry out the plan and, when I do, I am still hoping that you can go with me. I am writing you now concerning another proposition. One of the assistants here in my department is leaving on the first of January. He has a good position offered him with the museum in Chicago that he should accept and which, on my advice, he has accepted. I must fill his place and I can't think of any one as competent to fill it as you would be, Judson. You would be working directly under me in the Ornithological Department and I know we should get on together. The salary isn't that of a bank president—they don't pay you bird stuffers in five figures—but it is more than I should imagine you are getting in your brother's fish business. And, if you cared to, you might help it out by making those decoys of yours in your spare time.

He stated the amount of the salary—it was far from munificent, but it was larger than Carey's wage as bookkeeper—and went on to urge acceptance of the offer.

I shall hold the position open until I hear from you [he wrote]. I sincerely believe the opportunity is a good one. You and I have pulled in harness before, and you will like the work, for it is your kind. And, of course, there is always that South American trip waiting in the offing. Come on. I need you. Throw your account books out of the window and come out here and do a man's job. Write me at once. Better still, telegraph. One word will be enough, provided the word is "Yes."

Carey read the letter through. Then he read it again. It seemed unbelievable, an offer like this coming to him. The thought of what it meant was overwhelming. To work with "Big Jack" again, to devote, not a little, but all of his time to a labor which was not really labor but play, to be free to pursue his hobby at its completest, and to be paid for doing it! Why, it was a miracle! And it was offered to him—queer Carey Judson! Out there, away from Wellmouth and these people who had always known him, he would not be "queer," at least no queerer than Knight and his associates. It was what he had always longed to do, what, as a boy, he had begged his father to permit his doing.

His first impulse was to rush up to the telegraph office—that office would be closed if he did not hurry—and send the message, the one word, which his friend urged him to send. Then he decided that the next morning would do as well. Perhaps he should tell George before telegraphing acceptance. Yes, he ought to do that. George would not greatly mind his leaving the employ of J. C. Judson & Co. Any bookkeeper hired to take his place would be an improvement on the present incumbent. Ben Early would be glad to see him go. Yes, he would. He might not say so; no, he would express sorrow at his leaving. Carey could imagine with what suave condescension and guarded good wishes that sorrow would be expressed. He smiled at the fancy.

George would be glad to hear of his good fortune. It would relieve him of the care of his impractical brother. And Cora T. would be delighted to be rid of him. Emily—when she heard of it—she—

His train of joyful reverie came to a stop with a jerk. Emily! What difference could they make to him, her thoughts now? His joys and hopes were hers no longer. If this offer of Knight's had come to him before George had made his desperate plea—if it had come before the news of Aunt Susan's legacy! Oh, if only Aunt Susan had adhered to her original decision and had left the money to George, as she should have done! If George had not made his selfish demand for secrecy, had not silenced him—Carey—by reminding the latter of the debt of gratitude he owed his brother, then—why, then—

He threw the letter upon the bench and groaned in savage rebellion against the Fate which had always made, and was still making, a joke of him and his life. Again he regretted his lack of firmness in yielding so completely to George's pleadings. Then was the time when he should have refused to keep silent. He should have told his brother that Emily Sayles had seen the letter from the Cleveland lawyer, that she knew the Dain property was his, and, although acceding to the request that no one else should learn from him of George's peril and urgent need, he, Carey, must and would tell her why he must sacrifice his and her immediate happiness and plans to help the brother who had helped him.

Then—*then* he could have gone to her and made his explanation and begged her forgiveness for the broken promise and she would have been willing to wait until George's crisis was past. In her letter to him she had declared herself willing to wait. Now it was too late. She did not love him now. She hated and despised him—she must. Oh, how could he have been such a quixotic idiot! Now it was too late.

Well, was it, after all? Might he not go to her even now and tell the whole truth? Perhaps, even yet, when she knew that truth, she would forgive him. He had a mind to do it. Why should he sacrifice everything to George? Why not, for once, think of himself first and let George take his chance? George might still have the money; he did not care for the money at all. But for her, for Emily, he cared—oh, how he cared—and longed—and yearned! The momentary uplift which Professor Knight's letter had brought to him vanished. He did not care about the offer which had, when he read of it, seemed so wonderful. He cared about nothing —except her.

The temptation to go to her now, that very night, was strong. He was close to yielding, closer even than he had been at any time since he made his first rash decision. But he did not yield. He had given George his solemn promise. One promise he had broken already, but to break another would be too despicable. He would accept Knight's offer, go away, leave Wellmouth and its memories and its hateful, sneering people, and do the work he loved and knew that he could do well. That is what he would do. As for the debts he owed and upon the payment of which his hopes and strivings had been centered for a year, he might send on money from time to time and pay them in that way. He did not much care at that moment whether or not they were ever paid.

He rose from the packing box and lifted the lamp from the bracket. He was about to blow it out, preparatory to going back to his room at home to write Knight his acceptance of the offer, when the shop door opened and George Judson came in.

Carey was surprised to see him, even in his present state of mind he was surprised. During his long tenancy of the Higgins' workshop George had visited him there not more than two or three times. He had expressed no intention of coming that evening.

"Hello!" hailed George. "Just in time, I should say. Getting ready to leave, were you?"

Carey nodded. "Yes," he said. "What brought you down here, George?"

George shivered. "Great Scott, man!" he exclaimed. "This place is as cold as the doleful tombs. Have you been here all the evening without a fire?"

Carey shrugged. "Isn't there a fire?" he asked, absently. "No, I guess there isn't. I forgot to build one. Well, what did you come for, George? What do you want?"

"I want you to come right up to the house with me. I drove down to get you. Come on!"

"What do you want me at the house for?"

"I want you there because there are one or two things I want to talk over with you and I am blessed if I risk my health talking about them in this ice chest. Hurry up! Get your coat on and come."

Carey, slowly, and with his usual awkwardness, twisted himself into the coat. He picked up his hat and moved toward the door.

"What are those matters you want to talk over with me, George?" he asked. "Business matters? Because, if they are, you know perfectly well it is no use asking me about them. And I don't feel like it to-night, anyway."

His brother pulled him through the doorway.

"I didn't say I was going to ask you anything, did I?" he observed. "Wait till we get home and you'll see for yourself what I want of you. Come, lock up! Get a move on!"

The Judson horse and buggy were waiting at the gate. The brothers climbed into the buggy and George took up the reins. During the short drive home neither spoke. Carey was still deep in his gloomy musings and George seemed to be thinking and disinclined to talk.

They left the vehicle in the drive and entered by the side door. George led the way into the dining room. Carey noticed that the door to the sitting room was shut, a most unusual happening.

At that door George paused and laid a hand on his brother's shoulder.

"Go in there and wait, Carey," he said. "I want to see Hepsy a minute. No, don't wait here. Go in." He paused, and then, leaning forward, added, in a curiously earnest whisper and with an odd shake in his voice, "Old man, the next time you have things on your mind that I ought to know, tell them to me and save us all trouble."

Carey turned. "What!" he asked, sharply. "What do you mean?"

George did not reply. Instead he opened the door and, with a sudden push, propelled his brother into the sitting room. Then he shut the door between them and hurried out to the kitchen. Hepsibah, arrayed in her Sunday dolman and bonnet, was sitting there awaiting him.

"Maggie is out, isn't she?" asked George. "All right. Then, come on, Hepsy! You and I are going over to Trumet."

A minute or two later the horse and buggy moved out of the yard. And, in the sitting room, Carey Judson, white and shaken, was standing staring at Emily Sayles, who had risen from the rocker as he entered.

She was the first to speak. She had been expecting him and he had most certainly not expected to see her. She came forward smiling, and held out her hands to him.

"Well, Carey," she asked, "aren't you even going to say 'Good evening'?"

He did not take the offered hands. He gazed at her in uncomprehending bewilderment, his brain trying to adjust itself to the shock of seeing her, his imagination whirling amid all sorts of wild speculations as to her reasons for being there. He put his hand to his forehead and it struck the brim of his cap. He had forgotten that he was still wearing it. Mechanically, he took it off. But still he could not utter a word. As usual she seemed to understand.

"Yes, Carey," she said. "I am really here. You wouldn't come to see me, so I came to see you. And this time you can't run away and hide. Take off your coat and sit down. We have a great deal to say to each other."

He did not remove the coat, nor did he sit. He spoke, however.

"Why did you come?" he demanded. "I told you not to. You shouldn't have done it. There isn't any use in our talking. Oh, Emily, can't you understand there isn't? You —you are going to ask me questions. I can't answer them. *Why* did you do this? Did George—"

She interrupted. "Hush, hush!" she begged. "You are beginning to look—and speak—the way you did that dreadful night when you came to the house, and I never want to be reminded of that again. Take off your coat, and sit down and listen to me. Please do."

"No. No, I won't—I can't! Why *did* you come? Why couldn't you believe what I told you—what I wrote you? If George has—"

"Hush! Listen, dear, please. And don't say another word until you hear what I am going to say now. It is all right—everything is all right. I know now. I understand. George has told me. . . . Think—try and think what I am saying. George has told me—he has told me everything."

Again he put his hand to his forehead. It was the hand holding his cap, but he did not seem to be aware of that. The cap dangled before his face and the words he uttered came from behind it.

"I—I don't—I don't understand," he gasped. "You say George—you say he has—has—"

The cap fell to the floor.

"You say George has told you!" he cried. "He hasn't—he couldn't!"

"Yes. Yes, he has. He has told me everything. That is why I am here. He brought me here to meet you. He has told me all about your letting him have the money and why he had to have it—everything. I understand now, Carey. I do, truly. . . . There! Now you will take off your coat, won't you? And sit here and be calm and let me talk to you. . . . That's it. Now do listen—please."

She pulled the coat from his shoulders and laid it upon the table. He made no effort to help with the operation, but he did not resist, nor did he when she led him to the armchair by the rocker. He appeared to be moving in a fog and not in the least conscious of moving at all. She sat beside him. It was not until she had done so and leaned forward to speak again that he uttered a sound. Then he drew a long breath and attempted an apologetic smile.

"You—you will have to excuse me," he faltered. "I am queer, I know; but—but— Well, that is to be expected of Queer Judson, isn't it? . . . Humph! Emily, I don't seem to get what you are saying to me. If you mean to tell me that—that George has— Oh, but he hasn't!"

"Yes; yes, he has. Of course you don't understand, poor boy, but you will in a minute. Just now you mustn't talk or ask questions. I am going to tell you what has happened and why it happened. You will be good and listen to me, won't you?"

He sighed. "Why, I'll try," he said, with a slow shake of

the head. "Of course I don't believe—I can't believe you mean—what I mean. But I'll listen. Tell me."

"You must believe. And you will, because it is perfectly simple. Oh, Carey, if it had been any one but you there would never have been this terrible month for us both. Any one else would have— But there, you *are* you and I wouldn't have you any one else. When you came to me that night, in the storm, and spoke and looked and behaved as you did, I was frightened almost to death. I thought you must be insane; for a little while I really almost believed that. Then I tried to think of a reason and, when I could think at all, there was but one reason that seemed to me to account in the least for your breaking our engagement so suddenly, leaving me without a word of explanation or. . . . Well, never mind that. The only reason I could think of was concerned with the money your aunt had left you. I remembered your promise to me that you would not let your brother persuade you to give up that inheritance. I believed, for some reason or other, you had been forced to break that promise, give up the money and all your plans—our plans. If that was so then, because you were you, I could understand your feeling that you must give me up, too. For my sake you would feel that way; not for your own; I never believed that.

"But, if that were the truth, then why didn't you tell me your reason? Why didn't you give me the chance to say, what I should have said, that I didn't care about the money at all? Except that I felt it was yours, that it belonged to you, that you needed it and should have it, I did not care one bit. If you were as poor as poverty I should love you just the same—oh, I told you that, Carey! You know I told you that."

He would have interrupted, but she would not let him.

"Wait!" she said. "You must wait. I have only begun to tell you. Well, I tried and tried to see you; I came here when you were sick, once with mother and once alone, and you would not see me. Then I wrote you that letter and your answer was—was— No, never mind. I know why you wrote as you did. You couldn't trust yourself to write in any other way. You felt that I must not see you again and the only way to do that was to make me hate you. Oh, Carey, as if I ever could do that!"

He groaned. She went on, quickly.

"So, at last," she said, "I told mother. I hadn't told her before, even of—of that afternoon down on the beach. I had been waiting until you were there and we could tell her together. But I told her at last and she—Carey, dear, she is the one who has saved us. If it had not been for her—! Well, she listened and she asked me a lot of questions and then, without telling me a word of what she intended doing, she came alone, last Sunday afternoon, to this house and saw your brother. She told him everything, about our engagement, about your getting and showing me that letter from Mrs. Dain's lawyer, about your coming to me that dreadful night, about everything. And she told him what she suspected as to why you had acted as you had.

"That evening George came to see me. He was—well, he was not in the state you were in when you came—no one else *could* be just like that—but he was very much disturbed and conscience-stricken and worried. He told me of his business trouble—"

Carey broke in then. "What!" he cried. "He told you that! Why, he must have been crazy! No one should have known that; he told me no one but him and me must ever know it. He made me promise— Why, Emily, that was the reason I—"

"Yes, yes! I know all that, too. Of course I do. But, Carey, couldn't you have trusted me to know it? I can keep a secret. So can mother. We shall keep this one. George is perfectly safe as far as we are concerned. If you had told him then that you must tell me, all would have been so easy. Why didn't you tell him? Oh, why didn't you?"

He tried to explain. "I—I didn't see how I could," he stammered. "He was so—so desperate—and so fearful that his creditors might catch even the least rumor about it. And Cora didn't know. He said she mustn't know. He was afraid she might—well, might do almost anything. He is so very fond of her, he worships her."

"Yes," dryly, "I know he does. I don't. But never mind her. Carey, dear—"

He broke in once more, seeking justification, not for himself even then, but for his brother.

"Don't you *see*, Emily?" he urged. "I think—I think I might have told him about—about you if it hadn't been that he was in such a state that I did not dare say anything. He begged me to promise not to tell a living soul. And when he reminded me—I don't think he meant to do it, he is the last person to do such a thing—when he reminded me of all he had done for me, of what I owed him, I—I *had* to promise. Why, Emily, think what he has done for me! Think what I *do* owe him! How *could* I say no to anything he asked? How could I?"

"*You* couldn't, of course. Another person might have remembered what was owing to himself—yes, and to me, but not you, my dear. I understand why you promised then and why, afterward, you felt you must give up your future and your life's happiness to save his. George understands it, too. He told me so and, of course, when he did, after mother's talk with him, he came straight to me and made me understand. George is a Judson and—I am quoting mother now—there never was a Judson who wasn't honorable."

She paused. He said nothing. The whole revelation had come to him with the suddenness of a lightning flash. He was stunned by it. He did not realize, even now, what was beyond, what it might mean to him.

She saw that he did not, and she smiled, a smile with tears very close behind it.

"There, Carey," she said, softly. "Now you know that I know as much as you do—yes, and that your brother knows, too. Do you still want to break our engagement?

Shall I go away now, and—forget you, as you ordered me to do in your letter?"

He came out of the fog with a start. He sprang to his feet so suddenly that the chair fell backwards with a crash.

"Emily," he cried, "what do you mean? Do you mean that—that you—"

She was still smiling, although the tears were running down her cheeks.

"I mean," she said, "that unless you insist upon it I am going to marry you some day, Carey Judson, and I am quite willing to wait until that day comes."

The old clock on the mantelpiece had ticked many, many times before he or she descended from the clouds and spoke of earthly affairs. Even in the midst of his aerial excursion he broke in upon more interesting matters to utter inarticulate protests.

"But I don't see how you can do such a thing," he repeated. "I can't see why you do it. I haven't any money now, not a cent except what I can earn, and that will never be much. I am funny, you know—queer—I can't help it. I shall always be doing foolish things. And you, why you could marry *anybody!*"

She laughed, happily. "I am going to marry you," she said. "I am 'queer,' myself, I guess. At any rate, I shall be proud to be Queer Judson's wife."

"But I don't know *when* I can marry you. George must have that money of Aunt Susan's. He needs it. He—"

"Hush! Certainly he must have it. He is going to have it. We both understand that."

"And I shall never be anything but—eh? Why, I forgot! Where is that letter?"

He withdrew his arm from the position it had occupied for at least an hour and rummaged hastily in his coat pocket. A shower of papers, pencil stubs, bits of string and odds and ends were sent flying about them as the letter from Knight was dragged forth and exhibited. She read it eagerly and then, as he had done when he received it first, she read it over again. She dropped it in her lap and looked up at him with shining eyes.

"Why, Carey!" she cried. "Why, Carey, this is wonderful!"

He nodded. "Yes, it is," he agreed. "I could scarcely believe he was in earnest when I read it. To think he could find a place out there for a fellow like me! Yes, it is wonderful enough, surely. . . . Humph! You don't suppose he is doing it, not because he thinks I could really be of any use to him, but—well, just because he is sorry for me, or anything like that?"

She looked at him steadily. Then she shook her head. "I should like to scold you," she declared, "but I mustn't— to-night. He wants you, Carey, because he knows you are what you are and what you are capable of doing. And of course you will send that telegram the very first thing in the morning?"

He seemed doubtful. "Why, I don't know," he replied. "I was going to—that is, I think I should have done it after I had had a talk with George. But now—I don't know. I —well, dearest, now that—that I have got you again, I can't leave you. At least I can't seem to think of leaving you; even to be exhibited in a museum," he added, with one of his twisted smiles.

She was reading the letter for the third time. When the reading was finished she looked up once more and there was an odd, half-humorous, half-serious expression on her face.

"Perhaps you may not have to leave me," she said, quietly.

He stared, then gasped. *"What!"* he cried. "Why, Emily! Why— Oh, but you can't mean *that!* Think of what it would cost to live—in any sort of a city. And the salary is pretty small. It is bigger than I am getting—I won't say earning—now, but it is very small."

She nodded. "I know," she admitted; "but you can still make those beetle-heads and things. Professor Knight says you can. And *perhaps* some people might not be *too* particular who taught their children the piano. Mother always says I am a pretty good manager. . . . Well, we will ask mother; she always knows what to do in an emergency."

And just then the Judson horse and buggy plodded and rattled into the yard.

## CHAPTER XVIII

CAREY walked home with Emily that night. George, on his arrival, had asked no questions; a look at their faces was sufficient. He shook each of them by the hand and turned to leave the sitting room.

"The horse and buggy are outside here, Carey," he said. "When Emily is ready to go you can drive her home."

His brother and the young lady exchanged glances. "I think I had rather walk," she said. "It is such a beautiful night."

George, after another look, said, "Oh, all right," and went out. The walk home was not a hurried one. Carey bade her good night at the Sayles' door, a parting far different from his frenzied dash from that door into the wind and rain the night of the "equinoctial." His progress back along the road and up the slope of Lookout Hill was a peculiar one. If his sister-in-law could have witnessed it— fortunately it was witnessed by no one—she might have found further proof of her surmise that he had taken to drink. He walked sometimes on the sidewalk, sometimes in the middle of the road, and quite as often in the stretch of stubby dead grass and weeds which lay between. He whistled, he sang, he laughed aloud, and when he again entered the sitting room, his cap on one side, his pet lock of hair dangling about his nose and his trousers legs below the knees thickly plastered with burrs and "beggar ticks," he found his brother there awaiting him.

"Why—why, hello, George!" he exclaimed. "Haven't you gone to bed yet?"

George ignored the inane question. He looked him over from head to foot.

351

"You old idiot," he observed; "you're a sight. Did you know it?"

Carey grinned. "Am I?" he queried. "Well, I—generally am one, so your wife tells me. I don't care, George. Do you?"

"Not a bit. If it pleases you to look as if you had been crawling through the cow pasture on your hands and knees, I am satisfied. Anything that makes you happy I shan't find any fault with. . . . You old jackass! Why did you keep all this to yourself? Why in the devil didn't you speak out that night in the office, instead of hiding it from me and driving yourself to the insane asylum?"

Carey's grin disappeared. He looked contrite and troubled.

"George," he said, "I—I can't thank you for what you have done for me to-night. It is no use to try. Emily says you—well, if it hadn't been for you she and I would—would —George, I had given up hope. I had written her that— that—"

"I know what you wrote her. She told me; she told me everything. At least I can't imagine that she or her mother forgot any of the essentials. Carey, why didn't you tell me, yourself? When I asked you to promise not to tell a soul about lending me the money Aunt Susan left you, why didn't you tell me you wouldn't do any such thing?"

"Why—why, George, how could I? You were in such a terrible mess. Of course I had to promise. Anybody would have done it."

"They would, eh? I suppose anybody would have thrown over all their plans, and the girl they were to marry, and just let their whole life go to blazes and never have whimpered, or even hinted. Yes, they would! Carey, do you suppose if I had known— Say, what sort of a fellow do you think I am?"

Carey hastened to protest. "I know the sort you are, George," he declared. "That was just it. When I remembered what you had done for me—"

"Oh, be quiet! Do you suppose if I had known about

you and Emily Sayles—what there was between you, to say nothing of your getting that letter from Phillips and showing it to her—do you suppose I shouldn't have told you to tell her the whole story? She would have kept it to herself. She and her mother can keep a secret; they will keep this one."

"Yes," eagerly. "Yes, they will, George. I know they will. Emily said they would. They, and you and I, will be the only ones in Wellmouth who will ever know Aunt Susan didn't leave you her property. And this isn't going to make a bit of difference about your having that money, George. Not a bit. If I thought it would I should—well, I should go to Emily again and tell her it was all off. I should have to do that. But it won't!"

"No, it won't. And I must have that money for a while, Carey. I have counted on it and made my arrangements to use it, and I can't back out now without making a bigger smash even than I saw coming before. That money is going to tow me to land, old man. . . . There! That is enough for to-night. You have got a mighty fine girl—about the best there is, I guess—but she isn't good enough for you. No woman that ever lived was that."

Carey gasped. "What are you talking about, George?" he demanded, indignantly. "Emily is—why, when I think that a girl like her is willing to marry a—a failure like me, it—it makes me almost ashamed of her. I—"

"Oh, do shut up! You and I will have more talks later on. Go out in the kitchen and pick those burrs off your legs, if you can. If you can't, go to the barn and use the curry comb. . . . Go ahead! If you stay here I shall kick you, or break down and cry over you, or something. Perhaps both. . . . Good night, Carey. But don't you forget that I intend to get even—or as near even as I can—for all this. Give me a little time, and. . . . Well, good night."

Meanwhile Emily and her mother were discussing the "emergency." Emily, after parting with Carey at the door, went up to her mother's room and found Desire awake and eager to listen. She heard the tale which her daughter had to tell and was as happy in its ending as Emily knew she would be. The news of Carey's offer from Professor Knight she received with enthusiasm.

"It is just exactly what he deserves and precisely the sort of work he can do," she declared. "I am so glad for you both."

Emily nodded. "Yes," she agreed, "it is very wonderful. If—if only he did not have to go out there alone. Of course he must accept the offer, but—oh, well! we may not have to be separated so very long. The doctor says you are ever so much better, dear, and when you are strong enough per- haps we—you and I—can go there, too. Don't you think we could, mother?"

Mrs. Sayles was thinking and she thought a moment or two before she spoke. Then she said, with decision: "He mustn't go there alone. If ever a man needed a practical, common-sense wife to look out for him and take care of his home and his money that man is Carey Judson. . . . I must think about this—yes, I must think. He will be here to see you to-morrow evening, won't he? Yes, of course he will. Well, by that time I may see a way. No, I mustn't talk any more now and you must go to bed. Good night, my girl. I am—yes, I really am—as happy as you are."

And when Carey came to the Sayles' house that evening, quite oblivious of and caring nothing for, the eyes that peered from behind the window shades across the road, he found that Mrs. Sayles was sitting up past her usual hour for retiring and that she had something important to say to both Emily and himself.

"I have been thinking about you two, Carey," she said. "When you go out there to work with Professor Knight— Oh, by the way, have you sent him the telegram?"

Carey nodded. "I sent it this morning," he said. "He knows now that I am going to take the place. I hope he hasn't changed his mind. I shouldn't blame him much if he had, but—well, it would be a disappointment."

"He hasn't changed it. Unless he has changed a great deal since I used to know him when he visited his sister here, he knows his own mind. Have you told your brother of the offer?"

"No, not yet. I was afraid something might happen and I wanted to hear from 'Big Jack' again before I said anything to him."

"All right. George can wait. He will approve when he learns of it, I know. Now then; as I told Emily last night when she told me, you mustn't go out there alone. You aren't fit to be alone anywhere. You needn't thank me, it is the plain truth and not a compliment. As I see it, Emily ought to go with you. You and she should marry and go together."

Carey stared and Emily was startled. She shook her head.

"No, mother," she said. "Unless you can go, too—and, now that I have had time to think about it sanely, I realize that you mustn't attempt such a thing—unless, or until, you can go too, I shall stay here. Carey and I are willing to wait. Aren't we, Carey?"

Carey nodded. "Of course," he declared.

"You don't need to wait. I have been thinking, myself, and, daughter, I shan't let you wait on my account. Carey needs you and you ought to be with him. You will probably have to do some close figuring and go without much more than the bare necessities to get along on his salary, but that is all right. It will be good for both of you. My husband and I got along on a lot less than that when we were first married and I wouldn't trade the memory of those years for the ones that came after them. No, you and he must marry and go together."

Carey looked decidedly dubious and Emily's shake of the head was emphatic.

"No, mother," she said, "that's out of the question. I shall not leave you in this house alone. Even if we could get, or afford, a maid from Boston to come and keep house for you, I shouldn't consider it."

"Neither should I. But if we could get a capable, honest woman in Wellmouth here, one we have always known and liked, you might consider it, mightn't you? And I believe, I know such a woman and that she would be glad to come. In fact she has hinted that she would like to do that very thing. She has been here to see me two or three times in the past fortnight—when you were out, Emily—and she has told me that she doesn't believe she can stand working and living where she is much longer and, if she could find a home with what she calls her kind of folks, she would move in a minute. Wages, she says, would make little difference to her; she has saved all her life and she has a small income of her own. She and I are old friends and her living with me would suit us both. She would jump at the chance, I am sure."

Carey did not speak. He had guessed the answer to the riddle. Emily had not.

"What woman do you mean, mother?" she asked.

"I mean Hepsibah Ellis. You would be satisfied to leave me in her care, wouldn't you? There is no one on earth more capable."

Emily was astonished. She looked at Carey and then at her mother.

"Hepsibah!" she repeated. "Why, Hepsibah would not leave the Judsons. She has lived in that house since she was a girl."

"I know that. But there was no Mrs. George Judson and no Maggie there then. She likes George, but she can't get along with his wife. So long as Carey was with them it might be hard for her to leave, but when Carey goes I think she will go, no matter whether she comes here or not. And if she does come here you can leave me with an easy mind, Emily. You must come and visit me once in a while, if you can afford it, and, perhaps, by and by, if that doctor is right and I do get a little of my strength back, I can come and visit you. But I shall never go out there to live. In the first place, I do *not* believe in old people living with their married sons and daughters and, in the second, I shall never give up this house. It was my home when Simeon was alive, I am fond of it, it belongs to me and I belong in it. There! Now send Hepsy to me, Carey, and I think she and I can settle the matter in five minutes."

There was much more argument, but the next day Hepsibah called upon Mrs. Sayles and the matter was settled just as the latter had prophesied. Hepsy told Carey of the settlement that evening.

"It is just exactly what I'd rather do than anything," she announced. "I like Desire Sayles and I rather guess she likes me. And *she* is a lady, not a second-hand clam peddler trying to play at bein' one. And so you are goin' to marry Emily, are you, Carey Judson? Well, I was kind of in hopes it might work out that way some time or other, though I didn't hardly dare believe it. She's an awful nice girl and a sensible one and if anybody can make you eat your meals at a reg'lar time and behave like a rational Christian, I guess likely she can. But she'll have her hands full. . . . My, my! but all this is goin' to make that Cora T. set up and take notice. I wonder if her ears are burnin' down there in Washin'ton. I presume likely not. She's too busy wavin' her hand to the President when he goes out to ride. If his horse would only step on her, so's he'd take notice of her bein' there, she'd be happy. Well, if it does I hope it puts its foot down hard."

Carey and his brother had many more talks in the private office of J. C. Judson & Co., conferences which puzzled Mr. Early and made him suspicious and slightly jealous. George, on the whole, approved of the immediate marriage.

"The salary isn't very large," he said, "and it will cost you more to live out there than it does here, but I am for it just the same. You need a manager if anybody ever did, and with old John Knight to see that you don't put your pay envelope in your hat or your hair instead of your pocket, and with Emily to take it out of that pocket and make sure that the money is used to pay bills with, instead of being tossed to any Tom, Dick, and Harry that asks you for it, I guess you'll do pretty well. And, in a year or two," he added, earnestly, "I am beginning to believe I can pay you a good-sized part, at least, of Aunt Susan's hundred and twenty-five thousand. That engine game is commencing to look like a winner already. I hardly dare believe what they write me about it, but I guess it is true."

Carey was disturbed, as he always was when the legacy was mentioned.

"Now—now, George," he protested. "You mustn't talk like that. You keep that money as long as you want to. Besides, don't you see, you mustn't let Cora know that it isn't yours. She—well, you said yourself—"

George motioned him to stop. "You don't understand, Carey," he said. "If this engine gamble of mine goes the way they tell me it is sure to go, a little matter like a hundred thousand won't be bothering Cora in a few years from now. She and I will have so much that— Oh, well! that may be all moonshine, but whether it is or not you shall have the money Aunt Susan left you, Cora or no Cora. That is the least I can do for you. The very least."

Carey sighed. "Well, I wish you wouldn't talk about it," he said. "I—I don't know why, but I always hate to talk about money, or think about it. That banking business of mine made me feel that way, I suppose. This world would be better if there wasn't a dollar in it."

George laughed. "Yes, yes, I know," he said. "Some day before you leave here, Carey, I wish you would write out your ideas about money and give me what you have written. I should like to send it to *Harper's Bazar*. They would be glad to print it—on the back page with the other jokes."

Knowledge of the marriage—which was to take place just after Christmas—was kept a secret from every one except those immediately concerned and Mrs. Sayles and George and Hepsibah. Carey worked steadily at the books, but he found it very hard to keep his mind upon them. The scratcher was continually in use again. The edge which that implement put upon Ben Early's nerves was far keener than its own. He hinted and remonstrated and, occasionally, lost his temper and scolded, but Carey was always provokingly serene.

"Ben," he said, on one occasion, "you are going to miss me after I am gone, aren't you?"

The manager started in surprise.

"Gone!" he repeated. "Where are you going? What do you mean by that?"

Carey grinned. He was sitting upon the high stool and now he turned and began twisting the lock of hair which was always his plaything when troubled or amused.

"Why, I may leave you some time, Ben," he drawled. "We are here to-day and gone to-morrow; that is the quotation, isn't it? If I should go—or when I go—I shall buy a new one of these things," holding up the scratcher, "for the house and give you this one to remember me by. It is—er—dull and not ornamental, so it ought to call me to your memory, I should think."

To but one other person, except those who knew already, did he disclose his plans and the great secret. That person was Captain Tobias Higgins and the place of the disclosure was the platform of the railway station and the time a minute before the departure of the afternoon train. Tobias and Phœbe were starting for New York and Washington on the "vacation" they had told Carey was in contemplation.

Tobias was surprised, and pleased, although disappointed to learn that his workshop was to lose its tenant. He offered congratulations, declared Emily Sayles to be a fine girl and good enough to be anybody's wife, but he sighed, too.

"I hope your cruisin' away off in those latitudes is goin' to turn out all right, Carey," he said. "I guess likely 'twill. But if it don't, you come right back here and you and me will go into the beetle-head business the way it ought to be gone into. There's money in that—you mark my words there is. Them beetle-heads of yours—well, I've got one of 'em—the one you give me one time—stuck up over the picture of the old *Ambergris* down in the dinin' room. I whistle to it about every time I go in and out of that room and—well, it ain't whistled back yet, but it's gettin' ready to, I can see that. Don't you forget me and Chippy when you're out there in that bird stuffin' place. Write us, will you? And, say, Carey, you tell that Knight man that if his old museum is fallin' behind so fur's as trade's concerned, all he's got to do is to set you to whittling and charge ten cents admission to see you do it. He'll have to build on an extension to hold the crowds, if he does that. You tell him I said so."

One evening, a week or so later, Emily and Carey were together in the Sayles' sitting room. They heard a quick step on the path and a knock at the outer door and Emily went to open the latter. Hepsibah Ellis was standing there and she was evidently excited.

"Is Carey in there, Emily?" she asked. "Well, can I speak to him and you a minute? I've got some news to tell and I guess likely you both will think it's pretty interestin'."

She hurried into the sitting room without waiting for an invitation. Emily followed her, wondering what the interesting item of news might be. Hepsibah, standing in the middle of the braided mat by the door, nodded several times and drew a long breath. There was satisfaction in that breath, and triumph in her manner.

"Well," she announced, "I've done it."

Carey, of course, could not understand.

"What have you done, Hepsy?" he asked.

Hepsy nodded again.

"I've done what I've been waitin' to do and been lookin' for'ard to doin' for a fortni't," she proclaimed. "I've give my notice. That's what I've done."

The understanding was not made more clear by this pronouncement. Emily looked at Carey and he at her.

"What notice? What do you mean, Hepsy?" Emily asked.

Hepsibah nodded for at least the tenth time. Then she sniffed.

"*She* came on to-night's train," she said. "She gave

us a surprise party. We didn't expect her till to-morrow."

"She?" repeated Emily.

Carey knew whom she meant. There was but one "she" for Hepsibah Ellis.

"Cora!" he exclaimed. "Did Cora come to-night?"

"That's what she did. And she was all puffed up with vainglory about her doin's in Washin'ton and Philadelphia and the land knows where; I tell you she was! But *I* took her down soon as ever I got the chance. George was out to lodge meetin'—he wasn't expectin' her, you know—and that Maggie was out larkin' around as usual, so while she was eatin' supper and she and I were alone in the dinin' room I saw my chance and I took it. I told her I was goin' to leave, wasn't goin' to work in that house after next Saturday night."

Both her hearers were startled and perturbed.

"Why, Hepsibah!" cried Emily. "Why did you tell her that—now? You aren't coming here with mother until the end of the month. Did you tell her why you were leaving?"

"Of course I didn't! I didn't mention a word about you two gettin' married. I knew you or George would want to tell her that. I didn't say where I was going to live and work, either. She can find that out for herself by and by. But I've decided that I need a little vacation and a trip somewheres just as much as she ever did, or as Tobe Higgins and his wife, and I'm goin' to take one. I'm goin' up to Boston and stay a whole week, I am. I don't care what it costs me. But, oh, dear, I wish you could have heard the last thing I said to her. That is what tickles me so. I've been laughin' over it all the way up here."

She laughed again at the memory.

"Well, why not let us laugh, too," suggested Carey. "What did you say?"

"I said—oh, dear me, it's funny! We had it back and forth there for a spell, and finally she says: 'Well, I guess there isn't much doubt that I can get along without you perfectly well. You're not indispensable by any means; and as far as that goes, I've been thinkin' of gettin' a better-trained servant from Boston. Maggie thinks she knows of one that will suit us. I should have done it before,' says she, 'but I didn't like to hurt your feelin's. You have always said that you would never work for anybody but a Judson.' That give me my chance."

Hepsibah paused to indulge in another triumphant chuckle.

"'How do you know I ain't goin' to work for a Judson now?' says I. 'Maybe I am. Or, if I ain't, what I am goin' to do amounts to pretty much the same thing.' Then I marched out and left her starin'. She didn't know what I meant, but *I* do, and that's satisfaction enough for *me*."

(1)

## The End